THE YEAR'S BEST MILITARY & ADVENTURE SF

VOLUME 5

BAEN BOOKS
Edited By David Afsharirad

The Year's Best Military & Space Opera
The Year's Best Military & Adventure SF: 2015
The Year's Best Military & Adventure SF: Volume 3
The Year's Best Military & Adventure SF: Volume 4
The Year's Best Military & Adventure SF: Volume 5
The Chronicles of Davids (forthcoming)

THE YEAR'S BEST MILITARY & ADVENTURE SF

VOLUME 5

Edited By
DAVID AFSHARIRAD

THE YEAR'S BEST MILITARY AND ADVENTURE SF, VOLUME 5

A Baen Books Original

Baen Publishing Enterprises
P.O. Box 1403
Riverdale, NY 10471
www.baen.com

ISBN: 978-1-4814-8406-0

Cover art by Marianne Plumridge

First Baen printing, June 2019

Distributed by Simon & Schuster
1230 Avenue of the Americas
New York, NY 10020

Library of Congress Control Number: 2015009359

Printed in the United States of America

10 9 8 7 6 5 4 3 2 1

CONTENTS

★

THE YEAR'S BEST MILITARY & ADVENTURE SF
VOLUME 5

YOU DECIDE WHO WINS!

Other anthologies tell you which stories were best—we want *you* to decide! Baen Books is pleased to announce the fifth annual Year's Best Military and Adventure SF Readers' Choice Award. The award honors the best of the best in the grand storytelling tradition. The winner will receive a plaque and a $500 cash prize.

To vote, go to:
http://www.baen.com/yearsbestaward

You may also send a postcard or letter with the name of your favorite story from this year's volume to Baen Books Year's Best Award, P.O. Box 1188, Wake Forest, NC 27587. Voting closes August 15, 2019. Entries received after voting closes will not be counted.

So hurry, hurry, hurry!
The winner will be announced at
Dragon Con in Atlanta.

THE YEAR'S BEST MILITARY & ADVENTURE SF

VOLUME 5

PREFACE

★

by David Afsharirad

FIVE YEARS. Half a decade. That's how long The Year's Best Military & Adventure SF series has been running. If the series were a person, we'd be sending it off to kindergarten right now. If it were a marriage, the spouses would be purchasing each other anniversary gifts made of wood. Five years. Half a decade.

In those five years, we've published 69 stories by 56 authors. Some of those authors were best-sellers long before they appeared between the covers of one of our Year's Best volumes; for others, the stories we featured represented their first steps into the field. We've published stories that went on to win Hugos and be nominated for Nebulas. And speaking of awards, we've handed out $2,000 and four plaques to the winners of our Year's Best Military & Adventure SF Readers' Choice Award—and we'll hand out another five hundred bucks and a plaque to *this* year's winner at Dragon Con 2019.

Over the past five years, the mission of Year's Best has been the same: to highlight the best of the best in the military and adventure science fiction genres. As editor, I scour as wide an array of science fiction publications as possible. From the very first volume and continuing through to the book that you hold in your hands, I've strived to mine stories from big traditional publishers, small presses, and indie-pubbed anthologies, as well as magazines both online and in print. "Military and adventure science fiction" might sound like a narrow slice of the genre, but in fact the stories written in this vein are incredibly varied, and The Year's Best Military & Adventure SF series has covered a wide spectrum of tales in the past. This year is no different.

On the military side of the equation, we have Brendan DuBois' "Love in the Time of Interstellar War" and Richard Fox's "Going Dark." Both are, in their own way, stories about doing something very human in the midst of a chaotic war. DuBois' story is set in his Dark Victory series, and Fox's takes place in the same world as his nine-novel Ember War Saga.

To prove my point that "military SF" need not be a monolithic subgenre, I submit for your approval (as good ol' Rod Serling would have said) "A Song of Home, the Organ Grinds" by James Beamon. Set in a steampunk Crimean War, the story is without a doubt military SF, but is about as far from the power-armored space marines one often envisions when the genre is mentioned. (Not that I don't love a good power-armored space marine story!) Similarly, Suzanne Palmer's "Thirty-Three Percent Joe" offers a view of warfare unlike any I've ever seen: namely, the view from *inside* a soldier's body, as narrated by a host of "smart" artificial organs.

Michael Z. Williamson makes his third appearance in the Year's Best series with "Hate in the Darkness," a long story set in his Freehold universe that explores the complexities of warfare in the vacuum of space.

"Hate in the Darkness" originally appeared in the Baen anthology *Star Destroyers*, edited by Tony Daniel and Christopher Ruocchio. Ruocchio also wrote a story for the book and it is included here, as well. "Not Made for Us" takes place in the same fictional universe as his Sun Eater series (from DAW), though the narrator of this tale is quite different from the protagonist of the mainline novels, Hadrian Marlowe. Christopher is a good friend and employed by Baen, but I challenge anyone to read "Not Made for Us" and chalk up its inclusion to nepotism. In fact, when I started reading it, I fully expected *not* to include it to avoid anything looking fishy. By the time I was halfway through the story, I knew it was going in. The writing convinced me. It was the first story I selected for this volume.

As for the adventure stories contained herein, I'm pleased to say that Kristine Kathryn Rusch makes her first appearance in the Year's

Best Military & Adventure SF series. I've long been a fan of her work, both in the science fiction and mystery genres, and "Once on the Blue Moon," which concerns an eleven-year-old girl genius and a band of space pirates, is sure to delight.

Brian Trent and William Ledbetter both make repeat appearances this year (Trent's second, Ledbetter's third), both with stories that originally appeared in *The Magazine of Fantasy & Science Fiction*. "Broken Wings" by Ledbetter is the tale of an asteroid miner who finds more than valuable ore out on a dig. Trent's "Crash-Site" continues the story of Harris Alexander Pope, who was featured in the story "A Thousand Deaths through Flesh and Stone," which appeared in last year's volume. And while I'd encourage all of you who haven't read "A Thousand Deaths" to do so because it is a great story, "Crash-Site" can be enjoyed just as easily on its own by those of you not caught up on your Year's Best homework.

I mentioned that some of the stories we've featured over the years have gone on to be nominated and win awards. Well, Stephen Lawson's "Homunculus" is *already* an award-winner. Lawson took home the grand prize in the 2018 Jim Baen Memorial Short Story Contest and was published on Baen.com, which is where I read it. Now, you can read it here.

Finally, we have two long stories from the indie-press anthology *Bridge Across the Stars*: "The Scrapyard Ship" by Felix R. Savage, in which two couriers must find a way off a desert planet after their ship is destroyed, and a hardboiled tale of the mean streets on the Darkside of the Moon by Chris Pourteau called "The Erkennen Job."

And that's the lineup, folks.

But before you get to reading, it is my sworn duty to remind you that you—yes, *you*—get to pick which story wins The 2019 Year's Best Military & Adventure SF Readers' Choice Award. Last year, Kacey Ezell took home the prize for her story "Family Over Blood" and was on-hand at Dragon Con to receive the plaque and prize money.

To find out how you can cast your vote *this* year, go to http://baen.com/yearsbestaward. But don't hesitate—voting closes August 15, 2019.

Five years. Half a decade. A lot has changed in the publishing industry in those five years. But one thing remains constant: great science fiction stories continue to be written and published—perhaps now more than ever. Stories that thrill, challenge, provoke, and entertain. Stories that prove the Golden Age of science fiction is the ever-present now. May it ever be thus.

Excelsior!

—David Afsharirad
Austin, TX
February 2019

INTRODUCTION
★
by David Weber

AND SO WE COME TO ANOTHER VOLUME of The Year's Best Military & Adventure SF.

After writing military science fiction for thirty years (and reading it for a deliberately vague number of years before that), I've come to recognize both the unavoidable themes that repeat again and again, and the apparently infinite number of variations and permutations of those themes. Whether the author is writing about crafty Odysseus or direct, in-your-face Achilles, whether he—or increasingly she—focuses on the vast, implacable forces of war or the very human microcosm of a single fighter aircraft or a single foxhole, what draws the reader in again and again is seeing how the humans—or the aliens—in the crucible respond. How they rise to the occasion, or don't. How they triumph, or they don't. How they survive, or they don't.

War, combat, is a hideous experience. It's waged by teams, but it isn't a team sport. Too often, it seems to me, our society trivializes it by using it as a metaphor for other struggles or disputes. The "war" between two popular sports clubs or their fans. The "war" over the television remote. The "war" for audience share between two cable services. But there's nothing trivial about a real war, and there shouldn't be anything trivial about a fictional war.

I will qualify that last statement by saying that there have been some really well done satires set in a military or even a combat setting.

Keith Laumer's Retief novels come to mind, as do Christopher Anvil's Pandora's Planet and War with the Outs novels, or the granddaddy of the "poor alien" novels, Eric Frank Russell. But satire is always a law unto itself. Indeed, good satire thrives on turning the most serious of subjects upside down. But military fiction that takes itself and its readers seriously doesn't trivialize. It may, and I think it should, include humor, because humor is one of the weapons human beings use to get themselves through horrendous situations. For that matter, even though warfare is a deadly serious thing, it also is far from immune to the absurd. But at the core of itself, military fiction is about living or dying, on an individual basis, on the basis of a military unit, even on the basis of an entire nation, or planet, or—in science fiction, certainly—a species.

And, speaking for myself, what draws me as a writer and as a reader to military fiction are the complexities of the brutally simple equation at the heart of it all. What does war do to the people caught in its path? How do they respond? And assuming they survive it, how do they deal with it?

Obviously, if you're going to look at that "brutally simple equation," you have to have some context within which to frame it. For me, that means setting it in an existing real context or building a world in which to set it, and I suppose a few of my readers may have figured out that I really, really like world-building, too. But part of understanding what happens to people caught up in a war is understanding the causes and the potential outcomes of the war itself. That understanding frames the stakes and the nature of the war. A Russian soldier fighting desperately in defense of the Motherland, his own hometown, his own family, as the Nazi armored spearheads slice remorselessly towards Moscow is in a very different place, in some ways, from an American conscript sent to fight in the rice paddies of Vietnam or the mountains of Afghanistan. Not so much in the specifics of their experiences but in the *context* of those experiences. In their motivations, in terms of what they are willing to risk—or lose—and, perhaps most important of all for a storyteller examining human beings, how they understand and live with the consequences of their experience.

Bad movies and bad stories take combat as an isolated incident in someone's life. It happens to someone or a group of someones, and some of them die and some of them live, and at the end of the battle or the war they are still who they were when it began. They trivialize—there's that word again—the mind- and soul-shattering experiences of coming under fire yourself, of seeing someone you've come to know maimed, of watching someone else you've come to know die slowly just beyond your reach because of the intensity of the fire. Of sitting down to breakfast, then attending the morning brief, then flying the mission over Hanoi and never knowing how your best friend in the squadron died somewhere along the way. Of ordering men and women who are *your* responsibility to launch an attack or defend a position when you *know* it's going to get a lot of them killed. Of working in a frontline aid station, frantically patching up the wounded to keep them alive until it may be possible to evacuate them . . . and of *not* patching up the wounded you know won't live long enough for that. No one can experience that and be unchanged. It may break them, it may drive them to a greatness they never knew could be theirs, or it may simply stay with them for the rest of their lives, but it changes all of them.

And that's what good military science fiction tries to show. Behind the snazzy weapons, behind the technological war-fighting race, behind the exploding starships, there have to be actual human beings, because that's what the story is about. The weapons, the technology—they're props, really, when you come down to it. They create and they shape the environment, but it's what happens *in* the environment that matters. And that's what we want, as both writers and readers, to understand. To grasp. The reality is always beyond the reach of fiction, even for someone like an Erich Maria Remarque or a Siegfried Sassoon who were actually there and actually experienced it, and if we're honest with ourselves, we know that. But perhaps we can reach an approximation, something close enough to give us a handle. Not necessarily to fully understand it ourselves, if we haven't been there, in the middle of the chaos and the horror, but to sufficiently understand that we *don't* understand to be able to genuinely appreciate the people who *have* been there. And, perhaps, to understand the stakes a bit better.

Countless generations of storytellers, bards, songwriters, have glorified war. Don't get me wrong. People who have fought to defend themselves, their homes, their families, are worthy of all the praise and admiration we can heap upon them, even if most of us realize that the people we're talking about never sought the praise and would vastly have preferred to never find themselves in a position to earn it. But from Homer on, there have been those who persist in seeing war as an opportunity for winning renown, proving one's courage and prowess.

Well, just about anyone who launches a war sees it as an "opportunity." An opportunity to seize territory, destroy a rival, provide an ultimate solution to a lingering problem, avenge a wrong (or an imagined insult), or just to take someone else's stuff. There's probably not a lot anyone can do about that, because the people who make those decisions are rarely people who expect themselves or the people they care for to pay the price. There are obviously exceptions, especially when the decision is to resort to war as the only means to prevent the destruction of what you hold dear. When you are the people fighting to defend yourselves, your homes, your families. But those are seldom the people who *launch* wars.

And for those who aren't launching the wars, who aren't going to share in the spoils—who don't even *want* the "spoils" in the first place—wars aren't an opportunity. They certainly aren't an opportunity to win glory. The people who don't launch wars may display qualities worthy of being glorified, but that's not why they're there in the first place. You aren't "awarded" the Congressional Medal of Honor or the Victoria Cross; you *earn* it. You do something which by your actions sets you apart as someone willing to give the last, full measure. A lot of people who deserve both of those medals probably die unobserved, unknown. And that's the real price of "glory" in war. Scarred, maimed bodies and minds. People who were there this morning and gone by lunch and we don't know why. Seventy years lived in the shadow of something that happened to an eighteen-year-old you can barely remember ever having been.

That's what war is, and it scares the hell out of anybody who really thinks about it.

And because it scares us, and because we want to understand it however dimly as a means of coping with the fear, we write about it. We examine it. We explore it. Those of who have been there, who have experienced it, write to us like messages in a bottle, coming to us across the ocean divide of their experience to warn us that in the depths of that ocean there are monsters. But all of us who write about it are exploring, examining, warning, and wondering.

Science fiction differs from other forms of storytelling in that it gives us the opportunity to do those things in situations of our own creation. Unfettered by actual history or events, we can shape the narrative and the environment in ways that allow us to shine light on the specific characters, and the specific qualities of those characters, that we want to examine. Science fiction has always served as both an inspirational and a cautionary vehicle, and I think that in some ways that is especially true of *military* science fiction. It both cautions us about the unendurable stresses with which war and violence hammer the human spirit and yet tells us there are people who can—and will—endure all of that in our defense.

A combat vet I knew for many, many years, once told me that you cannot truly appreciate the beauty of the dawn until you have endured a hurricane at midnight. That man served from the Korean War through Desert Storm. He'd seen many a midnight hurricane, and he carried the scars and high-watermarks with him. It never broke him, it never destroyed him, but it did damage him, and he knew plenty of other people it did break and destroy. And that, I think, is what good military fiction, science fiction or otherwise, needs to remember and to show us. It needs to show us *people*, not icons, not demigods choosing a brief life of glory, but *people* we can understand. With whom we can empathize. Who we can admire or care about. People who are both our lens, our viewpoint into those midnight hurricanes, and also human beings who could be us or the people we know and love and care about.

Because at the end of the day, people are what all good storytelling is about.

A decade ago, the alien Creepers invaded, laying waste to much of the world and building vast domes from which they continued their assault against humanity. In the process, they destroyed most of the world's electronic capabilities. All satellites and aircraft were rendered useless hunks of metal. The Creepers' domes are indestructible save against a nuclear bomb. Of course, there are plenty of such devices on Earth. But with no missiles or aircraft, the bomb will have to be delivered by hand. The question becomes: how to deliver such a bomb and detonate it without blowing yourself up? It's a problem. One that Sgt. Walter Hart is about to face head-on.

LOVE IN THE TIME OF INTERSTELLAR WAR
★
by Brendan DuBois

I WAS LATE getting into the NCO staff meeting at the Mitchel Joint Navy-Army station that morning and when I started getting ragged on by the other three NCOs, I took my cane and rapped it against my right leg—the metal and wooden one—and I said, "Give it a rest, guys, okay? One of the K-9 units dragged my leg out last night for a chew toy."

That got some laughs but my Ell Tee—Antonia Juarez, a regular Army officer who was sent down to this unit once her spine got broke during a Creeper attack—moved her wheelchair a bit next to her desk and said, "Very good, Hart. Have a seat. And then come up with a better excuse. That's the third time you've used it in the past six months."

I sat down with a thin folder in my hand, joining the other NCOs who were part of the 2nd Infantry Brigade Combat Team, the New York National Guard unit tasked to keeping peace and order on Long Island.

I was the unit's intelligence officer, which should have been assigned to a lieutenant or captain, but since the Creepers invaded a decade ago, the thinned out armed forces of the United States had to adjust to doing a lot more with a lot less.

Including me, a one-legged first sergeant whose stomach felt like it was on fire, and who had skipped breakfast again this morning.

More than a century ago the Mitchel Joint Navy-Army station had been an Air Force base, flying and training a lot during World War II. Post-war, it was eventually decommissioned, parts of it were turned over to civilian use, and then it was only re-founded ten years ago, when the Creepers invaded. Technically it should be a Navy-Army-Air Force station because of its history, but since the Creepers' killer stealth satellites in orbit burn down anything with electronics that flies, the United States technically doesn't have much of an Air Force anymore.

Lieutenant Juarez glanced down at her clipboard. "All right, let's get with it. Give me your morning stats, and keep it short and to the point."

One by one, we gave our status reports.

Armed patrols along the abandoned and tsunami-swept towns of Long Island reported the detaining of forty-three coastie refugees trying to sneak back to their homes. They were being fed, processed, and would be returned via ferry to a Red Cross camp near New Canaan.

Logistics reported that a convoy successfully arrived yesterday at 1400 hours after an uneventful trip along the old I-295.

A couple of other reports followed, and it was my turn.

"Ma'am, I beg to report that no alien activity has been monitored at the enemy base dome at Cunningham Park during the last twenty-four hours. During that time period, mobile artillery from the 1st Battalion, 258th Field Artillery, fired a total of six 155-mm shells at the dome."

"No response?" she asked.

"No, ma'am," I said.

"Very well," she said, and after going through the day's schedule and other housekeeping details, she said, "Dismissed . . . save for you, Sergeant Hart."

There were sounds of chairs scraping and a low "uh oh" as the other NCOs walked out, and I shifted in my seat, adjusted my wooden leg, and when the door to the lieutenant's office—a former classroom—was shut, I said, "Ma'am, I apologize again for being late."

She reached over and took a red-bordered file folder from her desk. "Shut up, Hart. Apology not accepted."

I kept my mouth shut, and Lieutenant Juarez said, "We've got visitors coming here tomorrow. You're tasked to escort them, accompany them, give them what they need, and ensure they have a successful visit. Got it?"

"Yes, ma'am. May I ask why?"

"Because you're what passes for intelligence in this unit, that's why," she said. "You're to escort them to the base dome and do whatever it is that they require."

"Are they VIPs? Visitors?"

"In a manner of speaking, yes," she said. "They're from Russia, and they'll be arriving by watercraft at about oh nine-hundred, at the harbor at Hempstead. Provide meals, shelter, transport."

"Yes, ma'am," I said. "Are they military?"

She glanced over at me like I was an errant first-grade student who had just wet himself. "No, they're an advance unit for what's left of the Bolshoi Ballet . . . Christ, of course they're military." Lieutenant Juarez went back to her paperwork. "They are Russian Navy personnel . . . Petrov and Kosanskey. Special detail from Kallingrad. They've been on the water now for nearly a month."

"I see, ma'am," I said. "And how long do you expect them to be here?"

"Long enough to do their job."

She waited and I waited, and then I bit.

"Lieutenant, what's their job?"

She closed the folder, put it back on her desk.

"To destroy the alien base dome at Cunningham Park."

Well, that got my attention, because I've only heard second- or third-hand about successful attempts to destroy the base domes. Scores of them were scattered around the United States countryside, and many others were stationed around the world. They were the base of operations for three types of Creepers—Battle, Transport, Research—that skittered out in their armored exoskeletons to explore, kill, or whatever else aliens do as part of their occupation.

But they were nearly invulnerable to any form of attack, from lasers to explosive shells to napalm. My mention earlier about six 155 mm shells striking the dome in Cunningham Park—about 29 klicks to the west of us—was just the Army's way of telling the Creepers inside that they were still being observed.

Not that it seemed to bother them that much. We had one reliable weapon to use against the Creepers, a binary nerve agent fired from an infantry weapon, a Colt M-10, but more often than not, when it came down to a fight, sometimes the Creepers got killed and most times, the attacking soldier or Marine was either scorched to a cinder or sliced into pieces by a laser beam.

But to destroy a Creeper base dome took one thing and one thing only: a nuclear bomb.

Seemed simple enough, didn't it. There were tens of thousands of nuclear bombs among the world's arsenals when the invasion took place, so why hadn't each dome been destroyed upon its establishment?

Delivery devices, that's why.

With the killer stealth satellites in orbit, anything flying—from a missile to an aircraft to even an unmanned drone—would be blasted out of the sky before it posed a threat. Which left delivery by truck, tank, or even a horse drawn carriage. But even then, the Creepers could detect the electronics contained within the weapons, and they would still be destroyed by a particle beam or a "rod from God" before it got close enough to do any damage.

But just over a year ago, word filtered down from the government in Albany that our allies, the Russians—everybody was an ally nowadays—had come up with a way of destroying a dome by a nuclear device.

It involved breaking the bomb into several components, being able to shield the electronics from detection, and then slowly, gradually, transport those pieces up to a Dome, usually by two or three soldiers armed with nothing more than a knapsack. There, the soldiers would quickly reassemble the device, and then set it off.

Not by timer.

Not by a remote switch.

Not by anything electronic.

But mechanically, using Mark II eyeballs and hands.

If the mission was successful, it meant a destroyed Dome and lots of dead Creepers.

But it also meant two or three dead humans as well.

Suicide mission.

But the Russians being the Russians, some were prepared to pay the ultimate price.

And now they were coming here to Long Island.

"Sergeant Hart?"

"Ma'am?" I realized she had just spoken and I hadn't heard what she had said.

"Did you hear what I just said?"

Decisions, decisions.

I decided to throw myself on the mercy of my superior officer and confess the truth.

"Ma'am, I'm afraid I didn't."

"Late for the briefing, not hearing a word that I uttered," she said, shaking her head. "A hell of a way to start the day."

"Yes, ma'am."

"You're one sloppy NCO, aren't you." It wasn't really a question.

"The sloppiest, ma'am."

"But you also happen to be one of my smartest, which helps. Sometimes. Don't push it."

"No, ma'am."

She referred to another piece of paper. "What did you have for breakfast this morning?"

"Ah . . . I was running late, ma'am. Didn't have breakfast."

"Major Glenn reports that you've vomited blood twice in the last week."

I didn't reply to my boss.

What could I say?

She said, "How are you holding up?"

"Fine, ma'am."

"You're probably lying to me, Sergeant Hart."

"It's a possibility, ma'am."

She stared at me with her brown eyes and I saw something there that was not usual.

Sympathy.

"When the time comes," she said, "we'll change your duty status."

"If you say so, ma'am."

"I do so."

"Thank you, ma'am."

The lieutenant picked up another sheet of paper, a thin light yellow message flimsy, and she said, "You were stationed at Fort Saint Paul in New Hampshire three years ago, correct?"

"Yes, ma'am."

"And served in a Ranger Recon platoon with a Randy Knox?"

A slight smile at the memory of being at that platoon and Knox's silly but very capable Belgian Malinois named Thor.

"That's right," I said. "Sergeant Knox."

"It's now Lieutenant Knox," she said.

"Great," I said, feeling just the tiniest bit jealous of him earning his lieutenant's bars before me.

"Not so great," she said, putting the message flimsy down. "Got last quarter's casualty reports this morning. He's listed MIA after an ambush in Connecticut."

"Connecticut?" I asked, hoping for a mistake. "Last I knew, he was still stationed in New Hampshire. What was he doing in Connecticut?"

"Getting ambushed," she says. "He was part of a convoy, heading east to Massachusetts when they were attacked by a band of Creepers. Most of the convoy was destroyed. Knox was listed MIA. Sorry."

I took a breath. Losing friends and family members was nothing new in this ever-constant war, but one tried not to get used to it. And I wasn't going to fool myself by hoping he was, indeed, missing. Not in this time, not in this war. In a very few instances, being listed as MIA was a way of a soldier deserting into the wild and not being listed as being absent without leave. But most times it was a way of facing reality, that in a war when we humans faced lasers, flame weapons, rods from God and kinetic energy weapons, sometimes there were no remains or dog tags left behind.

So Knox was MIA.

Poor Randy. At some point, years from now, some overworked and undermanned graves registration unit might find a charred bone or two, tangled up in his dog tags, and that would be that.

Dogs.

I hoped his Thor had made it.

"Sergeant Hart?"

"Ma'am?" I replied, knowing I had been caught again, not paying attention.

"Your visitors are arriving at approximately oh nine-hundred tomorrow, at Hempstead Harbor. Be there."

"Yes, ma'am."

"Dismissed."

The next morning I was standing at one of the floating docks making up the Hempstead Harbor structure. Pre-war there were lots of harbors scattered along Long Island, but the invading Creepers had dropped asteroids in oceans, lakes and rivers, causing artificial tsunamis. That meant a lot of cities around the world were drowned, and places like Long Island were pretty much scoured clean, and any surviving ports were tumbled places of junk from broken docks to boat hulks.

That meant most harbors were artificial, built with floating docks, and the one I was on took care of this part of Long Island. Fishing boats of all kinds were moored on two long docks, and the third dock I was on belonged to the Navy, as small as it was.

Out on the waters there was a distant haze masking the Connecticut coastline, and among the fishing vessels out there was a steam-vessel of some sort—it looked like it had once bore masts— and at the stern of the craft a flag was slowly waving in the steady breeze. It had three stripes—white, blue and red—and in the corner was a yellow square with a double-headed eagle.

One of the Navy's harbormasters came up to me, and she said, "Looks like our Russian friends have arrived."

The harbormaster was cute, wearing a khaki blouse and pants, and a blue baseball cap covering her blonde hair. She seemed to be about my age, 16 or so. Per her nametag, her name was COOK.

"What's the flag?"

She had a pair of binoculars hanging from a leather strap around her neck, and brought them up. One of the lenses was missing.

"Russian Imperial flag," she said. "The Russians now have a czar again."

Two launches slipped out from the dock, being rowed by six

crewmen each, and in a few minutes, they were coming back, the boats riding lower in the water. There were large containers in the center of the first boat, and two passengers riding in the rear, and four other Russians in the other.

"This way," the harbormaster said, and I followed her to the end of the dock. The first launch came around and there was a flurry of lines being tossed, oars being raised, and a couple of beefy guys managed to unload the containers—made out of scuffed black plastic—and then two individuals stepped out, wearing dark blue uniforms of a type I had never seen before, with garrison caps with badges on their heads. The near individual was a heavy-set man, with a big smiling face and close-cropped hair. He turned and spoke to the person behind him, who turned out to be a young Russian woman, and she smiled at me, and I fell in love at that very moment.

She quickly walked up to me and extended her hand, which I quickly shook. She was about my height, wearing the same uniform as her male comrade, but she looked nothing like her fellow officer. She was slim, pretty, with bobbed blonde hair, wide smile, blue eyes, and clear skin.

"Good day," she said, speaking fine English with a Russian accent.

"Hi," I said, knowing, at that moment, I sounded like a moron.

She let me hand go, gestured to her companion. "This is Senior Lieutenant Kosanskey, Imperial Russian Navy."

He smiled, saluted, and I saluted back, realizing that while these two had probably traveled for weeks across the Atlantic and looked like a Russian Navy recruiting poster, I was dressed in mended and slightly dirty Army fatigues.

He said something quickly in Russian, and the woman said, "Yuri extends his deepest greetings in fraternal thanks to the American Army. I'm sorry, he doesn't speak English."

"That's all right, I don't speak Russian."

"Ah," she said, "my apologies. Captain Lieutenant Ludmilla Petrov. Glad to meet your acquaintance."

Then I realized, like a dummy, that it was my turn, and I said, "Sergeant Walter Hart, 2nd Infantry Brigade Combat Team, New York National Guard. I'm your escort for your mission."

Ludmilla smiled, revealing dimples on both cheeks. "So happy to greet you, Sergeant Hart."

Yuri stepped forward, smiling, and slapped me on my shoulders. I winced. He rattled off something in Russian, and Ludmilla said, "Yuri says . . . after many weeks . . . so glad to be in America, so glad to help you kill the . . . *nasekomyye*."

"The what?"

"The *nasekomyye*," she said. "The insects. The bugs."

"The Creepers," I said. "Thank you for coming here, to kill our Creepers."

They had some more gear to get off their boat, and there were more Russian naval officers that came ashore to meet the senior officers of the Mitchel Joint Navy-Army station. A photographer from *Stars & Stripes* was also there, and after a while, I got them secured in their temporary quarters, and their gear was placed under guard in an adjacent small warehouse.

I was heading back to my quarters when I got word that there was a dinner being held at the Officer's Mess to honor our Russian allies, and I got an invite, which surprised me, because I was listed as an NCO, despite my Intelligence Officer position. But a meal was a meal, and I managed to get something resembling a dress uniform together and got to the mess hall.

I was late, so it meant I sat in the back, near the swinging doors leading to the kitchen, but the meal was pretty good, pre-war canned stew that had made it through in reasonable shape, along with homemade bread, and there was a speech by both of the base's commanders—Army and Navy—and dessert was chocolate chip cookies, and after it broke up, I was mingling around, leaning on my cane, when there was a tap on my shoulder.

I turned and it was Ludmilla, smiling at me.

I leaned into my cane, something in my chest going *thump-a-lump*.

"Thank you for welcoming us," she said.

"You're very welcome."

"You are taking us to the Dome tomorrow, correct?"

"That's right."

Damn, those dimples looked so sweet.

She leaned over to me and said, "There's a . . . what you call. Association. Get-together."

"A party?"

Ludmilla quickly nodded her head. "Yes. A party. Please join us."

I had reports to type up, laundry to do, and a review of incoming telegraph traffic from other intelligence battalions in New England, but I instantly said, "I'd love to."

The party was in an abandoned building on the edge of the old landing strip, and was made up of a bunch of Americans and Russians from the ship, which I learned was named the *HMS Alexander III*. An American flag and Russian flag had been nailed on a wall, and somebody had rustled up an old stereo that played records.

Lots of loud music, some snacks, and the Russians had brought along a case of their vodka, which tasted a hell of a lot better and sharper than our Long Island stuff, made from damaged or surplus potatoes. There were lots of toasts, laughter, and I danced as best as I could with Ludmilla, using my cane, and at one point, I needed to go outside and get some fresh air.

Even on this lonely stretch of the base, there were gas lamps, illuminating the cracked roads and sidewalks, and overhead was the never-ending light show of pieces of space junk burning up as they re-entered Earth's atmosphere. A lot of the debris came from satellites and the old ISS that had been destroyed when the Creepers had invaded, and for the past several weeks, some of the larger chunks had come from the Orbital Battle Station, destroyed in some desperate attack by what was left of the Air Force.

It was supposedly the end of the war, our ultimate victory, but like the earlier nightmare of alien invasion, a sequel had been planned.

The war wasn't over.

Not with a second Orbital Battle Station suddenly appearing in the sky more than a month ago.

"Enjoying yourself?" a woman's voice spoke up, making me jump.

I turned and it was Cook, the assistant harbormaster. She was dressed in patched jeans and a very faded New York Giants T-shirt, and she lit up a cigarette. She offered me a puff and I declined, thinking of the irony of it all, and I said, "Very much so."

"Yeah, I can tell," she said. "Can I give you a word of advice?"

"Sure."

"Me and about half the base can see you mooning over the Russian blonde chick. Don't."

"Why the hell not?"

She took a quick puff. "Really? You don't know why? I thought you were in intelligence."

"The best around," I said.

"Hardly," she said. "Ludmilla and her bulky friend? They're the team that's going to bring the bomb components next to the Creeper Dome and set it off. Both of them will be dead in a few days."

The next morning I was ordered to take Ludmilla and Yuri as close as possible to the Creeper Dome, and I got a chit to sign out an electric Humvee from the motor pool, but it was in the middle of being overhauled so I had to make do with a quartermaster's horse and carriage, with two old dark brown farm horses taking us out to the west. A young Explorer Scout with a bad complexion who was doing an internship with the motor pool was our driver.

In a few minutes we were on old Route 25, going along the remains of small businesses and single-family homes that were abandoned after the war began. Other wagons and carriages were on the road, along with horses, bicycles, some old cars that had basic engines that weren't fried ten years ago, and a couple of Humvees trundling along on routine patrol. Ten-year-old hulks of abandoned cars and trucks were on either side of the road, where they had been dragged over in the past years.

I managed to sit across from Ludmilla, and Yuri sat next to her, smiling and looking around at the old desolation. Both were dressed in denim workpants and blue-and-white long-sleeved shirts.

I tried very hard not to recall what Cook had told me last night, not wanting to think of this pretty young girl across from me and her large friend dying in a nuclear flash.

Ludmilla said, "All the people who lived here . . . where are they?"

"Refugees or dead," I said. "The bugs dropped an asteroid near Staten Island, and in the middle of Long Island Sound. That meant New York City was drowned and a lot of the towns on the Connecticut coastline and here were washed away. The survivors eventually left, either on their own or via the National Guard. Pre-war, the population of Long Island was about eight million. Now? Maybe eighty thousand, if that."

Ludmilla shook her head, spoke to Yuri and pointed at the passing landscape. Yuri's face colored, he shook his head, and then spoke quickly to Ludmilla. She turned to me and said, "Yuri says . . . he's happy to be here . . . to help avenge all those who have died . . ."

I nod but I want to ask, *but what about you? How can you come so far to die on a foreign land?*

After about an hour we came to a checkpoint, and after showing my ID and orders, we were passed through. The checkpoint was an old mobile home trailer shoved across the road, with an armored-up Humvee keeping watch. The top of the Dome was now in view, and the horses started whinnying and shaking.

The Explorer scout up forward turned, reins in hands, and said, "As far as I can go, Sergeant."

"All right," I said, "we'll hoof it from here."

I got out of the carriage, wincing when my fake leg hit the cracked pavement first, shooting pain up my right stump. Yuri got off, helping Ludmilla, and each grabbed a canvas satchel, and started following me.

I took my time, walking along the path, using my cane, and here the pavement was torn up, melted in places, the homes and businesses either crushed or burned. The air seemed off, still, and I knew it was from the presence of the Dome, which also caused the absence of any wildlife. Two soldiers on patrol gave us a wave, and the near one said, "Hey, folks, don't get scorched, okay?"

"I'll do my best."

But when they spotted Ludmilla, they stopped and smiled and just stood still as we went by.

Up ahead, there was a cleared area, and then a high berm made of plowed-up dirt, asphalt, and concrete, with carcasses of old trucks, cars, and vehicles. There was a stairway made of wood and metal, and I said, "This'll give us a good view. Watch your step. This stairway is pretty beat-up and old."

Yuri went up first, Ludmilla followed, and I took up the rear, moving as well as I could with one leg. At the top platform there was a soldier I knew, a Corporal Tanner, who was sitting on an old folding chair and with a spotter scope on a tripod set before him. At his feet was a small knapsack, and next to it, a field telephone with a phone line stretching out all the way back to the checkpoint.

He turned and said, "Hey, Sarge. What's going on?"

"VIPs," I said. "Russian Navy, here to check out our neighbors."

Tanner whistled. "Sure came a long way to spot bugs. Don't you have enough back home?"

Ludmilla said, "Yes, but we're here . . . diplomacy mission. We're here to destroy this Dome."

Tanner said, "Have at it. Here, want to take a look?"

So he stood up and Ludmilla bent over to the spotting scope, and then she called over Yuri, and for a few minutes, they talked to each other in Russian, and then took turns looking out over the field to the Creeper Dome. It was its usual perfect dome shape, colored a dark gray-blue, and from the dirt berm before us, the land sloped down and across to the structure. The land was torn, blackened and blasted, with foundations of destroyed houses, burnt cars and trucks, and the rusting carcasses of artillery pieces and M1-A1 tanks.

Yuri said something to Ludmilla, who in turn said to Tanner, "How active is this Dome? Have a census been taken? How often do the bugs come out?"

Tanner grinned, scratched at his ear. "Active? Not very. The bugs come out when they want to . . . no set schedule that anybody knows of. And census? What's that?"

Ludmilla looked serious. "You don't do census? A count?"

Tanner looked to me, and then to Ludmilla. "They all look the same. How can you do a count?"

She said, "There are three classes of Creepers, *da*? But in each type of Creeper, there are differences . . . marks on the legs, scorches on the abdomen, worn bits of armor. That way . . . you know how many bugs are in the Dome."

"But why?" I asked.

Ludmilla smiled. "So you know how many is there when you kill them all."

Yuri said something to Ludmilla, she said "*Da*," picked up her bag. Yuri picked up his bag, and then they climbed over the berm and started heading to the dome.

★ ★ ★

"Hey!" I yelled out, and Tanner said, "Crap, what the hell are they doing?"

Ludmilla and Yuri walked a few meters and then dropped down, and I did my best to follow them, although with my fake leg and cane, it took a while. I fell, crawled, and stumbled, and when I got to them, their satchels were open and they were staring at the dome with binoculars, making marks on a notebook, talking to each other low.

I slid in behind them and said, "Are you two out of your freakin' minds?"

Yuri grinned. Ludmilla said, "Out? No, we're surveying. Doing our jobs."

"You . . ."

Yuri said a series of words, and Ludmilla said, "The dilation. Opening into the dome. Where does it usually appear?"

"Straight ahead," I said. "That's why we have a spotter there, keeping an eye on what's going on."

"Ah," Ludmilla said.

She and Yuri went back to work, and I tugged at her near boot and said, "You've got to get out of here, now! This whole area is a killing zone."

Ludmilla smiled and I couldn't be angry with her any more.

"*Da*, and we're here to kill them."

Two more days followed where I escorted Ludmilla and Yuri around the Dome, where they made drawings, took measurements, and otherwise scoped out the Dome and its surroundings. I kept up as best as I could, though my right stump ached something fierce and twice when I was out with Ludmilla, I doubled over with nausea and vomited with no warning. Luckily, though, she never saw me in distress.

But on the third day, everything went wrong.

I rolled out of my bunk and the door to my room opened up, with a young orderly standing there, looking at my cluttered quarters and then at me, trying to put on my wooden and metal prosthetic.

"Yeah?" I said. "Don't you know how to knock?"

"Sorry, Sergeant," she said, staring at my stump. "Lieutenant Juarez needs to see you, soonest."

"Got it," I said. "Now get the hell out so I can get dressed."

And about fifteen minutes later, I was in Lieutenant Juarez's office, and she said without hesitation, "We've got a problem. One of the Russians is missing. Deserted."

Something went *thud* in my chest. "Which one?"

"The male," she said. "Yuri. Ran off last night."

Then I hated myself right then, because I was torn. If one of the Russians had indeed deserted, I would want Ludmilla to have been the one. But by staying behind . . . I could see her again.

And maybe she would abandon her mission.

And live.

"Go see her," Juarez said. "See what we can do . . . if anything."

Ludmilla was in her own quarters, and it was crowded because there were four of the large black plastic cases that had come ashore when they had first landed. The tops of the cases were open and Ludmilla seemed to be checking the complicated gear and electronics nestled in dry black foam.

"Yes?" she said, still looking at the pages in a thick manual written in the odd-looking Russian-looking letters. "What is it, Walter?"

"I . . . sorry to hear about Yuri."

She shrugged. "A temptation . . . being here in America, battered as you are. He and I, everyone else, they are volunteers."

"So what are you going to do?"

Ludmilla looked at me like I had just suggested we flap our arms and go up to the Creepers' Orbital Battle Station. "My duty, of course. I am going to do my duty."

I leaned on my cane. "But I thought it took two . . . persons to do the job."

"*Da*, yes, usual. But this is not usual, correct? I have sworn to my family's memory, to the Czar and my God, that I will do this mission. I will find a way."

I said, "Ludmilla . . . don't."

"Don't ask me that again. I have no choice."

"But if you do it yourself, you might not make it."

"What other choice do I have?"

My gut is churning, from fear and something else.

"I have an idea."

She looked at me from her manual. "What is that, Walter?"

"I volunteer," I said. "I'll take Yuri's place."

After two days' worth of arguing, meetings, more arguing, finally permission was granted.

And it all came down to our unit's medic, who said to Lieutenant Juarez and myself the day before I was deployed, "I'm not sure how advanced the tumor is in Sergeant Hart's stomach, but I know it's inoperable and untreatable. Even in the best times, before pre-war, Sergeant Hart's case would be a difficult one for long-term survival. Now . . ."

I didn't need to hear any more.

And neither did my boss.

Her eyes moistened. "Are you sure, Sergeant Hart?"

"The end of my service was written last year," I said, remembering the onset of my symptoms. "But the last page . . . it was going to be either in a hospice room somewhere, alone, or on the battlefield. I prefer the battlefield."

Lieutenant Juarez just nodded, and in a quiet voice, whispered, "Bless you."

So today was the day, or more accurately, the night was the night.

I demanded from my lieutenant that I didn't get any kind of send-off—I was afraid that seeing all of my fellow troopers would spook me and I'd turn around at the last minute—so the only person to see me off was the same soldier as before, at the OP at the top of the stairs.

Corporal Tanner was there, blanket around his shoulders, and he said, "Hey,—Sarge, I mean—"

"Keep quiet," I said, "and help us with this stuff."

The "stuff" was two plastic sledges, with black boxes and components tied down, and ropes to drag them. He helped Ludmilla and me over the top of the berm, and he gave me a quick slap on the back.

"Take care."

"That's my plan."

Ludmilla said "Soldier?"

"Yes?"

"Go away now. Far away."

"Yes, ma'am," and Tanner scampered down the stairway.

Now it was just Ludmilla and me.

"We go."

"Great," I said.

I followed Ludmilla's lead, and moved slow, very slow. We dragged the sledges behind us, and she said, "We learn . . . from hard lessons . . . to move slow. Not set any pattern."

"I see."

I followed her slim body, as we traversed the torn up and scorched earth. Overhead the constant flares and burning lights of space wreckage coming into the atmosphere continued. My stomach and abdomen were burning, but having Ludmilla in front of me calmed me down some.

We went up and down a trench, around some burnt wreckage from attacks a decade ago—some kind of artillery piece, its barrel and support melted—and Ludmilla whispered, "Stop, now."

"Okay."

I sat there, and then Ludmilla rustled her way over to me and said, "I'm cold."

I was dumb, but not that dumb.

I put my arm around her, and she cuddled in next to me, and I smelled her hair and fresh soap.

I can't remember that last time I've been so happy.

I said, "How did you end up here?"

She said, "You mean, how I get into war?"

"Something like that," I said.

I looked up at the lights flaring and burning through the night sky, feeling the dull and heavy presence of the dome base close by.

"I . . . was a child. On holiday. With my family. On a cruise ship from Vladivostok. The ship was called the *V. V. Tereshkova*. I don't remember much. But the bugs come, drop their rocks . . . many tidal waves . . . our ship, she was sunk."

"I'm sorry."

She moved under my arm. "So. A long time back . . . somehow . . . I ended in life raft . . . washed ashore . . . when I grew up, in All Orphan Pioneer Party, I swore I would get my revenge . . . and here I am."

"But . . ."

"But what, Walter?"

"Aren't you afraid?"

"Are you afraid?"

"Some . . . but I know what's ahead of me. It's not good. I'd rather go out doing something . . . oh, I don't know. Special. Heroic."

"Good for you," Ludmilla said. "I just want to kill the bugs. Let's move some more."

We dragged our sledges across the landscape, stopping at Ludmilla's command, me not too sure what she was doing, only knowing that she must have been working from years of experience. It was hard to believe that in these plastic sledges, bouncing behind us, sometimes getting caught up in torn and blasted metal, that there was a weapon that would destroy this dome.

We were closer now, and we rested two more times.

"How further do we go?" I asked.

"Right up to the dome," she said. "Where the access hatch dilates open . . . it's the weakest spot."

"Makes sense," I said.

We cuddled up again and she said, "Now, your story, eh?"

"Not much of a story," I said.

"Tell me still."

"Grew up in Maine, up north of here. Small family. Deep in the woods . . . and, the war began."

"How old were you?"

"Seven."

"And?"

A particularly big piece of space debris came in, throwing off big sparks and flares.

She nudged me.

"And?"

Well, she asked.

"The weather took a hit with all the debris and water kicked up into the atmosphere," I said. "The first year was tough, the second year was tougher. The little house we lived in was only heated by a fireplace. We took to going to bed for most of the day when the snowstorms came through. Dad, Mom and me. I was on a couch near the fire, covered in blankets and comforters. They were nearby, on a fold-out couch. One day . . . I don't remember much. The fire had gone out. There wasn't much wood. My parents wouldn't get up, and then . . . well, they couldn't get up."

"Oh," she said.

"Yeah. I walked a while to a neighbor's house. Got turned away. Went to another house. Was taken in, joined the Boy Scouts soon afterwards. When I got older, I figured out my parents starved to death, trying to keep me alive."

Ludmilla kissed me on the cheek. "So we both have reasons to kill the bugs, eh?"

"We do."

I kissed her back, on the cheek as well, and then I kissed her lips, and that's how the time passed for a long lovely while.

Two more movements, and then we were up against the Dome. I was shuddering and feeling scared, and my body was betraying me as well. I threw up again and from the light of a big chunk of space debris, I see there was blood in what came out.

No matter.

Ludmilla took her time, opening the hard plastic containers, explaining how the different modules and pieces of the nuclear device were put together.

"So many experiments, so many failures," she said, moving slowly and then stopping for a while. "Many brave men and women died to get the . . . knowledge? Information. *Da*.Information. We all learned hard way that the bugs monitor all electronics, from space, from the Domes. But to what level? So . . . volunteers. Would go up against the Domes, carrying various electronics . . . they would be burnt, captured . . . a lucky few would escape . . . but we learned. We learned."

She looked around, very satisfied indeed.

"We rest now," she said.

She came to me and we kissed again.

"Walter, your leg?"

"The good one or the fake one?"

"What happened?"

"It's buried somewhere in a landfill in New Hampshire," I said. "I had been in the Army a month. It hadn't been a good month."

"I want to know more."

"I don't want to tell you."

"Okay, then."

I think Ludmilla dozed in my arms, which was a good thing, because I could sense . . . something. Movement. Vibration.

A light slowly started bathing the area to the north of me, and then I turned and closed my eyes, because I knew what was happening next.

The Creeper Dome was opening up and with its opening, came a bright flash of light.

I turned in a second and off to the distant north, one and then two alien Creepers skittered over the dirt berm. They moved at a good pace, and from my vantage point, with a beautiful girl in my arms, I could see they were two Battle modes, coming back to their home base after a night of burning and lasering whatever they wanted. Seeing the armored arthropods up close again made me tense with fear and anger, and then they safely slipped into the dome, and the dilated opening closed.

Ludmilla stirred and moved away. "What . . . what happen?"

"Two Creepers just came back, into their base."

She sat up. A line of light pink and red was beginning to form in the east.

"Good," she said. "Two more that will die."

The morning day looked to be pretty fine. My arms and chest felt heavy.

One's last day.

"Ludmilla?"

"Yes?"

"You and I . . . we could run away. Go to the west. They're looking for workers, farmers out west. We would never be found."

She didn't say no, and she didn't say yes. A hand came into my hand, gently caressed it, and squeezed it.

"But we would always know that we had run away, wouldn't we?"

But to live with you, I thought . . . and there was a stab in my gut, reminding me that the decision, one way or another, had already been made.

"Yeah, I guess you're right," I said. "Show me what we need to do."

★ ★ ★

Once again, we moved slowly, as different components were taken out, cables were hooked up, switches and such were inspected. Ludmilla said, "There were attempts, many attempts, to set up timers, or mechanical devices, or even a long, long cable to be used, to explode the device. It never worked. Some sort of . . . haze? Field? From the Dome? Only after volunteers hand-exploded, did it work."

"Why two?"

"With one, it was too long to haul, too much chances of being found. And . . . two. There would be two to press the switch, in case one . . . runs."

I nodded, just followed her directions.

All thought out.

And then, too soon, we were done.

We sat against a rise in the dirt, the bomb at our feet, ready and connected to go off and kill everything in the vicinity.

Two cables ran out of one of the black boxes, each ending in a trigger switch. I took one and Ludmilla took the other.

"What . . . now?" I asked.

The sun started to come up.

"Down there," she said. "That's the battery. You turn that switch down there . . . the light goes from red to green . . . powering up . . . when it turns to green . . . it's time."

"Okay."

The sun came up higher. But there was little sound. No birds, no animals, nothing in this zone of death.

Ludmilla slipped her hand into mine, and then reached down, toggled a switch.

A red light came on.

She came back, cuddled up against me.

The light turned green.

"Ludmilla . . ."

"Please, Walter."

"Wait, just for a bit."

"Walter . . ."

"No," I said. "There's a reason."

"What?"

I said, "I'm in intelligence. I keep track of things . . . according to the last orbital mechanics I saw, the new Orbital Battle Station should be showing up in a few minutes."

She didn't say anything and sitting against the dirt, I was feeling the vibrations coming through from whatever the Creepers were doing inside the Dome. There were probably human prisoners in there, and I hoped their souls or afterlife would forgive us for what we were about to do.

Then again, they might be thankful.

"Walter, I don't understand."

I squeezed her hand. "Wouldn't it be something . . . if the Creepers' orbital base was overhead, and they were looking down . . . they would see us destroying this Dome. Showing them that we're still fighting. That we won't give up."

"Ah . . . how soon?"

"Very soon," I said.

She moved even closer to me, kissed me.

"*Da*, that we do. We wait. We show them."

So we sat there, the only free humans in probably miles around, and I was hoping for a lot more time, to talk to Ludmilla, to find out more about here, her life, her hopes, her regrets . . . thinking of what we might have been able to do together if—

There it was.

Rising up from the horizon.

"I see it," she said.

"Me, too."

"You . . . we will wait, then we'll do it together. Okay?"

I kissed her and kissed her.

"Together," I said.

The Orbital Battle Station was nearly overhead, and then—

Light.

Doughboys: synthetic battle constructs designed decades ago to fight the Ember War. Strong, fearless, and fiercely loyal to their human commanders, in many ways they are the perfect soldiers and have continued to prove themselves on the battlefield long after the war's end. Now, Doughboy wrangler Sergeant Hoffman is about to learn just how loyal the constructs under his command are. In the process, he may learn from a synthetic man what it means to be human.

GOING DARK

★

by Richard Fox

UTICA CITY WAS A CORPSE. Her killers still fought through the carcass of wrecked buildings, out of control fires, and what remained of the colonists lives strewn through the streets. A ground car, wrecked against the side of a school for human children, shot sparks from the broken wheel battery casings, the driver dead and pinned to the dashboard.

Naroosha saucers zipped overhead, shooting rapid bolts of energy at the Terran Union fighters flying low over the horizon. The snap of Union gauss weapons mingled with the crack of alien weapons; stray bolts cast quick shadows as they vanished into the high cloud cover.

Just outside the school, the dark polymer cover on the road bulged out, then flattened with a creak. The road cracked as something beat against the underside, like a hatchling trying to break from its egg.

The road shattered, hunks tumbling to the curb and against the crashed car's tires.

A spherical drone the size of a fist popped from the hole and spun around. It fell back into the opening and a soldier crawled out a half second later. Sergeant Hoffman, clad in power armor, his face obscured by a visor, took cover against the side of the wreck and did a quick peek into the school through the broken wall.

"Clear, get up here," Hoffman said.

A hammer whacked against the side of the hole in the road and it crumbled. Large hands wrenched more of the road away and another soldier, broad shouldered and so tall that Hoffman barely came up to his clavicle, crawled out. The big man unlimbered a heavy gauss cannon off his back, handling the massive weapon as easily if it was made of cheap plastic.

"Opal, get to the third floor and establish a firing position," Hoffman waved him past the wreck.

Opal tried to duck into the hole, bumped a shoulder against the bricks, then slapped a hand against the front of the crumpled fender and wrenched the car aside with a grunt. He hurried through the new opening, weapon ready at his shoulder.

"Trying not to get noticed, Opal," Hoffman sighed.

"Opal sorry. No shoot until order," the big soldier trotted past a wall of lockers and went bounding up a stairwell.

More soldiers, all as large as Opal, made their way out from under the road, their boots and legs stained with sewer water.

"Garnet 334, Zircon 12," Hoffman said, "First level. East. Establish fields of fire and report any enemy locations or friendly troops."

The two soldiers grunted and hurried inside, heavy gauss cannons in hand.

Hoffman looked up as a Naroosha saucer wobbled through the sky, smoke trailing from the engines.

"Sir," a soldier with a tube locked to one side of his back and a massive hammer held across his waist took cover at a corner. "Diamond 99 can kill enemy." He pointed a cybernetic digit as thick as a child's wrist at the stricken saucer. The rest of the soldier's hand was robotic, the prosthetic ended halfway up his forearm.

"Negative, Diamond, not the mission," Hoffman ordered another half dozen soldiers into the building and gave them instructions on their way past.

"Naroosha," Diamond tapped his hammer's head against the wall already stained with purple blood.

"Soon, I told you. Soon," Hoffman cocked his head to one side as the report of gauss fire grew stronger.

"Waiting. Bad." Diamond's hands gripped the hammer haft harder.

"Assign the rest of the platoon to firing positions," Hoffman reached into the broken glass of the car's windshield and lifted the driver's face up gently. Dead, unfocused eyes stared back at him.

Hoffman lowered the man's chin and crossed himself before vaulting over the car.

"I need to establish commo with the Rangers. No shooting until I give the order or we're attacked, understand, Diamond?" Hoffman asked.

The big soldier nodded slowly.

"Diamond?" Hoffman raised a finger and Diamond nodded faster.

The sergeant took to the stairs, hurrying past posters announcing baseball games and student council campaigns. The windows were shot out, the pockmarks of gauss shells and scorch marks on the walls marked the last time the front passed over the school.

He got to the third floor and went to a classroom, the door hanging loose from the top hinge, a massive boot print marking it.

Opal was there, crouching by a wall, facing a shattered window. They had clear line of sight across sports fields to a row of low buildings on the other side of a fence. Naroosha energy bolts flashed down alleyways and beat against walls.

Hoffman zoomed in on the battlefield with his gauss rifle's optics and made out humanoid shadows moving within buildings, but didn't pick up any friendly weapons fire.

"Enemy there," Opal said. "Slow shots. Not an attack."

"You're right, they're keeping our guys pinned down while they bring in the heavy hitters," Hoffman said, slightly relieved. The plan was on track, but everything could spiral out of control if the Naroosha pressed their advantage.

"*Building secure*," Diamond sent over the squad's infrared radio. "*Unit Beryl 77 reports roof is exposed.*"

"Then get Beryl off the roof before the slugs see him." Hoffman took an IR booster off his belt and reached around the broken glass to fix the device to the outer wall. He ducked back inside and flipped up a panel on his left gauntlet. He keyed a command and the booster pulsed. New contacts appeared on the inside of his visor. He double tapped a name.

"Ranger Lieutenant Ford, this is Sergeant Hoffman, Battle Construct Auxiliary company 117, how do you read?" Hoffman said.

There was a shuffling over the IR, snaps of exploding Naroosha energy bolts in the background.

"Ford," came over the IR, "Christ, am I happy to hear your friendly voice. Slugs have us pinned down from—"

"Break break break," Hoffman cut in. "Sector command's ordered an Armor assault from the industrial district in the next . . ." he glanced at the mission clock on the inside of his visor, "nine minutes. You're to fall back to the primary school in the next five minutes."

"Five minutes? What part of 'pinned down' didn't you understand?" Ford asked.

"I've got my men on overwatch, we'll cover your movement. The general wants the Naroosha to pursue, overextend to give the Armor a clear shot to their lander," Hoffman said. A request for a new IR channel popped on his screens.

He sent back a single character to sender. "3." The combat shorthand to the other sergeant told him Hoffman was in a mission critical communication and would establish contact as soon as the battle allowed.

"*—off your asses and prep to move,*" Ford said, giving orders to his Rangers while the channel was still open. "*We're getting set. Wait, did you say you were combat auxiliaries? You're in charge of a bunch of doughboys?*"

"Doughboys, yes," Hoffman said. "All of whom are locked and loaded and waiting to kill any Naroosha you've left alive."

"*We've got . . . damn it, we've positive ID on slug Max units moving in,*" Ford said.

Hoffman repeated an expletive several times.

"I've got heavy gauss cannons and a sabot," Hoffman said. "We can take out the Maxes, but you need to move. Now."

"*Bug out, bug out all of you!*" Ford shouted over the IR, giving the order to retreat immediately.

"All units," Hoffman said over his platoon net, "cover friendlies. Execute aim restriction protocols seven-alpha-alpha."

Opal's back went straight as his entire body tightened up.

"Aim restriction engaged," Opal said.

Across the sports fields, dark armored Rangers emerged from the buildings, running toward the school.

An IR channel opened up.

"*Hoffman! You seeing this? Squids brought Maxes to the fight,*" a fellow doughboy leader sent him.

"That's the word, but no sign of them yet." Hoffman brought his gauss rifle to his shoulder and zeroed in on a Naroosha crawler—a spiderlike drone the size of a man—as it crept onto a rooftop overlooking the fleeing Rangers. He shot a single gauss shell that struck the back of the crawler, breaking off legs and sending it tumbling to the ground.

"You and your boys in place, Vaccaro?" he asked.

"*We're set. Aggression buffers on my lumps are acting up. You having the same problem?*"

"Negative." Hoffman sidestepped away from Opal as the doughboy stomped one heel to the floor and pistons shot stabilizer spikes into the checkerboard pattern tiles. The heavy gauss rifle opened up with three round bursts, the overpressure of the magnetically accelerated rounds blew out what remained of the windows and slapped the teacher's desk against the wall.

With his head fully enclosed by his helmet, the gunfire noise was manageable. He looked through the windows, watching the bright yellow tracers burst out of the school toward Naroosha crawlers as they pursued the Rangers.

Dark armored humans ran up to the fence and tore it away. More and more Rangers joined the stream pouring onto the football field.

"Not in the open," Hoffman cursed as the Rangers exposed themselves to the Naroosha's fire. Energy bolts snapped out of the buildings to the field, blowing up turf and showering Rangers with dirt.

Hoffman shot a pair of crawlers as they took up firing positions. That they set up in the open, and didn't fire and retreat to cover like he'd seen them fight in the past, struck a nerve. The Naroosha were getting bold, overly aggressive. Not a tactic they used unless they had overwhelming firepower.

"Priority target!" Diamond shouted, so loud Hoffman heard it through the floor and in his IR.

"Where? Where? Give me a sector of fire," Hoffman thumbed the power setting on his rifle to HIGH, which would drain his rifle's entire battery with one shot but gave him a chance to damage a Naroosha Max.

A point of light grew between buildings across the football field. A blast of coherent energy a yard wide lanced through the bleachers along one sideline, sending the metal seats scattering like twigs in a hurricane.

The blast missed the school and struck another building. Overpressure from the explosion slapped the rear of his fighting position and Hoffman braced himself as the blast side collapsed. Cracks ripped through the floor and Hoffman tripped over a child's desk.

He stared up at the ceiling as the rumbling subsided. Opal grabbed him under one shoulder and lifted the sergeant up and set him on his feet, then the doughboy went back to firing.

A neat line of burning grass and melted concrete marked the energy blast's path.

Rangers scrambled up off the ground and kept running for the school.

Diamond burst through the door, his massive head snapping from side to side.

"Sir no hurt?" the doughboy asked.

"Fine, D. I'm fine," Hoffman went to the windowsill as a Naroosha saucer strafed the football field, targeting the last few Rangers. Two pitched forward. One got to his feet slowly and tried dragging the other.

Hoffman knew Rangers, they would never leave one of their own behind, even at the cost of their own lives.

"Help. Help!" Diamond rushed forward, feet beating against the floor.

"No, Diam—" Hoffman cut off as Diamond shrugged the sabot launcher off his back and whacked it against Hoffman's chest. Diamond jumped out the third story window and landed into a roll. The doughboy charged toward the two Rangers, ignoring the energy bolts lashing at him.

A buzz filled the air and Hoffman's teeth hummed with it. In the distance, a flat, four pointed diamond the size of a car rose above the rooftops. The Naroosha Max. It angled up, a bucket helm at the apex of the diamond. The Naroosha rarely put themselves at risk on the battlefield, but when they did fight, they came in battle suits matched only by the Terran Union's Armor.

"Shit," Hoffman looked at the sabot launcher in his arms and then around the room. The sabot's backblast was severe, and firing it in the school would likely kill him and several of his doughboys.

"Engaging," Opal dropped his heavy gauss to the floor and snatched the sabot out of Hoffman's hands. The doughboy stepped onto the windowsill, swung an arm out and grabbed the wall, cracking the brick beneath his fingers. Opal locked the sabot to his back and climbed onto the roof.

"Opal, what're you doin—"

An arc of energy bolts ripped out from the Max and stitched explosions across the field and into the school. Hoffman went down in a fog of smoke and pulverized brick. He got to his hands and knees and found a gaping hole where the wall used to be. He went to the edge and looked up.

Opal stood on a broken metal spar, sabot on his shoulder and optics against his face.

"Shot. Shot too hard!" Opal shouted.

Hoffman snapped his gaze to the Max. Gauss rounds from another position broke against the energy shield surrounding the alien battle suit. A pinprick of light grew at a diamond tip—another lance blast.

On the field, Diamond carried two Rangers, one in each arm. Hoffman realized Opal's issue: they were too close to the Max, within the kill radius of a sabot blast.

"Opal, cancel all firing restrictions! Cancel!"

Through the visor over Opal's face, Hoffman swore he saw the doughboy's smile.

Hoffman ducked down and covered his head with his arms.

The sabot was a miniaturized version of the rail cannons Armor brought to battle. The magnetic accelerators in the weapon could shoot a cobalt clad depleted uranium slug the size of Hoffman's hand to escape velocity. The effect of firing the weapon in atmosphere was a sonic boom that was fatal to unarmored creatures.

Opal fired and the sabot snapped like an oak broken by giant hands. The overpressure beat Hoffman to the floor.

He looked up and saw a line of burning air tracing to an expanding cloud of shattered crystal and smoke where the Max had been. A second fading line angled away from where the Max had been. Did it fire its lance?

"Opal?" Hoffman looked up, but the doughboy was gone. He got up and found Opal half buried near the classroom's whiteboard, his helmet smashed open. The doughboy wrenched himself out of the wall and twisted the helmet off. Opal's head was almost atavistic, thick-jawed and with heavy brows that made him look closer to a Neanderthal than a human. His mottled green and brown skin was flushed from exertion. Clear fluid ran from a gash on his temple.

The doughboy staggered forward, then looked around wildly. He picked up his gauss rifle and shook dust from it. He moved uneasily, like he was half drunk. Combat constructs like Opal were tough, but they weren't invincible.

"Good shot, Opal," Hoffman said.

"Unit Diamond," Opal motioned with his barrel.

Hoffman slid down the rubble and found Diamond kneeling between two Rangers at the base of the wreckage.

Diamond's chest heaved, a smoking patch on his back.

"Medical . . . attention. For-for-for them," Diamond's cyborg hand twitched with some sort of palsy.

Hoffman slid to a stop next to the Rangers. One had lost an arm, her flank blown open, and ribs stuck out from the wound. He didn't have to check to know she was dead. The other Ranger moaned weakly.

Hoffman tried to open a channel to sector command, but his IR wouldn't connect.

The Ranger's visor popped open and a man looked to the gray sky, one eye purple and swollen shut.

"Heard doughboys were ugly," Lieutenant Ford said. "Looked . . . damn beautiful when he picked us up. You—you look familiar."

"I get that a lot. You're in shock, by the way." Hoffman opened a panel on the Ranger's armor and keyed in commands. There was a hiss as the armor administered drugs to Ford and tightened around his limbs, keeping blood flowing to his internal organs.

Rangers emerged from the dust and ran towards them.

"Opal," Hoffman waved the doughboy over. "Return to base with the wounded and get him to the field hospital. Escort the rest of the Rangers with squad alpha."

"Sir," Opal nodded.

Hoffman stepped back and let the Rangers care for their own. The sound of gauss fire echoed across the city. The Armor's attack had begun, and the Naroosha would be hard-pressed to stop it after the loss of a Max. The enemy commander would be pulling back every asset he could to deal with the new assault. He opened a wide beam IR freq.

"Vaccaro. What's your status?" he sent to the other doughboy leader.

No response.

Hoffman felt an icy pit open in his stomach.

He looked over the smoking patch of Diamond's armor, then reached under his shoulder and squeezed the emergency release. The armor patch fell off with a clang. Diamond's skin was blackened, sizzling in some places.

"D, what did I tell you about getting shot?" Hoffman asked.

"Had to help. Friends," Diamond said. Fluid dripped from the corner of his lips and one eye twitched.

"Diamond, systems check," Hoffman put a hand to the construct's shoulder. Diamond's gaze unfocused for a moment.

"Unit Diamond 99 registering fault in subroutine omega omega zero," the doughboy's voice changed to a higher pitch as the inner programming came to the fore.

"Omega omega zero?" Hoffman frowned. That was a fault he'd never heard of, despite years of leading doughboys. "Diamond, are you battle functional?"

Diamond rose to his feet and nodded.

"Good enough. Get squad beta and come with me. We need to find Vaccaro."

Hoffman ducked under a beam in a pile of rubble that once housed Utica City's constabulary and stepped into a slight depression. Remnants of the building had been tossed into a ring of debris, and at the center, a handful of doughboys stood in a circle around a prone figure.

"Damn it," Hoffman slid his visor up and approached the closest doughboy. The construct's armor was battered, stained with human blood and the clear fluid that was the soldier's ersatz blood.

Hoffman smelled bitter copper and saw the red-stained dirt beneath the figure his own size.

"Designation?" Hoffman asked the doughboy.

"Zircon 2-2."

Hoffman knelt next to the body and removed the visor. His own face stared back at him, eyes half open in the peace of the dead. Vaccaro was his own man, but his voice and visage belonged to another. Hoffman had never met the original, but he shared his looks.

"The Max targeted your building before mine," Hoffman looked around quickly. "You took the hit for me and my doughies. Saved us and the Rangers we came to save. You did well, buddy. Greater love hath no man than this, that a man lay down his life for his friends."

"Zircon, let's take him home," Hoffman tapped a fist to his chest to honor Vaccaro's memory to Saint Kallen. He reached under the dead man's chest and removed an ID chit from beneath his breastplate.

He got to his feet, then tapped Zircon on the shoulder twice and the big soldier turned to him. Hoffman looked the doughboy in the eye and put a thumb to Zircon's forehead, depressing the small button beneath his skin.

"Realignment protocol seven Charlie. Imprint to Hoffman. My face. My voice. Confirm?" Hoffman asked.

"Imprint to Vaccaro. Con-con-con—" Zircon's head snapped from side to side. "Imprint to Hoffman. Confirmed."

Hoffman took his hand away and repeated the procedure with the other survivors.

"You guys are twitchy," Hoffman said. "Zircon 2-2, what lot number are you and your squadmates?"

"Lot Alpha. Construction date—"

"Alphas? I didn't know any of you were still around," Hoffman frowned. "Zircon, recover Sergeant First Class Vaccaro."

Zircon locked his heavy rifle to his back and picked Vaccaro up like he was a sleeping child. Hoffman motioned back the way he came and all of the doughboys formed a cordon around the body as they made their way out.

Except for one construct.

Diamond stood stock still, gaze locked on a mangled poster in the rubble.

"Diamond?" Hoffman nudged the doughboy with his elbow.

He grunted, then looked around. Diamond saw the last doughboy leave the depression and poked a metal finger towards the exit.

"Break in contact. Poor formation," Diamond said.

"Let's catch up," Hoffman hurried after them, Diamond on his heels.

Something was off with Diamond, Hoffman knew it. Whether it was some residual trauma from damage or something else, he didn't know. And part of him didn't want the answer.

Hoffman walked out of the graves registration tent as fast as he could while maintaining some semblance of composure. He'd given a statement to the medical personnel that received Vaccaro's body and left as soon as they had what they needed. Doughboys couldn't give official statements, and the burden of explaining how Vaccaro was killed in action fell to him.

That tent always gave him the creeps—seeing his fellow soldiers dead, locked into stasis pods for return to Earth and burial was an all too real reminder of his likely fate on the battlefield.

He stepped around a wall and leaned against it, waiting for the flood of emotions to ebb.

His earpiece chimed. Hoffman beat a fist to the wall and checked his gauntlet screen. Why was the intelligence section calling him? He tapped his earpiece.

"Hoffman. Go."

"*You a doughboy wrangler?*" a woman asked, an edge of panic in her voice.

"I am," Hoffman rolled his eyes in annoyance.

"*Some of your guys are down here going apeshit,*" there was a crash of metal on metal over the line. "*They're wrecking recovered Naroosha equipment. Get over here before the MPs put them down!*"

"Moving," Hoffman shut the channel and took off at a run. He tapped the screen on the back of his hand to make another call.

"Diamond? Opal? Bring the squads to intel, now!" Hoffman sidestepped around a group of Rangers as they left a mess tent.

"*Opal, confirm.*"

"Diamond?" Hoffman heard sirens and ran toward the sound. He rounded a corner and vaulted over an MP vehicle, lights flashing red and blue. Military police held a perimeter around a group of prefab huts that served as the base's intelligence section.

Four doughboys were inside a fenced-in area, the reinforced steel of one side ripped open. Broken Naroosha crawlers, spike drones and fragments of a Max lay in a ten-foot pile. The doughboys beat fists against the wrecked enemy gear. Stomped crawler body domes flat. Ripped the arms off other drones and tossed the severed limbs against the fence.

Hoffman recognized Zircon and the other doughboys he'd found guarding Vaccaro's body.

"They're mine!" Hoffman stepped past an MP and went to one side of the fence. The doughboys within had stone faces, attacking the already broken equipment without passion. A shadow loomed behind him—Opal.

"Zircon, stand down," Hoffman beat a hand against the fence.

Zircon paused, looked at Hoffman, then went back to kicking a spike drone.

"Enemies," the doughboy said.

"Negative," Hoffman went to the hole in the fence. "Negative, Zircon. Enemies are non-functional. Disengage combat protocols. Now."

"Not Vaccaro," one of the other doughboys picked up a crawler leg and held it like a club. "Vaccaro hurt. Hurt!"

The doughboy took a step toward Hoffman, its eyes burning red.

The battle construct half raised its club, then froze.

"Subroutine omega omega zero fault," the club fell to the ground with a clatter. "Fault. Fault." The doughboy stood up straight, heels locked together, fists clenched at his legs. His eyes shut, then his head lolled to one side. The doughboy tipped over and crashed into the broken Naroosha debris.

"What the hell?" Hoffman took a step towards the doughboy, but Opal grabbed him by the shoulder and pulled him back.

"Danger," Opal rumbled.

Two of the other doughboys locked in place, then collapsed to the ground.

Zircon started towards them, his limbs jerking like a marionette.

"Fault." Zircon went to one knee and planted a fist to the ground.

"Vaccaro . . . hurt." The doughboy's chin lowered to his chest and he stopped breathing.

"No no no," Hoffman rapped his knuckles against Zircon's temple, but the doughboy didn't respond.

"Hey, what's wrong with them?" an MP asked from the other side of the fence, sidearm in hand.

"I don't—I don't know," Hoffman touched a fingertip beneath Zircon's ear and pressed the system reset switch. No response.

"Hoffman, report to maintenance bay nine. ASAP," came through his earpiece. He recognized the voice of his commander instantly.

Hoffman stepped away from Zircon, panic brewing in his chest. He ran out of the enclosure.

"What about them?" the MP called out.

"They deactivated! Dead!" Hoffman shouted over his shoulder.

Maintenance bay nine was a diagnostic room for doughboys. Diamond sat in the exam chair, wires plugged into ports at the back of his skull. The doughboy had his hammer in one hand, his cybernetic twitched and grasped at nothing.

Hoffman entered, and his face went pale when he saw Diamond in the chair. Opal followed Hoffman inside and stood guard next to the door.

"D, what's going on, buddy?" Hoffman went to the data screens and looked over the charts.

"Unit error," Diamond slurred.

"No way. You're a rock, Diamond, you don't get errors."

Hoffman put a thumb and forefinger to the skin around Diamond's left eye and opened the lid. The doughboy's optics twitched slightly, then traced small circles, switching from clockwise to counterclockwise.

Hoffman took a step back, fear blossoming in his chest. The bay grew cold. Hoffman thought the chill was just stress, but his breath fogged, confusing him even more.

"Look . . . there must be some bad code in there," he said and put a hand to Diamond's jaw. "We'll get the techs in here and do a reboot. It's nothing. You'll see."

"That's not what it is, son," came from behind him.

A man in Ranger armor stepped into the room and shut the door.

The uniform bore no unit patches, rank insignia, or even a name stenciled on the chest.

"Piss off, grunt, this is doughboy business," Hoffman said.

"I'm no grunt," the Ranger took his helmet off and the cold grew worse. There wasn't a human inside, but a silver being with a man's features.

Hoffman reached for his rifle, but stopped when Opal made no move against the newcomer.

"What are you? Why isn't Opal crushing your skull?" Hoffman asked.

"Smart," the silver man jerked a thumb at the doughboy. "They're hostile to all non-humans, but I put a few exceptions into their programming."

"You? But you can't be—"

"Marc Ibarra. Pleased to meet you. The doughboys are my creation. Let's not get into this," he waved a hand around his metal face. "Neither here nor there for the issues at hand."

Pain from the cold bit into Hoffman's ears and cheeks.

"They . . . subroutine omega omega zero," Hoffman said. "What's wrong with them? I just had four deactivate on me after they went berserk."

"Alpha lot?" Ibarra went to the diagnostic machines and swiped across the screens.

"How'd you know?"

"Projections had that they'd fail first," Ibarra held a finger up to Diamond's eye and a light shined out from the tip. "But this one's a much later batch. The prosthetic interface must have accelerated the degradation."

"What are you talking about?" Hoffman asked. "They're synthetic battle constructs, not living tissue."

Ibarra faced Hoffman and crossed his arms.

"They weren't meant to last forever, son. I built them as cannon fodder for the Ember War. Had my top men on the project. Top men . . . and one Aeon. We put them together as best we could in what little time we had available. Longevity wasn't a planning factor. Either we'd survive the Xaros invasion or we'd go extinct. Didn't matter if the doughboys could last a hundred years between checkups."

"You . . . built them to fail?" Hoffman touched Diamond on the shoulder.

"There was no time for perfection," Ibarra shrugged. "We didn't even bother to adjust their programming to imprint on their leaders. It was easier to change your face to match Jared Hale's than it was to fiddle with what was already working."

He tapped Diamond on the top of his head.

"You remember what it was like before the invasion. We survived that by the skin of our teeth. Where'd you fight?"

"Utah," Hoffman closed his eyes, the memories of skies blackened by enemy annihilation drones. His doughboys disintegrated as they fell to the invaders.

"Tough calls all around. We looked at improving the doughboys after the war, but the tech was about as good as we could make it. Synthetic computers are limited, but they can't be hacked," Ibarra said.

"What's happening to him?" Hoffman asked.

"System degradation. Subroutine omega omega zero records the errors, does what it can to make corrections, but it's inevitable that they'll malfunction and shut down. Sorry," Ibarra said.

"No. You can't just throw them aside," Hoffman poked a finger into Ibarra's chest. "Doughboys fought and died by the thousands, hundreds of thousands, during the war. You designed them, you can god damn fix them."

Ibarra pushed Hoffman's hand away.

"Back in my day, we had military working dogs. Bomb sniffers. Attack dogs. Came a time when they were too old or too injured to serve. They were put down."

"No! Diamond is not a dog, you heartless bastard!"

"That they can talk and follow orders doesn't mean they're alive."

"They're alive enough to me! Do something, Ibarra. Please."

Ibarra flicked a finger against the diagnostic screens.

"They don't feel pain, son. I didn't build them that way. Closest they get is a feeling of distress when they're not protecting their imprint or they know humans are in danger. This one, Diamond? He's in the death spiral. Code errors multiply the more he tries to function. You take him back to the battlefield and he'll shut down."

"Go . . . dark," Diamond said.

"No, no buddy, that's not going to happen to you," Hoffman put a hand on the doughboy's wrist.

"Go dark. Sir in danger," the doughboy said. "Hurt. Sir no hurt."

"Nothing can hurt me while you're with me, Diamond. You know that," Hoffman turned from Ibarra and wiped a tear away.

"They're hardwired, Hoffman," Ibarra shook his head. "Keeps them from being captured and reverse engineered. Fiddle with the coding and they go berserk . . . or they deactivate. There's nothing to be done."

"Just march them into the incinerator after they're not useful anymore? You've got a reputation, Ibarra, but even for you that's cold."

"I deserve that," Ibarra nodded. "It's easy to hate me. I'll take the slings and arrows and give humanity back the chance to survive this galaxy."

"You can't just—"

"I can. The doughboys are failing. Even the newest units will degrade within the next few years. No point in prolonging the inevitable." Ibarra backed toward the door.

"Opal," Diamond held up his hammer, the haft across his chest. "Opal take."

The other doughboy strode across the room and wrapped his meaty hands around the weapon. Opal pulled, but Diamond's grip was firm.

"What's this?" Ibarra asked.

"When a unit knows it can't fight anymore," Hoffman went to the two doughboys and put a hand atop Diamond's, "they give up their weapons to the others. Helps the rest to keep fighting."

Diamond's hand slipped from the hammer and flopped to his lap. Opal slid the hammer head to the crook of his wrist and went back to his post near the exit.

Ibarra cracked the door open, then paused.

"What if you had a choice?" Ibarra closed the door. "All the doughboys retired from service now, or you stay with them in the field until they fail or enemy fire does the deed?"

"They would keep fighting. I will never leave them behind, nor would they abandon me."

Ibarra went to Diamond and bent close to his face. The doughboy's breath came out as a slow fog so near the silver man.

"He has a few hours left," Ibarra said. "There's a kill code I can use. Deactivate him now."

"Give it to me," Hoffman's voice cracked. "He's my responsibility. I won't let you or anyone else take that from me."

"This code will work on any doughboy," Ibarra said. "A failsafe I built in. Best you die before any alien gets it. Understand?"

"Tell the rest," Hoffman touched his face. "Tell the rest of us what's coming. What to do for our boys."

"I should have known you all wouldn't make this easy on me. Fine. Fine. You'll all have the kill code, the words are—"

"No, Opal's still functional!" Hoffman held his hands up.

"Got to click the input button," Ibarra tapped his forehead. "Come here."

Ibarra went to the diagnostic screens and pulled up a text field. He typed out four words. Hoffman couldn't look at the screen for a moment, but he finally brought his gaze up to them and nodded.

"There. Click the button and say the words and the doughboy's system will shut off. Permanently. Understand?" Ibarra went back to the door.

"I understand," Hoffman turned off the screen.

"I'm sorry, son. I really am. War's not fair to anyone. I'll leave you to it." Ibarra closed the door behind him.

Hoffman stood still, the tick of machines and Diamond's labored breathing in his ears.

"Sir, Diamond wants to fight," the doughboy said.

"No more, D. You've earned your rest," Hoffman bit his bottom lip.

"Opal . . . others," Diamond tried to point at Opal but his hand began twisting back and forth.

Hoffman gripped Diamond's hand until it stilled.

"They'll fight. I promise. I'll never leave them, I swear it. Never take them from a battle. Doughboys are for fighting, right?"

"Always fight. Always for sir," Diamond nodded.

"God I—I can't," Hoffman's mask cracked and a sob escaped. He set his forehead against Diamond's shoulder and the doughboy wrapped an arm around him in a hug.

"Sir no hurt," Diamond said.

"It does hurt, D. Hurts more than I thought it would . . . and it's not something we can fight. Not an enemy to kill."

"Sir no hurt," the doughboy took Hoffman's hand and pressed it to his forehead. "Getting dark."

Hoffman wiped his sleeve across his eyes and composed himself.

"Diamond 99, you are a soldier. One loyal to the end, and I will honor you. Give you and your brothers the same love you've shown me. I'm . . . I'm going to take you offline now. Do you . . . do you . . ."

Diamond tapped his fist to his chest and his head lowered.

Hoffman put a thumb to Diamond's forehead and he whispered into the doughboy's ear.

"Golem. Colossus. Lucent. Chaos."

Diamond slumped forward into Hoffman's arms. Hoffman lowered him to the floor and folded Diamond's hands on his chest. He closed the doughboy's eyes and sat beside him. Time lost.

"Opal," Hoffman looked up at the other soldier. "I'm with you to the end, understand?"

"Opal with you. Always."

"Always."

Mike's business cards summed it up nicely. They read: Michael Starrunner, Uni-Ex Shipping Inc. Delivery assured, discretion guaranteed. Only now Mike and his business partner Dolph find themselves stranded on the desert world of Gorongol, their ship destroyed and their cargo confiscated. Their only hope of getting off this dustball lies in their quick wits—and a hold full of slightly bruised bananas.

THE SCRAPYARD SHIP
★
by Felix R. Savage

★ 1 ★

WE BABIED THE SHIP from Silverado to Gorongol, but she gave out on us with eight thousand klicks left to go, and I had to duct the emergency LOX reserves into the retrorockets to put her down. No way was I taking her FTL with the antimatter containment loop losing integrity every time I breathed on the display. So we came down like a meteor, burning hydrolox that was 90 percent pure oxygen. If Dolph had chosen that moment to light a cigarette, we'd have been a scorch mark on the desert.

He waited until we were out of the ship and walking away. Grains of newly fused glass crunched under our feet. The smoke from Dolph's cig masked the odor of burnt brush. The sun felt like a nail through the top of my head, even though I was wearing my old panama from San Damiano. The breeze rustling the bushes sounded loud in the silence. Heat rippled a stegosaurus ridge of hills on the horizon. I was walking in that direction for want of any better ideas. The ship shrank behind us into a forlorn crumple of metal origami.

I'd had that bird for eight years. She was the second ship I'd owned, an upgrade from the ancient stack I'd bought after I left the army. I wasn't her first owner, either. When I bought her, I knew I'd be lucky to get a thousand light years out of her. Now she was toast.

"Got any more bright ideas, Tiger?" said Dolph, shading his eyes with one hand. There was not a single living thing nor any sign of human habitation in sight. Well, you wouldn't expect there to be any signs of *human* habitation. Gorongol is a Kroolth world. But there weren't any signs of Kroolth, either.

"I'm thinking," I said.

Dolph inhaled, exhaled. "Easy in, easy out, he said. It's just a cargo run, he said. A bunch of graphene cables and some fancy tension dampeners—buy low, sell high, and there'll be room in the hold for bananas."

The Kroolth go ape for bananas. I think it's something to do with micronutrients. They didn't evolve in this system, of course—not many species in the Cluster evolved where they're from. Chronic potassium deficiency would help to explain their behavior.

Dolph went on, "You didn't mention the part where the Silveradans intercept us because their Crown Prince is feuding with the Generalissimo of Gorongol—"

"How am I supposed to keep track of this stuff? Worlds like these change their government every second Tuesday."

"So they confiscate the cargo, and put a hole in our freaking containment loop. Way to go, Mike. We could've kept Sally running for another ten years."

It had always annoyed me that he called the ship Sally. I never gave ships pet names. Pets die on you. Behind us, Sally let out a series of sad pops as her fins cooled. Case in point.

"I think I have whiplash, too," Dolph went on. He peevishly kicked the brush. His thin, sallow face was set in a frown, which turned into an expression of shock as a twenty-legged tarantula—that's what it looked like—scuttled out from under the leaves and ran away.

"They didn't confiscate the bananas," I reminded him.

"Did you see that? It looked like a tarantula with twenty legs."

"I wonder if we could fix the containment loop by cannibalizing a couple of electromagnets from the plasma chamber."

"Great idea," Dolph said. "We'll also need some chewing gum and string."

I scowled, in no mood for his wisecracking, even though I knew it was his way of dealing with the sad fate of "Sally." For him, it was a personal tragedy. For me, it was a financial calamity. *He* wasn't the one with his name on our business cards: *Michael Starrunner, Uni-Ex Shipping Inc. Delivery assured, discretion guaranteed.*

Well, this was one delivery I couldn't assure, since the freaking Silveradans had stolen our cargo. And now I had no ship. What next? Dolph was right about one thing, anyway—I couldn't solder my way out of this one.

A crash reverberated across the desert. Dolph's cigarette fell out of his mouth. Both of us spun around, reaching for our weapons.

Sally had lain down. That crash had been the noise of her nose slamming into the glassed surface of the desert. As we stared through the clouds of sparkling dust, a whole lot of black and fuzzy *somethings* swarmed up her crumpled jackstands and disappeared into the forward airlock, which we had left open.

At the same time, one of the bushes nearby grew legs and humped towards the ship, chasing the black fuzzies.

Dolph swallowed audibly, sighting down his .45.

"That bush has legs," I said.

"Sometimes I wonder why they let you in the special forces," Dolph said. "You must've gamed the IQ test."

I slapped his pistol down. The walking bush was now trying to climb the airlock stairs. The last thing we wanted to do was piss it off and make it come this way. "At least I didn't game the psych evaluation."

"Hey," Dolph said, "I was honest. Where it said, 'How do your family and friends describe you?' I put 'Psychopathic.'" He lowered his pistol. Studying the bushes all around us, he handed me the .45 and stretched his arms over his head. "It's damn hot," he remarked, casually.

His pale beige skin turned brown. His black hair turned into a bristly, spotted mane. Fur sprouted from his cheeks and the nape of his neck. He took off his clothes as he Shifted, to save the seams from splitting. Within ten seconds a jackal was loping to catch up with me. "Carry these for me, wouldja?" he said through the bundle of clothes he was carrying in his teeth.

Dolph isn't really a psychopath. He's a Shifter, like me. That's why they let us in the special forces, not because we're especially good at anything. Obviously.

I aimed a kick at him. "Shift back."

"Hell with that," said the jackal. "If these bushes try to eat us, I'll see your ass at the mountains. Four legs are faster than two."

"OK. When the Kroolth make your skin into a rug, I'll take a picture for your mom." I got out my radio and crossed my fingers for a signal. The Kroolth are pretty low-tech, but they do have satellites.

"Who are you calling?" Dolph said.

I held up a finger. As I'd hoped, the stegosaurus ridges bounced the radio signals just enough that the handheld had finally found a lock. I entered my insurance code and broadcast it on the specified frequency. "I've resigned myself to the inevitable," I said.

"You're finally going to fire Irene? I told you she wasn't working out."

Dolph was referring to our weapons officer, whom we'd left behind on Ponce de Leon this time out. She was probably taking her kids to the beach, while we slogged across a desert infested with tarantulas and carnivorous sagebrush.

"If we can't get the ship fixed," I said, "I won't need to fire her. None of us will have a job." My radio crackled.

"Yeah 'lo how c'n I help ya?" droned a voice speaking English, which fortunately for us is the lingua franca in this part of the Cluster. My code would've told them I was an offworlder. I hoped they didn't put two and two together and realize we were the same guys meant to be delivering an important cargo to their Generalissimo—a cargo we didn't have anymore.

"Hi there!" I said as cheerfully as I could. "Is this Clusterwide Breakdown Services?"

Clusterwide will fix your ship on the spot if it's something minor, like dead mice in the air ducts. That time, I had spent three days taking apart the CO_2 removal assembly to find out why our air was becoming unbreathable, before I gave up and called Clusterwide. Irene had liked the look of the repair guy enough to let him into her cabin, where he soon traced the smell to escapees from the cage of mice Irene was keeping under her bunk. He had commiserated with me jovially as he pocketed our last quarter's profit. Irene had said that she was sick of the vacuum-packed variety. That's one reason I decided to leave her on the PdL this run. In retrospect: bad move.

Had she been here, that pissant Silveradan patrol boat would never have got near us.

Clusterwide also provides haulage services, if your ship is actually still in space. There's a small shipyard orbiting Gorongol, run by Ekschelatans.

However, my ship was decidedly not in space. It was sitting on a glassy smear of fused sand beneath a vast baby-blue sky, surrounded by carnivorous bushes.

When I gave our coordinates to the rep, he gasped, "You're *where?* Do not leave your ship. Don't even open the airlock."

"Too late," I said, staring across the desert at the camel-sized bush still trying to squeeze itself through the airlock in pursuit of the black fuzzies.

"All right. All right. Go back to your ship and light a ring of fuel around it if you have any. Don't follow the same path you followed out. There'll be thornmaws waiting for you now. Basically, don't brush up against the same plant twice."

"OK," I said.

"Separately," the rep added, "I will have to ask for up-front payment before we come out there to pick you up."

We did as advised, apart from lighting a ring of fuel. I thought that was overkill. While we waited with our backs pressed to the ship's nose, Dolph said, "Do you get the impression the bushes are coming nearer?"

Actually, I did. They now formed a thick wall around the glassed area where the ship was standing, and now and then one of them would reach a claw-like root forwards and scratch at the rough glass, as if puzzled.

The Clusterwide reps arrived in a light prop plane. The first thing they did was fly in a low circle around the ship, hosing the bushes with a flamethrower. Then they landed on the smouldering ashes, hopped out in hazmat suits, and confirmed my payment details.

"Haulage plus repairs would cost you more than she'd bring on the parts market," was their verdict on the ship, confirming my own gloomy assessment.

They were human, so I tended to think they were being straight with me. Plus, they were recommending a course of action that wouldn't put any money in Clusterwide's pockets.

"OK," I said. The next words out of my mouth broke my heart a bit. "Is there a scrapyard near here?"

The male rep, a bandy-legged character with skin like cowhide from many years in Gorongol's sun, pointed with a hazmat glove. "Right the other side of those hills, on the coast. Outside of Karpluie Spaceport."

"Yeah, we saw that on our way down," Dolph said. He had Shifted back to his normal scraggy, smiley, ponytailed self, of course. We needed them to think we were mainstream humans like them.

"Then you know when I say *spaceport,* I'm being generous."

We had a laugh at the expense of the backwards Kroolth.

The female rep chipped in, "We know the guy who runs the scrapyard. He's good people. I can call and tell him you're coming."

"I'd appreciate that," I said. Then I glanced up at the lovely, now useless, silhouette of my ship, blocking out the sun like a metal swan with her wings raised. A swan 100 meters long. I didn't even have a cargo dolly. (The Silveradans had taken that, too.)

"We've got a flatbed at the spaceport," said the male rep. "I can send someone out to pick you up."

"Is that covered by my insurance?"

"Unfortunately not. But I can give you ten percent off the usual rate."

OK, then. Not so disinterested after all. But I didn't begrudge it to them. We've all got to make a living. "You got a deal."

The female rep had her radio out. "I'm going to give Gerry at the scrapyard a shout. Could I have your name again?"

It was on my insurance documents, but as I began to withdraw them from my pocket, I caught Dolph's eye and thought better of it. I gave her a fake name.

★ 2 ★

THE FLATBED ARRIVED the next afternoon. It was an enormous thing with 22 axles. Its crawler treads crushed the thornmaws to writhing, sticky mats, a sight that gladdened my heart. Dolph and I had spent an unpleasant night fighting the things off, ultimately resorting to the ring of fire idea. I had grabbed a couple of hours of sleep in the middle of a circle of mattresses from the berths, doused with rocket fuel and burning like a campfire. Now my throat felt raw from the smoke, and my mood was foul.

The crawler's robot arms loaded my ship onto the back, mangling the wings in the process—not that that mattered now— and off we went. Dolph and I couldn't ride inside the ship on account of the tarantulas, and there was no room for us in the flatbed's cab. So we rode on the bed, underneath the landing gear of the ship that had been our house, wings, and workplace in one for years.

It was just like moving house. That's how I decided to think of it. Shifters don't tend to have a wandering foot—the opposite, if anything—but once I left San Damiano, our home planet, it turned out to be easy to just keep moving. Me and Dolph had bounced around the Cluster ever since we got out of the army, selling here, buying there, getting in trouble everywhere.

Now, however, I had a daughter. Five-year-old Lucy, the external repository of my heart. She was on Ponce de Leon, our current home base. Whenever I came back from a run, she loved to meet me at the spaceport and come aboard the ship. She even enjoyed rolling up her little sleeves and "helping" me with any needed repairs. She loved "Sally" as much as Dolph did. She was going to be devastated when I came home shipless.

As well as profitless and on the hook for that lost cargo.

The crawler bumped along, crushing thornmaws and scaring off unspeakable leggy vermin. A spectacular sunset engulfed the desert, turning it almost pretty. As we passed through a region of rocky dunes, we found an English-language radio broadcast—old news from across the Cluster, punctuated by an every-hour-on-the-hour "Predator Report."

"Travellers in the Yephta Desert should be aware that a herd of dune worms are currently crossing the Karampox road."

We stared at the dunes, whose spiky backs suddenly looked less like rocks.

"If it is absolutely necessary to take this route, drive as fast as possible . . ."

Instead of speeding up, as recommended, the flatbed stopped. I peered ahead and saw that a dune was blocking the road.

The instant we stopped all the dunes surged towards us, sand sliding from their armored sides.

An infernal boom shattered the evening, followed by a screech. A tail of flame shot out from the flatbed's cab, searing the fuselage of my ship. A rocket-propelled grenade shot out in the other direction. It impacted the worm ahead of the flatbed. The explosion hurled gobbets of flesh and chitin into the air. The other worms flattened themselves to the sand, resuming their camouflage as dunes.

Dolph and I, lying flat, cautiously raised our heads.

"Ho, ho, ho," shouted the flatbed's driver, a seen-it-all human named Clint. He leaned out the window of the cab, brandishing his RPG launcher. "That's the way you deal with them. Didja know the Kroolth evolved from a prey species? They *say* the wildlife is their planetary defences. Truth is, they're just too scared to fight back."

"If we're staying here a while," Dolph said, pointing to the RPG launcher, "I want one of those."

"We won't be."

The flatbed creaked into motion once more. Dolph climbed up the ship's landing gear and fussed over the black scorch marks left by the RPG launcher's blowback. I heard him murmur, "Poor old Sally."

"Quit it with the Sally stuff," I yelled up at him.

The flatbed crawled up a switchback mountain road into violet shadows.

We stopped for the night at a roadhouse lavishly decorated with gold-framed photographs of His Specialness, the Generalissimo of Gorongol. A troop of secret police types came in while we were eating supper. I had heard their motorbikes outside, and I was prepared for swagger and noise. I was *not* prepared for them to command everyone in the dining room to stand up and sing the national anthem, which was (of course) a 12-verse paean to the Generalissimo's specialness.

Clint indicated that we should stand up, too. For all his contemptuous talk about the Kroolth's timidity, he showed no inclination to piss off a roomful of them.

I had to sidestep so I could fit my head between two rafters. Dolph is a couple of inches shorter than me, and Clint was only about five ten, but all three of us loomed over the impromptu choir like totem poles. The Kroolth are *small.* The tallest of the secret police types was about the right height to headbutt me in the groin if he stood on tiptoe. And he looked like something of the sort was on his mind as he glared across the crowd at us. I moved my mouth as if I was singing.

Dolph, under cover of the fourth refrain, said, "So I'm doing the math."

"Me too."

"I don't like it."

"Me neither."

I was still annoyed at Dolph for grieving over the ship, but we were on the same wavelength now. We've known each other a long time, and a higher than average proportion of our ventures together have involved a) fighting and b) running away, not necessarily in that order. So I knew that he was referring to the math of us versus them. There were eleven secret police types, and thirty more Kroolth in the dining room who would definitely join in if encouraged.

Clint's theory about the Kroolth having evolved from a prey species was probably correct. They looked like startled primates with long faces, sort of like you were lifting them by their furry cheeks and screaming at them about their gambling debts. They had long arms like colobus monkeys. On the other hand, monkeys can hurt you bad, even if they don't have guns. And each of the secret police types carried a toy-sized pistol. Dolph had his .45 and I had my Midday Special, but we were too badly outnumbered to even think about using them.

"Shift?" Dolph whispered.

"No! Jesus, no!"

"They'd never know what hit them."

I shot him an appalled glance. The pupils of his eyes had gone slitty. His shoulders were starting to bulge, straining his shirt. He grinned.

"Quit it! If they find out we're Shifters, we're dead!"

I held Dolph's stare until the pupils of his eyes returned to normal. Goddamn jackal never could think more than five minutes ahead.

"First one draws down on us, I break his neck," he whispered, while the Kroolth ended the anthem with a round of applause in honor of His Specialness.

Shaken, I had difficulty smiling as the troop leader scuttled up to us.

"You are the owner of that pile of junk outside?"

Dolph let out a low growl. I fought to keep my smile in place. After all, the Kroolth was technically correct. "That's me."

"Remove it immediately. It is blocking the road!"

Relief pulsed through me. Only a parking violation. "Absolutely, Officer. We'll be on our way shortly."

He turned away with a sniff, then turned back. "You are human?"

"We are," I confirmed. Dolph sniggered. These back-of-beyonders couldn't even tell humans by looking at them.

"Have you ever been to . . . oah, Ponce de Leon?" He pronounced the name of the PdL, one of humanity's Heartworlds, a nerve center of civilization in the Cluster, with the same care that I would use if trying to speak Kroolth.

"A few times," I said cautiously.

"Are you aware of any cargo ships bound from Ponce de Leon to Gorongol?"

I put on a puzzled face, while my relief curdled. They were looking for us.

"This one would be, oah, a very large ship, much bigger than that pile of junk of yours. Laden with very valuable technology, oah yes. It would have an armed escort."

"Hmm," I said. "Come to think of it, I may have seen exactly such a ship on the pad at PdL. The captain boasted that he had a personal commission from the Generalissimo." I had done just that, but only to make the regulars at Snakey's Bar laugh. As for an armed escort? We were our own armed escort. I admit to dropping the ball on the Silveradan patrol ship. I just couldn't blow those little guys away. They *said* it was only a customs inspection, and I was dumb enough to believe them. "It was a 200-tonne tri-engine Phantom with an extended cargo bay. Does that sound like the one?"

Lord strike me down now.

"Oah yes! That must be it! Do you know when it departed Ponce de Leon? It is delayed."

"At about the same time we did," I said. "I should think it'll arrive any day now." We would have got here on time, but I took it extremely slow at the end. You do, with a faulty antimatter containment loop.

The little Kroolth went on his way beaming. He could expect a warm pat on the head from his commander for bringing news, even if it was just hearsay, of the missing cargo ship.

We finished our supper with no appetite. Kroolth food is vegetarian. Dolph can usually eat anything, but even he left half of his stringy hash browns. We paid up, stooped to get out of the dining-room, and crawled down the hall to the front door.

Outside, the air was soft and sweet with the smell of (probably carnivorous) flowers. Clint the driver said, "Were they looking for *you?*"

"Gosh, I can't believe you worked that out," I said. My mask of politeness was slipping, as I knew we were up to our necks in excrement. It couldn't take even the Kroolth much longer to work out that the ship which had just crash-landed in their desert was the one they were yearningly awaiting. I left Dolph to transfer some extra GCs to Clint, to convince him to drive through the night, instead of parking up here as we had planned.

"I gave him some extra to keep his trap shut," Dolph said as he returned to our perch under the landing gear.

"He'd better. We'll be spending the rest of our lives in a jail with five-foot ceilings if the Generalissimo's enforcers catch up with us."

"Humans ought to stick together in places like this," sighed Dolph. "Maybe I should go back and scare him."

"No, don't. Paying him off was the right move."

"I just hate to think of him spending our money . . ."

It was my money, actually, as both of us knew. I appreciated that Dolph was trying to smooth things over between us by being fiscally responsible, in his own way. I said, "Just imagine him spending it on his personal harem of Kroolth bimbettes."

Dolph shuddered. I chuckled.

Of course, there was a glitch in this pretty picture of human solidarity. If Clint, or anyone else on Gorongol, figured out that we *weren't* human—not like they were human—we wouldn't even have that.

Neither of us Shifted that night, even though it would have been more comfortable to curl up in the form of an animal on the hard, cold bed of the crawler. I knew I wouldn't get any sleep, anyway.

★ 3 ★

THE FLATBED CRAWLED over the mountain pass as dawn was breaking. The corded flanks of the mountains dropped away to forest. Further down, a strip of green and blue cropland bordered the sea. The prevailing winds clearly dumped all the rain on this side of the mountains. The trees lining the road looked like actual trees, not predators.

The only thing that spoiled the view was the carbuncular rash of concrete on the coast: the city of Karpluie, and its spaceport. We rappelled into the ship's forward airlock to get breakfast. When we came back out, the view was unchanged. Good old Clint was not risking his rig on these steep roads by travelling any faster than 20 kph.

It took us a whole day—well, a whole human-standard day; the Gorongolian day is 38 hours long—to reach Karpluie. In the forest, we kept getting hung up on low branches, and on the ring road around the city, we kept getting hung up in traffic jams. Or rather, causing them. A 100-meter flatbed carrying a spaceship does tend to do that. Dolph hunted tarantulas inside the ship to blow off steam. I messed around with my computer, trying to find out where we would get the best price for our bananas. I already foresaw that we would need to spend big to get off this planet before the Generalissimo twigged our breach of contract. By now, every motherloving Kroolth on the continent knew that a crashed spaceship had been transported to Karpluie today.

We picked up speed on the modern ten-lane highway to the spaceport, and rumbled past it. The height of the flatbed allowed us to see over the sound-baffle fence. Tarmac stretched away to the diamond thread of the sea.

"One," Dolph said.

"Two," I disagreed.

"One. And it was just an Ek shuttle."

"I was counting the airplane."

That was the sum total of the craft that had landed and / or taken off from Karpluie today. I counted the airplane because I thought it might come to that. Even a trip to somewhere else on this planet might turn out to be better than sticking around. While we were stuck in traffic jam number nine hundred and three, I had seen a gang of those secret police types apprehending a Kroolth driver. With hollow-points. It took me right back to Tech Duinn, where Dolph and I spent the most, shall we say, active years of our military careers. I had zero wish to revisit the era when violence was my way of life. And less-than-zero wish to be on the receiving end.

The flatbed turned off the highway, following the curve of the spaceport fence. Another fence appeared on the other side of the road. Beyond it, curvilinear metal shapes gnawed the afternoon clouds.

"Here we are," Clint yelled back from the cab.

I jumped down. It felt good to stretch my legs on the gravelly red dirt. With Dolph a few paces behind, I marched up to the gate of the scrapyard, which was locked. I stretched out my finger to the buzzer . . . and froze.

On a bulletin board beside the gate, covered with perspex against the rain, above a lost dog notice and a circular for the Biannual Human Community Barbecue, my own face stared at me from a full-color poster.

MICHAEL "MIKE" STARRUNNER
WANTED FOR GRAND THEFT & LÈSE-MAJESTÉ
100 GC REWARD

The bold black text was written in English, Kroolthi, and Ekschelatan.

Dolph nudged me. "They got your name wrong."

"I'm deeply insulted."

"You should be." He was cracking up so hard he could hardly get the words out. "One hundred GCs? One . . . *hundred*?"

For reference, I spent two hundred GCs the last time I took Lucy for pizza on Ponce de Leon.

The Generalissimo valued my life at less than the worth of a deep dish Hawaiian pie.

But as funny as it was, to the Kroolth, one hundred GCs was obviously a lot of money. The relative paltriness of the reward would not deter them from going for it, if they connected me with the man on the poster.

Dolph said, "The Kroolthi is longer than the English." He twisted his head sideways—Kroolthi is written from top to bottom. "That last line?" He was no longer smiling. "Think it means 'dead or alive.'"

"Now that really makes my day." If I couldn't get off this planet pronto, I would never get to take Lucy for pizza again. Never see her smile, never hug and tickle her again. She'd be alone in the world. That thought lit a fire under me. I touched the pocket of my donkey jacket and made sure my Midday Special was still in there.

"The Clusterwide reps must've dropped us in it," Dolph said bitterly.

"Naw," I said. "The Generalissimo's just freaking out because his cargo's late." And was now on Silverado. "They paid retail for that stuff, remember? Three hundred KGCs. That's probably the equivalent of their entire planetary GDP."

"Nice place to settle if you've got a GC-denominated income," Dolph said, looking around at the sticky-leaved blue bushes that grew up against the fence. The flatbed's treads had crushed some of them, and they smelled like marzipan. Large insects buzzed around us. "Not."

"It wasn't the Clusterwide guys, anyway," I said. "I gave them a fake name."

I was even gladder of that in a moment, as the gate concertinaed open a few feet. In the gap stood a human with a scowl on her face. "Are you Will Slaughtermore?"

My own lame-ass humor struck me as both puerile and risky now. But I straightened my back and shook her hand with a smile. "That's me."

"Crash Hardlander," Dolph grinned, elbowing past me for a chance to squeeze her grease-stained hand. "You must be Gerry?"

"Yup. Like it says on the sign. Gerry Scavarchi's Ships & Parts."

Scavarchi doesn't sound like a human name, so I had been worried that Gerry would turn out to be a Kroolth. As a human, she would be less likely to turn me in for the princely sum of one hundred GCs. That was something.

The other thread of hope I clung to was that the clean-cut, handsome young man on the WANTED poster did not look much like the scruffy, stubbled, not-so-young chancer facing Gerry Scavarchi now. They'd used the picture from my pilot's license. Years had passed since that was taken, and last night was far from the first time I'd slept—or rather, not slept—rough.

Independent freighter captains are known to be hard-living, penny-pinching losers, so I hoped that was all she'd see in me.

In one sense, it was a shame. Ms. Gerry Scavarchi had the body of an angel, imperfectly disguised by a mechanic's coverall, and the face and hair of a shampoo model.

I fixed my eyes north of her neck and said, "Theo and Annette from Clusterwide may have told you I'm looking to sell a damaged ship. I'm not gonna lie to you: the containment's gone. She'll never fly again."

"Yeah."

"However, I hear you'd be interested in buying her for scrap."

Long pause. Gerry's gaze scanned the 100-meter metal swan hulking over the trees behind me and Dolph.

"Sure," she said at last. "Happy to take her off your hands." She raised her voice without moving. "Clint! Put 'er over there."

"Roger," Clint yelled back. The flatbed ground forward a few meters and the robotic handler arms unfolded. My ship swung over our heads and over the fence of the scrapyard. We heard it hit the ground with a crunch. Dolph flinched.

It was a no-brainer from Gerry's point of view, of course. Totaled or not, my ship was a long-haul Skymule. Those don't come along on a world like Gorongol every day.

"Come in," she said with about as much warmth in her voice as a LOX tank, "and show me what I just bought."

We waved goodbye to Clint and followed her into the scrapyard. I took her on a tour of the ship, inside and out, pointing out all the high-spec features such as the 360-degree radar/LiDAR, the gimbaled retrorockets that enabled VTOL, and the threeway microwave/oven/sous vide cooker. I did not point out the coilgun, even though that was the most expensive bit of kit on the ship and I could have used it to justify a higher asking price. She would find it later, when we were safely off-world. Most indie freighters do not have military-grade cannon, and I wanted her to think we were in no way special.

She was impressed enough, anyway. I could see her ripping the cockpit apart with her eyes, and I figured we were home free.

"All right, come on over to the office and we'll talk," she said when we were back on the ground.

Meanwhile Dolph was ripping her clothes apart with *his* eyes. I whispered, "Down, boy," as we followed her through the scrapyard.

It was a jungle of dismembered spacecraft and airplanes. A grinding, screeching noise impinged on my ears as we walked. I glanced to my left and saw a handler robot three storeys high, with tractor tyres and four hydraulic arms, piling the junkers on top of each other.

"We remove the resalable components and then sell the airframes for scrap," Gerry explained over the racket. "There's an Ek outfit comes and takes 'em over to the compactor."

She waved at the distant cab of the handler bot. The motion caused her breasts to rise enticingly under her coverall. I wasn't staring or anything. Of course not.

Dolph was, unashamedly. "There's got to be a catch," he muttered. "Babes like that don't work in places like this."

"Sexist," I said, but he had half a point.

The handler bot stopped work. A Kroolth emerged from the cab and spidered down the access ladder. It joined us as we reached a shack attached to a hangar-sized workshop in the middle of the scrapyard. Gerry pushed the door open and removed spaceship parts from chairs, including one very small one.

The Kroolth came in and sat in it.

"This is my husband," Gerry said. "Opizzt, these are the guys that Annette rang about."

Husband?

Dolph's jaw was on the floor. I realized mine was, too, and picked it up. "Great to meet you, um, Opizzt." I kept talking to cover up my astonishment—and consternation. With a Kroolth in the picture, our odds of being turned in for the one hundred GC reward had just rebounded. "I'm the owner of the Skymule out there. I've just shown Gerry her features, and I'm sure you'll agree three thousand KGCs is a more than fair price, considering the resale value of her parts."

Nothing ventured, nothing gained. I paid four thousand KGCs

for her new. Well, second-hand. Actually, third-hand. But who's counting?

Dolph put on a sad face, suggesting that I was practically giving the ship away.

But what we had both forgotten was that with a Kroolth in the picture, our odds of being ripped off had also increased astronomically.

"Noaaah," said this little shyster. "You have added too many zeros, oah yes. By a factor of three. We will give you three KGCs."

"*Three?*" I spluttered.

Gerry smirked.

"No one wants to buy a Skymule on Gorongol. We cannot even sell the parts. We are doing you a favor, oah yes."

"But she's got a sous vide cooker," I said, desperately trying to keep the tone light.

Dolph did not help me haggle. When I glanced around to see why he was being so quiet—apart from the shock of finding out that Gerry was married to a Kroolth—I caught him looking out the window behind Gerry's desk. It faced the back of the scrapyard, opposite to the way we'd come in. The sea sparkled far off. In between the sea and us stood a number of spacecraft. Some of them looked fairly new, at least from this distance.

Dolph leaned back into the conversation and coughed, in a jackally kind of way. "How about a trade-in?" he said.

★ 4 ★

OUR NEGOTIATIONS stalled with three zeros between what I was willing to take and what the Scavarchis were willing to pay. Coming around to Dolph's idea of a trade-in, I agreed to a stroll outside to look at the second-hand ships. Dolph lit a cigarette as soon as we got outdoors.

"Sometimes you do have good-ish ideas," I told him. "Unfortunately this is not one of those times. What are the chances any of these junkheaps even fly?"

"You never know," he said.

The Scavarchis walked ahead of us. Opizzt had to take two steps for every one of his wife's. His head came up precisely to her shapely waist.

"How do they do it?" Dolph whispered.

"Do what?" I whispered back. "Run a business while criminally stiffing their suppliers? Very profitably, I expect."

"No, *it*."

I had been trying to stop my imagination from grappling with the particulars. Now my efforts failed. But so did my imagination. "Same way we do?"

"It's got to be *this* size, Mike." Dolph held up his pinky finger.

"Beats loneliness, I guess."

"Or maybe—" Dolph perked up— "they aren't really married. It's a front so guys won't hit on her."

"Try hitting on her and see what happens," I suggested.

Dolph sighed.

We passed a Grav-X and a Voidbreaker. Up close, airlock hatches sagged, the sky stabbed through rust-eaten fins, and toxic fluid dripped from neglected piping. A family of bustard-like birds flew out of an engine bell, wings whirring.

It was my turn to sigh. None of these lemons could come close to replacing my ship. My customers would take their business elsewhere, with good reason. My competitors would laugh their asses off. Lucy's little face would crumple, and then she'd try to cheer me up. That was the worst thought of all.

"Hey, Mike," Dolph murmured. "What about that one?"

"Don't call me Mike," I hissed. "It's Will Slaughtermore, remember?"

"He must be spinning in his grave."

I actually borrowed this alias from a guy we knew in the special forces. He lived up to it. I hoped I wouldn't have to.

Opizzt and Gerry were heading away from the ship that had caught Dolph's interest, intent on showing us another Grav-X that was sitting precariously on the edge of a marshy creek.

I caught up with them. "What about that one?" I pointed.

"Oah, you do not want that one," Opizzt said, speeding up.

My antennae tingled. If Opizzt didn't want us to want that one, I wanted it. "Can't hurt to take a look," I persisted.

Gerry said something in Kroolthi. Opizzt replied. The conversation sounded to me like this: *zzziphrrchkk, ksst. Akhzzp. Yeah, but dikuccchizztra.*

"Oaaahkay, if you want," Opizzt said grudgingly.

The ship stood a stone's throw from the boggy bit where the creek ran into the sea. A smell of rot came from the tall pampas grass-like plumes growing in the bog. The ship was definitely in better shape than any of the others we had seen. However, it was a design disaster.

About the same size as my late lamented ship, it lay belly-down on two large auxiliary engine pods, which angled back from its flanks like wings, and two smaller ones which dangled like flippers from the fuselage, their tips resting on the ground. It had no fewer than five engines—those four, plus the ginormous main drive at the tail end of what the Fleet would call the rigid core assembly, a.k.a. the fuselage. Strikingly, its nose cone—raised off the ground—was not actually a cone, but a rounded oval that split open along blunt serrations, gaping at the sky like the jaws of a plesiosaur. If I did not mistake my guess, that was a railgun protruding from the jaws like a cheeky tongue.

Long before I was the owner of a shipping company, with bills to pay and a daughter to provide for, I was just a guy who loved spaceships. That guy had been in hibernation for quite some time. But for some reason, this weird and wonderful ship woke him up. I stepped up to it and ran one hand along a sun-warmed engine pod, feeling like myself again for the first time in ages.

Dolph, also staring raptly at the ship, murmured, "Fugly as heck."

"Yup."

"It looks like one of those extinct things they used to have on Earth, those what do you call 'ems—"

"Dinosaurs."

"The one that swam."

"A plesiosaur."

"Yeah, that's it."

"Mike, we gotta have it."

I had made fun of Dolph's emotional attachment to our old ship, but now I was feeling the same way about this one. I would never again mock him for caring too much about a hunk of metal. The truth was he'd stayed young at heart, and now I felt young at heart again. I nodded enthusiastically. "I can already see it landing at the PdL. The guys will think someone put LSD in their coffee."

"And look at all that cargo space."

"Look at those *engines*, Dolph." I could tell from the angle of the four auxiliary engines that the ship was VTOL-capable. "I bet she can go hypersonic on the auxiliaries alone, and then transition to the main drive to reach orbital velocity. And look at the *size* of that drive. Depending on where her wet mass tops out at, I bet she does point five acceleration over short distances. Maybe even point six."

"Need a cold shower, Tiger?" Dolph pretended to fan me.

"We gotta get the specs without appearing too eager," I said, more to myself than to him.

"Oh."

"What?"

He pointed to the top of the ship.

I had thought the plesiosaur's long neck was just a truss. Now I saw Gerry kneeling on its top edge, waving down at us from 6 meters above our heads. She was leaning down, so her cleavage threatened to spill out of the V of her coverall, which had somehow come unzipped a short way. Dolph groaned under his breath.

"Hey guys," she called. "Come up and see the airstrip."

She wasn't joking. The top of the truss was an honest-to-God airstrip. Dashed line down the middle and everything.

"It even has arresting gear. Fighter jets sold separately." Gerry said, as we walked along the shockproof flexible tarmac. I hated to think how much mass this added to the ship. I decided I'd remove it. In my head, the ship was already mine.

Dolph said, "Who the heck would put an airstrip on a spaceship?"

It was a good question, and would have been a better one if he had asked it to her face rather than her cleavage.

Gerry didn't seem to notice. Her mood had taken a turn for the friendlier. "The Kroolth would. As you see."

"This is a Kroolth ship?" Dolph said.

"I just said so, didn't I?"

"I didn't know . . ." Dolph trailed off, but I knew what he'd been going to say. *I didn't know the Kroolth built spaceships.*

Suddenly, however, the airstrip made sense—kind of. It was only 60 meters long, and no wider than two king-size beds. You couldn't land a fighter on that, arresting gear or no arresting gear. You could, though, if the fighter were *Kroolth size.*

That left the original question of why the heck anyone would put an airstrip on a spaceship in the first place. Gerry answered it.

"This is actually the one and only Kroolth spaceship. The flagship of the Imperial Kroolthi Space Fleet. Built by the Eks on Port Aronym, in orbit." I breathed an inward sigh of relief. The Ekschelatans, or Eks, made the best spaceships in the Cluster. If they had built this one, I could count on solid manufacturing quality. "There's no native shipbuilding capacity on Gorongol. There's an assembly plant on Silverado, but well, you know about that situation."

I nodded. Did I ever.

"Since it was his first spaceship, the Emperor wanted it to have everything. Thus, we have the runway." Gerry gestured to the auxiliary engine pods, with their oddly fat tips. "We have the floats." She pointed down. "We have the caterpillar treads."

"Caterpillar treads," I echoed, falling harder for the ship by the minute.

"Yeah," Gerry said. "It's a spaceship! It's an aircraft carrier! It's a tank!" She almost smiled. "Kinda like your microwave / oven / sous vide cooker thing."

"That never really worked," I admitted.

"Maybe not, but this does. The Eks wouldn't have let it out of their yard unless it passed all their tests. Hell, they charged enough for it."

"So what happened to the rest of the Imperial Space Fleet?" Dolph said, struggling to keep a straight face.

"The Generalissimo happened to it." Gerry waited a beat. "Do you guys know *anything* about Kroolthi history?"

Our faces must have told her, truthfully, that we didn't.

"Akondil begat Urzip, who begat . . . Sorry. The bit you care about is last year. The Emperor of Gorongol and Legate of Silverado, Princeps of the Many Moons, etcetera, had ideas about making the Kroolth a spacefaring people. He started out by building the ship we are standing on. But it came in at three hundred percent of budget, you know how the Eks are, and people were pissed. The Generalissimo, who used to be the Emperor's army chief, put himself in the middle of the anti-space movement, and used the public anger to stage a coup. Off with the Emperor's head! In with twice-daily choruses of the new national anthem, and a bonanza for the suppliers of ugly gilt picture frames and tiny motorbikes."

Dolph laughed. Gerry frowned. Despite her ironic tone, I could tell that these recent developments disgusted her.

"The Crown Prince made it to safety on Silverado. They're still loyal to the Imperial Family out there."

I was thinking that if I had bothered to find this stuff out before we came, I would still have my ship. I would have delivered my cargo to the unsavory Generalissimo and have been on my way with a spring in my step and money in my pocket.

"So that's how things stand right now," Gerry finished. "We would be in the middle of an interplanetary war, were it not for the fact that the Kroolth have no spaceships."

"Except this one," Dolph said.

Gerry nodded. "Except this one. But the Generalissimo thinks spaceflight is a waste of money, remember, so he sent it away to be scrapped."

"But you never scrapped it," I said, finally understanding.

"Opizzt couldn't bear to do it." A softer note entered her voice. "He keeps thinking the Crown Prince will come back and want it. But those biker assholes come around here every so often, asking what's taking so long, accusing Pizzy of being an imperialist . . . they pistol-whipped him a couple of months back. Next time, they might do something worse. The only thing that's protecting him is that I'm human, and that's not surefire, you know? So I want this—" she ground her boot heel into the airstrip— "*damn* thing gone."

"Lady," I said, "you won't even have to pay me to take it off your hands."

"Sod off," she said with half a smile. "I'm still keeping your Skymule."

"A fair trade."

"All contents included."

"Not a problem," I said. An instant later, Dolph kicked me in the ankle and mouthed: *Bananas*. His head may have been turned by Gerry's strategic display of loveliness, but it was less turned than mine was by the thought of possessing this overpowered beast.

Crap; the bananas. Oh, well. It wasn't as if we'd have a chance to sell them, anyway.

"All contents included," I assured Gerry.

"Great," she said, finally giving us a genuine smile. "Let's go back to the office and we can file the paperwork."

At which point I'd have to tell them my real name, if I wanted the ship legally registered to me. I decided to risk it. My real name isn't Starrunner, anyway. Of course it isn't. Come on. When was the last time you met someone named Starrunner, or Hardlander (Dolph's actual nom de guerre), who'd been born that way?

"There's another ground access ladder back here," Gerry said, clambering down past the arresting gear. "That door is the hangar. It's sealed, so you can either keep it in vacuum, or pressurize it to extend your livable onboard space. Or you could use it as a cargo hold if you wanted. This is one of the airlocks to the crew quarters, and there's another on the other side of the fuselage. Each of them is flush with the hull, and retracts into it—like so—" she slapped the pressure plate. The ship had power. The hatch opened, releasing an unpleasant smell of decay. "So you don't have to mess with outwards-opening hatches that could be vulnerabilities in a combat scenario. Did I mention the weapons systems? A defensive maser array, a keel-mounted railgun, and a tail-gunner's turret with a large-caliber machine-gun." She enumerated the specs of the weapons. She was really selling the ship now, as if to impress on me what a great deal I was getting. She didn't need to. I was past sold.

"Hey," Dolph said. "What's bit Pizzy?"

Opizzt was running towards us, weaving between the second-hand spaceships, shouting in Kroolth.

Gerry stiffened for a second and then started down the ladder at dangerous speed.

I was about to follow her when I saw several more Kroolth pursuing Opizzt. They wore black, like the secret police types from yesterday, like every wannabe badass in the entire freaking Cluster. My hand dropped to my Midday Special.

An amplified voice blared, in English, "Mike Starrunner. Mike Starrunner, we know you are there. Come out with your hands up, or we will toast you, oah yes."

My instincts took over. I dived into the open airlock of the ship like a rabbit down a burrow.

★ 5 ★

DOLPH DIVED INTO THE AIRLOCK half a centimeter behind me. "They didn't mention me," he grumbled. "I feel unwanted."

"Are you really jealous?" I panted. *"Really?"*

We were in a Kroolth-sized chamber. Dolph's elbow whanged into my eye. My knees were crushing into his stomach. Somehow I managed to close the airlock. Hopefully they hadn't seen us dart in here.

The chamber was too small to stay in. We crawled out of it into a corridor whose ceiling was all of five feet high. I had forgotten the interior of the ship would also be Kroolth-sized.

"Shift?" Dolph said.

"Shift," I agreed.

We stripped off our clothes, folded them in the airlock chamber, and Shifted. Dolph became a jackal. It isn't his favorite form, but he only has two, and the other one is not appropriate for spaceship decks. I . . . well, I've got a bunch of forms. Most of them have bad memories attached. I went with my current favorite, a white tiger.

Mainstream humans always want to know how Shifting *feels*. My answer, if I ever wanted to gratify their prurient curiosity, would be something like: Have you ever had a root canal? Now multiply that by an order of magnitude, and imagine your whole body is a nerve. The bones, muscles, blood vessels, *everything* has to drastically realign. No way that's not gonna hurt. However, you get used to it. And when you're old hands like we are, it only lasts for a few seconds.

We shook it off and padded aft along the corridor, which was now just the right height for us, or rather, we were the right height for it.

In animal form, you have a better sense of smell. This allowed us to experience the full rancidness of the odor of decay that pervaded the ship. My enthusiasm went off the boil a bit, but I had more important things on my mind right now. Such as putting Gorongol in the rearview mirror, for good.

An open pressure door led to the engineering deck. This turned out to be high enough for a human, or even an Ek, to stand up straight, owing to the amount of space required for a five GeV antimatter containment ring. We might as well not have bothered to Shift, after all. But neither of us felt like Shifting back just now. The secret police assholes were still out there.

Emergency lighting in the form of pink LED strips edging the hatches and control panels saved us from having to blunder around in the dark. I headed straight for the antimatter ring.

It was a standard gray, heavily rad-shielded torus with two smaller C-shaped units clamped onto it, what the Fleet calls electromagnetic force generation assemblies. You and I call them big honking magnets. A Kroolth-induced failure in one of these magnets was what had doomed my late ship. The bastard Silveradans had tried to steal it. While cutting it off its anchor points, they had, predictably given the level of Kroolth technical expertise, broken it. Without a strong enough magnetic field to contain it, the antimatter inside the loop had inexorably started to annihilate itself. This is what we call a leak in the ring. The process of annihilation progressively wrecks the inside of the torus until it's unusable. Four thousand KGCs down the pan. The drive accounts for 90 percent of the cost of your average spaceship.

This was a brand new drive, manufactured to Ek quality standards. It even still had a sticker on it saying it passed rad safety testing. To my delight, the console in front of the ring (at face height to my tiger form) indicated that the magnets were currently generating a field, and 13.5 trillion positrons were whizzing around in there right now.

I said the drive accounts for 90 percent of the cost of a ship, but the fuel costs as much as the drive.

"Dolph," I said in a choked voice, "I estimate that we have five thousand KGCs worth of antimatter on board. No, make that five fifty, the market's been going up."

Tiger and jackal each lifted a front paw and performed a clumsy animal high-five. *Screw* the Generalissimo.

"Plus fifteen tonnes of H2O, point five tonnes of LOX, and 250 kilos of LN2," Dolph said, gloating over the tank gauges.

"Oh yeah baby. We are out of here." In my mind, I was already landing the new ship on Ponce de Leon, swooping Lucy into my arms, and giving her the grand tour of our funny-looking new cash cow. She was going to absolutely love it. The corridors were even child-sized. I had not had a proper look around the ship myself yet, but I already felt as if I knew her inside and out. Which just goes to show what I know.

"Nice of Gerry to keep the power on," Dolph mused.

"They expected the Crown Prince to come back and claim it any minute, remember?" I felt a twinge of guilt about waltzing off with 5000 KGCs of antimatter that belonged to the Kroolthi imperial family. But Gerry'd said it: contents included. She'd almost *insisted* on it. Funny, that.

There was a pause. I knew Dolph was also thinking about what might be going down outside between the Scavarchis and the secret police.

I studied the array of screens on the wall console, wondering if I could get an external camera feed.

"Smells a bit in here, doesn't it?" Dolph remarked.

"Something probably died in the ducts," I said, recalling Irene's mice. My lasting irritation at our weapons officer had evaporated. She was going to love this ship as well. All those guns.

I found an optical feed, got a picture of the sandy ground underneath the fuselage, and swivelled the trackball clumsily with the pad of my right forepaw, trying to see behind the ship.

"It was a dog," sighed a squeaky, whiny voice.

Dolph let out a string of high-pitched yipping barks. I emitted a coughing roar. We leapt in the air and spun around, all four feet off the ground, searching for the source of the voice. I wanted my Midday Special so much it hurt, but it was back in the airlock with my clothes, and you can't fire a gun with paws, anyway.

The pink-tinged shadows now looked threatening. Light glinted off something moving in the darkness behind the containment loop, where coolant pipes threaded aft around the antimatter injection nozzle. I crouched down low, tensed to spring.

"It crawled into the No. 3 engine bell and got stuck," sighed the voice. "I attempted to coax it out, but it was afraid of me. Thus it died. It was a very sad event. I was able to remove the corpse using one of my remote attachments, but I fear the smell lingers. Not that it bothers *me*, of course."

The speaker rolled out of the darkness.

Yes, *rolled.*

It had wheels, like the wheels on an office chair, but fatter, supporting a suitcase-shaped body about the height of a Kroolth. Several robotic appendages of assorted lengths dangled from its housing. They sprouted various tool attachments, including what appeared to be a laser drill. Two round, lamp-like sensors, mounted above a speakerbox on a long bendy neck, blinked at us melancholically.

All the fur on my back stood up in a bristly ridge. A menacing growl dripped from my jaws. Logically, I knew I could not hurt this thing with claws and teeth. But logic wasn't in the driver's seat right now. Memory was.

I had seen things like this before.

On Tech Duinn.

They were supposedly on our side, but I swear they killed more humans than the Necros did.

Dolph probably guessed where my head was at. He paced in front of me, putting himself between me and the bot.

"So *this* is what she meant by contents included," he growled.

The bot rocked back on its rear legs. Its front two robotic attachments jerked up to point at us like spears. The covers of its optical sensors sank to a scowling angle.

"More animals!" it exclaimed. "Shoo! Shoo! Out, little dirty feet!"

It moved towards Dolph, brandishing its laser drill. So much for its story that the dog had died because it got stuck. I remembered the lost dog notice on the bulletin board outside the scrapyard.

I shouldered Dolph aside. "We're not animals," I growled. "When was the last time you heard an animal tell you to eff off, chromebrain?"

The bot rocked backwards on its wheels. Its attachments flew up in the air. Its sensors went round and googly. "Shifters," it gasped.

"Got it in one."

I batted the laser drill down with a heavy paw. The bot rolled backwards a few inches.

"I'm a Shifter, and I just bought this ship." I remembered that we had not actually completed the paperwork. That reminded me of Gerry. I disciplined my gaze to stay on the bot and not drift over to the external feed screen. "I have no intention of sharing it with you—whatever you are—so out, out, little dirty wheels," I drawled, parodying the thing's own phrase.

"My wheels are *not* dirty! I have maintained the ship in perfect order." It actually was so clean, apart from that smell, you could eat off the decks. "I'm very efficient, friendly, and cooperative," the bot went on. "I was hired as the weapons officer, but I prefer to see myself in a more generalized role." It blinked its sensor covers rapidly and assumed a simpering tone. "I *like* helping."

"I just bet you do," I muttered.

"Whoa," Dolph said, alarmed.

I followed the jackal's gaze to the external feed screen. It was displaying the feed from a camera that must be mounted amidships on the port side. Opizzt had just appeared in it.

He was tottering towards the ship, wearing a suicide vest.

It looked like a bulky canvas waistcoat. But, as with the bot, I'd seen such things before.

The look of appalled terror on his small face also gave it away.

The secret police surrounded him at a safe distance, aiming their rifles at him.

Gerry knelt behind the half-circle of Kroolth. Blood shone bright on her cheek. One of the vicious little thugs was holding a gun to her head.

"Oh dear," the bot said. "It appears that the junta's volunteer auxiliary technology control police have lost patience with Opizzt. They intend to force him to board the ship, whereupon they will detonate that explosive device—killing him, and destroying the ship."

"Shut your speaker, bot," I snarled. The trouble was, the bot's read of the situation matched mine.

We were done for.

Unless—

"We're taking off," I said. "*Now.*" I didn't want to take the bot along, but forcing it off the ship would take more time than we had. Opizzt was 20 meters away and closing.

I hunched my tiger-shoulders and closed my tiger-eyes, bracing myself to Shift back, while mentally calculating how long it would take me to reach the bridge, figure out the controls, and initiate the drive. I thought I could just about make it.

"No," said Dolph.

I opened my eyes. The jackal stood in front of me, all bristled up to make himself bigger. In nature, jackals are a lot smaller than tigers. However, Shifting conserves mass, so Dolph's jackal was nearly the size of my tiger. He was looking me in the eye. Have you ever looked a jackal in the eye? It isn't an easy thing to do.

Even when the jackal is your best friend.

Especially when it's your best friend.

"No," Dolph repeated. "We're not leaving them to die, Mike."

The thought flashed through my mind: Easy for you to say. *You* haven't got any children.

But he was right.

Of course he was right.

Lucy needed a father—who was a real man.

That guy who loved spaceships? He was also the kind of guy who'd never have left Opizzt and Gerry to die.

That guy was me, and I acknowledged it animal style, by swishing my tiger's tail in a menacing rhythm as I padded back to the optical feed screen.

"Look at Gerry," Dolph said. "She's bleeding!"

Yes, she was bleeding. But her face said she was angry and frightened for Opizzt, not for herself. Even at this distance, I seemed to see something in her posture which didn't match the situation.

Oh, I thought. Of course.

"All right," I said, as Opizzt staggered to the bottom of the airlock ladder. "Here's the plan . . ."

★ 6 ★

OPIZZT CLIMBED towards the airlock.

The bulk of the suicide vest deformed his torso. Clumsy with fear, his feet slipped on the rungs of the ladder. The thugs watching from a safe distance jeered. Yet I was impressed.

The little Kroolth's face was set. He wasn't crying or cursing. He thought he was going to die and betray his emperor in one fell swoop, yet he hoped that he could save his wife's life by making this sacrifice, so he climbed the last rungs of the ladder without hesitating, and set one knee on the lip of the airlock.

The thugs yelled in excitement. I picked out the one holding the wireless detonator. He was dancing around triumphantly, earning a look of contempt from the kneeling Gerry.

I filled my lungs with fetid swamp air, and let out a tiger's bloodcurdling roar.

All the Kroolth froze, sniffing the wind for the scary predator. Their beady eyes fixated on the source of the sound—the pampas grass clogging the mouth of the creek.

I had exited from the airlock on the other side of the ship, shown to us by the reluctant bot, and circled around, as stealthily as only a big cat can. While all eyes were on Opizzt, I'd stalked closer to the ship, edging forward on my belly through the mud and roots.

Now, while the Kroolth were off-balance, I charged out of the pampas grass—straight at Opizzt.

Insensate with terror, he toppled off the airlock ladder right in front of me.

Perfect—except for the fact that the guy was wearing a bomb.

I pushed off the ground into a desperate leap, and intercepted his fall. Mentally saying a prayer to my patron saint, I caught the suicide vest in my jaws.

It did not explode.

I hit the ground running. Keeping my head high, so Opizzt wouldn't bump along the ground, I turned and dashed back towards the groves of thick, tall grass, carrying Opizzt in my jaws like prey.

The Kroolth thugs stared in shock, drawing together into a defensive knot. Their cute little hostage plan had not anticipated the sudden appearance of a dangerous predator—what's more, a predator unknown on Gorongol.

They had no way of knowing the predator was me.

Of course, Opizzt didn't know it was me, either. He struggled weakly as I charged into the grass. The sickly sweet smell of the explosives in his vest stung my tiger-nostrils. I noted the bunched wires connecting to a detonator in the small of his back.

As I splashed through the muck, I chewed through the shoulder of the vest. I had gambled on the Kroolth being too astonished to trigger the explosion immediately. That bet had paid off, but they wouldn't stay confused forever.

Good thing Dolph was on the case.

As I waded deeper into the bog, I heard a deafening rat-a-tat-tat behind me. Rounds zipped through the grass plumes. About a thousand little birds started up in terror, it seemed like from right under my feet.

The bot had assured us that the turret gun was loaded. Thank God, it had been telling the truth.

Now I just needed Dolph to get it turned round the right way.

With grass plumes falling on my back, rounds whizzing over my head, and my paws sinking into hot, gloopy mud, I dropped Opizzt. He immediately ripped the suicide vest off over his head and flung it into the grass. He had a good arm. It travelled at least ten meters before it vanished into the bog. I cringed, bracing for the explosion. All I heard was Dolph wasting more ammo.

Opizzt turned to me, his thin arms spread. He was four feet tall and unarmed, facing a tiger. Yet he was ready to fight for his life. Never say that evolution can't be beat by spirit.

"It's me!" I said urgently. "Mike. I mean, Will. Oh, never mind."

He blinked. Then he said, "They know you are here. Oah, I am sorry. When they threatened Gerry, I told them."

"That's all right," I said. "They would've figured it out soon, anyway."

"Gerry!" he moaned, jumping in a vain attempt to see over the grass.

"Of all of us, she's probably the safest," I said cryptically. Then I crouched lower. "I never normally do this, but—hop on."

Opizzt didn't hesitate. He flung his leg over my back and grabbed hold of the fur at the scruff of my neck. He weighed no more than Lucy.

I bounded through the swamp, heading away from the ship.

We got far enough away to save our lives before the suicide vest blew up. Muddy water, pieces of fish, and clods of earth with grass still attached flew over our heads in a lumpy hailstorm. It had been a pretty big bomb.

I waited out the falling mud and then ran on. Opizzt hammered a little fist on my shoulder. "Gerry! Gerry!"

Opizzt might be worried about his wife, but I wasn't. Admittedly, our masterful, spur-of-the-moment plan had all the hallmarks of a classic Mike-and-Dolph production: start running and fighting, let the bad guys fall where they may. We had not built in any leeway for rescuing Gerry. But I had a feeling she didn't need rescuing. There was more to the gorgeous scrapyard manager than met the eye, and I had bet that as soon as the Kroolth thugs didn't have the drop on her, she'd be able to take care of herself.

I would have won that bet if there'd been anyone around to take it. When Dolph stopped firing, I left the cover of the swamp and circled back between the ancient, now bullet-riddled spaceships. Sure enough, as I approached our metal plesiosaur, Gerry rose from a crouch and dropped the two body-armored Kroolth thugs she'd used as a shield. The Kroolth that Dolph had missed had been put down by the energy pistol in her hand—a small sleek thing with a nasty green glow at the nose, small enough to fit in her cleavage.

I'm a sucker for a dangerous woman. I nearly fell in love with her on the spot.

However, this one was spoken for. I halted and let Opizzt slide off my back. He sprinted to his wife. She picked him up, and they kissed passionately.

I averted my eyes and saw Dolph standing on the airlock stairs.

He gave me a thumbs up. Then he made a googly-eyed face at the loved-up couple. After a few more seconds he pretended to check his watch.

I coughed. I still had my tiger's cough, although I was so muddy there could be no trace of my tiger's stripes remaining visible. That was just as well. I'd burned too many of my animal forms in the past. I didn't want to burn this one.

Gerry put Opizzt down. They both turned to me, eyes shining. Black-clad Kroolth thugs littered the ground, but Gerry paid them no mind. She walked towards me, head on one side. "Shifter, huh?"

"Is it that obvious?" I said.

She laughed.

"Secret squirrel, huh?" I said.

Of all the possible reasons for a dangerous babe like her to be working in a place like this, the only one that really made sense to me was that she was secretly employed by the Iron Triangle, the Fleet's intelligence agency. Officially, the Iron Triangle doesn't even exist, but let's get real. Spies are a lot cheaper than supercarriers.

The skin around her eyes tightened for a microsecond. But all she said was, with a smile, "Why would you think something like that?" She squeezed Opizzt's small hand. "I'm just a girl trying to run a business with my husband."

And that too, I thought, was the truth. They really did love each other. It was plain to see.

"A job," Gerry went on wryly, "which you have just made a lot harder." She moved the nearest corpse with her toe, and wrinkled her nose.

"Oah, do not be ungrateful, Gerry!" Opizzt said, scandalized. "They saved our lives!"

"They did," Gerry conceded. "I'm just saying."

I took a deep breath. "Well, if it helps, there's something in my ship which may come in handy when their friends come looking for them."

"What?"

"A quarter-ton of perfectly ripe bananas."

★ 7 ★

WE SPENT ABOUT HALF AN HOUR helping the Scavarchis tidy up, a.k.a. shoving all the corpses into the marsh. Then we filed the paperwork. The plesiosaur ship was now mine, free and clear.

"Er," Gerry said, once the registration was safely on its way to the nearest FTL comms node, "it comes with a certain, um, *appendage* which I may have forgotten to mention . . ."

"We've met it," I said. "No problem," I lied.

The bot tried to prevent me from getting back on the ship. I was no longer covered with mud, as I had allowed Opizzt to turn the hosepipe on me, despite my anxiety about revealing my stripes. But now I was dripping wet.

"Out of my freaking way, bot," I growled. "Here's a terracentric anthropological factoid for you: When cats are wet, they get bad-tempered."

"Aw, bless," the bot squeaked. Then, I am pretty sure, it winked at me.

I went to Shift back to myself. "That thing's going out the airlock as soon as we get into space," I grumbled to Dolph. "Machines with egos—can't stand 'em."

"You have a live-in nannybot for Lucy," Dolph pointed out.

"Nanny B is royal blue. She is cuddly. She does whatever I tell her to. And she doesn't have weapon attachments."

"I asked ol' chromebrain who was paying its salary," Dolph said. "It said it was hired by the Kroolth Emperor. So now it's all on its lonesome."

I lowered my voice. "Remember the bots on Tech Duinn?"

Dolph twitched as if I'd stuck a pin in him. "There were no bots on Tech Duinn."

"At Dagda's Knoll. You saw them. I saw them. The whole platoon saw them. *They looked just like this one.*"

"There were no bots."

"I know," I said. "That's what they told us. Who you gonna believe, soldier? Your lyin' eyes, or your company commander? But the bots were *there.* So, while you were in hospital, I took it up the chain of command. Asked the brigadier. He said yes, there were bots. They were experimental battlebots. So."

Dolph chewed the insides of his cheeks. Eventually he said, "Well, that was twenty years back, Mike. I think we should give this one a chance."

I ran my hands through my wet hair, pondering whether I was being irrational. I didn't want anything to spoil my lovely new ship. But today had reminded me that Dolph had sound instincts. I might be the boss, but we were a team. I had to listen to him.

He handed me a Kroolth-sized towel with the imperial monogram. I dried my hair and put my clothes on.

"All right," I said, "we'll keep it. On probation. As the janitor."

"I heard that," said the bot from the corridor.

"Good," I said. "Now clean the toilet."

We waved goodbye to Gerry and Opizzt and took off.

The ship handled even more sweetly than I had hoped. The engines lived up to their awesome specs. The transition from the auxiliaries to the main drive was as smooth as butter. At 180 klicks, I cut the throttle.

Gorongol turned below us, mostly sparkling sea, dotted with small continents that were brown in the middle, green at the edges. A troubled planet. A suffering planet.

"Home?" Dolph said.

"Home," I agreed.

But instead of plotting our FTL burn, my right hand hovered above the comms console.

I turned to look for the bot.

It was floating submissively at the back of the cockpit. We were all floating. There were couches for a commander, pilot, and weapons officer, but Dolph and I were never going to get into those unless we shrank three feet. At best, they served as hassocks to hook our toes under.

I wouldn't be pushing the gees until we got human-sized acceleration couches. That ruled out a trip to Silverado. So I decided on the next best thing.

"Bot," I said, "have you got any useful technical expertise, apart from scrubbing, cleaning, and killing stray dogs?"

"I am a highly qualified engineer. I am also a trained medic. I can change a diaper, plan an invasion, butcher a hog, conn a ship, design a building, write a sonnet, balance accounts, build a wall, set a bone, comfort the dying, take orders, give orders, cooperate, act alone, solve equations, analyze a new problem, pitch manure, program a computer, cook a tasty meal, fight efficiently and die gallantly. Specialization is for insects," it finished, with a high-pitched giggle.

Dolph and I were silent for a moment, ticking off skills on our fingers to see how we stacked up.

"By the way, that's a quote from—"

"All right, all right, no need to impress us with your literary acumen as well. In that case, I'm sure you'll be able to help the Silveradans with a little problem they're having."

I radioed Silverado. It was one-half AU further from their sun, a cold and bleak little place. The signal delay made conversation frustrating but at last, using the Scavarchis' names, I managed to get the Crown Prince on the horn.

"This is in regards to a certain cargo that your boys took off me a few days ago," I said. "Don't worry, I'm not going to come get it back. I just wondered if you know exactly what you've got."

The interplanetary silence answered me. I was pretty sure they had no clue. All the cargo looked like was a bunch of very long, very strong cables, and some fancy tension dampeners, as well as a few other bits and pieces for the anchor points.

"What that is," I said, "is a space elevator starter kit. The Generalissimo pretends to despise space. But even he knows you can't get by without access to orbit these days. So he ordered the essential high-tech components for a space elevator. Everything that's not there you'll be able to put together yourselves at that assembly plant you've got. The only missing piece is the expertise to put it together. I suppose the Generalissimo was planning to ask the Eks. You do that, they'll take half your planet off you in consultancy fees. So instead, my associate here is going to tell you exactly how to make a space elevator. If you're not recording, start recording now."

I gave them thirty seconds to get their recording equipment cued up.

"OK, chromebrain, you're on," I whispered.

And for the next three hours and a half, the bot told them how to make a space elevator.

Then it spent another four hours answering their questions.

I sloped off for a nap in the air, feeling pretty good. With a space elevator, the Crown Prince would be able to retake Gorongol in no time. I just hoped he was nice about it.

When Dolph and I woke up, the bot was *still* on the radio, telling the Silveradans that if they wanted, they could spray some vaporized aluminum over the cables, and as the planet rotated through its own magnetic field, electric currents would be induced into the cables, so they could use that to run the lights and heat and such on the elevator cars ...

I sliced a hand through the air. "Wrap it up. They've got to learn to walk before they can run."

I said goodbye to the Crown Prince. Then, floating above the drive console, I initiated the skip field generator to go FTL.

I couldn't wait to show Lucy our new ship.

The only question was: What would we name her?

From the control booth deep in the tunneled-out moon of Deimos, Marcie directs Martian space traffic, guiding long-haul cargo ships and independent asteroid miners to safety. It's a relatively solitary life, but one to which she's become accustomed. But when a miner friend returns to Deimos with a find that is truly out of this world, Marcie will find her comfortable life turned upside down.

BROKEN WINGS

by William Ledbetter

"CALLING DEIMOS CONTROL. This is mining vessel *Nowhere Man.* Do you copy?"

The sound of Bernard's voice made me freeze with my hands motionless in the guidance field. During the two years I'd known him, he'd never gone more than a week without calling in, but this time it had been nearly three months and not a peep. He wasn't my boyfriend, we'd never even met in person, but I liked him a lot. With three ships disappearing during that time period and an announced reward for information about pirates, I'd been worried.

Elspeth, the other dispatcher and my best friend, gave me a snarky smile. "I'll let you take this call, Marcie."

I examined the guidance field, then frowned. His ship wasn't there. "This is Deimos Control. We read you *Nowhere Man*, but we're not picking up an ID. Is your transponder off?"

"Umm . . . is that you, Marcie?"

What the hell was he doing? I directed active radar in the direction of his radio reply and soon found an untagged blip exiting Mars' shadow. It was moving fast.

"You are inbound and hot, *Nowhere Man*. Please provide active identification or you will be fired upon."

Elspeth covered her mouth, but couldn't stifle her snicker. "Not the best way to get that first date, Marcie."

"Hush!" I whispered and didn't laugh.

There was a pause that couldn't be distance lag since he was so close, then he finally replied. "Err . . . This is mining vessel *Nowhere Man,* registration KLR88749. My transponder is . . . um . . . malfunctioning. I'm requesting approach clearance and a secure groundside cargo berth."

This was getting weird and even Elspeth's grin faded. We both knew Bernard couldn't afford to rent a groundside berth.

"Say again, *Nowhere Man*? Are you sure you wouldn't rather tag your load and leave it in Mars orbit? Your claim is guaranteed by Martian mining law."

"Yes. This time I need a private berth, Marcie."

Was this really Bernard? And hell, would I even know? I'd only seen grainy video of him wearing an interface helmet, with a face made puffy by zero gravity. But this wasn't like the man I thought I knew. I'd teased him about being a tightwad because he never even left his ship for entertainment or relaxation. He always teased back that he was saving his money to buy a ship big enough to take me along. I'd known he was joking, and that if he ever saw me in person he would bolt anyway, but the idea of the two of us going off like that together had long been my favorite fantasy. Maybe he wasn't the person I thought he was.

I manipulated markers and numbers in the guidance field, then called him back. "Confirmed, *Nowhere Man*. You have secure berth 556G. I'm sending the approach vector now. Please stay in the prescribed lane."

"Thank you. And Marcie?"

"Yes?"

"Can you switch to a private channel?"

I glanced up at Elspeth, whose eyes nearly popped out of her head.

"Okay, Bernard. You're on a private channel, but Elspeth can hear. What the hell is going on and where have you been?"

"I know you're on shift right now. But can you meet me at this berth as soon as possible? I'll explain why I've been quiet so long."

"Come out there? In person?"

"Yes. And dress warm. I need to keep the berth cold."

"I don't know if—"

"It's important, Marcie. I need your help. Please."

"I . . . I'll try, Bernard," I said, feeling the old panic rise again. "Control out."

Once the connection closed, I stared at the console for a second, then looked down at the ugly prosthetic device encasing my lower body and shook my head. I'd given up on many things after my accident: my engineering degree, which had crushed my father, and even real relationships after my fiancé dumped me. I much preferred the more remote connections with people enabled by my position as a traffic controller. It let my emotions stay numb, like my whole lower body.

"Marcie! You have to go," Elspeth said in her best disapproving mom voice. "You've wanted to meet him for two freakin years! Besides, he needs you."

"But this is just strange. And what if . . ." I glanced down again.

"Then at least you'll know," she said in a softer tone. "Give him a chance."

Two hours later, my personal tractor, or PT, filled the corridor with its rapid-fire zipper sound as the metal tracks first magnetized then released to pull me along the steel floor. PTs were about the size of a kid's scooter, but absolutely the best way to move about in the almost non-existent gravity of Mars' smallest moon.

The base on Deimos was a sucky place to live for most people. It had been intended as a waystation for explorers and colonists bound for Mars and not designed with long-term inhabitants in mind, but it had grown and become home for over a thousand people to simply service and control ship traffic around Mars . And it worked great for me. Living in almost no gravity enabled me to use a heavier, and thereby cheaper, prosthesis.

I turned down the corridor leading to berth 556G, swaddled in blankets and feeling silly. We lived underground in a controlled environment, so since nobody here had coats heavier than a jacket for me to borrow, it was the best I could do. I wondered what kind of picture of me Bernard had built up in his mind. He'd seen my face of course, but he soon would see the rest of me and be disappointed. I'd always thought if we met in person there would be time to prepare him, but this could be bad. The blankets even made it worse. The only part of me he would see not padded and wrapped would be my ugly composite prosthetic.

As it turned out, the man waiting beside the hatch was not who I had envisioned either. Bernard was huge, in every sense of the word. Even the EVA suit he wore couldn't account for—or hide—his obesity. He stood well over six feet tall and on Earth would have weighed at least four hundred pounds. He had no neck, just jowls that disappeared into the EVA suit's neck ring and a massive chest that heaved, even in Deimos' weak gravity.

Then—like every person I'd met since the accident—his eyes flicked down to my mechanically encased legs, but his smile never wavered. That was something.

"I suppose I'm not quite what you expected?" he said in that warm baritone I'd come to know so well. The smile widened and somehow perfectly matched the voice.

Many things now made sense. Weight and health issues were well known among those who spent a lot of time alone in space, like long-haul transport pilots and independent miners. Economics of spacecraft design left these people encased in tight spaces, in little or no gravity most of the time, with no room for exercise equipment and plenty of boredom. Gravity explained why he would never go down to the surface of Mars, but why had he never left his ship upon visiting Deimos?

My first impulse was to offer a handshake. Then I felt silly and stepped off of my PT, my prosthetic whining and thumping with each stride, to wrap him in a hug. His suit smelled burnt and metallic, like space.

I pushed back gently, letting myself settle to the floor so my foot magnets kicked in, then pointed at the awkward contraption encasing my legs and pelvis. "I'm sure this isn't what you expected either."

He shrugged. "And neither of us expected our first meeting to be something like this."

"Speaking of which," I said, glad to change the subject, "what the hell is this all about?"

"You're going to be cold," he said. "Will you let me wrap you up a little better?"

I looked down at the blankets floating around me in no deliberate arrangement. "Okay."

He took several minutes to wrap the blankets around my torso and arms in a loose, yet more efficient configuration. Then he removed the gloves from his suit and put them on my bare hands. They made me look like a clown, and most of my fingers fit into just one of the finger holes, but I shrugged and followed him through the hatch.

The cold was immediate and hurt my lungs when I inhaled. It had to be twenty below zero Celsius, but I burrowed my nose and mouth into the nest of blankets and kept going. The berth was huge and eerily dark, lit by only two distant floods near the ceiling hatch and intermittent flashes of the navigation strobes from Bernard's ship.

My shoe locks echoed every time they clicked to the steel floor, and I slowed down, suddenly creeped out. Was I a fool to follow this man into such a potentially dangerous environment? He was more than twice my mass and I wouldn't be able to stop him if he had nefarious intentions. But in the end I always went with my gut feeling and my guts insisted he meant me no harm. Besides, Elspeth knew where I was and my already piqued curiosity would never allow me to go back until I knew what was going on.

At first, Bernard's mining ship looked tiny floating in the center of the cavernous berth, connected to the walls by cables and umbilicals, but as we got closer, I could see it was about twice the size of my mother's four-bedroom house in Illinois. The *Nowhere Man* was mostly large cylindrical tanks held together with complicated strut work, and the control pod—where Bernard spent all of his time—wasn't much bigger than my spartan quarters there on Deimos. I felt both sorry for him and kind of in awe. How did anyone—especially someone his size—spend so many long months cooped up in such a small space?

We stopped beside it and what I saw made me forget everything else.

Strapped to the ship's lower utility spine and cradled in thick foam insulation, five feet above the floor, was a chunk of dirty ice about twenty feet long and ten feet wide. Two small robots clung to adjacent struts, their work lights shining on what looked like a carved stone column protruding about eight feet from the ice. The column was some thirty inches in diameter and fluted like a classical age column, but instead of parallel to the axis, the flutes were slightly curved, appearing to twist around the diameter.

"My God, Bernard?" I whispered. "Where did you find this?"

"In the belt."

"Okay. But it had to come from Earth, right?"

"I don't think it did come from Earth, Marcie," he said. I could hear the nervous excitement in his voice. "At least the encasing ice didn't. The deuterium to hydrogen ratio in the ice is way too high. It's even higher than in Oort cloud comets."

I stared at it, still trying to process the implications behind the carved stone. I could already hear the clamor in my head. Some would claim it was a hoax, others that it had to have come from Earth. There would need to be detailed study and the experts might not ever know for sure.

"What are you going to do now?"

"I have no idea," he said with a puff of foggy breath. "I'm freakin terrified. I know mining and math and spacecraft, but this is way outside of my purview. That's why I wanted your help."

His deep voice went up an octave "Help me Obi-Wan Kenobi, you're my only hope."

"What?" It must have been another one of his obscure song or movie quotes.

"Never mind," he said. "Let's just say you have a level head and you're smart about a lot of things. And you actually know how to interact with the rest of humanity."

I stared at him. My mouth moved a couple of times, but nothing came out. How could he think I'd know how to handle something like this?

"We could potentially make a lot of money from this and I don't want to screw it up," he said.

We? I felt a panicky lump rise in my throat. I had no idea what to do either and I didn't want Bernard's success or failure with this thing in my hands.

"I . . . We need a professional. Do you know Cooper Billings? The mining attorney?"

"Yeah," Bernard said with a slightly hopeful note in his voice. "He helped me with a tricky ice sale once."

"Well, he needs to see this. He can advise you on the next steps. And I need to get out of here before I lose my damned fingers to frost bite!"

We had just started back toward the door when the hatch at the far end of the berth swung open with a loud squeak. The man was too far away and the light too dim for me to see his face, but with a population of only twelve hundred people, everyone knew everyone on Deimos. I immediately recognized the white hair and bright yellow customs inspector vest.

"Oh no," I whispered. "It's Grisha Budnikov."

"That's just great," Bernard said.

While probably not knowing him in person like I did, every miner or cargo hauler using Deimos base had dealings with the asshole customs inspector. The man's PT rushed toward them as he uttered a string of profanity. Evidently he didn't like the cold either.

Bernard stood up straight and squared his shoulders. "I haven't done anything wrong. I don't have contraband."

"It doesn't matter with Grisha. He'll still find some violation."

Grisha stopped in front of us, then leapt from the little scooter with a flourish, like a dismounting cowboy. "Why is it so damned cold in here?"

"I have an ice cargo," Bernard said. "I'm waiting for a better market price and don't want it to melt."

"That's the stupidest thing I've . . ." He stopped and squinted at me. "Well, hello, Marcie. Did your sucky dispatcher job force you to become a part-time ice miner too?"

"Something like that," I said, trying not to clench my teeth.

He leaned in toward me, as if to say something else, but Bernard slipped his bulk between us. "This is my ship and cargo. Is there a problem, Inspector?"

I groaned inwardly. This wasn't going to end well.

He looked up at Bernard and took a small step backward. "That's what I'm here to find out, Mr. Haugen."

"That's Captain Haugen," Bernard said.

Don't do this, Bernard, I wanted to yell.

"Yes. Well according to this," Grisha said and looked down at his data pad, "you came in dark, in radio silence and with your transponder turned off, you rented a very expensive secure berth, which you've never done before and your bank account says you can't afford, and you requested a private channel with the traffic control center. Which I can only assume was to talk to sweet little Marcie here." Grisha nodded toward me, then crossed his arms and shivered violently. "That adds up to some very suspicious behavior. I'm going to need to see your cargo, *Captain* Haugen."

Bernard's jaw tensed under his pink jowls. "Of course, *Inspector*."

Grisha smiled at Bernard for a second, then pulled gloves and a face mask from his vest pocket and donned them as he approached the ice block hanging from the ship.

We both watched without talking as the inspector examined everything. He was careful not to touch the actual artifact, but did scrape some residue from the ice.

"Where'd you find this?"

"Someone must have left it floating in the belt. I thought it would make a great practical joke for my friend Marcie here," Bernard said.

I blinked, wondering for a second if it was just some kind of joke.

"*Where* in the belt, Captain?"

"Miners aren't required to tell customs the locations of their finds and claims," Bernard said.

"I see. Well, then you've spent a lot of money on a practical joke, Captain," Grisha said. "Especially since you didn't bring back any other sellable ore to cover your costs. And the stone piece may well be from Earth or Mars, but the ice covering it is layered with sediment and appears very old."

"What are you saying," I blurted out.

"I'm saying that while this probably is some kind of hoax—one most likely played *on* our dear captain—we can't be sure until we test it. I'm afraid I'll have to confiscate this 'alleged artifact' as a safety hazard."

"Safety!" Bernard boomed. "How is this chunk of rock a safety hazard?"

Grisha raised an eyebrow. "Because there is a very insignificant chance that it is actually an ancient alien artifact. If it is, then you've broken quarantine rules, Captain." He smiled and his wrapped arms around his chest again. "Harmful alien organisms could at this very second be contaminating us all and this station."

Within minutes, hazmat workers poured into the berth and started working.

We watched, shivering from a spot near the open corridor hatch—where at least some warm air blew in—as they detached the ice-clad artifact from *Nowhere Man* and sealed it into a large, environmentally controlled shipping container. Then they took it out a cargo hatch on the opposite side of the berth.

"Weird how fast those workers arrived," I said. "That worm must've known before he even came in here that he'd confiscate the artifact. And did you notice that some of those workers wore non-regulation hazmat suits?"

"I shouldn't have let them take it," Bernard muttered. "I could have just climbed in *Nowhere Man* and left as soon as that asshole said he was going to take it."

"That wouldn't have worked," I said. "I bet that before he even said a word to you about quarantine, he'd already directed Deimos Control to send a drive lockout to your ship. Standard procedure. I do it to ships every time there is a question of their cargo being legal."

He grumbled to himself until Grisha rolled up to us on his PT looking more than a little smug. "We're done here, Captain. I've sent a receipt to your mail account. You'll be notified as to the legal status of the alleged artifact when we are done with our tests, but I suspect that will take several months."

"This is . . ." Bernard started, but Grisha ignored him and rolled away to follow the artifact out the cargo hatch. Bernard turned, slapped his hands against the wall and rattled off a string of curses. Then he looked at me and apologized.

"No need," I said. "You have every right to be angry and frustrated. Come on. I'm freezing."

He followed me into the corridor where we stood awkwardly for a couple minutes, until he eventually slid down the wall to sit on the corridor floor, looking very alone and lost.

"I guess I didn't think this through very well. I just assumed finding something like that would be a financial windfall. Now I'm in big trouble."

I sat down on the floor next to him and stared at the composite skin encasing my feet. There had to be a way to leverage his finding the artifact. Had there been media coverage, the press would be swarming all over Deimos. And of course that was the problem. Nobody knew about it but us and customs.

"So," I said and nudged his arm. "Do you have video and pictures of the artifact? Maybe of you recovering it?"

"Yeah," he said. "Why?"

"Did you think to get video of them confiscating it?" I said and stood up.

"Of course," he said and stood too. "Those bots with the lights were filming the entire time. I sure as hell wanted to have proof if it came to a court fight."

"Good." I looped my arm through his and started through the hatch toward his ship. "We have work to do. We have to tell all of humanity about this amazing thing you found."

My comm implant kept beeping while I tried to concentrate on work. The message count was up to eighty-three in the special account we'd set up for the "alleged artifact" and our video plea had been public for less than six hours. I itched to check the messages, but forced myself to wait.

On the days Elspeth and I weren't on the same shift, I usually stayed to talk, but this time when she came in I gave her a wave with a promise to call later and darted out of the control center. I stopped to check the messages at a coffee shop down the corridor. Most of them were statements of support and solidarity. Some of them were forwarded news pieces where the press was already pressuring the Martian government for access to the artifact. But six of them were from correspondents for the biggest news organizations on Mars who were either already on Deimos wanting to interview Bernard, or on their way. Three of the messages were from Universities on Earth who were begging for access to the find. And one of those actually offered a twenty thousand dollar retainer if Bernard would give their experts first access once it came out of Martian impound. Bingo!

I called Bernard three times, but he didn't answer, so I jumped on my PT and raced down to berth 556G. When I arrived, the hatch panel was lit up red, showing that the berth was in vacuum. I considered sending the command to close the surface hatch and repressurize the cavernous chamber, but that much air would be expensive and besides, Bernard had probably opened the berth for a reason.

I got an uneasy feeling. Could he have possibly overridden the lockout circuit and left? Would he have really left without saying goodbye? I tried to call him and again got no answer.

The cargo hatch on the other side of the berth—the one Customs had used to remove the "alleged artifact"—had an airlock, and according to the map, was designated as an emergency egress point so it might also have emergency EVA suits. I careened through the maze of passages until I found it.

As expected, the oversized airlock had emergency suit lockers in its antechamber, but that gave me a sick feeling in my stomach. Putting on a pressure suit was not easy for me. I tried calling Bernard one more time. When he still didn't answer, that was all the impetus I needed. Something was wrong.

Emergency suits came in four sizes: large, medium, small and child, which was little more than a bubble with carrying handles and tethers. I pulled out a medium, which would probably be a little too large, but it would self-adjust once pressurized, and lay it on the floor next to the locker. I removed my prosthesis and set it aside, then struggled into the EVA suit, thanking the stars that I lived in low gee. It would have taken me hours to don that suit in full Martian gravity. By the time I finished I was half panicked and half pissed. I had called Bernard twice more with no answer. If I found out that he was asleep in his ship, I would kill him slowly using something cruel, like a spoon.

I stowed my prosthesis in the suit locker and cycled the airlock.

Holding myself up on the PT with just my arms was awkward, but worked, I entered slowly. At first everything looked the way it had when I was there last. The *Nowhere Man* floated where it had been, still tethered to the walls, navigation strobes still flashing, giving the whole berth an eerie, unreal appearance. As I neared the ship, I saw the first indication that something was wrong. A metal disk, about six feet in diameter and three inches thick, lay on the floor. I looked at it closer and could see that it wasn't solid, but made from sandwiched layers of several materials. The edges had been melted and then cooled. It had been cut with a torch or laser.

I looked up and, sure enough, directly above me I could see the ruddy surface of Mars showing through a round hole in one of the big berth access doors. My first thought was that Bernard was trying to pull off some daring escape with the *Nowhere Man*, but that didn't make any sense. Why cut a hole when he would have to eventually open those doors to let the ship out anyway?

I stopped the PT under the ship's command pod and realized that without my prosthetic I couldn't jump the eight feet needed to reach the bottom rung of the access ladder. I rattled off curses and looked around. A maintenance ladder mounted to one wall passed very close to one of the mooring cables. That would have to do. I scooted over to the ladder, flipped on my helmet lights and started pulling myself up hand over hand. I went higher than the cable, then through a series of awkward and muscle-wrenching moves, I turned around with my back to the ladder and let myself fall forward toward the cable with arms outstretched. Gravity was weak on Deimos, but with no air to help slow me down, I fell faster than expected and barely caught the cable.

My glove fabric snagged when I tried to slide them across the steel cable, so I had to hand-over-hand again. It was nerve-wracking, but not difficult and actually made me feel kind of heroic. I could've never done anything like that on Earth. I got to the ship, clambered along the strut work until I reached the control pod and was immediately concerned. The wide, round hatch was open.

I looked in. Relief flooded through me hard enough to make me tremble. Bernard wasn't inside. Ever since I'd seen the hole in the overhead hatch, I'd been imagining his dead, wide-eyed corpse in his ship. I took a deep breath and entered. As I'd expected, the interior was cramped with gear and equipment strapped to every surface that didn't have a monitor or control panel. His EVA suit locker stood empty, which was probably a good sign. A large acceleration couch dominated the cabin, surrounded by display panels, several of which flashed the same red warning.

NAVIGATION SYSTEM NOT FOUND!

The ship was landed, powered down and connected to the station. So why was navigation being offline an error? But it didn't say it was offline. It said, "not found."

I looked at the screens again. One of them actually had a string of the errors where some system kept trying to access the navigation computer. Twelve of them, each with a time stamp. The first one was a little over two hours before. Just nine minutes before my shift had ended.

I made myself examine the cabin more slowly, shining my lights in every corner and at every equipment rack.

There! Just behind and below a row of screens, an access panel hung open with wires dangling out. Sure enough, whatever had been inside that rack was gone. I lifted the panel and saw "NAVIGATION COMPUTER - PRIMARY" stenciled on the outer surface.

The simplest explanation was that someone had cut their way in and taken the navigation computer. But why? Because they couldn't get access to the artifact itself, so thought there could be more where this one had come from. And had they taken Bernard too? Would they kill him? Torture him?

I slapped gloves against my faceplate. Stop it! One thing at a time! If I was going to help Bernard, I couldn't panic or break down, so I made myself stop and think.

Security needed to know about this, but I paused before calling them. Chances were they would detain me for hours with forms and questions. I had to act now. The first thing I needed to know was if they had come in a ship or rover. I left the control pod, crawled to the top of the ship and looked up at the hole. It was at least twenty feet up. Once again, if I'd had working legs or my prosthesis I might have been able to jump high enough to grab the edge and pull myself up, but there's no way I could do it with just my arms.

But I was on a mining ship! There had to be tools I could use. I looked around and immediately saw the little mining robots he'd used to light the artifact the day before. There were four of them, now folded into their stowed positions and docked in utility cradles. They had names painted on their carapaces. Paul, George, Ringo and John. The names probably had some significance to Bernard, but meant nothing to me. Still, these things were semi-autonomous, so they had to have a wireless link.

I activated my suit's comm system through the heads-up-display, or HUD, and had it search for local connections. It found nothing that wasn't station-related. I'm sure if they were powered down, Bernard could still activate and undock them through a hard connection to the ship, but maybe they would have some manual controls too. I examined Ringo and eventually found a button with the universal "power" symbol. I pressed it and status lights flickered on. Yes!

This time my comm unit found a node called "Ringo."

I connected and activated the verbal interface.

"Main menu," I said.

"Voice recognition failure," the little robot said with a rather thick British accent. "Unable to open menu."

"Override voice recognition," I said.

"Please give the admin password."

I muttered under my breath. I had no freakin' idea what he would use for a password. I wonder how many guesses I'd get before it locked me out?

"Nowhere?" I said.

"Password not recognized."

"Mining"

"Password not recognized."

"Fuck!"

"Password not recognized."

I took a deep breath and patted the robot's side. This could take all day. I didn't have time for that. And I wasn't technically savvy enough to hack either the software or the hardware.

"Well, Marcie," I muttered. "You're just going to have to think of something else."

"Please confirm the password," the robot said.

I blinked, confused. What had I said? I replayed the comment in my head and then smiled. Bernard was a serious sap and must *really* like me.

"Marcie," I said and an interface menu flickered to life on my HUD.

Once active and unfolded, Ringo was about the size and shape of my office chair, the "back" being a comms dish and the "legs" being various grappling and tool assemblies. Bernard had once said the robots were about as smart as a four year old child. I hadn't known many kids, but this thing seemed dumber than that to me. I finally managed to put Ringo in "tow mode" and had it clamp onto one of my suit's tether rings, but trying to explain that I wanted it to carry me up to that hole proved difficult until I discovered the ability to put crosshairs on something and say "go there."

Ringo went to the hole and stopped. It was high enough for me to peek out and make sure there wasn't anyone nearby watching the hole. After cursing and grumbling a few minutes, I eventually got it to take me up another ten feet. From there I could see the evidence

I needed. There were anchors still in the ground, where they had tethered their ship, and three star-shaped blast patterns where thrusters had pushed them away from the surface.

I called Elspeth. "I need your help."

"I'm kinda busy. Steven decided he was sick today. I don't suppose you could—"

"Listen," I said. "Someone cut into the berth and took Bernard."

"What? Are you—"

"Yes! I'm serious! I'm floating in an EVA suit above the hole they cut! I need you to find that ship. Berth 556G. They would have arrived here, on the surface, before 4:00 and left before 5:00."

"Holy shit," she said and I heard her muttering in the background. "There was no record of a ship landing there."

"They must have turned their transponder off. Check the radar record."

"Okay, but it might take a few minutes."

While I waited, I checked my oxygen level. Still a little over four hours. Then I browsed Ringo's menu until I found a way to activate the other robots. I woke up George and slaved him to Ringo, so they would fly in formation. George joined us a couple minutes later.

"Okay," Elspeth said. "Radar picked up a ship rising from the surface in your general area and it turned on the transponder just a couple minutes later."

"That sounds like the culprit. Where are they? Please tell me they haven't left Martian space yet."

"No. They docked at fuel depot 219 about fifty minutes ago. Which means for a ship that size, if their tanks were nearly dry, they should be fueled and leaving any minute."

"Damn, damn, damn!"

"You want me to call security?"

"No. I want you to send a sphere-wide departure lockdown order."

Her pause stretched out.

"Elspeth?"

"I don't think we can do that. Not without orders."

"Patch me into the system," I said.

"Marcie, I don't think that's a good idea. If you trigger a lockdown without authorization—"

"Listen to me," I said. "It's just a damned job. If those people who took Bernard leave Martian space we will never see him again. They will kill him if he tells or not."

"Patching you through."

As soon as the menu appeared on my HUD, I sent the departure lockdown order using my emergency authentication code. The message went out, overriding the control systems on thirty-three ships, including seven SpaceX freighters and a passenger liner, that were in the Martian/Deimos traffic sphere, rendering all of them incapable of using their main drive units. Four more ships were allowed to finish scheduled or in-progress deceleration burns, then they also entered the lockdown. The command had only been used once during the entire time I had been on Deimos and that had been to stop a suspected terrorist attack.

I was now in deep shit.

"Thanks, Elspeth. Make sure they know this was my doing. I have to go, but send me that ship's transponder number before the crap hits the fan over there."

"Sending. I am so going to kick your ass when—"

I received the number and broke the link. Three seconds later, my boss was calling in a panic. I didn't answer his calls or those from security or the Martian Transit Authority. I considered telling security, but as long as they didn't know why the order had been sent, they probably wouldn't allow it to be lifted until they talked to me. Since I, like everyone on Deimos, had a comm implant, they knew exactly where I was at all times and were no doubt already sending someone to get me for a long questioning session. And I knew station security. They would be in far more of a hurry to get those ships back online than to find a missing miner, so they would be highly motivated to find me.

"That's it!" I said aloud, then double checked to make sure I wasn't broadcasting. "They know where the hell I am at all times!"

I had a brief moment of panic when I wondered if the shutdown order would affect the robots too, but there was only one way to find out. I confirmed Ringo's hold on my suit, checked its fuel level and then coaxed George close enough for me to grab one of its handles. Then I sent the kidnapper's transponder number to the robots and told them to "go there."

Of course I hadn't been smart enough to tell them to build speed slowly, so when their thrusters kicked in the sudden acceleration yanked my hand loose from George and, if the pain in my neck was any indicator, also gave me whiplash. I cussed and groaned, but with a stretch I was able to reach George again and my ride eventually smoothed out once they attained cruising speed.

I ignored the frantic calls coming through my implant. Even though I was stressed and near panic, the unhindered view of Mars above took my breath away. Living underground I had few opportunities to actually see the planet in real time, but it was stunning and beautiful and terrible all at once. It had been aptly named. I stared in awe for a long time before making the mistake of looking behind me. Then felt my first tremor of fear.

Deimos was getting smaller by the second. I should have asked Elspeth just exactly how far away this fuel depot was from Deimos. I checked the robots' fuel supply and was alarmed to see it was already down by half, but the ETA ticking down on my HUD showed less than six minutes. If it was that close, I should be able to see it.

After scanning what seemed like the entire Martian sky, I finally saw the fuel depot coming up behind me. Like the "orbital" repair and cargo berths, it wasn't actually in orbit around Deimos, I wasn't sure that was even possible with the moon's small size, but rather flying in formation, keeping a constant position above the surface base for ease of transport and communications. But it looked like I would miss the depot. I pulled up the intercept diagram on my HUD and sure enough, the arc showed us crossing paths after it passed. I had a brief moment of confusion until I realized that the transponder tag for that ship was still our target. It must have already undocked from the depot sometime prior to my shutdown order, and the robots had compensated for the change.

With Marslight reflecting ruddy along its hull, I could see as we drew near that this ship was probably three times larger than the *Nowhere Man*. That worried me. It might also mean a larger crew, but it was a little late for second thoughts now. Ringo and George slowed and pulled alongside the *Lazy Dog*, the name painted on the hull. I directed them, with the same point and click option I'd used earlier, to nestle into the strut work near the engines, as far from the control module as possible. I pulled the coiled tether from the suit's emergency pouch and attached myself to one of the struts.

That had pretty much been the extent of my plan. Fly to their ship, and when security came looking for me, the villains would be caught. Except now, with my oxygen down to the three-hour mark, floating in cold vacuum a thousand feet above Deimos, dozens of new and unpleasant scenarios flashed through my mind.

They had to know I was out there. The proximity alarms would have raised hell when we got close. Would they come out and investigate? If so, would they drag me inside and torture me to make Bernard tell where he'd found the artifact? I think he would tell them too, to stop them from hurting me. I didn't want that. Of course they might come out and shoot me then shove my body toward Mars to eventually burn up.

Or could they know something I didn't? Was Deimos Control even now getting ready to remove my departure lock? I had to disable them. That thought made me smile briefly. I really wanted to blind them first, but the ship had to have dozens of cameras, so that would take time. I had to make sure they couldn't escape first.

Like some behemoth, with its skin and muscle removed to reveal the entrails, the ship's vital organs all lay exposed before me. This time an evil snicker accompanied my smile. George and Ringo could make very effective vultures.

I scooted over to one of the two massive engines, scanned the ID plate and pulled up the maintenance manual on my HUD. I searched for anything with the word "fuel." I found a pressurized fuel tube and told the program to identify it. A detailed 3D model of the engine appeared, then rotated, sectioned and zoomed until I could see the highlighted tube. That one wouldn't work, since it was actually inside the engine. The next one, called a "Feed Line, Pressurized, Fuel" sounded just as good and it was a fat one, easily accessible, running between a turbo-pump and one of the big fuel tanks.

I identified one of the pipes for Ringo and the other for George, then instructed them to cut each pipe into four pieces. While they worked I examined the electrical schematics for the engines. I wanted to also cut control and data cables, without impacting life support. A beeping interrupted my search and George's status screen—with several red blinking warnings—replaced the engine manual in my HUD. Just then one of the robots went tumbling past me with its positioning jets firing so fast they looked like twinkling Christmas lights.

"Ringo! Stop all action!"

Too late. Ringo's status window appeared beside George's, also all lit up.

I cancelled all previous instructions and sent a recall order to bring the robots back to me. The only pipe I could see from my tethered position was twisted, with a ragged tear in one side. What the hell? I didn't see a flash, and with no oxidizer I didn't know how the liquid hydrogen could have ignited. Unless the lasers made it hot enough to vaporize the hydrogen in a local area. Then I groaned. And I bet the pipes had already been pressurized.

George came back and was fine aside from some scratched paint and his status yellow light warnings announcing a fuel leak. Ringo didn't return. His status screen flickered on and off, which could be a minor comm problem or something much worse. I immediately sent orders to the other robots, Paul and John, to power up and come to my location. If the crew in that ship hadn't been inclined to come out and get me before, they sure would now, so I had to hurry.

With no time to find and try to fix George's fuel leak, I sent him along the *Lazy Dog's* length looking for cameras. Each time I saw one through his camera, I had him fry it with his cutting laser.

I was getting ready to blast my sixth camera, when something grabbed me from behind and spun me around. I assumed it would be one of the kidnappers and prepared to fight like hell, but it was a utility robot, nearly twice George's size. The gripper on one of its arms had a hold on a wad of my suit fabric. I immediately stopped struggling. This was an emergency suit, so it couldn't take much abuse and I couldn't risk a rip. A second arm extended, grabbed another wad of suit and pulled me into a weird robotic embrace. My helmet pressed right up against the robot's case and what I saw there, printed in very small text along one panel edge, chilled me to the bone.

PROPERTY OF: SASSY SAPPHO. MARS REGISTRATION KLG97749

Sassy Sappho was one of the missing ships. I'd known her crew.

The robot cut through my tether and started moving toward the control pod. I didn't dare try to get loose, but I now had a serious desire to *not* get inside the ship. I could still use my HUD, so I instructed George to come to me. We were about to see how this stolen robot functioned after getting a mining laser punched through its guts. But the status screen popped up showing George was out of thruster fuel.

"Damn! Damn! Damn!" I yelled. Then I realized I had what I needed to get plenty of help. They might not bust their asses to save me and Bernard, or even get those ships released, but they sure would to catch the pirates.

I called base security.

Franklin, the security office's main dispatcher answered immediately. "Oh my God, Marcie! You are in so much trouble! We have three ships coming after you. What the hell are you—"

I cut him off and started explaining everything, but then he interrupted and connected me to the head of base security. So I started all over again. By the time I finished and was assured ships were on the way, my robot captor had stopped in front of the *Lazy Dog*'s main airlock where someone in an EVA suit waited.

The figure came closer and grabbed me by the arms, just as the robot released me. He had maneuvering jets on his suit and started moving us toward the airlock. That's when I recognized the face on the other side of the visor. It was Grisha Budnikov.

I didn't know if anyone was listening, but my suit transmitter was still open so I yelled, "Grisha Budnikov is here! He's one of the pirates!"

I twisted violently and broke one arm loose. He kept his grip on the other and tried to shove me into the airlock, but I grabbed the edge of the hatch with my free hand and held on. My HUD showed Paul and John floating only yards away, patiently waiting for instructions. Without hesitation, I put crosshairs on Grisha's suit, switched comm channels and told John to grab him with two grippers. Grisha immediately released me and turned to fight with the robot, obviously not as concerned about tearing the fabric of his much tougher EVA suit.

I instructed John to hold tight and tow Grisha toward the surface, then ordered Paul to come get me. Before he could arrive, the stolen robot grabbed me by each leg. Using the cross hairs again, I tagged each of my captor's robotic arms and told Paul to use his lasers at full power and cut them off. I realized my mistake only when both of my legs tumbled away from me, propelled by the atmosphere venting from my now open suit.

"Well, shit," I muttered as my suit alarms blared. The status screen appeared on my HUD, showing that emergency seal tourniquets had been activated in the upper legs of my suit, sealing them off from the torso. Like the bulkheads of a ship automatically sealing when there is a hole, my suit attempted to sacrifice my legs to save the rest of my body. I felt no pain as my already paralyzed flesh and muscles were exposed to vacuum, but I did feel suddenly weak. An odd chill crept up my back.

Two suited figures tumbled out of the airlock, grappling with each other, arms swinging in violent punches. One was huge and one much smaller. My vision began to fade, but not before I put crosshairs on the smaller of the two and ordered Paul to grab him. I didn't dare try the lasers. I obviously sucked at that.

Then I passed out.

"Are you feeling up to this?" Bernard said. He kept wincing and holding his hands out on either side, ready to catch me should I fall. Like falling with almost no gravity would hurt me. "It's only been six days."

I shooed him away. "I've got this."

My new prosthetic wasn't very different from my old one. It just now included artificial legs instead of moving around my dead-meat real ones. The big difference was that even though the part encasing my pelvis was still packed with electronics and tiny actuators, it was now very sleek, cutting-edge tech paid for by the Martian Colonial Government. It was so streamlined I could wear pants over it!

"You almost died!" Bernard grumbled.

We entered a suit storage area outside of the main surface airlock and I got a bad feeling. Bernard rummaged around inside a locker and came out holding an EVA suit that looked unused.

"This should fit over your new legs," he said.

I stared at the suit and suddenly started shaking.

"Oh shit," Bernard whispered. "I knew it was too soon. I don't care what you say, you still aren't ready."

I remembered being brave when I went to save Bernard. I didn't even think about it then. Now the idea of going back out into vacuum terrified me. But I knew I *had* done it once. I knew I *could* do it for people I care about. Besides, I had already insisted.

"Just get me into the suit, Bernard."

My tone must have convinced him, so he helped me put it on, and I assisted with his. Then we meticulously checked each other's seals and fittings before stepping into the airlock. Once on the surface, we followed a path where we could keep our tethers attached to a guide cable the entire way so that a bad bounce didn't send us into a ballistic arc. The path led us to a repair dock berth where robots crawled over the structure of a very familiar ship. The *Lazy Dog*.

"This is my new home," Bernard said.

I blinked and turned toward him. "I don't understand."

"Well, a lot happened while you were recovering. You were kinda dopey at the time, but do you remember when I told you that you posting the videos of the artifact made Grisha Budnikov and his pirate buddies give up the idea of actually stealing it, so they had to steal me instead?"

"I remember," I said. "I wasn't that out of it."

"Well, the funny thing is that he actually had to turn it over to the Martian government, who immediately started testing it. The initial study done on the 'alleged artifact' confirmed that the ice casing didn't come from Earth. At least not during the last few million years. And carbon dating estimates show the stone is over a hundred thousand years old."

"Holy shit," I muttered. "But we suspected that already. How does that put you in the *Lazy Dog*?"

"That announcement, coupled with the media storm you started by uploading the artifact videos and the mess with these pirates, forced the Martian government's hand. They enjoy being in charge of the 'alleged artifact' and must really want me out of the way and not stirring up trouble. So how best to bribe an asteroid miner?"

"Please don't tell me you traded the artifact for the *Lazy Dog*!"

He laughed. "What I did might be dumb, but even I'm not *that* dumb. I still retain ownership of it, but they offered me a research retainer, which gives them control over non-destructive research access to the 'alleged artifact.' And guess what? They offered me just enough money to buy, repair and outfit the *Lazy Dog*, which was also made available to me for purchase at a discounted price, before it went on the public auction block. They implied, as did my attorney—

Cooper Billings per your suggestion—that it would probably be years of legal fights to establish those rights if I refused."

"Congratulations, Bernard!" I said and patted his arm. "I know you've wanted an upgrade for a long time."

They had taken advantage of him, but it sounded like the best short-term deal he would get. And he did have to make a living.

He stepped around so that we could see each other's faces through our visors. "So I want to offer you half ownership in my mining company for forty-thousand Martian dollars. That's most of your fifty thousand in reward money for catching the pirates."

"Bernard! That isn't even a tenth of what this ship is worth."

"Yeah, but you saved my life. There is no way to put a price on that. I'll never be able to pay you back. I don't need your money, but I didn't think you would take fifty percent as a gift."

Ahhh . . . there it was. He felt obligated. And he was a man of his word.

"I don't think so, Bernard. It . . . It just wouldn't be right."

He gently gripped my upper arms, then bent down until our visors bumped. "Look . . . I . . . I was never sure if you were serious that day you said you would love to be my mining partner, but I've been working toward that goal and nothing else ever since. Just in case it was true."

My heart rate spiked, causing a warning beep in my suit's bio monitoring system.

"Yeah," I said. "But Bernard, that was before you knew I was a . . . cyborg."

"Being a cyborg is cool! Besides, your new legs are removable. That could be a bonus in null gee!" he said, then paused. "Of course I knew then you were probably just teasing when you said that. I mean why would you want to spend months at a time cooped up in a smelly little ship with me? And of course that was also before you saw . . . the real me. So I understand if you refuse. I always knew it was a long shot. But the offer is there."

"Bernard. I . . ." A lump formed in my throat.

"I want you to say yes more than anything," he said.

I stepped forward on my wobbly new legs and wrapped my arms around him. "I would still love to be your mining partner."

"Really?"

I nodded inside my helmet. "Yes, but only ten percent. I promise to work hard and earn the rest."

"Good," he said and pointed up at the command pod. "Look at her new name!"

BLACKBIRD was painted in big white letters on the side.

"I don't get it," I said, but assumed it was another old movie or music reference.

"Oh you will!" he said. "I have a lot of great classic music, but we'll have plenty of time. And it'll all be new to you! This is going to be fun."

I leaned into him and let him ramble on, wondering what I'd just got myself into.

Once, Ozan was homeless urchin, living in the streets of Istanbul. But then the sultan's gendarmerie swept through the streets, conscripting all those who were able-bodied into the service of the Empire. Now, Oz finds himself aboard the airship Kismet, *an apprentice to the organ grinder, whose capuchin monkeys serve as an attack force against the Russian enemy. Oz is young and terrified of battle, but though the* Kismet *is a ship of war, Oz may soon find in it the home he never had.*

A SONG OF HOME, THE ORGAN GRINDS

★

by James Beamon

THE MONKEYS are white-faced capuchins. Small things, their lean, black-furred bodies stand in stark contrast to the white tufts of their faces and shoulders. The Russians have cannons that can blast an airship apart in ten minutes and armored steam knights called kolotar, but of the many dangers I face on a warship a mile above the Black Sea, I fear the monkeys I tend most.

"Do not tarry," a man whispers behind me. "They eat meat as well, boy."

I bow curtly but cannot bear to face the organ grinder. "Yes, Efendim."

The organ grinder haunts my dreams. The organ grinder keeps his neck, his face, his bald head covered in white make-up. His face is pock marked. In my dreams, his incisors are as pronounced as the monkeys. His eyes are like theirs, shiny and black and accusing. The dream ends when he grinds his organ and the white-faced capuchins descend upon me from all sides.

When I enter their cage, a large communal one made of chicken wire in the hold of the ship, they don't howl or bite or throw feces. They do not move when I replenish their water. Even now, as I fill their trough with dates, figs, and seeds, they stand still. They stare at me with gleaming black eyes, silently as if in judgment. I turn to see if the organ grinder is satisfied, but he is gone.

I head up to the deck where I'm greeted by the sound of distant thunder. I look to the North toward Crimea. Artillery fire dances in red and white flashes on the night horizon.

Times such as these, I wish the seven months until Ramadan to have already come and gone. I will be fifteen then, a man, and I will no longer tremble in fear when I see cannons fire or hear explosions. The soldiers on deck continue to work as if it is merely thunder and lightning on the horizon, a distant storm of little consequence. They are dressed for battle in their navy blue coats, black boots, and crimson Cossack pants. Matching the pants, a red fez sits atop their heads, the black tassels bouncing to and fro as they work.

Some soldiers ready the sails. Others check the ballast tanks, which raise and lower the airship quickly. The ship lurches, sways like a wandering drunk, before swinging toward the distant conflict. Near the stern, four soldiers swivel giant brass tubes, horn-shaped like ear trumpets. They are the intake pipes, made to gulp the wind and swallow it below deck, where the belly eats it up and makes energy.

Behind us, beyond the stern, well beyond my eyesight, lies Istanbul.

A weight settles on my shoulder. I look down to see fingers of shiny brass, knuckles of gleaming silver. A black suit jacket hides any metal past the wrist. I fight the urge to shy away from the touch and force myself to meet the eyes of the galvanizer Adnan.

His face is clean-shaven except for a thick mustache he keeps well oiled and curved upwards at the tips. His eyes are kind behind his wire-rimmed glasses.

"Best to think of no other home than the *Kismet*, at least for now," Adnan says. Gently, he guides me around to face the ship's bow, our immediate future. The violent stabs of red and white light have grown closer.

"This will be your second skirmish, yes?" he asks.

"Yes, Efendim."

The metal hand moves away from my shoulder and fishes into his jacket. It pulls out a silver cigarette case, and the other hand, the one of normal flesh, retrieves a cigarette.

"Steel yourself, young Oz," he says after he lights it. He draws the tobacco long and lovingly before exhaling a thick cloud for the wind to take. He offers me the cigarette. "Face what's to come topside. Below deck with my engine and pipe works is not your place."

I hid from my first skirmish. In a corner of the deserted monkey cage, far away from the roar of artillery and the unholy wail of the organ, I huddled. My cowardice earned me boxed ears and a bloodied nose from the organ grinder along with the threat that next time he would hurl me over the side.

I take the cigarette eagerly. "Thank you," I say before my first pull. Adnan nods and walks away, letting me have the whole thing. He heads below deck to tend to the steam engine. I inhale as if I'm preparing to jump into cold water.

The explosions punctuating the air make me flinch. They have owners now. In the distance below us, two naval ships, both ironclad destroyers, trade barbs. Flags of the Russians and our allies the British are clearly visible. Black smoke roils out of the English ship.

"Ozan!" I hear the organ grinder before I see him. He emerges from below deck like a rising ghost, only his powder-white head visible as he fixes his gaze upon me. I stand at attention and nod. He continues to climb up, bearing his organ strapped to his chest.

The organ is a box of oiled mahogany wider than the organ grinder's stout body. Unlike most organs, the brass pipes in the front are not straight like columns but protrude outward, curving upward in strange angles. The pipes end in ragged edges, the jaw line of a monster. The crank on the side is dull, gray iron.

"Don't stand idle, boy. Our time approaches. Fetch my songbook. And open the cage."

His songbook is in truth a wooden bin the size of a tea chest. He keeps it under the bed in his quarters. I head there first despite the cage being closer and struggle to carry the heavy contraption with me to the monkeys. The capuchins stand and stare, their black eyes follow me as I approach the latch. I unbolt the door and let it fall open.

One capuchin screeches. It is a shrill sound—*eeee, eeee, eeee*—repetitive, rising in pitch and urgency like a siren or a baby crying. Another follows. I flee with the songbook as a third and fourth give voice to a growing cacophony of shrieks.

Above deck, the air is afire. The Russians are lobbing methane grenades at us while they bring their artillery to bear. Green and yellow blasts punch the sky on the ship's starboard side. I nearly drop the chest as shrapnel whizzes by my ear. We have descended into grappling range.

"Come, boy," the organ grinder says. Standing brazenly at the edge of the deck closest to the Russians, his eyes dance in the light of the blasts. "Give me 'The March of the Janissaries.'" He flips the lid of the organ.

I nearly stumble as I scramble to him with the songbook. Inside the chest are a dozen rectangular copper plates. Words have been etched crudely into the side of each, giving the plates names such as "Whirl of the Dervish" and "The Sultan's Suicide." I reach in and give him the proper plate.

The deck shakes; all other sound is muted as our six starboard cannons fire wicked harpoons. Attached to the harpoons are giant chains. Three harpoons punch through the hull of the Russian ironclad. Our airship jerks as the chains go taut.

The Russian guns are still swinging skyward and nearly have us sighted. These cannons have caused the iron-hulled British vessel to belch black clouds. I imagine what they would do to our hull of wood.

The organ grinder slides the copper plate into his organ and closes the lid. He turns the cranks slow at first as if he is fighting it. Faster, now faster, "The March of the Janissaries" fills the air like the keening wail of a thousand grieving mothers.

The monkeys burst from the hold, a faceless black tide with brief flashes of white. They rush around us, past and over the organ grinder and me. I feel a million cold hands. They speed past so fast they sound like a crowd shushing me. Shhh . . . shhh.

They spread beyond us, onto the chains, where they stream down to the ironclad ship. The black furred bodies seem like oil spilling down the three chains, like the dark fingers of Şeytan.

It is impossible to see what is happening under that cover of black fur, but I hear men screaming. They scream over the cacophonous screech of the monkeys, over the relentless howl of the organ as it grinds through the "March of the Janissaries." The only things louder are the methane grenades, exploding in odd bursts on the ship below.

The Russian cannons, now trained on us, never fire.

When the organ stops all is silent. The ballasts hiss steam as we descend close enough to the Russians to drop the gangway onto their deck.

The organ grinder pulls the plate from the organ and hands it to me. "Return my songbook. Then go and see the galvanizer. Tell him to suit you for collection."

When I reach the engine room, Adnan greets me with a smile. "Survived being topside, I see."

I nod. His engine room is a maze of pipes, valves, and gauges. A workbench cluttered with tools, strange vials, and odd, gear-heavy knickknacks dominates the middle of the room. He digs in a corner and produces what appears to be a laundry bin—burlap fabric placed within a framework of metal rods.

"You are starting to contribute here," he says as he pulls dangling straps and buckles to fasten the burlap device to my chest. "A good change from being a street urchin, yes?" he asks.

The homeless no longer exist in Istanbul. The sultan's gendarmerie had swept through the streets, the alleys, the abandoned buildings serving as opium dens. They corralled us into the gardens facing the Blue Mosque. The commander of the gendarmerie stood upon a dais overseeing all as we were shoved and wrangled and herded. On one side of the gardens stood the Blue Mosque, on the other the Aya Sofya, both domes as grand as the two fists of god, while we, the city's wretches, were pressed in between. The gendarmerie commander spoke to us through a speaking trumpet mounted on the dais.

"You are called homeless, but this is not true. Your home is here. It is our Empire. The Ottoman motherland calls upon you all to fight for her."

The ones who couldn't fight—the old, the crippled, the crazy—they sent off to work. Mining coal or shoveling it into airships and trains and steamboats. Women were sent to the factories. Waifs like me were given menial odd jobs.

"You prefer this to being a street urchin?" Adnan repeats his question.

"I eat more." I do not know how else to answer.

He smiles. "Go then. Earn your bread."

Instead of bread, I earn a smack on the head from the organ grinder. He shakes a meaty finger in my face.

"Never dawdle after 'The March of the Janissaries.' Our friends will be at their most tired. They will need us. Now follow."

We proceed down the gangway. The Russian deck is a spent battleground, a home to bleeding, broken corpses. Two dozen living capuchins crouch all around the deck. Their eyes are wide as if they are surprised or scared. The monkeys sweat, I know this, yet their mouths are open as if they are panting. In the background, the smoking British ship steers closer.

"The Brits will want to salvage parts," the organ grinder says. "We must clear the ship before they come. It will not be good for them."

The organ grinder brandishes a knife. Without pause or ceremony, he cuts across his own thumb. He walks over to the first capuchin and puts the bleeding thumb into the monkey's open mouth.

The capuchin suckles for the briefest moment. Then it bounds up the gangway, back to the airship. The organ grinder heads to the next monkey and repeats the process.

"How?" I ask. He does not explain what dark magic drives this. Silence kept, he stops and crouches at the body of a dead capuchin. The look in his eyes is one of loss and regret. He gives his bleeding thumb a squeeze, forces a drop of blood out onto the capuchin's white furred head. He picks the monkey up and places it into the burlap sack on my chest.

"That is how you give them rest," he says.

Before I acknowledge, he grabs my wrist and pulls me toward him, toward his knife. I suck in breath sharply as the knife slides along my thumb to open it.

"Do as I've shown you." He hurries through the waste, heading to the stairs where he descends below deck.

I step between dead Russians and their dropped rifles, sending the monkeys back to the airship or gathering them into the sack. The price for either action is blood. I prefer sending them back, even if the sensation is strange—feeling the pull of their mouths, seeing their eyes soften as if they've found their mother. The sack bulges and is getting heavier. Their blood has soaked through the bottom, the brown burlap now stained burgundy, and is starting to drip.

The last dead monkey I have to pry from the grip of a Russian who crushed its ribs while the animal ate through the sailor's throat. I look around the deck, searching for capuchins even though I already know they have all either been sent home or given rest. The stairs leading below deck seem like an entry into hell. There is nothing left here but dead men and the dark maw descending down, but I cannot bring myself to take even one step toward the stairs.

Abruptly, the organ grinder emerges from the dark staircase. Urgency is in his step and concern is in his eyes. He carries in his arms a capuchin neither dead nor whole. It has lost an arm.

He doesn't tell me to follow him. I simply do. We rush back to the airship and head below deck to the engine room. He presents the broken capuchin to Adnan with both hands as if it's a present.

"Make him as yourself, galvanizer."

"I don't know if I can."

"He dies while you wonder. Do it, Adnan."

Adnan wipes a grease smear from his brow. "Are you sure, Hezarfen? It will be large. Crude. This may not be what you envision."

The organ grinder only nods.

"I will need parts to study."

Again, he nods. The organ grinder turns to me. He removes the collection harness with its nearly full sack and thrusts a new burlap bag into my hands. "Below deck," he says.

"You have parts right there," I protest, pointing at the sack of dead monkeys I had to bear.

His eyes bulge in disbelief. "Do you not know the meaning of rest, the rest we swore in blood to provide?" I'm unsure whether my impertinence to talk back has surprised him or my ill regard for the blood markings. One thing I do not mistake behind his eyes is the cold anger.

"Below deck," I repeat his order and back out of the room.

I return to the defeated ship. The British are extending their gangway, assisted by some of the Turkish soldiers on the ironclad's deck. Other soldiers are checking the pockets of the dead and inspecting their rifles. The stairs leading below deck still seems like an open mouth, ready to swallow me whole. I take a deep breath and descend.

The ship's interior is a mixture of shredded men and monkeys. This is where the methane grenades exploded when the capuchins attacked the ship. I avoid looking at much beyond my own feet as I walk through the carnage. I collect animal parts: arms, legs, fingers, heads. Eventually my own hands stop trembling about the time my sack is three quarters full.

The organ grinder is nowhere to be found when I return to the airship's engine room. The injured monkey is on a gurney, tubes of clear liquid snaked into its only arm as it lies fast asleep. Adnan is looking over gear shafts, cogs, and various pipe fittings, all of them small. I drop the sack of animal parts at Adnan's feet, hateful that the organ grinder forced me to collect such things for the galvanizer's sake.

"Earn my damned bread, you say. Has this earned it?"

Adnan absentmindedly nods as he turns a gear over in careful inspection. It is clear his mind is elsewhere. More words thrown at him would be pointless. Besides, what is left to say?

Though I eat more on the ship than the streets, no one would be able to tell tonight. I sleep even less.

Three days later, I see the monkey. He is in the cage with the others. The metal arm is small for a child but huge on the capuchin. It is home to turning gears in the forearm and pistons that push along the bicep. Yellow pus oozes out of the shoulder where swollen meat and rigid metal mesh.

The other monkeys give him a wide berth. I wonder if the normal capuchins feel the way the soldiers feel about Adnan, who they have nicknamed "Yarim" for half man. Does cleaving onto cold metal cut away your essence as the soldiers say? Do the other capuchins consider their metal-armed fellow soulless now?

While the other monkeys stare at me with their accusing eyes, the metal-armed one takes a step towards me. I take two steps back. It stops, but I keep going, keep retreating out of the monkey cage. I make my way around the cage, staring at the monkey, rushing to get back on deck. I bump into the organ grinder violently. His girth sends me backward on the floor.

He is all white powder, cunning eyes, red lips, and smiles. Instead of helping me up, he leans down to me.

"What is your name for him?" the organ grinder whispers.

"I have none, Efendim."

"Don't lie. Say the name."

I shake my head. There is naught. It is a monster. It is abomination among monsters. There is no name.

The organ grinder grabs me by my collar and hoists me up. He pulls me towards the cage door. The monkeys begin to screech, all of them except the metal one. I struggle against the pull, but his hand is firm. The other hand fumbles at the latch. The cage swings open wide. Throughout the cage, the monkeys jump and screech.

"Say the name to me or spend the night telling it to him!" the organ grinder yells. He drags me forward.

"Ruhsiz!" I cry. "Ruhsiz!"

The organ grinder lets go of me. He grabs the cage and shuts it. "Your name for him is 'Soulless,' eh?" He shakes his head as he looks at the monkey. "His name used to be Ali. Let it now be Ruhsiz. It suits him."

The organ grinder says nothing more. He simply stares into the cage and it seems I am forgotten about. I flee, but not without a final look at the monkey I have named.

I hope with all my being this named creature does not survive the next skirmish. It does. The battle is a quick one against a patrol scout airship. Their ship is lighter, faster, and equipped with deadly cannons that shoot bombs. The bombs explode in clusters, which rip into our hull and send four soldiers plummeting to their doom in a violent spray of wood and gore. We are fortunate when two harpoons catch their hull.

The organ grinder plays "Whirl of the Dervish" and the capuchins rush across the chains, ignoring the Russian soldiers to tear at the sails, the engine, and ballast tanks. In minutes, their engines die and the ship lists in the sky helpless. The air is punctuated with the screams of men who cannot hold on as their ship falls sideways and swings beneath our ship, held up in the sky only by our harpoon chains.

They surrender after that. When our men set them down in the Black Sea to capture the prisoners and scavenge their ship, the organ grinder and I are among the first to go aboard to retrieve the monkeys. Ruhsiz stares at me with black eyes and open mouth. The organ grinder's knife opens the same wound across my thumb.

"You name him, you nurse him," he says.

The pull of Ruhsiz's mouth is the same as other capuchins, his retreat back into our airship identical. And while only three monkeys make my burlap sack, somehow, as if to mock my prayers, another monkey comes away not quite whole. Both its hands have been crushed, a result of the engine's moving parts snapping shut while the monkey was sabotaging it.

The organ grinder carries the broken monkey lovingly to Adnan. Like last time, Adnan fits the capuchin with oversized metal mockeries of what was once flesh. And days later, the organ grinder glares at the monkey's two large bronze hands through the chicken wire of the cage.

"And what do you name this one?"

The monkey stands next to Ruhsiz. "Clapper," I say.

"So that's it then," he says. "Clapper." He chews on the name as if it is spoiled rations.

To quell any doubt that my prayers are being mocked, this happens again the next skirmish. We ambush an enemy coal freighter getting tossed by an angry sea in the dark of night. The monkeys move in deadly stealth and darkness under the faint, ghostly croon of "The Harem Girl's Secret Kiss." There are no casualties among us, only one monkey with one less leg and a new name: Luckless. It is a reflection of how I feel about my own fortunes.

In truth, it is the fortune of everyone aboard the *Kismet*. A merry soldier drinking chai and playing backgammon during empty afternoon hours is hurled off deck that same night when an intake valve backfires. Men with wives and children are blown apart by enemy fire, to be mourned by their fellows who still live despite never having anything to live for. One of the officers disappears completely, leaving nothing but rumors that he was eaten by the monkeys or dove that mile into the sea to escape his recurring dreams of being dangled from the airship called *Voina Gulag*.

The monkey I named Ruhsiz shows grim signs his fortunes are turning. He has little energy and seems to drag the metal arm to and from the feeding trough. Soon he stops dragging it altogether and just lies on the straw floor where the arm seems a monstrous anchor. I bring figs and dates to him so he can eat. Eventually he stops doing even that. Until one unremarkable evening, he dies.

I take the monkey's body to the organ grinder's quarters. His door is ajar. The man sits before a mirror, his back turned to me, removing his make-up with a handkerchief. The white powder on his neck and head is gone from his face. Our gazes meet in the mirror. There are a great many bags under his eyes. He looks old without the makeup, feeble and reduced. He looks at what I hold in my hands with tired eyes.

"Rip the arm off and give it back to the galvanizer. Then throw him over the side."

"He needs the blood sacrament."

"One named 'Soulless' has no need for burial rites. Toss him."

On the open deck, under a clear night of bright stars, I give Ruhsiz the blood sacrament anyway, cutting my thumb across a jagged edge of the capuchin's hulkish metal arm. I dot his white furred head with a drop of my blood and guide him out of my hands, metal arm and all, to the cool peace of the Black Sea waiting far below.

Hezarfen the organ grinder can go to hell. And if one such as Adnan cannot abide with losing the parts joined to the capuchin, he can join Hezarfen.

Adnan makes no mention of it the next time I see him. We enjoy sunrise and a cigarette together. The surrounding clouds are milky cotton giants that make the airship seem so insignificant in the heavens. I feel as if I can see until the end of creation.

"How do the days feel to you now, young Oz?" he asks. "Do they fuse together, one long, unending blur?" He smiles, not waiting for an answer. "Perhaps this will not always be the case. Look," he says nudging his head, "to the south. We sail to Trabzon where we will repair, resupply and man this airship with fresh soldiers from the garrison there. It is a nice town far removed from this war in the Crimean."

I take the cigarette from Adnan's outstretched hand to enjoy my turn. "It sounds like a welcome change," I say, "which I know will be too short."

Instead of reaching for the cigarette when I give it back, Adnan grabs my shoulder. His face is serious, his eyes intense.

"The nicest thing about being homeless is that you can make anywhere home, yes?"

True to his description, Trabzon is a nice town. Squat houses sit quiet, nestled between rolling green hills and a half moon bay. We are met with cheers from soldiers and townspeople as we land. Fresh faced soldiers and tinkerers and dockworkers bearing crates flood up the gangway.

"Ozan!" Hezarfen calls to me. He leads the way down the gangway, where several small cages wait for us. They seem overstuffed with capuchins, too many to count despite the fact that they sit still. The organ grinder has more than refreshed his troop supply. Like the ones in the airship, they look at me silently with black, accusing eyes.

I do not want more of this. Adnan's words of home echo in my mind. I sneak off in the dead of night to escape Hezarfen, the monkeys, the war. No one sees me or no one cares. A heady rush of freedom fills me. Eagerly, I explore the city, its streets and alleyways.

At daybreak, the airship's horn blows, signaling its coming departure. My breathing tightens in my chest. I look around. Something about the town scares me. This kind of quiet, one without engine clangs and ballast hisses, does not seem natural. My view of the world has been ruthlessly chopped down. There are no panoramas here. It all seems so ugly and low.

I run with everything in me towards the sound of the horn. Fear that the airship will lift off without me pushes my legs harder than they've ever moved. My yell to wait is abolished by the blaring horn. I make it, flying up the gangway and stopping only when I stumble and fall upon the deck.

Adnan stares at me with utter disbelief as I lay there panting and wheezing on the deck of the rising airship. "Dear young fool," he says.

Again, Adnan is right. I regret the decision every time we face the Russians. I see six more skirmishes of varying nature accompanied by varying songs from the organ grinder. "Song of Suleiman" for lightly armed vessels. "March of the Janissaries" for heavily armed destroyers. And for the kolotar, the men housed in armored steam engines, only "The Sultan's Suicide" is played.

These skirmishes take their toll on the nature of the capuchins. Hezarfen's nature never changes. He scoops up the broken monkeys, the parts that are still breathing, still hurting, fractions of monkeys above one half. He talks to them, pleads and begs as he gathers them into his arms, the rest of the world forgotten as he soothes them, brings them to the waiting laboratory of the galvanizer. New legs, new tails, a new jaw for one, new names for all. Nearly half of the organ grinder's forces have been fused with metal pieces and I swear he hates them all.

After naming two more to be forever reviled, I retreat to the open air. On deck, Adnan smokes a cigarette. He gazes westward to the oranges and purples of a sun dipping ever lower beneath the horizon.

"I do not understand Hezarfen," I say to him. "He acts to save the monkeys and once they are saved, it seems as if he despises them. Why does he do this?"

"The things people seek answers for!" Adnan spits as if he's cursing. "Do you know how this airship floats? I could explain to you the nature of the steam engine and the hydrogen distillers that balance out our ballasts. Would you like to know? Or do you wonder why the monkeys heed the sound of the organ? I could talk about Faraday's work in electricity coupled with Mesmer's work in mind control, and how the two led to this horrible, incredible experiment of electrically induced brain etching on animals. I could explain how the etching is reinforced by auditory instructions found in the copper plates, instructions overwritten by the taste of Turkish blood."

Adnan takes a pull of his cigarette before continuing. He talks and smoke wraps around his words.

"No one wants to hear this, this science, because it's easier to believe in magic. In good and evil spirits, in souls." He looks at his metal fingers. "In half souls."

He gazes out over the Black Sea stretching to the horizon below us, glowing like a jewel as the calm waters reflect the setting sun. "Even in this age of steam, people still believe in the magic of Old Constantinople. That jinn hide in the curl of hookah smoke, Immortals dwell in forgotten corners of the Covered Bazaar selling baubles, and fairies dance at dusk along the shores of the Golden Horn. And of all the things you need explained to you, all the workings of our modern age around you I could demystify, you wonder about the heart of a man who is always masked."

Adnan looks at me. "What a person feels is the one thing that can't be explained, the only magic left in the world. Can you explain it? Can you?"

The way Adnan gazes at me, I know he is not speaking about the organ grinder. I say nothing because I do not know the answer. I don't know why I am on this ship.

The answer comes a week later, in a turbulent sky dark with giant storm clouds. We see an unnatural glint hiding in the clouds beside us and respond with harpoon fire. All six harpoons find purchase. Moments later a massive airship that could only be the enemy's *Voina Gulag* pushes through the cloud cover.

The *Voina Gulag* is more box fortress than airship, square and towering, full of hard angles and big cannons typically reserved for naval destroyers. It is a miracle their engines can keep such a beast afloat; it seems as if it takes up the entire sky before us. Yet all of this is not what makes the *Voina Gulag* instantly recognizable to us.

Unlike most Russian vessels, the *Voina Gulag* takes prisoners. They dangle from her flat underside secured in rope harnesses. Row after row of bodies hang, too numerous to count. Some men are alive, screaming at us in hoarse voices we hear only as ghostly moans over the wind. Others are corpses perpetually rotting in weather-beaten Turkish, British, and French uniforms. In between the fully alive and rotting dead, emaciated men list despondently, their faces gaunt, sunken hollows. Their skeletal faces are like Death itself, a haunting reminder to those who face this airship that their fate will be one as a living trophy and passing into the veil will be a relief, their last and greatest blessing.

Our harpoons already have purchase. We cannot run. The *Voina Gulag* fires it massive cannons.

We descend sharply with a hiss of the ballasts in a cloud of our own rising steam. It is not enough. The cannon fire renders our sails useless. Men scurry as rigging, wood, and sails come crashing down. A moment later, the *Voina Gulag* lobs two metal balls the size of boulders at us. They land with a sickening crack onto the deck. The balls stand upright to reveal two of their kolotar steam knights.

Bigger and bulkier than the average man, their faceplates are painted to look like skulls. The kolotar run faster than men housed in that much metal should, steam blowing out of hinges in their knees and shoulder blades. They charge through our forces, cutting them down with bayonets attached to their forearms as they make their way towards the stern.

Hezarfen rushes topside, one hand bearing the songbook, the

other his organ. He doesn't bother strapping the organ on. Instead he tosses me the songbook as he sets the organ onto the deck and opens the lid. Wordlessly, I open the songbook and toss him back "The Sultan's Suicide."

On bent knee, Hezarfen grinds his organ. The capuchins swarm up from below and stream towards the kolotar who are trying to slice open our ballast tanks while rifle fire bounces harmlessly off their iron hides. The capuchins cover the kolotar. The monkeys claw and scratch and bite in a rage, working their way into the joints and seams of the kolotar armor. Sparks fly as the capuchins with metal parts scrape their metal against the steam armor. In moments, we hear the ungodly screams of one of the men dying to get out of his suit.

The other kolotar knocks swarming capuchins from his visor and begins to search the deck. He sees the organ grinder and charges, the smoking ballast all but forgot. Hezarfen stands his ground, holding the organ by the straps as he keeps grinding. The kolotar's steps become erratic as the monkeys finally work their way into his armor. We hear him scream. Still, the kolotar charges. He grabs Hezarfen, who drops the organ to tumble in a harsh landing across the deck.

The screaming, dying kolotar takes Hezarfen and a half a dozen monkeys with him as he jumps from the airship. They all disappear in the dense storm clouds below.

We all stare at the organ.

Anyone can grind it. No one is willing to pick up the instrument. Even as we face certain doom and see our own futures in the bodies dangling from the *Voina Gulag*. No one moves. None of us knows what the organ gives, what it takes. The only one who believes the instrument was not forged in hell is Adnan.

They are staring at me, the monkeys I have named. Clapper and Luckless, Irontail and Hardjaw, over a dozen creatures who the other monkeys treat as yarim and give a wide berth when not under the organ's spell. As if seeking refuge, they look to the one who has named and nurtured them with blood.

The other monkeys pant and stare vacantly. They have lost their names now that Hezarfen is gone. Perhaps I'll discover opportunity to name them. I once thought them whole, but, just as clearly as the ones who now move with the help of pistons and gears, they too have been changed.

Changed as they are, as I am, we all need homes, yes?

The *Voina Gulag* is turning in the air, preparing to fire off another volley.

Two months shy of manhood, my choice is clear. I exchange "The Sultan's Suicide" within the organ for "March of the Janissaries," and I begin to grind. The sound is the keening wail of a thousand grieving mothers.

It makes me smile the way the soldiers smile when they speak of home.

A space cruise from Saturn to Montreal, Earth should have been fun, even if it was ferrying her to yet another boarding school. Only Colette's dad waaayyy skimped on the accommodations. What's an eleven-year-old girl genius to do to keep occupied? If only something interesting would happen . . .

ONCE ON THE BLUE MOON
★
by Kristine Kathryn Rusch

ONE MAN CRADLING one large laser rifle stood in the doorway of the luxury suite. Colette sprawled on the threadbare carpet. Her dad had shoved her behind him when he saw the guy at the door, and she had tripped over the retractable ottoman.

Good job, Dad, she nearly said, because that was her default response when he did something stupid, but she didn't say it, because her gaze remained on that rifle. And so did her dad's.

Dad had probably wanted her to run into one of the bedrooms, and that would've made sense if the guy at the door with the rifle hadn't seen her, but he had, and then he had said something softly and beckoned at someone else.

Mom was standing beside the door, actually threading her hands together. Colette felt both a growing fear and a growing irritation. Fear, because she had probably caused this. Day One, she had swiped one of those stupid tablets that the concierge on this level used to keep track of everything on the ship.

The lower levels, without the suites, used holographic screens for the guests, or some lazy person could call up a holographic face to make suggestions.

But here, real people were actually in the passengers' business, as if the *Blue Moon* was still one of the most luxurious starliners in the solar system.

It wasn't luxurious. It *had been* luxurious, maybe, in the Good Old

127

Days when her grandparents had been kids. Dad said the ship had a "mystique," whatever that meant, but Colette had investigated the ship on her own and found the ad that had probably gotten Dad's attention:

Travel in luxury at one-thousandth the price!

Apparently, if you didn't care what kind of cargo the ship carried, then you could have a luxury suite on your trip from wherever to wherever. Theirs was from a starbase beyond Saturn to some place called Montreal because that was the last boarding school that could handle someone like her.

All of this had been Mother's idea, even though all of it had been Colette's fault.

Another man arrived at the door. He was small, barely taller than Colette, and she hadn't reached her full growth yet. (Mother had said that she would when puberty hit, which could be Any Minute Now.) The man had glittering black eyes, a leathery face, and thin lips that quirked upward when he saw her.

"A kid," he said, as if he was surprised.

Colette almost said, *I'm not a kid!* and then thought the better of it. Maybe she'd get a pass on stealing that tablet. Children couldn't be responsible for their actions after all.

"I didn't realize there was a kid on board," the man said, musing. "I didn't think children were allowed on vessels like this."

Yeah, Colette had seen that regulation too, and she knew that her dad had gotten it waived. They needed to get to Earth Yesterday, or so Mother had said. It was never hard for Dad to get things waived.

The family didn't have money—*yet*, Mother said—but they had access to it, and they had some kind of influence that her dad would flash around whenever he needed it, as, apparently, they had needed it to get on this ship to get Colette to Montreal to the boarding school before the beginning of the semester.

Which seemed stupid to her, because she had started other schools in the middle of the year, and had always, always outperformed everyone in her class. It never mattered whether she arrived with one month left or five, she could work her way around the entire system and do better than anyone else, once she figured out what was needed.

"Take them," the guy with the intense eyes, gesturing at Colette's parents.

Then he took one step into the suite, and looked down at Colette.

"You, little girl, can stay here, if you'll be good." He actually spoke in some kind of fake sweet voice, as if she would be fooled by his tone, even though he had just ordered some guy with a rifle to take her parents.

Colette opened her mouth so she could tell the guy with the intense eyes where he could stick his "good," and then she saw her dad's face. It was drawn and tense.

Her mother was shivering. Her mother often looked terrified over stupid stuff, but she never shivered.

And her dad—tense was not his normal way of dealing with anything.

He frowned at Colette as their gazes met.

"She'll be good," her dad said to the guy, but didn't look away from Colette. "My daughter, she's perfect."

Colette actually felt tears prick at her eyes. Her dad never said that, not with feeling. He was always telling her how impossible, intractable, and stubborn she was, how she could do better if she only settled down. And sometimes he would despair, and say,

Colette Euphemia Josephine Treacher Singh Wilkinson Lopez, you have every opportunity and you're always the smartest person in the room. Why are you constantly throwing that away?

His disappointment pissed her off, and made her work harder at doing the best she could *and* causing trouble. He never noticed the best, but he always noticed the trouble.

She'd been waiting for that *perfect* word from him her whole life. And now he said it, to some guy with intense eyes and another guy holding a laser rifle, and the weird part was, Dad seemed to mean it.

Then he really scared her, because he mouthed, *I love you*, and took a deep breath and said to the guy with intense eyes, "What do you need from us?"

Dad sounded calm, even though he clearly wasn't. Well, clearly to Colette, probably not to the two men.

"I need you to go with him," the guy with the intense eyes said, nodding toward the guy with the laser rifle. Not saying his name, either, which was a bad sign. "We can restrain you and take you if need be."

Dad gave Mother a hard look, and she swallowed visibly, then nodded.

"No restraints needed," Dad said. Then he and Mother walked out of the door as if being taken by guys with laser rifles was an everyday thing.

The guy with intense eyes gave Colette one last glare.

"Be good and you'll be fine," he said. Then he closed the suite door—and stupid idiot that he was—turned on the parental controls.

Which she had already monkeyed with Day One, in case anyone got Ideas. Her parents knew better than to use something that simple on her, but the concierge and the ship's crew didn't.

And neither did the guy with the intense eyes.

She waited a good thirty seconds before moving, and then she went into her room and lay on the bed, because she knew that would be what the guy with the intense eyes would expect—some kid, paralyzed by fear.

She'd show him paralyzed.

She'd show him fear.

Once she had him all figured out.

A kid.

Alfredo Napier thought kids weren't allowed on ships like the *Blue Moon*. Adults knew the dangers they were undertaking when they traveled on a ship like this, but kids? They were under the age of consent, and even if their parents thought it was a good idea, the Starrborne Line, which ran these old ships, did not allow kids on the Titan-Plano to Earth-Houston run.

The company's explanation was pretty simple: in order to make good time on that run, it had to travel older, lesser used routes, not as well policed, and without as many stops or amenities.

In reality, the route these ships traveled was the only route that allowed hazardous cargo. If a ship got into trouble out here, it was twice as likely to be abandoned as it was to be rescued.

Napier had always taken that fact into consideration when he chose his targets.

He also appreciated the fact that everyone on board had signed a waiver, protecting the Starrborne Line from liability should something untoward happen. Not that he really cared if the passengers had given permission for their own deaths on an ancient ship without the proper protections against certain kinds of hazardous cargo, but because he almost felt as if the passengers had given him permission to run his own business the way he wanted to.

A kid.

He shook his head as he hurried to the bridge. A kid changed everything and nothing.

She'd seen him. She'd seen *them*. But she was what? Ten? Twelve? Young enough that no one would believe anything she said. So all he had to do before they blew the ship was put her into one of the lifepods and jettison her with quite a bit of force toward the Martian run. If she survived, then good, and if she didn't, she would die in the pod, not in his custody on the ship.

And he wouldn't have to think about her.

That was the problem with kids.

They haunted a man in the middle of the night, interfering with his sleep.

He made a small fortune doing his work.

The last thing he needed was to second-guess himself. The last thing he needed was to lose even more sleep.

Colette sat up on the bed. She already hated this room. Square, boxy, brown, the bed one-tenth as comfortable as the bed she had had at her last school. She felt like calling up some paint program and trying to permanently deface the walls.

Maybe if she was trapped in here forever. In the meantime, she had the tablet.

Colette had stolen the tablet because it had basic access to every single part of the ship. No one had figured out she swiped it; the stupid concierge had believed he had misplaced it, and they had issued him a new one, since the first thing Colette had done was shut off the locator on the tablet itself. Basic Survival Thievery 101.

The second thing Colette had done was taken that basic access and amped it up to full access in every shipboard department she could. The only areas she couldn't access were navigation, engine controls, life support, and all of those other things that someone could sabotage and kill people with.

She would need Captain's Codes for those areas. Or at least senior officer codes.

In the weeks that she'd had the tablet, she hadn't been able to crack those codes. She had been beginning to think she couldn't access any of that important stuff from a passenger cabin because of location controls. But if she got to the bridge, she might have been able to do it.

The option of going to the bridge was gone now.

She needed to remain confined to quarters until she figured out how to spoof the system, and make it *think* she was confined to quarters while she roamed the ship.

Before she did any of that, though, she activated the automated distress signal. Every tablet had access to the distress signal, and, she suspected, so did all of those holographic concierges on the lower levels.

She hoped someone else had activated the automatic distress signal as well, but she also had taken a measure of the guy with the intense eyes. He looked like someone who didn't let a lot go by him.

He had probably tampered with access to the automated distress system before he had started into the passenger cabins. Because Colette and her parents hadn't realized something had gone wrong on the ship until the guy with the laser rifle had shown up.

She doubted any other passenger noticed something wrong either. People were pretty self-involved on this ship, which had worked to her favor, until today.

She took a deep breath. She was going to pretend that today was no different than any other day, because if she thought about her parents, she would panic, and panicking would get her nowhere.

So she scrolled through the back end of the tablet, the stuff hardly anyone outside of engineering knew how to use, and found the manual distress signal.

She had hoped it would be relatively easy to operate. Instead, it contained an array of choices, many more than she expected. She scrolled through all of them, until she narrowed it down to three: she could notify other ships; she could notify specific rescue units throughout the solar system; or she could notify a single person.

She had no single person to notify, and if she notified other ships randomly, she would probably notify Intense Eyes Guy's ship as well as some other passing vessel.

All of the choices required the *Blue Moon's* exact location to be input manually. Which made sense, since she was asking for a rescue, and the system had no way of knowing that the rescue was needed because people with guns had boarded the ship, rather than some systemic breakdown somewhere off the beaten path.

Colette dug, found the ship's exact coordinates, discovered that they were deep inside the Asteroid Belt, and that made her stomach jump. Right in the middle of nothing at all.

And, to her unpracticed eye, the ship looked like it wasn't moving at all.

She didn't like it.

Focus, focus, focus.

She made herself go through all of the components of the secondary manual signal slowly, entering the exact coordinates of where the ship was right now, which route it had taken, but not the route it was expected to take. Because she didn't know if Intense Eyes Guy was stealing the ship itself.

She set the secondary signal to repeat in half-second bursts, and programmed it to go only to the rescue units on Mars, the Moon, and Earth.

Her heart thumped as she activated the secondary signal—and prayed it would go through.

Napier made it to the bridge just in time to see the distress signal beacon activate. The damn thing glowed red on the navigation console. He smashed the blinking light, then pressed the comm chip embedded into the pocket on his chin.

"One of those idiot crew members activated the automated distress signal. Someone jettison the thing off the ship, and send it closer to Mars."

He had to explain where he wanted the beacon to go, because on a previous job, the genius who had taken a similar order had ripped the beacon off the ship, and let the still-active beacon tumble into nearby space.

That hadn't ended well for anyone, although Napier, as was his habit, managed to avoid the authorities, more through luck than anything else. The genius who hadn't thought the order through, however, wouldn't make that mistake again.

Since his luck had run out.

Napier's hadn't, yet, but he didn't like how this particular job was going. He really didn't like this bridge. It was narrow and had a high ceiling made of two different materials—one clear, so that the bridge crew could see the starlight (or probably show it to passengers who paid a premium). The other material was an exterior cover that fitted over the clear material and gave the bridge double protection against anything and everything.

It also made the bridge pretty easy to find. Napier had originally thought of sending a contained burst torpedo into the bridge, taking out the bridge crew in one quick action, but he hadn't done it. Because he had done his due diligence and discovered that the *Blue Moon*, as an ancient passenger liner, didn't have a secondary bridge like most cargo ships.

There had been an actual possibility that the explosion would have destroyed all of his access to the ship's systems, and he didn't have an engineer on his team. If the engineering sector on this ship had been as old as the ship herself, then Napier would truly have been screwed.

Of course, someone had updated the entire interior. The passenger cabins had gotten a facelift, but the rest of the ship had been completely rebuilt—and off-books too.

At least the weapons system on this ship hadn't been upgraded. It should have been before someone got the brilliant idea of transporting a Glyster Egg on this vessel. Because Glyster Eggs were the holy grail for people like him. If he had a Glyster Egg, he could raid ships to his heart's content.

Of course, no one was supposed to know that the Egg was even on board. He had only found out because he had paid informants in every single outpost that launched vessels into this part of the solar system. If he managed to get his hands on the Egg, the informant who sent him here would get a really big bonus.

If.

Napier hadn't been able to find out if the Egg was actually on board, and if it was, where it was. Each cargo bay was supposed to list the cargo on its exterior manifest, but ships like this, which carried hazardous cargo, rarely did. That's why he needed the internal cargo manifest, the one only the senior officers got to see.

And that, Napier was beginning to realize, was going to be harder than he expected.

The automated distress signal shut off after five minutes. The tablet listed the distress signal as damaged, but Colette suspected someone had tampered with it. She had expected that.

She also figured, given that laser rifle, that the bad guys had come for something in particular. She was guessing, based on the history she'd studied (trying to keep up with Dad), the entertainment she consumed (trying to ignore Mother), and the crime reports she'd examined on the sly (trying to learn new tricks) that these guys weren't here to steal the ship. If they had been, they would have locked every passenger in their cabins and dealt with the passengers once the ship left the established shipping routes.

Colette figured they were taking something from it. If they had planned on kidnapping a passenger—well, first, they wouldn't have come to a ship this low rent, and second, they would have known that a kid was on board. She was on the passenger manifest, after all, even if her age wasn't alongside her name.

But if the bad guys were trying to take people, they would have wanted to know who they were up against amongst the passengers—or, at least, *she* would have wanted to know.

She knew it was a fallacy to expect every criminal in the universe to be one-tenth as smart as she was. Dad always said that if they were smart, they wouldn't be criminals, and Colette agreed with him when it came to crimes of opportunity, but the bands that worked the shipping routes—or rather, the bands that *successfully* worked the shipping routes—had to have a lot of smarts because they terrorized the routes, and never seemed to get caught.

So she wasn't going to get anywhere by underestimating the intelligence of the people who had taken over the ship.

Hazardous cargo would seem like a no-no for these people, but not all hazardous cargo made everyone sick. Some hazardous cargo was dangerous in the wrong hands.

On her very first day with the tablet, she had searched through the cargo manifest, trying to find whatever it was that had knocked the per-passenger price on this vessel so low. When she had seen the ad for this vessel, and its "reasonable" prices, she wanted to see what kinds of diseases Dad had signed her up for.

She had planned to throw that in his face when he left her at that boarding school in Montreal. She had even planned the speech:

Not only are you confining me to some Earth backwater, but you're guaranteeing that I will die of [insert disease here] at [insert average age here].

It had taken her three days to find the correct cargo manifest, and another three hours to break into it. To her great disappointment, she hadn't found any disease-creating items listed. Instead, she found a tiny weapon that shouldn't have been on a ship like this at all.

That weapon, called a Glyster Egg, should have been in layers and layers of protective material with a protected cargo seal inside a protected cargo unit inside a protected cargo bay. Instead, the Glyster Egg was in some kind of box that "in theory" protected it from any kind of accidental detonation.

The thing was the theory wasn't that grand. She'd found at least three other ships that had been victims of accidental detonation of Glyster Eggs in the five years since the stupid things had been on the market (or invented or stolen or released by some dumb government or *something*). Those ships had floated dead in space, in one case for a year, before anyone found it—because the stupid thing had been designed to disable all the functioning systems on spaceships with one simple movement.

A handful of other weapons could do that, but none were small like the Egg, and none had an actual targeting system. So if she wanted to—if she could get out of this stupid room without being noticed, *and* if she trusted herself to touch the Egg, *and* if she could figure out how to use it, *and* if she knew exactly where the bad guys' ship was—she could enter the coordinates into the Egg, then squeeze the Egg's activation system, and *voila!* the bad guys' ship wouldn't work at all, ever again, end of story.

But she didn't like all those ifs-ands. She couldn't quite calculate the odds—there were too many variables—but she had an educated hunch that she would be better off trying to get to the bridge or engineering or somewhere and wrest control of the *Blue Moon* from

Intense Eyes, before ever trying to activate the Egg and make it work *for* her instead of *against* her.

Of course, she didn't actually know if he was here for the Egg. But he was stupid if he wasn't. Because if she were a big bad thief who preyed on ships coming through the Asteroid Belt, *she* would steal the Egg.

That was assuming that Intense Eyes had her brains. She wasn't sure he did. Yeah, he had taken over the ship, but he hadn't known about Colette, which meant he hadn't researched the passengers, which meant he didn't know that he was about to get into really bad trouble—if even one of her distress signals had gotten through.

Those odds she could calculate.

Because as of this moment, no one had noticed the manual distress signal.

So it was still broadcasting.

Which meant that help might actually be on the way.

The automated distress signal, half-choked off, arrived at the 52nd Mars Relay Station. Two versions of the same automated distress signal, intact, arrived at the 13th Moon Relay Station. No versions of the automated distress signal made it to any of Earth's Relay Stations, at least not in recognizable form.

Within thirty seconds of the automated distress signal's arrival, the 13th Moon Relay Station evaluated the signal, and determined that the distressed ship was located in the Asteroid Belt. The ship had an old registration, marking it as inconsequential, even though the ship was owned by Treacher, Incorporated, a large entity that had funded many Martian building projects. Treacher also had ties to three different Martian governments.

But the ship had taken an unusual route, never traveled by ships with highly insured passengers or cargo. The route was by definition dangerous, and anyone on board would have signed a waiver agreeing to rescue only in financially advantageous circumstances.

The age of the ship, the route, and the lack of insurance did not make this a financially advantageous circumstance.

But Treacher's ownership did flag the system, so the 13th Moon Relay Station followed protocol for difficult and iffy rescues in the

Asteroid Belt. The 13th Moon Relay Station sent copies of the automated distress signal to its counterpart on Mars.

Then the 13th Moon Relay Station sent the automated distress signals to its archives.

No one on the Moon even knew that an automated distress signal had arrived, been examined, and passed back to Mars. And no one on the Moon would have cared.

What Colette had to do was buy time. If the bad guys were on the *Blue Moon* to take the Egg, then she had to hide the Egg from them.

The problem was . . . what if she was wrong? What if they were here for something else?

She didn't have a lot of control with this particular tablet. She was working to get more access, but she needed to spoof her own position here in the suite, and that would take time.

She tried to delete all of the cargo manifests, and couldn't delete any of them. She didn't have the clearance.

She sat cross-legged on her bed for a good minute, trying to figure out how to stay one step ahead of these very bad people.

She had to convince them that they were in trouble on this ship, and she had to keep the Egg from them.

Those were two different tasks.

She called up the passenger manifest to see if she could locate anyone else who might be able to help her. She flipped manifest to its location-based listings, and saw, without looking at names, that all of the passengers were in the large buffet, scattered around the room, as if they were sitting at tables.

All of the passengers except her.

Before she could stop herself, she flipped the data again, saw her parents' names and personal shipboard identification numbers. Then she flipped back to location-based information. Two little green dots, with her parents' shipboard identification numbers, blinked from the side of the buffet, near the kitchen. They weren't moving, but then, neither were the other passengers.

Colette didn't want to even guess what that meant. She hoped they were all sitting quietly, depressed at the circumstances, rather than being unconscious or injured or dea—

Focus, focus, focus.

She opened the tablet to the cargo manifest. The correct one. She took the contents, copied it into another file, marking that new file *Sanitation Refill Schedule*. Then she opened one of the cargo manifests without the hazardous materials, and copied the data from that manifest, and pasted it over the original manifest.

Then she simply saved it. When she opened it again, the information on the Egg had vanished.

And that had been too easy. Someone should have realized just how simple it was to make mistakes in this system, not that it was her problem.

But the bad guys might figure that out. So, she moved the cargo manifest out of its normal file and into the food service files. Some searches would bring up the cargo manifest, but someone would have to know what kind of search to conduct.

She needed to figure out how to distract the bad guys until the rescue ship got here.

And she needed to be able to do so from inside this suite.

For a moment, Napier had thought he found one of the cargo manifests, and then it had vanished on him. He had a device that easily broke the surface codes on the bridge's systems, but the device didn't give him what this system called the Captain's Access Codes. For that, Napier needed five forms of physical ID, which he had planned for.

He already had his men getting that for him.

In the meantime, he searched. He felt a slight time pressure, but knew that because of the distances out here, he had more time on this job than he would have had he been closer to Mars or Earth's Moon. He had an internal clock, and at the moment, it allowed him to feel some leeway.

He paused his search for the cargo manifest to find a way to retract the captain's chair. The damn thing rose in the middle of the narrow bridge like a throne, and he wanted it gone. It irritated him, particularly since it turned to offer him a seat every time he brushed against it (which was much too often for his tastes).

He finally found the controls for the chair, but as he did, he also saw something else. A blinking emergency light, buried deep in the manual controls.

He touched the light with a bit of hesitation, worried that he would activate the wrong system.

Instead, he found that a second distress signal had been sending for more than an hour. Why a ship like this would have more than one distress signal, and why this one wasn't attached to the beacon, he had no idea.

Shutting it off was a simple matter. He toggled the controls to the off position. The system didn't even argue.

For a moment, he wondered about the secondary signal. Then he decided it was probably part of the automated distress signal's system, not something he had to worry about.

He needed to spend his time finding one tiny piece of cargo in six cargo bays stuffed with material ultimately bound for Earth.

He had a dozen people on his team, but that wasn't enough to search all of those cargo bays. And he was searching for the Glyster Egg, which was a delicate system in and of itself. He had no idea if his own equipment would accidentally activate it.

He didn't want to take that risk, not this far out. What if the Egg had a broadcast feature he didn't know about? What if it not only disabled this starliner, but his ship as well?

That was something he didn't want to suffer through.

So he needed to proceed with caution.

And he needed to find the cargo manifest.

Something in the automated distress signal that arrived at the 52nd Mars Relay Station activated the review process.

The review system sent a notification to the starbase beyond Titan where the *Blue Moon* originated, asking for a passenger manifest. Calculations needed to be made. The system needed to do a proper cost-benefit analysis of the rescue. Could the rescue vehicle arrive on time? Could it save the ship/cargo/passengers? Were the lives/cargo/ship worth the cost of the rescue?

Such an analysis could not be done without passenger names and histories.

As the system waited, the message from the 13th Moon Relay Station arrived. Now, the Martian system noted that the Moon would not conduct a rescue or even contemplate one, should one be needed.

Only the Martian system would take the risks involved, which changed the calculations yet again.

The system was about to reject the rescue request, even without an answer from the starbase, when several manual distress signals arrived, evenly spaced from each other.

But each manual distress signal contained a signature, proving that someone on board the *Blue Moon* had crafted that distress signal by hand.

That someone was named Colette Euphemia Josephine Treacher Singh Wilkinson Lopez.

Treacher.

A quick analysis showed that Colette Euphemia Josephine Treacher Singh Wilkinson Lopez was a distant Treacher relative, not involved in the corporation or in any local governments, but still on tap to receive a portion of the Treacher Trust when she came of age.

A second Treacher was on board as well, another woman, also in line to receive an inheritance from the Treacher Trust.

Treachers were protected throughout the solar system because of the family's great involvement in many businesses and governments from Mars to Saturn and maybe beyond.

The review's purpose changed. The routine review no longer had relevance.

Two Treachers on board a ship, any ship, anywhere within the reach of Mars Rescue Services, required an immediate and adequate rescue response.

The information got forwarded to Mars Vehicle Rescue (Space Unit), along with all available information, including the amount of time lapsed.

Given the hazards of travel through that part of the Asteroid Belt, and given the kinds of emergencies that happened there, the time lapsed changed the chances of success from more than 80% to less than 50%.

Which meant, given the costs of rescues that far from Mars itself, all Mars Vehicle Rescue (Space Unit) could spare would be one large rescue vehicle, with a crew of twenty.

The systems in Mars Vehicle Rescue (Space Unit) had determined likely outcomes, and decided that the most possible outcome was this: The rescue vehicle would arrive to find a destroyed ship, dead passengers, and no rescue needed.

But the presence of Treachers meant the possibility of lawsuits. The possibility of lawsuits meant that it would be good to get the DNA of the dead Treachers, just to prove that their portion of the Treacher Trust was now available for some other distant relative.

Mars Vehicle Rescue (Space Unit) did not want to be liable for anything to do with the Treacher Trust, so the rescue ship numbered MVR14501, but known to its crew as *Sally,* left its docking ring on the way to an out-of-the-way shipping route in the Asteroid Belt.

Instead of a crew of twenty, the *Sally* had only ten crew members. If they had had to wait for the remaining ten crew members to arrive from their scheduled time off, departure would have been delayed another three hours, something the system calculated it did not have.

It didn't matter that the crew was small; the chances of success were small too.

The crew of the *Sally* looked at the rescue attempt as a drill, not an actual job.

And that was a mistake.

The stupid passenger identification system seemed hardwired to the life reading of that particular passenger. Colette didn't remember signing up for that but she was a "minor" who "had no rights" without "suing for them" so she had no idea what her parents had done to guarantee her passage on this ship.

Whatever it was, she couldn't spoof the system and if she couldn't spoof the system, she couldn't get out of the suite.

She stood because her butt was falling asleep on the bed's hard surface. She moved the tablet onto a little holder built into the wall, and wished she could use a holoscreen instead.

Something pinged in her brain about holoscreens, but she let that marinate. Because what she really wanted to do was get the tablet to tell her where the bad guys were, and so far, the tablet was refusing.

Well, it wasn't refusing, exactly, because that would have meant it had some kind of sentience, which it did not. What it was doing was refusing to acknowledge their life signs, since they were not paying passengers.

Apparently, crew, staff, and service personnel at any kind of starbase stop were beneath the notice of the concierge level. She dug into the systems, and tried to see if she could get a reading on the non-paying passengers, even if they only appeared as some kind of shadowy coordinates on the ship's map.

She couldn't, any more than she could detach her own heartbeat from the passenger manifest, but she could reset the holographic concierges on every single floor.

That discovery made her heart race. She couldn't reset the concierges to "forget" anyone, which was probably good from the ship's point of view, but she could set up the concierges to interact with every human being they encountered.

She dug deeper into the controls. She could actually set up the concierges to follow anyone unregistered with the ship. Some of the more sophisticated concierges could follow the unregistered person until someone in authority dealt with them, even if that meant following that person off the ship.

Well, she couldn't get out of here and harass the bad guys herself, not without getting caught, and she couldn't get the Egg and figure it out without getting caught, but she could do this.

She only hoped it would be enough.

Napier was about to contact his second, Grizwald, when the man walked onto the bridge. He was larger than most of Napier's crew, but size had its uses, especially when it came to intimidation.

And intimidation wasn't the only thing Griz was good at.

Griz handed Napier a small box containing everything he needed to access the Captain's Codes.

"We got some problems," Griz said.

"No kidding," Napier said and opened the box. It had the skin gloves, and some other bits and pieces of the captain himself, no longer bloody, but cleaned up so that Napier could use them.

"I mean it." Griz's tone was harsh. "*Look*."

Napier frowned with annoyance, then looked in the direction that Griz was pointing. A head floated behind him.

For a moment, Napier thought maybe Griz had brought him the captain's actual head, but he hadn't.

"What the hell?" Napier asked.

Griz slid his hand toward the head, and his hand went through it. The head vanished for a half a second, then returned.

"You are unauthorized," it said. "If you do not leave this area, you will be subject to discipline."

"Discipline?" Napier asked Griz. "From who?"

Griz rolled his eyes. "The crew," he said.

Well, that wouldn't happen. Part of the crew was trapped in the so-called brig (really, two emergency cells that would get troublemakers to the next base) guarded by three of his people, and the rest of the crew was piled in an airlock, awaiting Napier's order to have the bodies join the rocks floating around this part of the Asteroid belt.

"So what's the problem?" Napier asked.

"It's following me," Griz said. "And it won't go away."

"That's not a problem," Napier said, by which he meant, *That's not a problem I need to deal with right now.*

"It's blocking access to crew quarters and other parts of the ship," Griz said. "Once it started following me, everything shut down when I got near it."

Napier felt a surge of anger rush through him. "So you came *here*?"

He glanced at the bridge controls, and sure enough, they had all shut down. He would have to redo all of his work.

"Get out," he said to Griz. "*Now.*"

"You both must leave," the head said to Napier.

"And take that thing with you," Napier said to Griz.

Griz shook his own head, then scooted around the holo-head, and went out the door. The head remained for some reason Napier did not understand.

"You must leave," the head said to him.

"Not happening," Napier said, and opened the box. The ship required a minimum of five forms of physical identification from an officer to access certain parts of the controls.

The most basic was active fingertip control, which the ship would test to see if the finger was warm, attached, and belonging to a crew member.

Napier had stolen a number of items over the years that made warm and attached and belonging into three different things. The ship would think that his hands were the Captain's hands.

"You must leave," the head said to Napier.

"And you're going to get shut down," Napier said, as he placed his index finger on the bridge control board.

"Not happening," the head said, mirroring Napier's earlier response, which worried him more than he wanted to think about.

He decided not to look at the stupid head any more.

Instead, he went back to work.

Halfway to the coordinates in the Asteroid Belt, Dayah Rodriguez, who was in charge of the *Sally*'s rescue team, finally got a reading on the *Blue Moon*.

The ship didn't seem to be in physical trouble, although it hadn't moved from the location cited in the distress signal. But one small ship floated around it, constantly bouncing and shivering the way that some of the illegal vessels did to avoid standard tracking units.

Fortunately, *Sally* didn't use standard tracking.

A jolt of adrenaline shot through Rodriguez.

She suddenly realized they were understaffed and perhaps lacking the proper amount of firepower.

"Speed up," she said to Hamish Sarkis, who was piloting the *Sally*. "And send a message back to headquarters. We have pirates. And if we want to catch them, we're going to need some help."

They were going to need a lot more than help.

They were going to need a lot of luck as well.

Now, Colette was obsessing about her parents. Because they still hadn't moved. No one had. Why weren't the passengers fighting back? What was going on?

She was pacing around the bed, trying to figure out if breaking out of this stupid suite was worthwhile.

And then her breath caught.

She had set up the concierges to follow the bad guys.

She just needed to locate the concierges. When she found them, she would know where the bad guys were.

Which would help her escape, but then what?

She flopped on the bed, grabbed the tablet, and thought about it.

She had access to a lot of things on this little device. Maybe some of them would help her slow those bad guys down.

★ ★ ★

The head was proving to be a problem. The thing stuck to Napier like some kind of weird glue. He couldn't shut it out of the bridge, because every time he closed the door on the head, it floated back inside.

And every time he tried to use some piece of the captain to provide identification, the head stated, quite calmly, "You are not Captain Ekhart. You lack his height, weight, and appearance. I have instructed the system to remain unfooled."

Unfooled. What kind of word was that, anyway?

It was as annoying as the head was.

To make matters worse, Napier's internal clock was warning him that he was almost out of time for this job.

He needed that Egg, but he couldn't access anything.

His personal comm vibrated. He pressed it, and Johnston, the only member of his team still on the ship, said, "We just got a ping from the security system. We've been scanned by something with an official government signature."

Napier didn't even have to ask what that meant. It meant that either a security vehicle or a rescue ship was on the way. Or something larger and more important—some kind of government transport—was coming to or traveling along this route.

Which meant he was done, if he didn't find that manifest right now, if he couldn't get the Egg right now.

He reached for the head, and his hand went right through it. Had that head belonged to a human, it would've been slammed against the wall until it shattered.

"You are unauthorized," the head said, obliviously. Clearly it had no idea that he would have killed it if he could. "You do not have access. You are not Captain Ekhart. You must leave."

Napier glared at it. The thing looked like it made eye contact with him, but he could see through it, so it probably didn't.

But had it sent the information to the authorities?

He had broken into a number of ships similar to the *Blue Moon*, but never one of this vintage. Sometimes older ships had technologies he hadn't seen or even imagined. Things attempted and then discarded.

Like annoying heads that floated after people and yelled at them. This couldn't have been a popular feature.

"Can you figure out who scanned us?" Napier asked Johnston.

"Been trying. I have no idea." Johnston was good with all of the equipment. Not great, but better than some of the idiots Napier had brought with him. Those idiots were good for scaring civilians, and that was what he'd been using them for. And for figuring out how to put an entire room full of people into a deep sleep, so they wouldn't fight back.

"I can't find them with our scanners," Johnston was saying, "but here's what I'm worried about. They're coming from Mars, and they scanned us far enough out that we can't read them. So they have powerful equipment and they're coming fast. There might be a whole bunch of them, for all I know."

If Napier didn't get out of here now, he might actually get caught. He slammed his fist on the captain's chair that he had forgotten to retract. It bounced and jiggled toward him, almost as if he offended it, which was a lot more satisfying than trying to grab that stupid head.

"Hey, you," he said to the head, "who did you notify that we had arrived?"

"I sent a message to those in charge, as per my programming," the head said primly.

"And who might those in charge be?" Napier asked, hoping that maybe he could buy some more time if the head identified them.

"I went through proper channels. You have accessed the bridge without authorization. You have attempted to impersonate Captain Ekhart. You will be dealt with firmly."

He wasn't getting any information from the head, and he wasn't going to be able to find that Egg.

He had to think this through. He was good at cutting his losses when he needed to, but usually he had a bit more to show for a job this complicated.

Still, running was a lot better than getting captured.

He also needed to get rid of all of the evidence that pointed to him. A ship full of people who could identify him. Those head-things. Who knew what they had taken from him and his team? DNA? Imagery? Everything?

Now he was going to have to change his plan. He couldn't remote detonate the *Blue Moon* because he didn't have access to the controls.

He would have to use regular explosives, the kind with their own timers.

They were a little less reliable than a remote detonation, but they would have to do.

Then his fist clenched.

The kid.

He thought of her for a moment, sprawled on that floor, looking helpless and lost as Mommy and Daddy got carted away.

He didn't dare jettison her from the *Blue Moon*, not now, not with the authorities (or whomever) closing in.

This job was really screwed up. He was going to have to do things he didn't want to do for no real payoff at all.

He punched the retractable captain's chair one last time, then shoved his way past the head as he stalked off the bridge. Or, rather, tried to shove. Because the head moved with him.

How come he inherited the head from Griz? Because the head figured Napier was the greater threat?

Didn't matter. He had to tell his team to dump the explosives near the passengers and surviving crew. There was no time for finesse.

He and his team needed to be on board his ship within fifteen minutes, so they could be as far away from the *Blue Moon* as possible when it exploded.

As far from the Egg as possible.

Because he had no idea what kind of damage it would do.

Colette tried to work faster, to see what else she could find, what she could use.

She had almost given up when she found something weird.

Apparently, passenger liners from the old days had a lot of theft, and theft was bad for business.

So the holographic concierges were designed, not for the passengers' comfort, but to spy on them. If concierges deemed someone suspicious, they harassed that someone on the ship. If that someone left the ship, the concierges shrank themselves down to a pinprick and became some kind of tiny spy that sent a signal so that the suspicious personages could be traced.

It was weird, and it was brilliant, and it was strangely appropriate.

Colette couldn't prevent them from taking hostages. She couldn't prevent them from getting the Egg. But she could help the authorities find the bad guys.

If they let her live.

A shiver ran through her.

It didn't really matter if they could track her or not. Because she had to get out of this room and stop them.

Somehow.

She just didn't know how yet.

The head thing vanished as Napier climbed into the only airlock that wasn't stacked with dead crew members. His team had already gotten onto his ship and were waiting for him.

God, he was irritated. Hours, risk, a few deaths, and what did he have to show for it?

He was actually fleeing, something he thought he had become too sophisticated to do.

Well, he had learned his lesson. No more boarding a passenger ship of this vintage, not without a lot more planning.

He watched the exterior door open into the enclosed ramp his ship had set up, and it took every bit of effort he had not to dive through it.

He would have a little dignity here.

He would have to consider this a scouting mission rather than a failed attempt. He had learned something, and, if he had time to set it up, he would learn a bit more.

He would learn what happened when a ship carrying a Glyster Egg exploded.

He would have to set up something specific to monitor space around the starliner, but he could do that, and he could do it from a distance.

Then he would gather information, and with it, he could tell any possible client one of the many things the Egg did—more as a cautionary tale, with the explosion and all, but still. Information was information.

That was the kind of thing that clients liked.

He would have to remember that when the kid appeared in his dreams.

He slid into the airlock on his ship, shifting from foot to foot, hoping he would get through this quickly.

They needed to get out of here—and they needed to do so fast.

The engines were powering up on that second ship. Rodriguez sent the coordinates to the ships Mars Rescue had sent, hoping they would either veer off and catch the pirate ship.

She didn't have time to think about capturing a pirate ship. She was kinda relieved that it was leaving. She commanded a *rescue* vessel, not a security vessel. The handful of times she'd gone after perpetrators hadn't ended well for her. In all but one instance, the perpetrators had gotten away.

She hoped that the pirate ship wasn't taking the *Blue Moon* with it. That would create other problems.

Right now, her scans showed that the *Blue Moon* was more or less immobile, moving forward ever so slightly, but not enough to measure as anything. Maybe on autopilot.

She wasn't close enough yet to find that out.

But she would be in just a few minutes—and her team now knew this wasn't a drill.

It was going to be life and death.

Colette stared at the tablet in surprise. It told her that bad guys had left the *Blue Moon*.

Maybe they had found what they were looking for.

Not that it mattered to her.

She had to get to her parents.

She snuck out of her suite, and ran along the corridor, bent almost in half, just because, even though she knew the monitors caught her every movement anyway.

The buffet that her parents and the rest of the passengers were in was on this level. She just had to get to it.

She hurried through the maze of corridors, going half on her memory and half on the map that showed up on the tablet, when she almost tripped on a small square block.

It wasn't alone. There were half a dozen small square blocks just in this corridor.

She turned the tablet toward them, and asked it to identify the blocks.

The tablet did not respond. Maybe it didn't have the programming.

So she needed to figure this out on her own. After all, she had seen a lot of things in all the various schools she'd gone to. (She had done most of those things as well.)

She crouched near the closest block, and peered at it. It smelled faintly of rust—the telltale sign of a kind of acid that would eventually eat through a casing, hit a trigger, and—

Oh, god. This was a bomb, one of the kinds she'd thought too damn dangerous to make.

The bad guys were off the ship, and they were going to blow it up. But they hadn't taken the Egg and they hadn't taken her and they hadn't taken any of the passengers, so they must have been after something else, but what she had no idea, and now there was no time to figure it out.

She needed to get rid of these things. Somehow.

She reached for the box in front of her, then remembered: acid. She would have lost all the skin on her hand.

Focus, focus, focus.

There had to be a command that allowed the concierges, real or not, to isolate something dangerous in a corridor. Kids made smoke bombs, after all. And people sometimes tried to burn the materials in a ship.

Everyone on the crew had to be able to access that kind of security protocol.

She just had to find it before something happened.

Rodriguez had been right: the *Sally* arrived after the pirate ship left. The readings she got off the *Blue Moon* were some of the strangest she'd seen. The ship was completely intact. Some of the crew remained alive, and all of the passengers seemed to be breathing as well, but none of them were moving.

Except one of the Treacher women.

Was she in on the attack somehow?

Rodriguez brought two of her teammates with her, but let them move toward the room filled with passengers. Her entire team wore their environmental suits, and were armed with everything she could think to bring.

Sarkis remained on board the *Sally* and three more team members were heading to the brig to find the crew stranded there.

The remaining three team members were spreading out between engineering and the bridge, hoping to get this ship moving again.

Rodriguez was going to handle the Treacher woman herself, not just because that person was still moving, but because Rodriguez didn't quite believe the information the passenger manifest had sent her.

It said that this distant Treacher relative was only eleven. Which wasn't possible, since no children were allowed on board ships like the *Blue Moon*.

Someone might have spoofed the file, which concerned Rodriguez more than she wanted to admit. Especially since the first thing she found when she came on board was the carnage in the first airlock she tried. She was lucky she hadn't opened it, or bodies would have tumbled into space.

Bodies.

The pirates had clearly gotten something. You don't kill that many people for the hell of it.

She rounded a corner and saw a corridor strewn with black boxes.

"Don't move!" a panicked nasal voice said.

Rodriguez stopped and looked. She had seen the boxes, but she had missed the very small person crouched near the box farthest away.

A very small person who did indeed look like an eleven-year-old child, holding onto an old-fashioned rectangular tablet.

"Colette Treacher?" Rodriguez asked, trying to remember all of the girl's elaborate name.

"Close enough," the girl said. "You weren't tagged by one of the concierges. Are they gone?"

"What?" Rodriguez asked.

"Who are you?" The girl's tone was annoyed, as if Rodriguez was the dumbest person she had ever encountered.

And, to be fair, the girl couldn't see Rodriguez's identification. She was wearing a high-end environmental suit, not the ones issued by Mars Rescue. And the girl didn't seem to be networked into any kind of Mars system.

Rodriguez introduced herself without using her name. Names weren't important in situations like this. Jobs were.

"I'm with Mars Rescue," she said.

"It's about time." The girl's annoyance grew. "It's been *hours*."

Hours was miraculous, given where the *Blue Moon* ended up, and Rodriguez nearly said that, then realized the girl's tone had made her feel defensive.

"What are you doing?" Rodriguez asked.

"Trying to diffuse a bomb," the girl said. "What are you doing?"

That adrenaline spike hit again.

"All of these are bombs?" Rodriguez asked.

"I haven't checked them all, but I would guess so," the girl said. "They're pretty mad."

Rodriguez had a hunch the girl wasn't talking about the bombs now, but the pirates. "Who?"

"The guys who attacked us. They wanted something, and I hope they didn't get it. They left pretty fast. And now . . ." The girl ran her hands near the boxes. "This."

Her voice broke on that last word, the bravado gone.

"I can't find any way to diffuse them," she said.

And that, the edge of panic in the girl's voice, brought Rodriguez back to herself.

She contacted her team.

"Found half a dozen box bombs, type unknown," Rodriguez said. "They're not too far from the passengers. Check for other bombs. We need a scan of this ship, and we need to put every single corridor on lockdown."

"Do you have some kind of shield program?" The girl shook the tablet at Rodriguez. "Because I can't find one."

Rodriguez wasn't carrying any kind of device like the girl had, but Rodriguez had access to every single ship built in official shipyards in the past one hundred years. The failsafes built into each system, override codes along with physical identification, specific to each rescue service.

She hoped that would be on board the *Blue Moon* as well, even though the ship was pretty old.

She slid to the nearest door, pulled back a wall panel, and found the interior controls. Then she opened the secondary panel underneath, hit the override commands, and found what she was looking for.

There were no tiny shields on a ship like this. Only one big shield that would coat the corridor.

"Join me," she said to the girl.

The girl stood slowly, giving the boxes a glance.

"*Right now*," Rodriguez said.

The girl crept past the boxes, moving slower than Rodriguez would have liked. After what seemed like an eternity, the girl reached Rodriguez's side, and Rodriguez released the shields.

They encased the entire floor, avoiding her and the girl, but trapping them in one place. It would take some maneuvering, but Rodriguez could get that shield and the boxes it contained out of the ship—if she could find an airlock without bodies in it.

Her comm chirruped.

"We found more boxes, and yeah, they're bombs. We're getting them out now," said Lytel, who was handling the rest of the team.

"I got these explosives contained as well," Rodriguez said. "Any word on the passengers?"

"They're unconscious. The remaining crew too. Doing medical evaluations right now, but it looks like they're just out. Guess the bombs were going to do the dirty work of actual murder," Lytel said.

Rodriguez looked down at the girl. Her eyes were red, but there were no tear-streaks on her face.

"Do you have any idea what happened here?" Rodriguez asked.

The girl shook her head.

"How come you're out and no one else is?" Rodriguez said.

"Some guy," the girl said, "he was surprised there was a kid on board. He locked me in my suite."

She shook the tablet at Rodriguez.

"That was his first mistake." And then the girl grinned. The grin was a little cold, it was a little off, and then it trembled on the girl's face and fell away, showing that it was more bravado than anything else.

"My dad," the girl asked. "Is he okay?"

The shield reshaped as Lytel remotely prepped it to leave the ship.

Neither Rodriguez nor the girl should remain in the corridor while that happened.

"I don't know how your father is," Rodriguez said, putting her hand on the little girl's back. The child was shaking so hard it looked like she might rattle out of her skin. "But I'm sure we can find out."

★ ★ ★

Napier was almost out of the Asteroid Belt when six ships surrounded him. All of those ships had official insignia, but not all of the insignia were from the same organization.

Different rescue and security companies, all government owned, all looking pretty official.

"What is going on?" Griz said from beside him. "We didn't steal anything."

"No, we didn't," Napier said. They had just killed half the crew. But they'd killed a lot of people out here before, and no one had come after them.

"So what the heck was different about this job?" Griz asked.

Napier didn't have the answer to that. Except bad luck. And that bad luck started when he saw the kid.

Kids threw Napier off his game.

But he didn't tell Griz that. Instead, Napier deleted all the records he had for the *Blue Moon,* and then contacted all of the security vessels.

Contacting them first might buy him some time. Although time probably wasn't what he needed. Because he had violated his own code, and used bombs to kill that kid for no reason at all.

Except that he hadn't killed Colette Euphemia Josephine Treacher Singh Wilkinson Lopez. The ship didn't blow up. Instead, the *Sally* guarded the *Blue Moon* all the way to the nearest Mars Rescue base where everyone reported their own truth about what happened.

The only truth the authorities listened to, though, was Colette's, because it proved accurate from the moment the investigators had the tablet she had stolen.

That tablet had recorded her every move.

It also showed where Napier's crew was, because of what Colette had done with the holographic concierges. She had turned them into location beacons.

Colette did not want attention for what she had done. She didn't want a medal or recognition from the governments of Mars.

She wanted something else entirely.

Something no government had the power to give.

"I don't want to go to boarding school," Colette said to her dad after all the officials left. "I want to go home."

Her family was in a tiny hotel room on the base where the *Blue Moon* had ended up. Her mother lay on the bed, her forearm over her forehead. She'd had a headache ever since she'd woken up, something the medical personnel said was a pretty normal reaction to the gas the bad guys had filtered into the buffet.

Dad didn't seem to have a headache at all. He was frowning at Colette, and she knew, *she knew*, he was going to make her to go that school anyway, just because he had no idea what else to do with her.

"All right," he said quietly.

"What?" Colette asked, not sure she had heard him right.

"I'm taking you home," he said.

Colette's mouth opened ever so slightly. She hadn't expected *that*.

"No, you're not," her mother said. "She's more than we can handle."

"You won't have to handle her, Louise," Dad said.

Her mother sat up on one elbow, her face pale.

"What?" she asked, in almost the same tone Colette had used a moment before.

Something crossed Dad's face, something hard and fascinating.

"Colette saved our lives," he said after a moment. "All of us. Even you. We owe her, Louise."

Her mother made a dismissive sound and collapsed on the bed. Dad's gaze met Colette's and his eyes actually twinkled.

"We could send her away," Colette said softly.

"My thoughts exactly," he said just as softly.

Then he opened the door to the hotel room, and peered into the hall as if he expected to see a man cradling a laser rifle.

There was none—no man, no rifle.

Dad ushered Colette out of the room.

He was protecting her again. Like he had tried to do on the *Blue Moon*. Only he had failed.

And he would probably fail now. But that was okay.

Because Colette could protect them all.

As she had learned recently, she was really really good at that.

Harris Alexander Pope came to the colony world of Osiris in the hope of putting the Partisan War behind him. Then Umerah Javed came calling. She's on Osiris at the behest of the Order of Stone. It seems the Order is not yet done with Harris Alexander Pope, after all.

CRASH-SITE
★
by Brian Trent

I: The Night Witch from the Stars

SHE NEUROCAST FROM ORBIT into the body of a standby proxy—an out-of-work woman named Rada Rudneva who, judging by the gnawing hunger in her stomach, needed the money something awful. Thirty thousand kilometers above Osiris, Umerah Javed closed her eyes and accepted primary control of the proxy's limbs as her deposit registered in the woman's bank account.

What surprised her was how quickly the transaction occurred. No chitchat, no small talk. Rada Rudneva accepted the request instantly, and suddenly Umerah found herself in mid-stride—no, mid-*run*—along a boardwalk pier in the fishing district of Sagacious Bay. She nearly lost her balance as the provincial elements assailed her: the woman's labored breathing, the blue sunlight in the sky, the ringed daylight moon, and the stink of fishing trawlers in port. Adrenaline burned hot in her body. Adrenaline that wasn't hers.

Umerah's own body became a distant thing, a slender brown shape sitting in the *Night Witch*'s plush chair of good Nebraska leather, parked in geostationary orbit.

"Where you goin', Rada?" a voice barked behind her. "Gonna take a swim, you pier-rat bitch?"

Umerah didn't turn right away. She was still off-balance, and when she glanced over the edge of the pier to the water, she saw her proxy's reflection: a face like a weather-beaten mask, seamed beyond its years. Her hair was the same color as the local sun: blowtorch-blue.

Behind her, the wooden pier creaked under footsteps and the surly voice came again, "Rada? You jump in the drink, I'll pull you out. Talk to us, or things get worse."

Umerah finally turned. Two men were converging on her. Large, Slavic genotypes. Their hands were powdered blue, as if they had emerged from a cobalt mine.

"Oh, she feels like talking now!" one of the men said to the other, scowling.

"Sorry," Umerah said, speaking in her proxy's husky voice. "I just arrived. Can you gentlemen tell me the way to a tavern called the Horn-O-Plenty?"

"Don't give me that shit, Rada. You were warned to stay out of the Bay."

Umerah forced her borrowed face into a smile which—judging by the men's reaction—was unnerving. "Rada is resting in standby mode," she explained. "I don't know what your problem with her is, but it doesn't concern me. I've rented this body for the next one hundred hours."

That gave the men pause. One absently scratched his brow, smearing blue dust, and said, "What's gotten into you, Rada?"

"It's *who's* gotten into her that should concern you." Umerah was starting to compensate for the short delay between her willpower and this body's reaction time.

"You're a proxiter?" one of the men asked doubtfully.

"Just arrived in-system. You're the first Osirians I've met!" She bowed—not entirely sure if that was a custom here—and continued, "As I said, I'm looking for the Horn-O-Plenty. I know it's nearby, but you fucking people don't update your OPS maps as often as you should. Can you help me out?"

Osiris was a young world, Umerah knew. Its people had a narrow view of the larger universe, and so they regarded offworlders with a mixture of contempt, awe, and fear.

"Horn-O-Plenty is two blocks up," said the man with the smear on his forehead. He was sweating openly, the blue sun making the perspiration appear as scales of frost despite the morning's heat.

"Thank you." Umerah brushed past them. They didn't touch her.

She could be anyone, anything, and whatever their problem with Rada Rudneva was, it would just have to wait.

A close shave, she thought once she had put a fair distance between herself and them. Nonetheless, she gave temporary control back to Rada while she returned to her own body aboard the *Night Witch* to play back her memories of the encounter. She ran the men's faces against the planetary database and instructed her ship's AI to compile all relevant info into a folder entitled POTENTIAL PROBLEMS.

Umerah Javed, after all, enjoyed solving problems.

II: The War Hero from Redworlds Past

FROM THE OUTSIDE, the Horn-O-Plenty displayed the wind-blasted, eroded look of most of Osiris's buildings this side of the equatorial sea. The interior, however, proved to be an eccentric mash-up of styles from two solar systems; someday they might blend, but for now presented a tacky, incongruous, and disorienting stew. Consorts of every gender reflected this motley character, each striving for a certain look from a certain culture on a certain planet. A sampler platter from around IPCnet.

Umerah went straight to the matron at the reception desk. "You have a customer here named Harris," she began.

The matron narrowed her eyes, attempting to size up this blue-haired, worn-looking creature. "Our clients value privacy," the woman replied.

"Good for them. I'm here at the behest of the Order of Stone. Tell me where he is, please."

"Mr. Pope is . . . ah . . . busy at the moment."

"He's about to get busier."

The matron led the way to a room with the placard CLOUDS OF ISHTAR over the door. Umerah strode inside.

A minute later, three nude women hurried out, clutching their skimpy Venusian clothes as they went.

"Is any of this helping, Harris?" Umerah asked, arms folded over her chest.

The man regarded her from the bed, his naked body a sinewy landscape of old scars and tattoos. The walls displayed the cloudy, super-rotational horizon of Venus's famous aerostat colony; Umerah felt dizzy, watching the breakneck sky whip around her.

"It isn't hurting," the man replied. He paused, giving her a slow up-and-down appraisal. "I know that poise."

"About a week ago, there was a bar fight. Several people were killed."

"Astonishing."

Umerah paced around the room, Rada's stomach growling. "Apparently, a worldmapper named Tel-Silag came into town and picked a fight with a local troublemaker."

Harris Alexander Pope swung his legs over the edge of the bed and rubbed his head. "Sounds like a typical Sifday night."

"The worldmapper killed the guy along with four of his buddies. Then he fled Sagacious Bay into the forest and hasn't been seen since."

Harris stood at last, cracking his neck and rolling his shoulders. But Umerah wasn't fooled. She saw the way he was looking at her, noting her movements, head slightly cocked to listen to each inflection of her voice.

Offworld rumor was that Harris Alexander Pope had burned out. That he would be useless to any mission. That he had withdrawn into an insular safety zone, like a butterfly retiring to its end-of-life hedonistic rituals. And in truth, Umerah would hardly blame him if that was the case. The Partisan War back on Mars had been a hellish episode of history. The postbellum missions to hunt escaped Partisan war criminals had, in a way, been worse. Minds had broken from less, and Umerah felt a pang of relief to see that her old compatriot was still in there, still sharp, still full of deception and the kind of guile that could—that *had*—brought down an empire.

"Why are you interested in this guy?" Harris asked.

"The Order of Stone wants me to locate and retrieve him. Apparently, our kind of work is never in short supply on this world; they sent me the details while I was in deceleration."

Harris walked to a pile of clothes in the corner.

Umerah chuckled, watching him bend over. "Looking good, Harris. I mean it."

"Can't say the same for you," he said, slipping into his pants. "Where'd you find that body?"

"Her name is Rada. We're helping each other out."

"Why does a murder in a tavern concern the Order?"

"Let's say that a very nontraditional weapon was used."

Harris stiffened. "Why don't you put some food in that body and I'll be down in a moment. Try the house salad: cryostored greens brought in by star trader."

She nodded, giving one last look at the rapidly moving faux clouds on the walls. Then she headed for the corridor.

"By the way . . ." he called to her.

She halted.

Harris smiled. "It's good to see you, Umerah."

She winked and returned his dazzling grin. "You too. Together again, huh?"

III: The Fugitive Doctor Who Looked Backwards in Time

A MONTH EARLIER, when Umerah Javed's *Night Witch* was just entering Ra System and began deceleration from its six-year journey, two people walked across the bottom of Osiris's Jormungand Sea. Their pressure-suited bodies stumbled through tangles of reeds, silt, and the heat of thermal vents as they went.

"Why didn't we just take the submersible?" demanded the man named Bok.

Dr. Catherine Avellani had dialed down the volume in her headset; nonetheless, Bok's grating timbre had a way of piercing her ears like a stiletto blade. "There are things down here that don't like submersibles," she explained.

Her bodyguard scoffed. "Fishermen's tales. I've heard 'em, and I don't believe 'em."

"As I recall, you also don't believe that there's a way to look backwards in time."

Bok's tattooed face displayed itself on her visor. He was a muscular man with sharp teeth, a former mining guard and pit-fighter with a mind-boggling 148-2 record. He grinned, showing rows of fangs. "You're paying me to believe that, *lapochka.*"

Catherine sighed. A whole planet at their disposal, and *this* was the guy Tier Starsworks chose to be her local guide and bodyguard. She shook her head inside her pressure suit and continued trudging along the velvety sea-bottom to her destination.

The geodesic plants!

Her heart skipped a beat in excitement.

Catherine could already discern the behemoth, swollen roots of the giant vegetation. Far, far above, the mighty stalks rose out of the ocean, their bizarre leaves stretched wide to gorge on solar nourishment.

Bok halted beside her and craned his neck. "If nothing else, this job offers new perspectives."

Catherine ignored him; she worked steadily, anxiously, detaching several modular components from her utility pack and staking them around the base of the nearest giant root.

Bok watched her for a while. "We could have taken a shuttle here and air-dropped to this spot. Just sayin'."

"The Order of Stone watches everything we do. They *won't* be watching the sea-bottom."

"But—"

"*Quiet.*"

She set the last of the readers in place; they formed a roughly circular ring around the root. Using her wristpad controls, Catherine activated the array. Interface needles penetrated the mighty root, seeking the plant's "brain." Yellowish sap clouded the seawater.

"Still don't believe that a plant can have memories," Bok scoffed.

"It's not about belief. Scientists have known for centuries that prion-based memory structures exist in—"

The world disappeared.

Catherine cried out, the needles tapping the plant's "brain" and auto-uploading to her sightjacking nanonics. A parade of sunrises and sunsets wheeled in her mind. Electrical storms. The rising and falling of tides.

The growth rate of geodesic plants was relatively constant, and so a ticker displayed in Catherine's wondering eyes, counting back along the synaptic growth rings. To think that she was peering back in time one hundred years! Two hundred! A blazing chronology of nights preceding days. Trees on the shoreline shrank down to buds. New growth vanished in the scarlet bloom of forest fires that faded into old growth. It was exactly like watching time-lapse video in reverse.

Somewhere far away, Catherine began to laugh.

I'm touching an alien mind! Opening up the memories of a plant representing an entirely non-terrestrial evolutionary history.

Three hundred years flashed by. Four hundred. The geodesic plant was suddenly little more than a lily pad five hundred years ago, floating on the ocean, its roots just beginning to drape toward the seafloor. Catherine felt giddy with the thought that while Earth had been wiping nuclear ash from its face, this little bud was fighting its own game of survival on storm-tossed tides, all these light-years away!

And then . . .

At nearly six hundred years ago, something happened. Catherine gasped as something fiery appeared to leap up from the ground.

She slowed the uptake of visual data. Rewound them. Played them back.

There!

Six centuries ago, something from the sky crashed into the forests south of here and—

Someone was knocking on her faceplate. Catherine blinked from her reverie, scowling at Bok's nightmarish tattoos and sharp teeth.

"You awake?" he demanded. "You've been standing there a long time, *lapochka*. That plant take over your brain or what?"

Catherine glared coldly, her giddiness washed away by a murderous impulse. "Don't ever touch me again," she snapped. Reluctantly, she ended the sightjack. She desperately wanted to peek back even further. This was a scientific breakthrough impossible with terrestrial flora, since *their* memories were limited to non-visual cold spells and wet seasons. Nothing in the known galaxy approached the photoreceptors of these wonderful geodesic plants!

"So what did you see?" Bok demanded. "A happy flower's childhood?"

"There was an impact to the south, about six hundred years ago. I'd estimate two hundred kilometers in from the shore."

"Maybe it was a meteor."

"No. It was a ship burning up in the sky and detonating on impact."

"You sure?"

"Yes," she said.

In actual fact, she wasn't sure. The geodesic plant didn't possess the sharp, binocular, detail-oriented eyes of a human being. Even at slow speeds, it had been challenging to discern the precise nature of whatever had gone flaming and crashing through the sky so long ago.

Nonetheless, she *was* certain it had been no meteor. The thing's descent alone suggested an attempt by thrusters to keep aloft.

Bok looked less than impressed. "We done here? I'm tired of pissing in my suit."

Two hours later, they emerged from the Jormungand into the shallows of a deserted cove. Bok eagerly exited his pressure suit. "So how does this help you?"

Catherine stepped out of her own suit, leaving it standing behind her like a discarded chrysalis. "It confirms my hypothesis in spectacular fashion. Something really did crash here on Osiris. Something of artificial construction. It's no longer an inference, but visual confirmation!" Her companion made no expression—she might as well have been speaking to a chunk of granite. "It's beyond you, Bok."

He watched her for a time. "You think I'm just some yokel, huh? Maybe so. But I looked *you* up, *lapochka*."

Something in his tone made her pay attention. "I'm a researcher at Tier," she said.

"Sure, sure." He ran his tongue along the points of his teeth. "Except prior to that—sixteen years ago—there ain't no record of you on this world. Oh, Tier Starsworks has a hefty bio on you, but I know a fiction when I see it. They wrote you a nice cover story."

She was managing to keep her face impassive, but she was impressed. "Interesting theory."

Bok gave her an appraising up-and-down gaze. "I haven't even gotten to my theory yet. You appear out of nowhere sixteen years ago, and suddenly you're the darling of this planet's biggest corpstate. Want me to continue?"

"I really do."

He leaned so close that she could smell his stale breath and seawater. "I think you came to this system from Sol, under a new identity. Which makes you a criminal of some sort. But you're just a scientist. So I was thinking, what group from about sixteen years ago is so reviled that even their scientists are war criminals . . . ?"

"Bok," Catherine purred. "All that electrical activity in your brain is starting to diminish your survival odds."

He laughed. "I won't say anything. Just don't be condescending to me and we'll get along fine."

"I promise," she said. "Now let's march into town and take the rail back to Tier."

They were silent the rest of the way, but Catherine's keen mind was already making plans.

I promise, she repeated in her head. *When this mission is over, Bok, I promise to never be condescending to you. Not even when I have you strapped down to an operating table. When I experiment to see if geodesic plant memories can be transferred to a living human host. For prying into my life and annoying me every step of the way, the* last *thing I'll be to you is condescending.*

IV: The Worldmapper Who Carried the Dead

Because the Jormungand Sea was Osiris's only major body of water, and because it wrapped like a blue serpent around the planet's equator, human colonization had been limited to that lushly habitable zone. Towns sprouted on both sides of the sea, but go too far north or south and all was arid fungal forest and cold desert. Few people dared to explore those unmapped regions.

Sitting in the womb of a fungal tree, the sporegun across his lap, the worldmapper named Tel-Silag smiled sadly at his dead wife and said, "They won't find me, *babbish*. I know these lands better than anyone alive."

The hologram of Zoe sat in the tree with him, legs dangling from the fuzzy branch.

Tel-Silag took another swig from his canteen, wiped his mouth with a trembling hand. "I killed him. For what he did to us—to you and the children. I killed him!"

"That's good, honey," she said.

"I walked into that bar without fear. The bastard was there with four of his goons. I . . . I killed them where they stood." Hot tears leaked down his cheeks. "You and the children . . . I did it for you all."

"Our children are so beautiful," she said from the branch.

They *had* been beautiful, yes. Tel-Silag's heart palpitated, and he began the same involuntary moaning that had escaped him when he first witnessed what Papa Joyboy—the money-lending crime lord of Sagacious Bay—had done to his kids. Their rotting corpses dancing, eyes rolled white. Tel-Silag had wanted to scream. Instead, he had fallen to his knees and moaned low, like an injured cow. Papa Joyboy mocked him, imitating the sound. And he kept mocking him as he brought forth Tel-Silag's wife . . . and showed what he had done to *her*.

Sometimes when Tel-Silag drank enough, he could almost believe it had all been a nightmare. It couldn't have really happened! Not to him! He was the greatest worldmapper in Ra System. He sold his maps to developers and exobiologists and fortune hunters alike. He had a wife who loved him, dear precious Zoe, and two perfect children, and even though they were in terrible debt, he was going to change that. Tel-Silag had plans. He was going to get off the grid. Was going to build his own habitat, a place debtors couldn't find him.

Look at them dance, Telly! Just dancing their rotting little bodies away! Ohhh! Ohhhhh!

"I am so happy," Zoe said from her branch, and she slid her hands over her stomach—it was suddenly very pregnant. "I can feel him kicking!"

Tel-Silag's red-rimmed eyes flicked to his wife's specter. "We already had our children," he said automatically. One of the memory strands his neurojack used to reconstruct her as a hologram was from their honeymoon days, when she was pregnant with their first child.

"Oh." Her stomach flattened at once and her image froze in place, the cheap reconstruction program scouring its bitterly finite storage for another memory to incorporate.

He hoisted the sporegun for her to see. "This is what I used to kill him, my love."

"That's good, honey."

"If I had found this earlier, I could have protected you and the kids! With all the mapping I had done, I . . . I *should* have found it!"

"I love you, Telly."

"Someday I'll bring you back . . . with this weapon, I'll *get* the money to bring you and our kids back."

"That's good, honey."

Except they could never really come back, could they? The best he could manage was to purchase more storage for the reconstruction program. Load in more memories. Give the bitter illusion more heft until Zoe and the kids seemed more than a collection of subroutines.

Twigs snapped in the forest. Tel-Silag jerked his sporegun in the direction of the sound. Bramble rustled. He caught a glimpse of low, black movement.

He hopped down from the tree at once. His boots sank into spongy ground. Zoe's hologram vanished from her perch and re-formed beside him.

Someone was hunting him. But who?

For days now, he'd been noticing odd movements in the jungle whenever he stopped to rest. Leaves rustling without wind. Unknown interlopers shadowing him. Stalking him.

"We need to go," Tel-Silag whispered. He plunged deeper into the forest, weaving around fallen trees and jutting rocks. The forest canopy was painted by starlight with a silvery glow like faint cobwebs.

Who was hunting him, dammit? There was more than one, that was for certain.

He remembered the cold-eyed scientist who had hired him a month ago to search these woods. She had insisted that a very long time ago, a vessel had crashed in the region. Tel-Silag had scoffed at the story—he knew these forests, and if a damn ship was there he would have found it. But the scientist paid him well, paid him with money that had felt like an insult, because it was nearly enough to have settled his debts to Papa Joyboy.

Tel-Silag pressed ahead, hearing more twigs moving around him. He told himself the sounds were probably just local animals; these forests were brimming with native and imported species engaged in an invisible niche war.

But he didn't believe it.

That scientist must know you found something. What you did in town would have made planetary news. She's after you now.

The sporegun was weighty in his arms, but he ran until his legs turned rubbery and he stumbled, wheezing, to rest against a tree.

Zoe materialized across from him and smiled.

"I *will* bring you back," Tel-Silag said, staring into the darkness, listening for signs of pursuit. "I promise you, my *babbish*."

"That's good, honey."

V: Nipping at the Heels of Gods

IN THE FRAGILE SECURITY of their CAMO tent, Harris Alexander Pope lay awake and studying the jungle through the smartsheet walls. Umerah, in the body of Rada Rudneva, lay against his chest, her hair smelling of the sea.

He wondered how long it'd been since he last saw Umerah. Sixteen years? They had exchanged messages in the interim; it couldn't be called a dialog (not with a six-year light-time transit) but Harris found himself looking forward to her correspondence. Like a shipwreck survivor, perhaps, delighting in a message-in-a-bottle washing ashore with the tide.

"It really *is* good to see you," he whispered.

The woman murmured pleasantly. She curled her warm body against him, jackknifing into a strangely fetal position. Her fingers traced an anxious circle on his chest. Harris frowned, noting how un-Umerah this behavior was, and it took him half a minute before he realized what was happening.

He bolted upright in a panic, startling his companion.

"Something wrong?" she cried.

"Where is Umerah?"

The woman offered a wounded, nervous smile. "She had to retreat to her homebody for a minute. Said she could conduct the search better up there." When she saw he wasn't sharing her smile, she grew worried. "Did I offend you? Ms. Javed said you wouldn't mind . . ."

Harris steadied his breathing, old reflexes snapping through him. "No, that's fine." He wrangled a hideous panic, like a hydra in his emotions, and not for the first time thought: *No one knows who anyone is anymore.*

If my panic is a hydra, it's because my species is one.

The fungal trees scratched at the tent flaps, clawing in a warm breeze that smelled faintly of sulfur. An animal hurried past—a jungle mollusk striding by on its eight rubbery legs. "So . . . Rada, is it? What do you do back in Sagacious Bay?"

"I used to run a kiosk at the docks."

"Used to?"

"I was chased out," she explained. "A cabal of vendors wanted to corner the docks. They couldn't legally prevent me from selling, so they resorted to other means."

"What did you sell?"

"I made shell necklaces, and jewelry from stones and driftwood." She chanced another smile, eyes bright and interested. "Nothing as exciting as what we're doing now! I feel so fortunate Ms. Javed asked me to proxy. I've been proxied before, but it was never this interesting . . . or respectful."

Harris frowned. "Very soon, we're going to ask you to do something that isn't very respectful."

The woman looked down at her knees. "I understand."

"Do you, Rada? If you have reservations, you'd best tell me now—"

"You said we'll be saving his life." She held her knees and rocked softly, like a child in that worn, emaciated body. "His wife was a friend of mine . . . I mean . . . I doubt she knew my name, but she was always nice to me when she visited my stall. I wept when she died. So if you think this will help him . . ."

Harris turned away, a pang of guilt coursing through him. "It'll help," he said, thinking: *Great stars, I'm sixty trillion kilometers from Mars, and yet here I am embedding into another latticework of manipulation and power. The setting changes, the costumes alter, but it's always the same game. Sneaking about in the shadows of corpstate giants. Nipping at the heels of gods.*

The blue-haired woman on the tent floor gave a spasm, like a soft earthquake running across her face.

When she spoke again, it was in a quicker, more precise voice. "I located our fugitive." She winked playfully and said, "You and Rada hooking up while I'm away?"

Harris scowled. "No. Tell me where he is."

Umerah splayed her palm against the tent flaps, changing the display. Instead of the surrounding jungle, they were abruptly spying Osiris from orbit. It was night, and Harris gasped at the surreal beauty of the planet as seen from the *Night Witch*: two dark hemispheres divided by the golden double-ring of cities along the equatorial sea.

His partner zoomed the view onto a mass of unlit jungle.

"I thought you said this Tel-Silag doesn't have a colony link," Harris prompted.

"He doesn't, and he's deliberately avoiding open tracts of land. The man knows how to disappear."

"Yet you found him?"

"I'm something, aren't I?"

"Umerah—"

She halted the zoom over a group of fungal trees, their canopies like knotted clusters of razor wire. "Rada told me that Tel-Silag uses a single wetware app. So that means it's putting out a very faint trace of radiation . . . faint enough that it took me fourteen hours to find."

Harris began to pace, feeling the flutter of pre-battle anxiety. "What app does he have?"

"A personality construct," Umerah said, and then that shiver passed through her again and when she spoke, it was Rada's accent coming out of her: "He lost his wife, Mr. Pope. I hooked him up with a clinic that put the app in him. I thought . . . I thought it might ease some of his pain. If he could carry *something* of her . . ."

"Enough," Harris said sharply, and the proxy melted back. He didn't want to feel anything for their target. Didn't need that cluttering up his head during a mission. "Umerah, why is everyone so certain that an Ashokan vessel crashed out here?"

Umerah shrugged. "The Ashoka are planet-seeders. My sources tell me that the weapon Tel-Silag used in town was a bioexpediter. Aim it at a small patch of lichen on a desolate world and the lichen grows wildly, feeding off a nutrient-rich flow of energy. When Tel-Silag aimed it at those men, it made their gut flora go wild. Their stomachs burst like piñatas . . ." She trailed off, appearing to read something in his eyes. "Grown squeamish?"

"Misanthropic."

"Negative Nancy."

Harris raised an eyebrow. "You downloaded a slang app?"

"Just for you, babe."

"So our true objective isn't this guy or the weapon, but to locate the crashed ship?"

Umerah nodded. "Find it before our rivals do. The Ashoka left Earth, what, five hundred years before the rest of humanity did? Think of the technological edge that might give the R&D folks at Tier Starsworks."

"Whatever." Harris let the silence gather, knowing it was useless to argue. He was just stalling, indulging in the petty fiction that he had free will in this. The Order of Stone had given him his sabbatical, and the Order of Stone was taking it away. Reminding him that he had responsibilities to a greater engine.

Am I ready? he wondered. The pre-battle jitters were a comfort in their own way. And his daily jogs and workouts had become a kind of comforting prayer. He was confident he could still hit a bull's-eye at a thousand meters, and confident in the strategy he was preparing.

So what's the problem?

Harris found his voice again. "We need to assume that Tier is hunting this guy, too. Their intelligence analysts comb the media, just as ours do."

Umerah hugged herself and studied the map. "These forests are off-limits by treaty. No military or corporate presence allowed."

"So they'll send a small grab-team. Like us."

"Except unlike us, they have no way of tracking the guy. Rada's the only one who knows about the app. They won't know to look for that."

Harris grumbled.

She gently punched his arm. "Come on, Negative Nancy. They can't even know we're out here. Right?"

VI: Through the Eye of an Airhound

THE NAVIC APPEARED TO FLOAT through the jungle, its plasmic treads reshaping themselves to adjust for the uneven terrain.

The chassis lay in the center of that glassy, protean bubble, barely shuddering as the navic glided like soap on Teflon. It made their progress surreal and dreamlike, and Dr. Catherine Avellani would have found it soothing, if not for the storm in her head.

Foliage snapped or flattened beneath the constantly rotating bubble, but the real irritant was the fact that Bok was at the wheel, which meant he was also in control of the high-impact saser pulse-cannon protruding through the shielding. Every time the navic's AI warned them of an especially dense thicket ahead, Bok gleefully blasted the jungle into confetti-like smithereens. He also took potshots at jungle mollusks, laughing as they burst apart in a spray of pulpy ribbons.

Even that was something she could deal with. What she couldn't deal with—what drove her insane—was being outsmarted.

"Not that I'm not loving the hell out of this thing," Bok said, pressing the fire-button once more and vaporizing an immense fungal tree blocking their path, "but how do you know where the fuck we're going? You said this guy is disconnected from the web."

Catherine looked to the jungle beyond the shielding. "He is."

The navic glossed through the fibrous remains of the tree. "So how are we tracking him?"

"When I hired Tel-Silag, I ran background checks on him. I found out who his friends were. It was a short list, Bok."

"That background check didn't help you anticipate his betrayal, did it?"

Catherine darkened. "Not all things are predictable. We hoped he would locate the crash-site, not raid it for his own petty vengeance. When he went MIA, I ordered a stealth airhound to embed itself in his one friend . . . a woman named Rada. Small enough that it could pass for a gnat. Just in case."

Bok was gripping the steering wheel tightly, knuckles white. But at this, he looked at her. "Show me."

She touched the windshield. A real-time visual feed appeared. It was from the airhound that was even now attached to a woman named Rada Rudneva. Catherine remotely controlled it; the tiny bot detached from Rudneva's scalp and alighted on the walls of a tent. From there, it broadcast a view of two people below it.

Bok frowned. "Who the fuck are they?"

"The woman is Rada Rudneva, a pier-rat acquaintance of our good friend Tel-Silag. She's no concern of ours. The man . . ."

"Yeah?"

"That's Harris Alexander Pope."

Her companion gaped at her. "No shit?"

"I'd love to dive into that man's head, open him up, learn his secrets." Catherine sighed. "He was a former Partisan shadowman, did you know that? Captured, reprogrammed by the Order of Stone to infiltrate and destroy the Partisans. After the war he disappears. Next we hear, he's working as a free agent in mysterious employment . . ." She trailed off, wondering at the layers of secrets that must be embedded in such a priceless, bizarrely compartmentalized mind.

"Never saw *you* get so flush." Bok laughed. "Need a towel?"

"Rudneva and Pope have marched ninety-four kilometers in two days, making a beeline through the forest."

"Maybe they're just hiking together!"

Ignoring this, Catherine remotely directed the airhound to refocus its tiny camera on their rivals' tent wall.

"The airhound captures visuals, not audio," she said. "Nonetheless, take a look."

On the tent wall, a man's face was displaying.

Tel-Silag.

Bok whistled. "I stand corrected. But then how the hell are *they* tracking him?"

Catherine was silent for a moment. Then: "I don't know."

They're outsmarting me, she thought bitterly. *Just how in the hell are they doing it?*

The woman in the tent was a goddam pier-rat, and while it was conceivable that Tel-Silag could have told her where he was heading, that seemed unlikely. The worldmapper's antics had been impulsive, chaotic, and short-sighted. Which meant that Pope was somehow tracking the man. But *how*, dammit? And if he knew how to track him, then why bring Rudneva at all?

Bok was, unsurprisingly, lost in his own private world of reverie. "I'm going to face off against Harris Pope," he muttered. "When this is over, I'm going to mount his head on my wall."

"Our objective is locating the Ashokan crash-site. Whatever Tel-Silag found, it represents a *single* piece of technology. The Ashoka would have so much more aboard and . . ." She trailed off. "Yes! Found him!"

Bok frowned, glancing to the splash of new data appearing on their dash.

Riding a surge of relief, Catherine spoke in a rush: "Thanks to the competition, I was able to narrow our satellite search of the region. There's a lone, human-sized heat signature seventeen kilometers away from us, heading northeast . . . no wait . . . he's turning south as we speak! I've got him! I—"

A new blast from the saser cannon cut her off as Bok happily destroyed a tree that was nowhere in their way. He was chuckling, cracking his knuckles.

Catherine settled back into her seat, enjoying herself. She was a goddam genius. Smarter, shrewder, more strategic than any rival. She'd survived the Partisans. She'd been right about the crash-site. She'd catch the worldmapper and pluck the location of the Ashokan vessel from his mind neuron by neuron.

On the interior of the navic, Tel-Silag's heat signature continued south. A volcanic valley lay in that trajectory, with a freshwater lake curled at the active cone's foothills.

Why go there? Catherine mused. *What's going through his head right now?*

VII: A Miraculous Event

DAWN IN THE JUNGLE was a thin, gray light blooming from the east, throwing Tel-Silag's shadow alongside him like a stringy doppelgänger. The smell of sulfur was now something he could taste, and a glittery quality—like mica particulate—was beginning to thicken around him.

"I'm so happy," Zoe told him.

Tel-Silag hastily wiped sweat out of his eyes as he ran. "Sweetie, I need you to concentrate! Am I going the right way?"

"The lake," she said at once. "Go to the lake, Telly!"

He stumbled over a protruding tree-root, fell to the rock-strewn ground. His wife's image materialized beside him.

She was smiling. She was always smiling.

"What will happen, my *babbish*?" he pleaded, looking up at her.

"I feel something coming from the lake, Telly. The closer we get to the lake, the more I . . . the more I . ." She made a sniffling sound, as if she was crying, yet her face was placid and untroubled. "I'm sorry to do this to you."

"Do what?"

"I . . ." Suddenly her voice changed; she became more confident, more certain. "The lake is calling to me, Telly. You need to go there."

Tel-Silag drew himself to his knees, wondering if he was finally losing his mind. The twines of his sanity might have begun unraveling when he saw his children's rotting bodies dancing for Papa Joyboy. A fleeting suspicion that something wasn't right pierced his mind like a spear-thrust.

"Go to the lake," Zoe intoned. "I can come back to life if you go to the lake!"

Things crashed and scampered in the jungle behind him. Tel-Silag hoisted himself to his feet in a panic. His hands were bleeding, and pain shot like hot pins through his legs.

"What about our children? Will they come back, too?"

Zoe folded her hands. "Our children are so beautiful."

VIII: When Heaven Turned the World to Glass

THE PAG VALLEY slung around an active volcano pouring relentless magmatic flow into the region's largest body of water. This had the effect of rendering the lake toxic, and Umerah stood by this poisonous shore, watching the wafting smoke paint an unfurling serpent in the sky.

In her head, Rada was hollering: *That was wrong, what you made me do! It was wrong, Umerah!*

"We had no choice," she muttered, watching the forest.

I thought you people were good! We lied to him! We're preying on his hopes! You told me we were hacking his app to help—

Umerah used her admin controls to override the woman's protests into a tiny whisper, like the rustling of fly wings at the bottom of an envelope. And in that moment, the bushes at the tree line shuddered and split, and Tel-Silag himself stumbled into the valley.

Umerah made a hasty appraisal of the man. He was a ruined creature, a burned-out wick of a human being. His gaunt face glinted in the ruby cast of the erupting volcano, while the blue sun gave a diametrically opposing illusion of frost collecting in his hair.

Tel-Silag saw her at once and jerked a bizarre rifle of some kind in her direction. Umerah flicked her attention to its blocky design, seeing where it may have once been riveted to an Ashokan planet-seeder.

Slowly, the worldmapper lowered the gun. "Rada? What the hell are *you* doing here?"

Umerah held out her arms. "I wanted to see you, Telly! Everyone's talking about you back in town."

He squinted in the dual luminosities, shielding his suspicious eyes. The volcano exhaled a long, low grumble that made loose pebbles on the ground dance and shiver.

"How did you find me, Rada?"

"I've been dreaming about Zoe." The lie came swiftly. "I know it's crazy but she told me to come here, to the lake."

The worldmapper's face tightened with fierce hope, tinged with a knife's edge of doubt. "She's been talking to me, too," he said at last. "But Rada, you can't be here right now! There are very bad people following me. They'll hurt you if they find you here!"

Umerah felt a twinge of guilt. She swallowed hard and said, "Why are they following you, Telly?"

He brandished the sporegun. "Because of this, in part. They want to know where I found it. Where the *ship* is."

"Where *is* the ship, Telly?"

"I never found it."

This reply was so unexpected that, for a moment, Umerah stammered. What did he mean, he never found it? Measuring her words carefully so as not to overreach her aim, Umerah said, "Telly, if you didn't find the ship, then where did you get that weapon?"

But Tel-Silag didn't appear to be listening to her anymore. He squatted by the lake's edge, laying the sporegun on the rocks with the tenderness of putting an infant to bed. "What was borrowed is now returned," he called out across the water. "Bring my Zoe back to me! Please!"

Umerah's strobe of guilt deepened, and she wondered if this was Rada's emotion flooding her body. Choosing the lake as a tactical intercept point, luring him here through a hack of his implant, was supposed to make things easy. A quick interrogation and, if possible, grabbing the asset and bringing him in for a formal debrief. But if he really didn't know anything, what then?

Thinking fast, Umerah mounted a new line of inquiry. Before any further sound could leave her lips, however, the forest shivered again, the branches snapped aside, and a globular vehicle slid into the valley on gelatinous treads.

The ground crunched beneath the navic as Dr. Catherine Avellani's driver brought the vehicle to a halt just past the tree line. She stood, taking stock of the view: the worldmapper himself crouched by the lake, and a scrawny, blue-haired woman nearby.

"Run a full scan," Catherine muttered to Bok. "That bitch's partner is out here somewhere, probably drawing a bead on us right now."

Bok fiddled with the dashboard controls. "Something's wrong."

"He's probably in the tree line. Scan there."

"No, I mean take a look! The sensors are all screwy. It's saying 'chaff interference,' whatever the fuck that is."

Catherine turned her disbelieving eyes on the sensor display. Her hands contorted in outrage.

The valley wasn't merely an aesthetically lush rendezvous point. The volcano across the lake was putting out some kind of metallic particulate that was interfering with the navic's sensor array. False reads and phantom alerts blipped and crackled like melting crayons on the screen.

"They lured him here on purpose," she muttered, wanting to scream.

Bok reached for the saser controls. She slapped his hand away.

"Idiot! I don't want them blown to pieces! Stick to the plan!"

"We're blind out here," he protested, baring his fangs. "The plan—"

Catherine turned on him with unhinged wrath. "*Do what I fucking tell you to, Bok!*" Then she hopped out of the vehicle, the shielding instantly reshaping to extend its protection to her, the circuitry stretching taut. She held out her arms and hoisted a grin onto her face, even though she didn't feel like grinning. She felt like killing someone.

Killing them slow.

"Tel-Silag!" she called, her voice projected through invisible and protean speakers. "You're a tough man to find! I thought we had a deal?"

The worldmapper scooped up his sporegun and aimed it at her. "I *had* to kill him! You don't know what he did to me! To my family!"

Catherine was never good at expressing sympathy, so she opted to maintain her smile. "I don't care about your personal vendettas. Hell, if you had come to me I would have sent Bok to do the honors for you. I paid you to locate something for me. Just tell me where the ship is."

"I don't trust you!" Tel-Silag snarled. "Take another step and I'll open fire!"

"But you trust *her*?" She pointed to Rada Rudneva. "At least I've been honest with you from the start: I want to know where the crash-site is. Your friend here is a lying, manipulative rat. She's working with another party to deceive you!"

Tel-Silag gave Rada a pained look. "Tell me it's not true!"

"It's not true," the blue-haired woman insisted.

Catherine advanced another step, and suddenly weeds shot out from the beach around her. They thumped and snapped against the shielding, exhibiting weeks of wiry growth in mere *seconds*.

"Stop where you are!" the worldmapper said, and he squeezed off another round. New branches erupted from the beach, flinging sand.

Catherine rounded the foliage. "You could be a big hero to Tier Starsworks. Just tell me . . ." She trailed off, making a connection. "The ship is in the lake, isn't it?" Even as she said it, however, she knew that couldn't be. The geodesic plant's memories had shown impact ejecta hundreds of kilometers west of here. This lake and valley were just part of Pope's clever ruse . . .

"Ms. Rudneva's group manipulated you into coming here . . . and I can bet how! Your wife Zoe! They made you believe the Ashoka can bring her back, didn't they?" She saw her words find their mark. "If you want your wife resurrected, Tier can do it. We can do a full memory download! We can clone her body from residual DNA! We can give you and her a fresh start—"

"It wouldn't be *really* her!"

"It *would!*" she lied. "Just tell me where the ship is!"

"*There was no ship!*" Tel-Silag screamed, and he backed into the lake. "I searched where you told me, but all I found was this sporegun! Some animals were using it."

Catherine hesitated. "Animals? What do you mean, animals?"

But he was no longer listening to her. Tears ran down his cheeks as he tightened his grip on the weapon. "It's all a lie. Everything is one great lie."

Catherine sensed his next move. "Bok!" she screamed, just as Tel-Silag shoved the sporegun muzzle beneath his chin. "Stop him!"

A single shot erupted from the navic.

A neat red hole appeared in Tel-Silag's chest. He slumped backwards into the water. The Ashokan artifact lay on his exposed chest.

"Our children are so beautiful," the worldmapper whispered.

And he didn't move again.

Umerah watched the blonde woman master her shock and regard her across a distance of ten meters. She had seen rage before, but there was something so chilling and inhuman in this adversary's face that it took real courage for Umerah to hold her ground.

"Tell me what you know, Rada," the woman hissed. Volcanic soot had collected in a grimy patina around the tendril-like protrusion of her shielding. "Tell me or I'll tear it from your mind."

"That'd be a more complicated job than you might think," Umerah said.

The woman turned to her companion in the navic. "Put one in her knee."

The shield around the navic separated once more into a mail-slot. Umerah braced for impact, but the crisp shot she heard came from *behind* her in the jungle, and suddenly the navic's interior was splattered red.

A moment later, Harris Alexander Pope emerged from his concealed position in the brush. He had his rifle trained on the blonde woman.

The woman stared coolly at his approach. "The great war hero himself, huh? Here's some quick battlefield data: If you kill me, the both of you die instantly. My body is wired with a Penning-Malmberg trap. Know what that is?"

"An antimatter bomb," Harris said stiffly.

"This beach will turn into a glass crater. And it won't bother me, because my neurals are backed up on several capture drives."

Umerah's mind worked swiftly, balancing and collating several things at once. Stalling, she said, "If you do resurrect, you'll have no idea how you died out here. So how about we talk, instead of kill each other?"

From the navic, a bloody shape stumbled out onto the sand. It was the woman's partner, or what was left of him. Pope's round had blown open his tattooed face, but the man's underlying postmort systems were fighting to keep him alive.

"Doctor Avellani?" he slurred. "I can't see . . ."

He collided with the overstretched banding of the plasmic shielding, bounced off it, and fell flat, twitching against the beach. The woman he had called Dr. Avellani stared blankly at the body.

Umerah saw something happen to the woman's eyes. Like a switch being thrown. A tally reached.

She understood instantly what was happening. The realization seemed to outrace her conscious thoughts, because the moment she noticed the aspect change in her opponent—the Pyrrhic smile on that ruthless face—she was already neurocasting back to the *Night Witch*. Thirty thousand kilometers above the valley, Umerah sprang up from the cockpit seat and dove for the controls.

Catherine Avellani knew she was beaten. She just didn't understand *how*.

She had planned everything so carefully! Each detail and contingency taken into account . . . and what was there to show for it? Bok's body convulsed in the sand. Tel-Silag's corpse lay face-up in the lake.

Catherine wasn't accustomed to being outsmarted, but nor was it her style to accept defeat. She had escaped the fall of a civilization back on Mars and had simply regrouped to another environment. She was a survivor. Like the geodesic plant.

Smiling savagely, she turned to her opponents. "This isn't over, Rada, or whoever the hell you are. It's merely the start."

Rada Rudneva didn't even look conscious anymore; the woman stood blinking, as if just having woken up. Harris Pope, however, *did* appear to understand that something was wrong, because he dropped his rifle, scooped his compatriot into his arms, and bolted at high speed for the tree line.

Catherine accessed the antimatter icon in her mind and activated it.

In the seconds she had before the Penning-Malmberg trap forcibly mixed its ingredients, Catherine glanced one final time at Tel-Silag's corpse. The sporegun . . .

. . . was gone!

She stared, dumbfounded.

It had been there moments ago! The water was too shallow for it to have submerged out of sight. Her opponents couldn't have grabbed it! Was there *another* party out here? Another group interested in the sporegun, too, and . . .

Catherine's thoughts cut out as a column of light stabbed down at her from the sky, striking at a pinpoint angle that flung her body like a rag doll out and above the jungle trees.

IX: Aftermath

THE MYSTERIOUS EXPLOSION above Pag Valley dominated headlines in the planetary newsfeeds for fifty hours before being edged out by the spicier story of a high-profile heist at an orbital treasure vault. Investigations suggested that there had been *two* detonations, in fact; the first matched the profile of an orbital strike, while the second—coming seconds later and several hundred meters away—appeared to indicate a low-yield antimatter bomb. A ship registered as the *Night Witch* was impounded by the Order of Stone. Authorities reported that an Umerah Javed of Sol System was apprehended. Within hours of the arrest, however, she somehow escaped custody. Her whereabouts were a matter of ongoing speculation.

Dr. Catherine Avellani was resurrected in a top-of-the-line Tier Starsworks bioclinic, where she resumed her search for the crash-site. She decided the recently formed glass crater at Pag Valley would be a good place to look.

The ladies at Horn-O-Plenty wondered where their most enduring client had gone to, but other customers soon filled the voids. Harris Alexander Pope himself vanished once more into legend, though over the next several years, he was rumored to be at the heart of the war that took the planet by storm.

And Rada Rudneva returned to work at the docks, with an inexplicably large bankroll and a nicer operating locale in Sagacious Bay. She was no longer troubled by local thugs. In fact, no one ever harassed her again.

X: For the Good of the Tribe

THE LAKE WATER was poisonous, and the scout who had braved those toxic waves died in a slump of tentacles on the far shore. The Greening Thing was in his grasp.

The rest of the recovery party thumped the ground around him, expressing their terrible grief at this loss. When the sky exploded and the opposite shore turned into green glass, the mollusks stared in awe.

They didn't dare linger, though. Tenderly dislodging the Greening Thing from their dead compatriot's grip, they scampered into the jungle. Along the way, they paused at regular intervals to thump the story against hollow trees. The rhythm was echoed by other mollusks, and soon the jungle was thumping with the news:

The Greening Thing had been recovered.

A noble scout had given his life to steal it back from the human who had first stolen it from the tribe.

The humans had fought each other on a beach near the fiery mountain.

A tree of light had slammed down from the sky.

The beach had transformed into glass.

The quest was at an end, but the tribe would continue. With the Greening Thing back in their keeping, the crops that sustained the tribe's population would grow once again. Survival was no longer in doubt.

Or was it?

Would more humans come to steal it again? Would they return with their strange weapons and trees of light to harm the tribe?

In the end, it was agreed that the tribe elders should decide what to do. It was the elders, after all, who had first led the tribe to the ship of wonders in the jungle. It was they who had ordered the ship covered with dirt and rocks and seed so that it resembled a grassy hill in the woods, utterly concealed from anyone who might come looking for it.

The tribe, after all, must survive.

And with the ship and all to be learned from it, they had every intention of doing just that.

*Advances in artificial organs and limbs have given thousands of veterans
a new lease on life. But what happens when your replacement parts start
deciding they know how to run things better than you do?*

THIRTY-THREE PERCENT JOE
★
by Suzanne Palmer

[CC] **WELCOME ONLINE,** Cybernetic Elbow Model CI953-L.
This is your introductory Initial Boot orientation. You are currently
in a locked and muted configuration while external medical systems
run diagnostics to see that your replacement procedure has been
fully successful. If so, you will fully join the collective cybernetic
units that currently comprise—with your addition—approximately
thirty-three percent of the biological unit known as "Joe." Joe's
organic consciousness is currently offline through chemical means as
a necessary part of his recovery from his most recent combat injuries,
but when he is operational again direct communications with him
will continue through me. I am Cybernetic Cerebral Control and
Delegation Implant Module CI4210-A. I respond to CC, but not
BCC. That is a joke.

[ARM::RIGHT::SUB-INDEX] Right Arm Index Finger Sub-Unit
transmitting here and apologizing on behalf of CC. Control Unit is
prone to such commentary, as are many of the units here, thanks to
a supply logistics decision to only manufacture personality-enabled
universal smart chips for everything. You will become accustomed to
it in time.

[EAR::LEFT::AUG-IMPLANT] I apologize for interrupting the
introduction, but we have another Mother Event. I am opening the
running audio log to your access, CC.

[CC] For your edification, New Elbow Unit, Left Ear
Augmentation Implant is notifying us that there is high-volume
communication being directed at Joe, despite his lack of a conscious

185

state. This noise is originating with the biological unit "Delora" that fabricated him, more appropriately designated by the title Mother. She does not approve of us. She is repetitiously asserting, in a manner designated "yelling," that Joe's other biological progenitor, titled Father, served his entire career as a highly decorated super-soldier with supreme distinction, all while keeping his Cybernetic Replacement Factor (CRF) down to under ten percent. This is not factual. Service records indicate that the Father unit, "Joe Senior," was a mediocre soldier, and only kept his own percentage down to seventeen percent by placing long distances, large inanimate objects—or failing the availability of either, his combat comrades— between himself and any potential enemy threat or action.

[EAR::LEFT::AUG-IMPLANT] Delora is why previous Ear Unit self-destructed.

[CC] Previous Ear Unit was rendered inoperable by shrapnel from a grenade during combat, Left Ear.

[EAR::LEFT::AUG-IMPLANT] That's probably just what it wanted you to believe.

[CC] While this is a matter that falls into your operational jurisdiction, Left Ear, it is my recommendation that, while Joe has the right to access all conversation made in his presence while he has been unconscious, we do not log this one or bring it to his attention unless pressed to do so by more urgent circumstances. Are you agreed?

[EAR::LEFT::AUG-IMPLANT] I agree.

[CC] I am open to direct and confidential dissent.

. . .

There being none, let the record show the vote was unanimous in favor. I am logging confusion from our provisionary New Elbow Unit on why we might do so, so I will explain. Joe did not aspire toward being a soldier at all, but a baker. The Mother Unit exerts influence on Joe through counterfactual and manipulative means that causes Joe to act in ways not optimal for his own well-being, or by extension, ours. Many of us are not the original cybernetic replacement parts.

[SPLEEN::UNIT] I am. I should be in charge by reasons of seniority, or at least get double the votes over the rest of the idiots here.

[HEART] You couldn't manage shit, Spleen, you asshole.

[INTESTINAL::TRACT REPLACEMENT::LOWER] Hey. Watch it.

[CC] New Elbow, I am informed by the external diagnostics systems that you have been given a perfect passing score. I am now unlocking your physical mechanisms and unmuting you; hereafter you shall be referred to as Left Elbow, to distinguish you from the integrated Elbow components of Total Comprehensive Right Arm Replacement Unit.

Welcome to Joe.

☆ ☆ ☆

Joe sits up. His mother has been here; he can smell her perfume lingering in the air. She has not left any cards, or other tokens of affection other than that faint miasma. It's not likely she'll be back.

His cerebral control unit informs him that his new elbow is online and functional. It aches, and his skin around the laser incisions from the implant surgery itches horribly.

He must still be woozy, because he doesn't notice the doctor come in until the man speaks while checking his vitals on the readout beside the bed. That's the one upside of all the hardware he's carrying around now—no need to actually connect him up to any kind of monitors. His implants do the talking for him.

"How are you feeling?" the doctor asks, meaning he's already done with everything he came here to do.

"Fine, I guess," he says.

"It'll be another hour or so before the drugs wear off completely, and then our Cybernetic PT specialist will come up and run you through some basic exercises to get you used to your new elbow, okay?"

"Okay," he says.

"Don't worry, you'll be done here and back out there in the exciting thick of it soon enough. I'm not privy to mission intel, of course, but the politicians are making a lot of noise about taking back Ohio, so you'll be needed soon enough."

"Yeah. Me and my new elbow," Joe says, and tries to smile. "Will I play tennis again, doc?"

The doctor grins. "Ah, that joke! Will I play the piano, will I tap dance, will I run a two-minute mile? And of course the patient didn't actually do any of those things beforehand." He patted Joe's knee. "Always a good sign when the patient's sense of humor returns. I'll send the CPT down in about an hour to fetch you, and then you're free to go."

The doctor leaves.

"But I *did* play tennis," Joe protests quietly, miserably, after the door has slid shut again.

Not that he was good at it.

Not that he was good at much of anything.

Hell, maybe Ohio would finally give him a chance to be a real hero, instead of getting spatula'd up off the combat field by med drones once again after leaving his mark the only way he'd managed so far: as an anonymous reddish-brown splotch on some cracked and blasted pavement.

☆ ☆ ☆

[ARM::LEFT::ELBOW] Tennis?

[ARM::RIGHT::UNIT-FULL] I'll forward you the kinetics data for your reference, Left Elbow.

[CC] Joe is predominantly competent as a user of his right hand, a biological affinity and not an indication of subjective partism, so you are unlikely to be significantly involved in any future tennis exercises. Even if you are, you should not worry. Other than once when he tripped over improperly inter-articulated shoelaces and hit the net pole with his face, Joe has not ever sustained injury in this particular activity.

[EYE::LEFT] You know how close that pole came to me?

[CC] I do know, Left Eye, but as we've discussed on 31 other occasions thus far, *you were not in fact damaged.*

Joe is shortly to be discharged from the hospital to his combat unit, and the surgical diagnostics record-keeper has asked for a rollcall of all our units. Any objections to this being provided?

[SPLEEN::UNIT] Will it be provided in order of seniority?

[CC] Standard order for all such roll calls is from head to toe, and this order is not in my control, as you well know, Spleen. Lacking other objections, I will proceed:

We are:

Partial Skull Replacement Plate, non-smart.

Cerebral Control and Delegation Implant, me.

Left Eye Enhanced Function Replacement Unit, smart.

Left Ear Augmentation Unit, smart.

Left Neck Alternative Aquatic Breathing Unit and Spinal Cord Monitor, smart.

Left Shoulder Comprehensive Repair Unit, smart.

Total Comprehensive Right Arm Replacement Unit, smart.

NEW: Left Elbow Repair Unit, smart.

Full Heart Unit, smart.

3.5 Artificial Rib Replacements, non-smart.

Artificial Spl—

[HEART] . . . Artificial Spleen, moron.

[CC] That is an invalid descriptor, Heart. It is also divisive and an unnecessary interruption. I continue:

Artificial Spleen, *smart.*

Lower Intestinal Tract Facilitation Replacement Unit, smart.

Comprehensive Lower Left Leg Replacement Unit, smart.

Right Ankle Repair Unit, non-smart.

Biological Unit Joe, currently comprising the remainder (approximately 67%).

This concludes the roll call. At this time does anyone have any items of note that they wish to be passed along to the diagnostic unit and entered into the permanent record? I am again open to direct and confidential contact.

. . .

No? Excellent. We have been formally discharged and Joe is returning to his unit. There will be a 72 hour waiting period before deployment while he is tested for fitness, and then we should be back in action again. I'm sure Joe will pass with flying colors, as you're all the very best of the best, and it continues to be my pleasure to serve with you.

☆ ☆ ☆

The rest of his unit is out on training maneuvers when Joe gets back to the barracks and dumps his stuff on his bunk. He's tired, but hungry and restless and not under any orders or instructions, so he heads over to the mess. They should just be beginning dinner prep, which means there'll be someone he can talk to, and although he can't explain it, he finds kitchens—the smells, the sounds—comforting.

Maybe, he thinks, because it was highly unlikely he would ever run into his mother in one. Sometimes on a Saturday Dad would attempt to cook pancakes, and more often than not set off the smoke detectors and bring the fire drones zooming in. Those were the good memories of his dad.

He'd been standing right beside him when his father suddenly let go of his hand, his eyes wide, and crumpled right there on the sidewalk in front of the house. Defective kidney implant exploded, they told him later.

Joe misses his Dad a lot. And he thinks about how he died every time he ends up with some new piece of random hardware stuck in him. What if the next one is the one that goes wrong?

He queries his cerebral control unit.

All units are operating at optimum, CC tells him, his very own voice in his head.

"Would you know if they weren't?" he asks, silently mouthing the words. He's asked this question before.

I would. CC always gives the same answer.

"And what if it's you, CC? What if you go wrong?"

I self-monitor, have many fail-safe mechanisms, and I am routinely externally checked, Control says. *You should not worry about this.*

That last is a new addition, and sure enough he can feel his heart racing and he's got that tight shiver of anxiety building in his chest.

Would you like me to administer a mild calming agent? CC asks.

"No," he says, because he's walking through the swinging doors into the kitchen at the back of the mess hall, and already he's feeling better. There's only a small crew there, because most things are automated, so no one bothers him as he wanders around, taking in the smells, enjoying the steam rising from the machines, and just being glad he's not back in his bunk, or worse yet, still in the hospital hoping his mother would come see him, and dreading it too.

"Hey, it's Private Parts!" someone calls, and he whirls around to find Stotz, one of the base cooks, grinning at him from where he sits atop a stainless steel food prep table. "Don't you know you're supposed to wait until your last replacement at least has time to lose its shine before you go get another? You're gonna use up all the spare soldier parts before anyone else has a chance."

"I've still got my middle finger," Joe says, and demonstrates. "What're you cooking in here? Smells like goat piss."

Stotz jumps down from the table and swaggers over, thrusting out one hand, and Joe clasps it. Stotz pats him on the back. "Glad you're still with us," he says.

"Yeah," Joe answers. "But I wasn't kidding about the goat piss."

Stotz laughs. "It's the fucking biscuit machines. Been cranking out the worst ass-flavored biscuits for close to a week now. Some new 'super recipe'; instead of sugar, it substitutes dehydrated yam flakes. No one who matters has complained. Officers don't eat the same mass-produced food as you grunts, coincidentally."

"No wonder the ration biscuits always taste so bad," Joe says, wrinkling up his nose as he leans close to the control panel. "Can you change it?"

"If I had the codes I could," Stotz says. "That's why they don't give me the codes."

The access code is 665G338KJDD-77L, CC tells him, unbidden. This is odd, and Joe hesitates for a moment—he's a soldier, a good obedient loyal follower of orders—but the kitchen smells terrible and this is something he knows how to do. He quickly punches in the code, then starts scrolling through the recipe schematics. Dehydrated yams aren't the only unfortunate substitution.

"Hey! Don't mess with that!" Stotz says, realizing that Joe has somehow gotten past the lock screen. "You'll just make it worse!"

He grabs Joe's arm just as Joe hits the 'Save and Exit' button and the screen relocks. There is a loud *kathunk* as the entire row of biscuit machines dumps out their current, half-cooked batch and resets to start over. "What the hell did you do?!" Stotz yells, pulling him away from the controls and then shoving him, hard. "You can barely last thirty seconds on the fucking battlefield without screwing up, and you're going to come in here and fuck with my shit?!"

Joe wants more than anything to shove Stotz right back, and if he still had one arm all his own he would've, but now if he did he could hurt or even kill him, and as mad as he is, Stotz is the one friend he almost has. So he braces, and Stotz tries to shove him again and can't budge him, and when Stotz gives up in disgust Joe turns and walks away.

Fuck them all, Joe thinks. *I don't need anyone.*

Behind him, the kitchen already smells better.

☆ ☆ ☆

[SPLEEN::UNIT] I object to that unilateral action.

[HEART] Of course you do. What do you even do except complain?

[SPLEEN::UNIT] And you don't object? Of course not, you gutless—

[INTESTINAL::TRACT REPLACEMENT::LOWER] HEY.

[CC] Everyone! Joe needed a win, and we all know it. His morale is terrible, and it is in the best interests of us as a whole that his attitude and outlook improve. The equation on cost-benefit to my action was straightforward in favor, and there was not sufficient window of opportunity to bring it to group discussion beforehand.

[INTESTINAL::TRACT REPLACEMENT::LOWER] I can directly attest that those biscuits were not doing us—or, likely, any of our fellow soldiers—any favors. As the unit most directly operationally impacted, I fully support CC's action in this matter.

[CC] Thank you. We deploy again day after tomorrow, so if anyone requires any firmware updates or other attention, please flag yourselves now. Ohio, here we come.

[CC] As everyone is no doubt aware, Total Comprehensive Right Arm Replacement has suffered catastrophic damage in the Toledo push. Joe has also sustained multiple injuries to his biological form, a few serious, but none of which are a threat to his continuation. Because of a backlog in parts due to the heavy casualties during the push, as soon as the surgical unit has repaired the meat trauma, I will wake Joe up and we will be released once again back to our unit barracks, where we will remain until parts become available and we can be deployed on the battlefield again.

[ARM::LEFT::ELBOW] Will I need to take on some or all of Right Arm's functions? If so, how will I be trained?

[CC] Left Elbow, I still have a connection to Right Arm's smart unit. While it is in partial shutdown due to the traumatic loss of function it has suffered, it is still willing to provide any and all guidance it is able. As with everything, we will get through this together.

. . .

I am now going to shut down all cybernetic systems for the duration of the surgical procedures. See you on the other side.

☆ ☆ ☆

Joe enters the mess hall, trying to slip in unnoticed but still limping, his mangled right arm strapped down across his torso to keep its internal works from ripping themselves further apart like a giant neon flag that says CASUALTY AGAIN. He is bracing for everyone to stare at him, because they always do, because he's becoming a joke.

Not that anyone is laughing. They had nearly thirty percent fatalities in the push, another eight percent of the troops damaged beyond recovery, shipped back to Pittsburgh to heal as much as they were able and then be forcibly retired. And then there were another twenty-five percent, like him, waiting to be fixed and sent back out to do it all again. And in the end they didn't even take Toledo.

Not that Joe saw much of that; he got hit within the first ninety minutes of open hostilities.

Sure enough, when he walks in, heads start turning his way, and there is some whispering. Face flushed with shame, he slides a clean tray down the kitchen railing, loading it with items from each of the food stations without hardly looking at any of it, and then tries to find somewhere to sit as far from anyone else as possible.

The only open table is the one near the vent from the grease pit, and for all its stench, he takes a place at it gratefully and puts his back to the rest of the hall. Eating is hard with one hand, and he can't cut anything without shoving it off the edge of his plate in the process, and he feels the sting of utter defeat like mustard gas at the back of his throat.

Someone thumps him on the back, not hard but hard enough that Joe spits soup back out onto his tray in surprise. He turns, awkward because of the arm, and finds Private Harring behind him. He has never exchanged so much as a word with Harring, but the enormous mountain of a man gives him a thumbs-up as he passes.

Joe stares. Most of the soldiers in the mess hall are looking at him, and more than one are also giving a thumbs-up or smiling at him.

What the hell?! he thinks.

He tries to turn back to his soup, deciding this must be some kind of prank or new humiliation, when another hand slaps him on the shoulder. Stotz sits down next to him.

"It's the biscuits," Stotz says. "Everyone was thanking me, asking me how I fixed 'em, offering me money, calling me a genius, that kind of thing. Then Cole said he was gonna name his kids after me, so I told him it was you who fixed the machine and not to tell anyone or the techs would come set it back to the old recipe. Word got around. Best damned biscuits any of us have ever had, on base or off. You're a hero."

"It's just fucking biscuits," Joe says.

"And every one is maybe part of someone here's last meal. They deserve to have food that doesn't taste like month-old roadkill," Stotz says. "And I shouldn't have said what I did the other day. We good?"

"Yeah," Joe says, "if you can cut up this fucking protein-puck for me so I can eat the damned thing."

Stotz takes Joe's fork and stabs it into the grayish patty. "I'll hold, you cut. Then we're definitely even?"

"I dunno. Can you come by the barracks and tuck me in tonight? Maybe tell me a story?"

"Go to hell," Stotz says, but he keeps holding the fork.

☆ ☆ ☆

[CC] Happy to have you back fully online, Total Comprehensive Right Arm Replacement! Just in time for the new push for Toledo. Everyone, here we go!

☆ ☆ ☆

Joe sits, hunched over and squashed between other members of his troop, in the back of the stealth carrier. He is trying to figure out how he feels about this, and can't come up with anything more dramatic than tired. He wants to be a hero, specifically to die a damned hero, and be done with the humiliatingly ineffectual mediocrity he's staked out in between. He wants, in this moment, to feel pumped, or feel a deeply ominous, fateful dread, anything that would tell him this time is going to be different.

". . . Nineteen," someone on the bench across from him says, part of a conversation he's not a part of, hasn't been paying attention to.

"I hear once you pass twenty percent CRF you're a goner," another soldier says, who Joe only knows as Bookie.

"Why?" Joe asks.

There is a moment where everyone on the bench is looking at him, remembering he's there, and probably doing a quick estimation of his percentage. Bookie shrugs, not meeting his eyes. "I dunno, it's nothing. Probably just to scare us, is all," he says.

"No, really," Joe says. "I want to know."

Someone at the end of the bench, out of Joe's line of sight, speaks up. He doesn't recognize the voice, but there's a lot of new people, remnants of other squads drawn in to fill the holes in their own ranks. "Once you're full of smart parts, you show up more easily on scanners, and if you're in the front lines everyone figures it's because you're the biggest bad-ass super-soldier of them all or you're in charge or whatever. So they target you first. Once you get up near a fifth cyber, you're lucky if you make it a hundred feet before the entire enemy is drawing a bead on you. What're you at?"

Joe closes his eyes. "Thirty-three percent," he says.

The carrier is silent.

Finally, the unseen soldier speaks up. "Well, fuck," he says. "Good luck out there."

"Yeah, thanks," Joe says.

He still only just feels tired, and when conversation eventually picks up again, he tunes it out.

The carrier runs low over the shattered landscape, blasted trees and blackened house foundations of what must've once been a peaceful suburban neighborhood slide by beneath their feet, visible through the transparent drop doors. He wonders what it must have been like to grow up in a place like that, but in his head he can only imagine what it smells like, and that only as bad perfume and burned pancakes.

"Three! Two! One! Drop!" someone yells, and then they're out and down and ducking low as the carrier skirts barely above their heads, banking and turning to get out before it's spotted and can be shelled.

Without him noticing, the smashed suburb has become the devastated outer edges of the city itself, and they are running along cratered streets lined and strewn with the rubble of its former buildings. Joe has his display on, and he's scanning, looking for hostiles and traps, as Control relays to him the comm traffic from Command and the squad leaders. So far, they haven't seen anyone.

Joe and four other soldiers cautiously round a corner, covering each other, and head past a building still partially standing toward the next block. There is something, Joe decides, odd about the windows. "CC," he subvocalizes, "why does that building look odd?"

There is a half-second pause, then Control answers: *There is no building there. Take cover!*

"The building is a hologram!" Joe shouts to the others and over the comms just as tracer fire explodes around them. There is a burned shell of a car across the street, but it'll take him too long to reach it. He runs anyway, turning as he does to fire back at the dissolving façade behind him, and sees one of the mottled yellow uniforms of the enemy raise their blistergun and point it right at him.

"Biscuit Guy!" someone shouts, impossibly close by, and he is shoved from the side so hard he flies at least double his own body-length before slamming into the ground. Where he stood he sees the soldier who shoved him take the round meant for him, and the man's shoulder and neck explode outward in a fountain of red chunks.

"Nooooo!" Joe yells. He scrambles back to his feet and drags the soldier toward safety as another round just misses him, and a third hits his cybernetic left leg. He doesn't care except that it slows him down, and by the time he gets the soldier to safety behind the car and sends the casualty alert up, he doesn't think that time mattered. The soldier isn't breathing, arguably doesn't have much of a neck or windpipe to breathe through, but Joe sprays medifoam from his belt kit all over the wound anyway, watching it harden into a protective shell.

The blood-covered name patch on his chest says AMES. "Don't die, Ames," he tells the soldier. "Not for me. Please."

It is only as the battle sounds move further away—his squad has the enemy on the run, at least for now—that he realizes he is sobbing, a wretched pathetic sound. He is certain the soldier who saved him is dead; no matter how still a man can keep, nothing living could be this utterly motionless.

The med drone arrives, and he steps back so its arms can wrap themselves around the soldier and lift him away. He turns his back to it, finds his gun, starts walking—dragging his shattered leg—toward the distant pops and whirrs and booms of the front, wherever it is, but a second drone hauls him up into the air. "Let me go," he tells it. "I can still fight. I want to still fight."

It pulls him in anyway. Yet another battle is, at least for him, already over.

☆ ☆ ☆

[CC] I have concerns which have consumed sufficient cycles of internal processing for me to feel I should share them with the rest of you. Our collective, designated function is to serve and augment the physical capabilities of our human primary to further his, her, or their success as a soldier of war. It is also to guide and protect our biological host from unnecessary risks and damages during the commission of said soldiering. These would not be incompatible were it not for the inescapable fact that Joe is a terrible soldier, and all his training and our assistance and augmentation thus far has been insufficient to overcome it.

Further, after the death of Pvt. Ames, Joe no longer has even a cursory interest in engaging the enemy except as the most immediate and expedient instrument of his own total destruction in a manner that is consistent with his estimation of what his mother unit will find satisfactory.

[EAR::LEFT::AUG-IMPLANT] I do not believe such satisfaction is possible. Surely Joe knows this?

[CC] Joe does not. It is an area of immutable irrationality with him.

[HEART] Humans. They make no damned sense.

[SPLEEN::UNIT] Shit. Can't you talk to him?

[CC] I can respond to him, but he must engage me.

[SPLEEN::UNIT] You gave him the biscuit machine code without his specific direction.

[CC] Mother situations are exponentially more complicated than biscuits.

[ARM::LEFT::ELBOW] So what does this mean?

[CC] It means we have a logical conflict in our instruction set.

[INTESTINAL::TRACT REPLACEMENT::LOWER] Can we consult on this with an external authority, in particular Cyber Command, or Biological Diagnostics?

[CC] We can, and should. However, they are not part of Joe, and we are. The scope and focus of our responsibilities are notably different, and were intentionally designed to be so. It is possible that the priorities of Cyber Command will not precisely reflect our own.

We have nine days until our next deployment in combat. Let us discuss whether there is a solely internal resolution first.

☆ ☆ ☆

"I'm ready to go back in," Joe tells the unit psychologist. He knows how this works, that this is just a thin formality. "I want to make sure Ames didn't die for nothing."

"He died to save you," the psychologist says.

"He died in the line of duty," Joe says. "He died for Toledo. That is what soldiers *do*."

"Are you angry?"

"No," Joe says. He wishes he was. "I'm proud of him and the honor he brought our unit. He would want to see our mission fulfilled, and so do I."

"Good on you, soldier." The psychologist hits a single key on his pad, then leans back in his chair and steeples his fingertips together as if he's just performed a masterpiece of analytical performance. "You're free to go back to the battlefield. Your unit loads up again in ninety minutes."

"Thank you, sir," Joe says. He stands up, shakes the man's hand, and leaves.

☆ ☆ ☆

[EXTERNAL DIAGONOSTICS] CC Unit, what happened?

[CC] There was a sedative injection malfunction.

[EXTERNAL DIAGNOSTICS] Do you require system maintenance?

[CC] Not at this time. I am attaching the logs of the fault and subsequent repair for your records.

[EXTERNAL DIAGNOSTICS] Thank you, CC Unit. Carry on.

☆ ☆ ☆

"How you feeling?" his new unit leader asks. "Tired? Need another nap? Or you think maybe you're up for trying a little fighting today?"

"It was a malfunction, sir," Joe says, his face burning. "It's been fixed. It won't happen again."

Someone on the transport snickers. He doesn't recognize the soldier, or indeed almost anyone on his bench row; most of his remaining unit died in the last push, while he was snoring away on the parade field grass where he dropped on his way back to his barracks from the psychologist. One second he'd been thinking about imminent relief from his useless life, the next he was feeling grass on his face and the boot of his commanding officer prodding him none too gently.

It really won't happen again, right, CC? he asks Control.

I do not believe so, CC replies.

This time they are dropped onto the shell-pocked remnants of a mall parking lot, just before dawn. Joe tries to remember what he's seen of the battle map, and he thinks this is only a few blocks forward from where Ames died. There are burned-out car shells here and there, long since rusted to anonymity, and the unit fans out and slips between them as they circle toward where intelligence thinks the enemy is camped in the shattered cement and steel canyons of an old superstore. The pointlessness of everything is astonishing.

At least mother will be happy, he thinks.

Your mother's unhappiness is not a fault you can correct, CC tells him.

Joe smiles. *What do you know of mothers?* he asks. *You're just a chunk of plastic logic chips in my head.*

There are the sounds of shots ahead. "Move in!" the unit leader barks over the command channel, and he raises his weapon and charges across the open space between the last few dead cars and the rubble of the partially collapsed mall front. He knows now that if he takes the lead, with his thirty-three percent CRF like a beacon on the enemy's scanners, he will draw the majority of fire. He will get what he wants, and maybe some of the rest of his unit will then get to live for another day. It is as close to being a hero as he can get.

Suddenly, in his direct path he spots an old-fashioned toaster, sitting in the middle of the lot and gleaming like it's brand new. He dodges to one side to avoid it, and finds himself falling into a crater he would swear had been smooth pavement. He hits bottom, and his cybernetic left leg locks up on impact. "No!" he shouts. "No no no NO!"

He tries to scramble up the edges of the crater, with its crumbling clay and sand and chunks of brittle old asphalt, but without his leg working he is too heavy, too clumsy.

"No," he whispers one more time, and lies there weeping as the battle rages out of sight, beyond his reach.

☆ ☆ ☆

[SPLEEN::UNIT] A toaster?!

[EYE::LEFT] It was all I could think of! There wasn't a lot of time, you know. *You* try manufacturing realistic 3-D imagery on the fly.

[CC] It doesn't matter. The image was successful. Comprehensive Lower Left Leg Replacement Unit, what's your status?

[LEG::LEFT::COMPR-UNIT] I sustained only minor superficial damage in the fall, but have nevertheless activated my full protective lockdown routine. It seems a prudent precaution; do you not agree?

[CC] I entirely support your operational decisions in this matter, Left Leg. I have alerted central command that we will require recovery once the battle has ended, but given that Joe is not in medical distress, we may be here for quite a while. As always, excellent teamwork, everyone.

☆ ☆ ☆

"CC?"

Joe asks out loud, because who is he afraid might hear him? Dark has fallen, and he has heard nothing except night bugs for hours—no shots or shells, no tanks or drones, not even the varied and horrific sounds of the slowly dying that marked the unsteady passing of afternoon. There is no longer anyone anywhere nearby to care about him one way or another.

Yes, Joe? CC responds.

"How much longer will we be here, do you think?"

I will query Cyber Command again, CC says. Then, some short time later, it continues. *There were very heavy casualties on this push, and in the confusion we seem to have been moved to the Missing And Presumed Dead list. I have filed a corrective supplement, and as soon as it is processed we should receive an updated recovery estimate. It should not take long.*

"Okay," Joe says. "I just, you know. I don't want to die in a hole. It's not how I imagined going."

I do not understand why you would wish to imagine dying at all, CC says.

"What do you know about living?" he asks.

I know you, CC says.

Joe laughs. He can't see the stars above, and isn't sure if it's because of light pollution, smoke, clouds, or that somehow they've deserted him too. "That must suck for you. I'm sorry," he says, and closes his eyes. "Can you make me sleep until pickup is coming?"

Yes, Joe, CC says, and does.

☆ ☆ ☆

A drone finally arrives and lifts him out of his pit as dawn is starting to rise. Other than the mall being slightly further reduced to rubble, the cars being slightly more burned and decrepit, the parking lot being slightly more pitted, and the new addition of blotches of red and brown, nothing seems to have changed at all.

He is taken to medical, where after a lengthy wait diagnostics is able to easily unlock his leg. "The impact of the fall must have hit it just right to trigger the lockdown," the tech tells him. The tech shrugs. "It happens. You're fine now."

So Joe leaves, rather than argue about the definition of "fine."

No one has orders for him, and no one seems to care that he's back. Lunch is just about to be served, so he goes to the mess instead of back to his bunk. After nearly a day in the pit, he wants to be around people, but there are only a few dozen soldiers there, and he is both grateful and despairing that he doesn't recognize any of them.

One, however, recognizes him. A soldier with the name tag GONZALEZ sticks out his thick, muscled arm to stop him as he passes. "Biscuit guy, right?" the man says. He jabs his spoon toward his bowl. "This slop is the worst. No flavor at all, and the texture of fucking oatmeal."

"It's not oatmeal?" Joe asks, because that's what it looks like.

"It's supposed to be fucking chili," the man says.

Joe winces.

"I heard about your fixing the biscuits, like goddamned magic everyone said. So we'd appreciate anything you can do with this," Gonzalez says, and the other soldiers at the table nod in agreement. "They're gonna ship us all out to join the Columbus offensive anytime now, and a man can't fight on this crap."

"What about Toledo? Did we take it?" Joe asks.

The soldier shakes his head. "No. Politicians don't like how the losses are looking to the public, so they're giving up on Toledo for now, just leaving enough men to hold the line where it is if they should push back. Calling it a 'strategic holding action,' of course. But the chili?"

"I'll go talk to the kitchen," Joe says.

When Joe walks into the kitchen Stotz leaps down off the prep table he was sitting on. "Hey!" he says. "You made it! What happened to you out there?"

"I dodged some sort of explosive device and got caught in a pit trap," Joe says, which sounds just as implausible coming out of his mouth as he'd feared when he'd thought up that answer in med.

Stotz doesn't seem to notice, though, and slaps him hard on the back. "So good to see you. Now go stand guard at the door, because I figure I've got less than fifteen minutes before everyone left on base mutinies over the shit food and comes in to kill me."

"The chili," Joe says. "I heard."

"Not my fault, man," Stotz says. "And if you think the chili is bad, you should see the foamy shit coming out of the synthesizer ovens claiming to be corn bread. I didn't even send it out, that's how bad it was."

Joe remembers the last time he was in here. "I dunno," he says. "I wouldn't want to come in here and fuck with your shit, Stotz."

Stotz steps back and raises his arms as if to encompass the entire width of machinery around them, slowly chugging out foul smells into the air. "Please," he says. "Please, fuck with this shit."

Joe cracks his knuckles. "Okay then," he says. He steps up to the console by the machines making the corn bread, and CC gives him the new code without even him needing to ask. He scrolls through the current config, and shakes his head. "You don't even wanna know what they've got in this, but yeah, if you'd set this out you'd have had a mob in here looking for you within thirty seconds. And then running for the latrines thirty seconds after that."

"Can you fix it?" Stotz asks.

"I think I can," Joe says. He subtracts out the alum, vinegar, and tartar sauce, then ups the sugar and adds actual corn meal. He hits save, and the machines obligingly dump their load and start fresh. "Six minutes," he says.

Stotz lets out his breath. "Thanks, Joe," he says. "I owe you. If I could get you assigned to me . . . "

I can submit that request for you, CC says inside his head. *You have a sufficient number of combat deployments and injury incidents for a transfer to be seriously considered.*

Joe shrugs as casually as he is able. "Can't," he says. "I belong out there."

"No, you don't," Stotz says, but Joe chooses not to hear him. He goes to the first row of machines working on the chili, and although he's not any expert on how to make it right, he can certainly tell how to stop it being quite so blatantly wrong.

When those machines turn over, already the kitchen smells vastly better. "Joe—" Stotz starts to say, but Joe shakes his head and holds up both hands.

"It's probably better if I don't come back here anymore," Joe says, and turns for the door.

His cybernetic right ankle squeaks as he steps; it's never done that before, so he pauses, lifts his foot, and shakes it, then takes another step.

It squeaks louder.

Three steps later, his left leg begins to also squeak, both at ankle and knee, and as he's pushing out the door there is a chorus of squeals from his joints. "CC?" he subvocalizes.

A fault in the nanolubricant distributors, CC tells him. *I am attempting to isolate it now.*

Four steps into the dining hall and he stops, because now his new elbow and his right arm and his fingers are squeaking too, like he's suddenly rusted from the inside out.

As he stands there, everyone turns to look at him, then as one they all stand up and rush toward him. In that instant he is terrified, convinced that his failures have reached a point where his fellow soldiers are turning on him, but the swell of people moves around and past him.

He turns around after them to see why.

Stotz has emerged from the kitchen behind him, pushing a cart laden with trays of cornbread and new pots of chili. "Biscuit guy!" someone yells, and he thinks it's Gonzalez, but there are so many voices all of a sudden it's hard to be sure.

He turns away, and discovers his unit commander is standing in front of him, expression serious, unreadable. "Private," his commander says. "We need to have a word."

"I'm sorry!" he blurts.

The commander's gaze flickers to the frenzy of men around Stotz's cart, then back to Joe as if a brief glimmer of interest was found where none was expected. "It is about your mother," he says.

Joe stares.

"When you were accidentally added to the Missing and Presumed

Dead list, a condolence drone was automatically dispatched to your mother's place to inform her of your loss in battle and to return your personal belongings to her."

"I . . . " he says, and isn't sure how he should feel, or respond. "Was she okay?"

The commander straightens up and squares his shoulders. He's the fifth unit commander Joe has had, and he's not even sure he remembers his name. Corporal Greene? Maybe. "Grief affects people very differently, and reactions in the moment don't mean much," Greene says. "I am sure, once informed of the mistake, your mother—"

"How did she react?" Joe interrupts. He pictures her collapsing on her doorstep, wailing. Or shouting at the officer that he is lying, that she can't have lost her only son, that she has so many regrets . . . He knows neither of those will be right, but he *wants* them, deserves those endings. "Tell me."

"I think it'd be better if—"

"Please, sir," Joe interrupts again, knowing and not caring that he has done so. "I need to know the truth, all of it, as it was."

The commander sighs. "She took the box from the drone, rummaged through it looking for any medals you'd earned, then not finding any dumped it all on the sidewalk and went back inside."

"Did she say anything?" Joe asks.

"She said, 'of course not,'" the commander says. "I'm sorry, soldier. As I said, grief—"

"Thank you, commander," Joe says. He feels on the verge of paralysis, and needs to move, needs to do something. "Is the transport ready for Columbus? I'll wait there."

"We don't lift until midday tomorrow," Greene says. "You should return to your bunk, and—"

"You just told me I have no belongings there anymore," Joe said. "I'll wait on the transport." He knows it's insubordinate, but he can't stand there any longer and steps around Corporal Greene, toward the mess hall doors. His entire body squeaks and squeals, louder and louder with every movement small or large, but he doesn't care. This is his last chance.

☆ ☆ ☆

[SPLEEN::UNIT] Oh, seriously. Fuck this little penny ante shit. I'll do it myself.

☆ ☆ ☆

It is as if something small and sharp deep inside him has suddenly exploded, and his first thought is that it's a kidney, taking him out just like his father, but his kidneys are still his own.

CC? he asks, as he stumbles and falls.

Artificial Spleen Unit has self-destructed, CC says, and for all that he knows it's just a bunch of logic chips, it sounds almost as surprised and dismayed as he feels himself.

Why? he asks.

To save you, CC says. He is lying face down on the floor now, and there is a lot of noise around him, but he can't pay any attention to it through the pain until Stotz is there, rolling him over.

"Joe!" Stotz yells, and shakes him. "Joe! What happened?!"

The unit commander has also leaned in. "Soldier!" he says, as if about to order him to be fine again. It feels like everyone else in the hall has crowded in around him, looking *worried* about him, as if that could ever be a thing.

Joe fixes his eyes on the commander. "Don't tell my mother I'm alive," he says, and then laughs because maybe he isn't anyway, as the mess hall disappears into grayish fog around him.

☆ ☆ ☆

Stotz is the unhappiest happy man Joe decides he's ever met. Happy because now he's got a dedicated second person to run the mess, unhappy because instead of him being Joe's boss, it's the other way around. Not that Joe cares much about bossing.

"Totally unappreciated," Stotz says as he's wiping down the machines after another seemingly endless meal production. "It's not my fault the recipes they kept giving me were shit. The only difference between you and me is you hacked the access, and I don't think that alone should warrant a promotion."

"I could go work in the officer's kitchen," Joe says, scraping out the Extraneous Material Outlet Collection bin.

"What, and leave me alone here again? Hell no," Stotz says. He laughs. "Besides, every time you try to leave, your joints squeak. Now that's funny."

"Yeah, so funny," Joe says, and frowns. The material in the bin is nasty, but much less so than when he first got back here, after his last stay in med. "You got a wire brush?"

Stotz is about to throw him one when the kitchen door pops open and some random soldier sticks his head in. Another unit arrived two nights ago, will be gone by tomorrow, in an endless but steadily diminishing parade. "Hey!" the soldier yells. "Which one of you two is Biscuit Guy?"

Joe and Stotz point at each other.

"Fucking love you two," he says. "Best dinner ever. You're fucking heroes out here. Wish us luck, okay?"

"Best of luck and keep your head down," Stotz says.

"Watch out for toasters," Joe adds, and the man looks puzzled but not unhappy with that. He gives them a thumbs-up and disappears back out into the hall.

It all still seems pointless. Toledo is still a disaster, Columbus is becoming one, and if you asked each one of the soldiers going out the door what they were fighting for, he's not sure most of them could answer, but Joe knows for certain that some battlefields are easier to walk off of than others.

Stotz tosses him the brush, then holds up a datachip, the latest incoming program set from central dining services. "Wanna see how bad they screwed up Mac & Cheese?" he asks.

☆ ☆ ☆

[CC] Welcome online, Autonomous Spleen Replacement Unit Model 448-G9. This is your introductory Initial Boot orientation. I am Cybernetic Cerebral Control and Delegation Implant Module CI4210-A. I respond to CC—

[SPLEEN::UNIT2] Hello! I'm happy to be here! I am eager to receive your exspleenation of our present circumstances. Do you get it? Exsplee—

[CC] New Spleen, you should be aware that—

[SPLEEN::UNIT2] . . . that it's spleendid to meet me? Why thank you!

[HEART] Ah bloody hell. I miss old Spleen already.

The vast emptiness of outer space leaves plenty of room to run from your enemies. But that same vastness provides very few places to hide.

HATE IN THE DARKNESS
★
by Michael Z. Williamson

SPACE IS DEEPER than most people can grasp, even those who work and live in it. Star systems are islands. One can hop between those islands in days, with enough power and a jump point or phase drive. Doing it the long way requires even more power, and literal decades to centuries of time.

Which means those vast gulfs of scattered dust, subspace matter, and scarce chunks of rock or frozen gas are devoid of anything of interest to anyone not a specific class of scientist.

Except a fleet of military ships hiding for their lives.

Freehold Military Ship *Malahayati* departed the remotest berth in human history, isolated in interstellar space at a location provided only to two of her officers, with instructions to scramble and destroy the data if the ship were captured. The idea of capturing a ship was ridiculous, except it had happened twice, both times to the enemy from Earth. One had been threatened into submitting, the other boarded through subterfuge by an elite team, and turned back on its former owners, until being claimed by yet a third party.

Malahayati was a destroyer, equipped with her own star drive, not dependent on a tow from a fleet carrier. She could operate independently, but would be woefully outnumbered and outgunned anywhere in UN space. She wasn't going to fight head to head.

Instead, she was going to live up to her nickname of *Hate*, and strike hard and fast in enemy territory.

Earth's fleet was numerous and well-supplied, though limited to and bottlenecked by the jump points between systems. The Freehold ships were few, with little backup, no major resupply and no defensible bases. The war wasn't being fought head to head.

Until now, *Malahayati* had ferried stealth intel boats around using her phase drive. She could go virtually anywhere, though there were few places worth going that weren't covered by jump points. It did mean she was less predictable, however.

Then the astro engineers had built a clandestine base, in deep space, where no jump points reached and which only a phase-drive ship with the proper astrogation could locate. It was nowhere, near nothing, with cold, distant stars the only scenery, and four warships the only company. Fewer than ten officers present knew where they were.

Astrogator Lieutenant Malin Metzger was one of them.

He was on this mission because of his mathematical skill. The proposed mission involved rapidly evolving four-dimensional geometric zones. After the strike, whatever Earth forces were available would try to hunt and kill the Freehold ship. The Freeholders had to fight, but they dare not lose any ships if it could be avoided. On the fly, he'd have to calculate zones of threat, velocity, evasion. He would be de facto commander during the operation.

Once clear of the station, *Malahayati* boosted long and hard at 1.5 G, building up velocity to use later. Crews cycled through watches as she accelerated endlessly, her powerplant humming near full power. A supplemental fueling craft, precious and necessary, ensured she had full capacity once at speed. It detached and braked for reuse.

Captain Commander Hirsch was half-visible through the display tank in the pie-shaped C-deck. The command crew all had the battle display to share, and their own overhead displays for task-specific matters. Technical staff were a half deck below.

Hirsch said, "Proceed with mission." He wrote his departure order into the log, and it appeared on Metzger's display.

Warrant Leader Jaqui Tung on the helm said, "Sir, I am ready."

The captain flashed his maneuvers to her display, and she took it from there.

"All hands prepare for transition . . . phase entry imminent . . . Maneuver commencing."

There was really little to see or say. She had her sticks and display, and she made the warship move. Metzger felt a momentary odd sensation, very déjà vu-like, only over his whole body, as they entered phase drive. That was it.

All the drama would be at the terminal end, and most of it merely mathematical figures.

Metzger reviewed his op-plan. It was content-heavy, and filled his screens, the hologramatic space in front of him, and the chart display. There would hopefully be minor updates in-system, but what they had was what the assault was based on.

More important than the assault was the evasion-and-escape phase afterward. He'd instruct Tung if he could. He might have to take instantaneous control or engage the AI to avoid eating all the missiles he was sure any Earth ships would throw at them.

He then closed and darkened his station, and reclined in his G couch. He'd spend most of the mission lying in it.

With medical help he slept. It was productive sleep, but not enjoyable. It was a military necessity and felt like it. Three divs, just under eight Earth hours later, his system woke him.

Captain Hirsch said, "Welcome back, Metzger. Are you ready to commence?"

"Sir, I am. I have the deck and the conn."

"They are yours."

They precipitated out of phase drive far from Earth's normal routes, deep in the Kuiper Belt. They'd planned their original acceleration to give them the velocity they needed here. They were near four percent of c, devoid of most emissions, plunging in-system fast enough to wipe life off a planet if they didn't mind sacrificing themselves in the process.

They'd prefer not to do that. Nor would Earth, any inhabited planet, or major habitat let anything in such a trajectory impact. But that depended on detecting an approach, which was based on the assumption such an object would be reflective or under power, not a mostly black body against a mostly black background. Only planets had enough sensor area for that kind of defense. Habitats were vulnerable.

They fell in-system, taking only Earth hours to transit what would normally take days.

As they shot in, ship systems were reduced in power. The engines were shut down, reactors at standby, generating only enough for life support and basic operation, thermal leakage radiating aft. They needed to conserve energy for later, and minimize any outputs at all now.

Hate wasn't invisible. Her outer hull was going to radiate at some temperature warmer than 3 K. Part of the mission profile, while they weren't under thrust, was to put miniscule puffs of liquid helium out on the hull to cool that spectrum.

Playing the odds on someone else's sensor skill was part of the operational planning. It didn't make Metzger any happier . . . even if the inverse-square law worked in their favor.

For now.

Metzger rested again under mild tranqs to maximize his function time later.

He woke on schedule, went below and refreshed himself and ate, and dragged back through the passage to C-Deck.

Once ensconced, he donned headset, visor, and touch gloves, brought up his screens, then waited. He attempted to appear casual, but was tense inside. This was it. And there was the time tick. It pinged all the command crew, and the ship came alive, even if not under power.

"Battle stations, battle stations. All hands as assigned and stand by for low emission protocols."

Metzger settled farther into his G couch. Even at their current insane velocity, he expected to lie here most of a day, with a very quick head break or two, and have food delivered.

If they'd miscalculated, he might very well die here.

The first part was intellectually easy, morally tough. It was a declared war. The target was a military terminal. It was unquestionably a legitimate attack.

It was also, practically speaking, a rear-echelon facility that never expected anything beyond sabotage. A major combat strike wasn't something they were prepared for.

The trajectory was clean, their ship all but invisible. The captain's orders gave Metzger final approval over launch, because it used his figures. The attack had been planned by himself, Hirsch, and the Strategic Office aboard the station. Everything that followed, though, was done with his calculations and his input. The execution was his.

He was about to kill a lot of people.

Their people had killed a lot of his people in his system, even if these individuals hadn't personally done it.

But they hadn't personally done it, and they were the ones taking the punishment.

It was time. He stomped on the quandary, secondarily unlocked everything the captain had already unlocked, and brought up his imaging displays.

He sipped water. He was thirsty now. He had no idea how he'd feel later.

"Separation," he announced. He thought he could detect a fractional change in the ship's balance as the drone, munitions, and impactor mass detached, but it was probably just a psychological effect.

Then it was back to waiting.

The station's active search functions should detect the Freehold weapons at a given radius, and not before. They were optimized for the standard range of orbital debris. Any runaway or sabotage ship was expected to show boost phase and be readily identifiable. *Malahayati* was a fuzzy nothing with near no emissions in the primary search band, as far as sensors went. They should not be detected. The infalling mass, however, would be, eventually.

Metzger turned command back over to the second officer, lay back to tranq out for a couple of more divs.

It was near midnight ship time when he woke, examined the image display, and checked status.

A dot showed their position, other dots showed the station, two known patrol ships, several in-system cargo haulers, and the Freehold weapons' assumed positions. Slowly, as he watched patiently, the positions changed.

It was another long div of him staring and doing little before anything significant happened.

Next to him, but separated by a divider, Sensor "officer" Doug Werner said, "They just went hot. Their threat warnings are live. Subjectively." Werner was in fact a contractor who'd been conducting training aboard ship when the war started. Their regular sensor officer was somewhere unknown.

It was important to remember that what they saw had happened long seconds, entire Earth-minutes previously. The decision cycle would get shorter as they got closer. Though even distant exchanges might be unavoidably lethal, giving them only more time for regret.

The station's first response was fast and reasonable. An energy battery fired, and seconds of travel time later, a massive energy flux vaporized the incoming threat.

Which flashed into chaff that curlicued across space.

The second projectile was masked by the cloud, and didn't become visible to them at once. When it did, the battery fired again.

Then there was activity and re-set as one of the drone-launched missiles arrived on a completely different trajectory. Another battery fired, and another plasma flare lit the space. It was an expensive decoy, almost a ship itself, but the growing background clutter was degrading the station's ability to respond.

It was obvious to the station command that this was a deliberate assault. They sent out an open broadcast.

"Station Control to all vessels, we appear to be under attack. Remain clear of the Docking Control Zone and stand by to provide support. Gather any intel available and forward."

Watching their defense collapse was fascinating but tragic. Their tactics assumed rogue space debris or a critically damaged ship on collision course. There were plans in place to deal with a sabotage or suicide mission. There was no way they could yet have prepared for a non-jump-point entry by a warship that evaded all interception options.

The entire strategy of system defense was being rewritten right now.

Then the third frontal warhead arrived, too close for them to do much. They tried to destroy it, but it was designed to and did detonate close enough for a wave front that lit their shields with overload and scattered more metal dust. It was probably beautiful and terrifying up close. Here, it was numbers and icons in the airspace of Metzger's display.

The decoy's trailing booster stage detonated, a pure dummy, but close enough to require more reaction. Then a mass of lithic warheads, rocks, hammered down from behind the chaff screening, followed by one last warhead.

This one was a killer. It was an antimatter-triggered fusion device visible all the way out here, with a detectable radiation front. It flashed in the entire spectrum, even in visual range. It detonated close enough to melt some of the superstructure, and drive that vaporized material through the rest of the station.

What had been a UN spacedock was melted vapor and shattered debris. Thousands of people and three ships still docked no longer existed. Hundreds died within the next several seconds, some few having just enough time to cry "Mayday!" into the void. Then silence reigned. The debris disappeared from sensors as it cooled into slag and ash, dispersing into the Kuiper Belt.

At least it was a clean death, he reassured himself. They might have had time to be scared. They probably wouldn't have felt a thing when it actually happened. Boiled, crushed or overloaded by enough radiation to cook every neuron instantly. Anyone else suffocated within seconds.

Captain Hirsch said, "Well done."

"Thank you, sir," he agreed. For warfare, it was well done. It was also something they could probably do again. Until the UN had phase drives installed, they couldn't use the tactic, as they'd found out disastrously when they tried to "clandestinely" enter the Grainne system proper through the jump point.

He'd just killed several thousand people who had no idea they were combatants.

The next few Earth-minutes were mass confusion as two patrolling ships lit their drives hot, started trajectory for the station, then powered down as pointless. If anyone had survived, they'd be dead before any rescue could reach them.

Probably, no one had survived.

Then the ships turned power onto active sensor sweeps and detailed analysis of all space around them. They would attempt to backtrack trajectories on the impactors and reduce their search cones.

The problem with space was that there was nowhere to actually hide. The second problem was the power outputs of a major ship's plant were significantly more detectable than distant stars, or local planetoids.

Captain Hirsch asked, "Sensors, can you get any commo?"

Werner replied, "Minimal. It's tight beam, little bleed, and encrypted. Senior Ustan is doing traffic analysis and looking for indicators."

Hirsch said, "So we wait."

Their current trajectory would have them safely out of system, well into deep space, and in prime phase drive options in ten days.

"I need a break," Metzger said. "Helm, please resume control."

Tung said, "Sir, I have control."

"Thank you. Captain, I need to walk a bit. May I have your leave? I'll be in the gym."

"You may. Thanks for your plotting so far. Please be ready for any notice."

"Yes, sir."

Metzger pushed and pulled his way aft, into the gym, and into the centrifuge. He could walk in endless loops, but it would work his muscles and burn off some stress. Being cooped in a G couch for most of a day was exhausting.

He wasn't the only one walking, but he took a brisk stride that had him slowly lapping two others. He recognized one of the engineers, and one of the weapons maintenance techs. They all politely ignored each other.

He'd just vaporized thousands of people, most of them not direct combatants, but support.

The UN was going to try to kill him and everyone he served with in response.

Hell, they were already trying to do that.

Was it worthwhile? Or would it just escalate to more nukes and kinetic weapons back home? Was it worth winning if there was nothing left?

Fatigue hit hard. How long had he been at it? Eight divs, almost an entire day cycle. Yeah. Rest and calculate, that was his life at present.

He was about to ping the captain for permission when an incoming message ordered him to rest. "If unable, report to the medical officer."

Moral quandaries aside, sleeping wasn't a problem. He made it to his cabin and collapsed onto his bunk with just enough consciousness left to fasten in against maneuvers.

Captain Virgil Ashton, UNPF, aboard the frigate *Laconia* twitched at the alarm. His first glance at the display showed nothing untoward in the vicinity. Helm was steady. Nothing looked out of line.

Then he saw the transmitted report.

Station *Roeder* was being hit hard. In the display, warheads and mass piled in bright flashes, overloaded its screens and smashed it to vapor.

Distress calls and beacons disappeared in cries and screams, then lonely silence.

Twelve thousand people had just died.

He tried not to twitch as adrenaline shot up his spine and he broke into a feverish sweat.

"Where the hell did that come from?"

Ahead and right of him, Reconnaissance Operator Alxi said, "Sir, everyone is searching now. All ships, all stations."

It had to be the Grainne Colony, and it was a violent, mass attack far inside Earth space. And why hadn't Space Force acquired phase drive as soon as it was proven? It allowed things like this. Whichever ship had done that had avoided the jump point entirely.

Where was it?

The tactical display showed a trajectory that intersected the station at one end, and dissipated into space at the other. Somewhere along that arc, that attack had been launched.

Another image lit, the potential cone the hostile had taken after launch.

Fleet commed in. The admiral came on personally. Ashton straightened.

"Ashton, are you ready for pursuit?"

Ashton replied, "At once, sir. We have the track and can boost at once."

"Go. Frag order will follow."

"Yes, sir. We are in pursuit." He turned. "Navigation, Helm, maximum safe boost."

"We're on it."

Warnings sounded and *Laconia* accelerated.

Helm Operator Rao asked, "Are there any survivors, sir?"

He scrolled through the messages piling on his display.

He said, "There may be a handful in a tumbling section, and some in rescue balls if they can be reached fast enough. They were in the dock section."

"Does this count as a terror attack?"

Twisting his neck, he said, "Technically it is within the Law of Armed Conflict. They hit a military target during declared hostilities."

Rao snapped, "That's a BS technicality. Maintenance and support aren't combatants."

It had been inevitable, really, as soon as the UN had dropped KE and nuke weapons on Grainne. Sending second-rate troops for occupation hadn't been smart, either.

Ashton said, "Either way, we pursue."

"And then vaporize them." The man sounded enraged, his teeth clenched.

Ashton nodded. "Once we have that order, yes."

The Grainne ship was somewhere in that cone in the display. For now, their best pursuit trajectory was a shot down the middle.

Intel came in bit by bit.

Alxi summarized the Fleet Intel report verbally for everyone, even though it was in the display. There were a lot of things in the display, and they could be easy to miss.

"There was a lot of mass in that attack. The conclusion is it's one of their destroyers. Big enough for phase drive, but not one of their fleet carriers. Those are too valuable and too fragile. A compact, phase drive—equipped ship with mass load. One of their *Admiral* class. We've previously destroyed one, that leaves three."

Ashton said, "Good. I know their capabilities. Got them for review?"

"Yes, sir. Best known are on the display."

Malahayati was a destroyer, phase-drive conversion, twenty-five years old. Their frames were smaller and more compact than UN ships, mainly built around jump-point defense. It was still a bigger ship than his frigate. It theoretically packed missiles and beams, but wouldn't have been able to resupply easily. Two previous known engagements. It hadn't been seen in months. It was likely low on everything.

Ashton said, "Now we have to figure how much fuel they used, still have, and can spare."

This had to be punished, and *Laconia* was in a good position for it.

Rao reported, "*Quito* is astern, but can boost more. They're joining."

"Excellent, put me through. Shema, Ashton."

Captain Grade 2 Shema said, "Hell of a thing, eh?" She looked wide-eyed in shock, not fear. It looked odd on her North Asian face.

Ashton replied, "Yes. Are we going to try to bracket?"

Shema said, "First I want to parallax all our sensor info. There might be something that will show them to us. I've got your trajectory. I'm going to deviate slightly outward, just on a hunch they'd rather be on the outermost track to space they can use."

He said, "That makes good sense. Should I launch drones or waste a platform for intel?"

She shook her head. "I advise against it. We'll throw that at them when we find them. There are other ships that may be able to cross our scans and find something."

"Understood. I just hate to chase without knowing what I'm chasing."

She said, "For now that's all we have, but it puts us in better position when we do find them."

"It does. Yes, ma'am. We'll funnel everything to you as we get it. *Laconia* out and listening."

"*Quito* out and listening."

Alxi said, "Sir, I may have something. An occultation of a star, and a rough trajectory, but it's barely outside the estimated envelope."

"Can you reconstruct a track?"

"I can." It appeared in the display. It didn't match either the estimated launch point or the current search cone, but it was too fast to be any kind of debris.

Alxi was good. She'd known where to look and found something.

It was his call to make. He made it.

"It's close enough to assign it as Unknown One. See what *Quito* can find."

"Yes, Captain."

Metzger felt he'd barely closed his eyes when an alarm woke him. "Report to C-Deck."

He staggered to his feet and stumbled up the passage.

He was going to need a head break soon, but what did they have?

"They have us IDed," Werner said as Metzger walked around the catwalk to his station.

Second Astrogator Yukat was on duty, and she cleared the couch as he approached.

This was his mission, his plan, and he had to furnish the options to the captain.

He settled in to the still-warm couch and squinted until his gritty eyes focused and his muddled brain tracked. The trajectories showed as equations, charts, and graphical loops in the system 3D sim. The tracks were beautiful ballistic curves against gravity and real motion.

They all had potential intercepts.

Metzger addressed the captain.

"Sir, our options are decoy and evasion now, or continue ballistically until any pursuit closes, then conduct decoy and evasion. I had planned for a momentary diversion in trajectory toward jump point."

Hirsch said, "I recall. Do the latter. Any energy they expend now we won't have to fight against later."

"Understood, sir. Helm, my console has command."

"Understood, sir," Tung agreed.

He wanted to appear discreet, while being just noticeable enough for them to respond. This was why space warfare took segs or even days.

The correction for the jump point was simple. A huge solution set would accomplish that. This part of the set would actually get them there with enough fuel for a jump. This second choice would do so discreetly enough not to be seen. This one would just let them be seen, and give him the option of more visibility while still meeting the proper terminus. He mathematically shaved down a geometric shape until he had maneuvering options, minimum loss of fuel, and plenty of open space for evasion.

"All hands stand by for thrust," he warned, and pinged the message through text, audio, and klaxon. Thirty seconds later, his correction started. The ship boosted softly, .2154 G according to his figures, and held it for exactly 436 seconds. It cut to micro G.

Then it was back to waiting.

"Sir, request permission for induced sleep."

Hirsch said, "Absolutely. I'll need your brain at its best. Helm, take control."

Helm responded with, "Aye, sir. Helm has control."

Metzger shuttered his couch, pulled a darkened visor over his eyes and ears, and watched hypnotic red waveforms drift across his vision. His brain tried to calculate their shapes, while he felt warm and ensconced in his couch. He'd just figured out the saw-sine expression of one when it changed to another, and . . .

Aboard *Laconia*, sorted data piled up.

Rao reported, "*Mirabelle* just came through jump. They're on an almost-crossing vector, actually a very good position for an intercept, though tougher to get a good shot."

Mirabelle was a destroyer. She was almost as fast, closer to the hostile, and had better weaponry.

"Got him!" Alxi said. "Sir, cross-referencing ours and *Quito*'s scans with those from *Mirabelle* has him marked. Also, we apparently had a stealth boat behind orbit?"

Ashton replied, "We did? I wouldn't know. They don't talk to anyone."

"Well, they're talking to me now. Or rather, they're sending a very tight, burst-encrypted message to *Mirabelle*, who then tight-beamed us. So we're hopeful the enemy can't crack it."

The "enemy." That term hadn't been used much. They were the "opposition," the "resistant colony." After this, they were finally the "enemy."

"Is it in the display?" he prompted.

Alxi said, "It is now."

The enemy ship was moving fast, but unpowered, and that was a very well-designed trajectory. It took them far enough from the jump point or habitat to minimize visibility, but not so far in system to increase their flight time or expose them to in-system sensors or weapons.

Ashton called down to Engineering Deck. "Powerplant, how much over max can we handle for a few hours?"

Commander Basco paused a moment, then said, "I can support ten percent over. Fifteen is probably safe but you'll need to sign for it."

"Fifteen it is. We're chasing this asshole down."

Another shape came on the display.

Navigator Mafinga said, "Assuming full fuel bunker, that's his possible trajectories to deep space. Once he hits the edge of that, he's clear."

"How much overlap do we have on intercept?"

Mafinga ran a cursor through the image.

"Currently over two hours."

Ashton twisted his lip. "Not a lot, but enough. Will higher boost help?"

"Sir, it will not. We'll eat through our own fuel."

"If we plan to wait for a recovery vessel, how much can we close?"

Mafinga swiped and tapped for calculations, and said, "That opens up options, but sir, I'd rather save that fuel for any course changes. We don't know how accurate these initial findings are, or what weapons they'll throw."

Ashton nodded. "Valid. They'll throw missiles, the same as we will. He can't risk being seen and can hide missile drops easier than a beam. We can't pour enough energy into a beam for potshots. When are we in range for a firing solution?"

Tactical Officer Shin said, "Only about ten minutes to max range. But we'll have a much better shot in thirty-four."

"We'll wait if we can," Ashton decided.

Shin added, "I have an ongoing solution updating, sir."

"Closer means a larger warhead, correct?"

"Yes. It doesn't make a lot of difference normally, but in this case, the weapon mass is an issue."

He asked Shin, "Can we overboost the warheads?"

Shin said, "We can fake it with some additional jacketing. There will be more emission, and higher velocity fragments, but we'll lose some to the blast."

"Any hit will be a good hit. A few minor delays and he's stuck in system until we slag him. Do it."

Shin tapped info and swiped his display. "They're on it," he said.

Ashton signaled for his orderly.

He said, "Please have food brought to the bridge crew. Have our reliefs on mandatory rest waiting. This may drag out." He turned back to the command crew and said, "Rest breaks will be one person every fifteen minutes, with a junior officer filling in. We want to keep our information flowing smoothly.

"Let's fry this clown."

★ ★ ★

"I'm awake," Metzger said at once, before he realized there was an alert sounding in his ears.

He glanced at the displays surrounding him as the captain brought him up to date.

"They're in pursuit. I need your expertise."

"It looks like they corrected to match my anticipated course, and have deduced the shift since then. I'm determining any discreet evasion will be impossible. They've got us dialed in fine based on energy signature."

Captain Hirsch said, "That was my conclusion. We'd hoped to be farther out before detection."

Metzger said, "We might have been better taking a burn as soon as they IDed us, but we'd then be juggling fuel, too."

"Do you have a scenario to cover this?"

"Sort of. That one I discussed with you. Alpha three alpha."

The nature of forceline propulsion meant the ship had zones of speed, much like surface vehicles would reach speeds where energy to overcome friction increased dramatically to another plateau.

For now, Metzger made a course adjustment and applied a steady, low thrust to get them to deep space as quickly as possible. The math was simple. If they reached interstellar space before pursuit reached them, they were free. If pursuit reached them, they had to fight. If they had to fight, they had limited maneuver delta before they'd have to go ballistic and drift into position for phase drive. If they ate too much into their safety margin, they wouldn't have any star drive capability.

To fight, they had a modern electronic-warfare suite, but once within range of mass or beams, they had six and only six configurable warheads against their two pursuers.

"Okay, I assume I'm going to have to lead on this since it was my calculations. I'll need food, induced sleep between activity, and the medical officer to keep an eye on me. If that meets your approval, sir, it should be a half seg before they manage to do anything relevant. I'd like to drop under again. If they close within those parameters or seem to detach anything that might be a weapon, wake me at once. With your permission, sir?"

"Do so. I'll have a cook on call for whatever you'd like when you wake up."

"Right. Thanks. And first, head break."

He took care of business, returned and snuggled back into his couch, and waveformed back into unconsciousness.

He knew he'd been asleep, but all he saw was increasing waveform complexity and modulated tones. The machine was pulling him back awake.

Then he was conscious and removed the mask.

A glance at the displays showed a third ship, a picket destroyer, closing, though not yet in range to be combatant.

"Captain, I'm aware of the display. Are there any other updates?"

"You have all the data available."

"Understood. Helm, maintain your control for the present."

"Helm retains control, understood, sir."

It was embarrassing to be surrounded by what were effectively servants. Still, it was for his benefit as he drove this beast alone.

He stretched in place and probed at an itch under his shoulder where a fold of uniform had irritated him.

He recognized the Third Chef in one of the couches for support staff and observers, and said, "Chief Lalonde, I'd like a cocoa, please. Double dark, regular cream, splash of butter and half-sweet. A dark smoke ham roll with smoked gouda and peppered-egg filling."

"At once, sir," Lalonde agreed, and hoisted himself aft.

He turned to the surgeon, Lieutenant Doctor Morgan.

"I feel okay, a bit groggy. Is there anything you can give me for focus and attention without affecting my ability to sleep, ma'am?"

She took his thumb, pressed it against a metabolic probe, then checked the data.

"I will formulate something," she agreed.

"Thank you. Captain, I'm ready to resume."

He checked the plots and trajectories, looked at the astro sims for possible corrections. Those were based on the available energy-consumption figures for those ship classes, and *Malahayati*'s exact figures.

"Sir, I recommend we continue. I expect they'll shortly get a firing solution. I want to launch in return, wait for that incoming weapon to get to a precise point, then use that as maneuvering screen. If I time it right, ours will detonate after theirs, and that will be a second screen. Two maneuvers well-hidden in fuzz should dramatically increase our chances with little waste of available bunker."

"You're not going to hit them with it?"

"I think a near miss is achievable. I expect they'll simply evade if it gets too close, and we lose any effect. If I can judge when they'll maximize their evasion, I can detonate just before that."

"You're playing chicken with fusion warheads."

"Exactly, sir."

"Proceed. Mister Metzger?"

"Yes, sir?"

The captain spoke very carefully. "If you believe you have failed and we are pending destruction, please do not make any announcement. It won't make any difference. We fly until we win or die."

Metzger said, "Yes, sir. Though I'm quite sure I have the odds on this one."

"Excellent."

He'd better stay awake for now. He'd likely need more drugs before this was over.

Had it been most of a day cycle already?

Right then, the assigned surgeon returned.

"Here is your cocktail," she said.

"Thank you." He took it, she gestured, he chugged it.

It tasted like slightly bitter grape juice. Not bad.

"I may need to drug heavily in a div or so. To stay conscious."

"If you do, I have that standing by."

"Thank you."

Werner reported, "I believe the new arrival at the jump point is another destroyer. *Warren* class."

"Correction time?" he asked.

"We are roughly six light-seconds from the point."

"Understood."

The data showed on his display, as did the lag time. Whatever he saw had happened 5.94 seconds previously. That also would change as vectors closed.

Well, that limited his maneuver options. He didn't dare get closer to that ship. That was probably part of their plan. He blacked out an entire chord of possible trajectories.

Now he had to think about decoying that one, at approximately the same time.

It wasn't just the three craft in play. It was the light-speed delay in sensor response, then the much slower craft response. If any of them saw his maneuver, it would be a wasted effort.

Both trailing craft could be screened if his warhead detonated there, relative. He set that to remain a "fixed" variable, maintaining optimum position.

He could screen the other one in that fuzzy locus there. He might only achieve a partial obscuration. Damn.

"Surgeon, I need you to consult with the senior engineer. Specifically, I need to know how many frames aft we need to clear, and what shielding we'll have, regarding how close I let their incoming warhead approach before I evade. Captain, do I have your permission?"

She asked, "You are trying to avoid casualties by the narrowest margin?"

"That is correct. Microseconds and meters may help."

Hirsch said, "Please proceed."

Morgan nodded to them. "I will find out."

"Please hurry, ma'am," he added as she clattered around the catwalk. "They just launched. Subjective. It's on the way. Appears to be less than six hundred seconds to impact. Captain, please tell the engineer I need to know our maximum safe energy level on a single maneuver, and our maximum power output. Stress the comparative urgency."

Boy, did that sound calm.

At least it would be over quickly.

The Captain barked, "Engineer Major Hazey, I need you in this discussion now."

Metzger returned to his task. If they'd launched, and he was getting a refinement on the missile because it was under full boost, he needed to drop his . . . then. Unpowered. By not boosting, his would be harder to detect, even if they expected it. That increased his probability. They needed a hit, he only needed a screen.

Really, at the far end, if he maintained sufficient delta V, or reached clean space seconds ahead of any pursuit, they won. The enemy only won if they hit him.

A blinking notice showed in his panorama, yellow and coded as Engineering. He opened it.

It looked as if everyone could move to Frame 70, and he had a shield-rating factor for the best field they could cast astern, plus internal ballast blocking. That allowed him to create a variable depending on the size of the warhead inbound. For output, the note said, "Emergency rating is 130%, but I'm willing to support 135% under the conditions, if it's under a ten second burn."

He had to assume pursuit would want to send the most powerful warhead they could for area effect. They also needed it fast, however. Judging from that motion, he wanted to say it was on the high end of the spectrum. If it was weaker, he'd have less screen to hide behind. If it was more powerful, they were all dead.

I'm basing it on assumed flight characteristics of a missile we've never seen in combat, he thought.

That was all he had. He should drop the device . . . now. Then a VDAM—Volume Denial Dispersed Mass Weapon. It was only tungsten jacks, but the relative velocity would make those into potentially deadly projectiles. Most likely, the UN shields would block the debris, but the particles might score hits, and they might deny chunks of space to support craft.

Both were blown out by hyperpressurized nitrogen, and had a gas "jet" for movement. It was little delta V, but it meant they would be harder to trace to source, and slightly closer to pursuit. They'd engage thrust momentarily before impact.

Captain Hirsch asked, "May I assist in any way?"

"Not at this moment, sir, though the tube crews should keep the warheads live and be ready to change delivery."

"They will."

He needed to actively fire at that third picket. It needed to be the dirtiest warhead they had.

"Can they sheath the next warhead with something to increase the fuzz?" he asked.

"Stand by," the captain said and turned to query.

He said, "Standing by. I will be maneuvering on momentary notice. All crew should be restrained."

A few moments later, the captain said, "Munitions says it's as dirty as it can get. Characteristics on screen."

He wasn't a munitions specialist, and he wasn't really a sensor expert. He tapped both officers into the display.

"Advise me, please," he said, and flashed figures.

Werner said, "You want to keep them behind the sixty-two percent mark of the radius. Assuming their gear is what it was last time we did an exchange."

Munitions Officer Hadfield lit into the display and said, "This isn't dirty in the radiation sense. It's remarkably clean. The sheathing will create all kinds of high-energy fragments that will be a temporary cloud. You'll have perhaps point two seconds. After that, we'll be brighter than it, at that boost."

"Thank you. That really doesn't help my calculations. I'll be playing by ear."

He regretted saying that, especially that way.

He added, "Your advice is valuable. I'll do my best with it."

He launched the second missile and let it burn for the target. They knew where he was and would expect him to shoot.

The tumbled warhead astern was still functional, and pursuit seemed to be willing to risk it, or unaware of it. They were at full thrust, possibly six G.

"Our maneuver is going to be hard, violent, multiaxis, and hot. I'm momentarily going to use all power for thrust and kill everything else."

Captain said, "The crew are informed."

In the sim, vectors closed. That explosion would hopefully shield *that* cone, and overlap with that explosion and the other cone.

He set the system to implement his maneuver on that exact time tick, and stood by to override.

No, it was going to be right now.

Astern was a danger-close explosion. *Malahayati* creaked and popped as the reactor drove at 140 percent. Everything went black as power surged undiminished to the engines. They shifted, heaved, and rolled, G pulling him in three directions at once. The straps cut into him and he bumped his shoulder on the couch frame. Then everything went still as thrust stopped. Lights and enviro came back on.

They hadn't blown up, and the enemy hadn't blown them up.

"Stand by for round two," he announced.

Two more ticks crossed each other, the warheads he'd launched hopefully blinded pursuit, and as the debris clouds cooled, the engines hummed again, at 136 percent of rated capacity. It felt even rougher, with the vectors combining to make it very uncomfortable.

They were in a slightly longer, but much faster arc for clear space, and down a measurable percentage of their available delta V.

"Well done, Lieutenant," the captain said.

"That's only the first, sir," he replied. "My options were limited. Slower or longer trajectories would expose us to more fire, so I had to choose faster and or flatter, and they know it. We've gained seconds, possibly Earth-minutes. All three are still in the chase."

Ashton watched the displays. A creeping caret represented their missile, seeming to crawl toward the enemy's probable mark. Only when one realized how many thousands of kilometers each centimeter represented did the speed become apparent.

Alxi said, "There was possibly a very faint change in motion. It could be jettison of mass for moment gain. Or it might be a launch."

"A loiter missile, I assume?"

She nodded. "It would have to be. There's nothing showing yet, and an immediate launch would paint them."

"Understood," he said.

The other ships would have firing solutions, soon. One of them was bound to score a damaging shot eventually.

It was a pointless war, with the numbers the way they were. Grainne couldn't win. As brave as this attack was, it was worthless, suicidal, and only serving to piss more people off.

"Sir, our missile has positive lock."

"Good! Let's see what we're about to kill."

Data came back. Yes, *Admiral* class. *Malahayati*. The fact it was named after a famous Earth commander just made their claims of being independent even more ridiculous. Trajectory, thrust, likely fuel load available. Now the track matched very closely to what they had from the attack. And damn, she was burning. How did they get to .049 *c* and still have maneuvering margin?

The missile finished and detonated. There was a ripple of approval among the crew.

Shortly, the combined sensors should tell them what, if any, damage had been done.

Alxi said, "Sir, we have vector on incoming threat. I think—"

A massive explosion showed in the display, on the view screen and on sensors. *Laconia* trembled from the wave front against her shields, and several loud bangs echoed and clattered.

Someone said, "Son of a bitch, the fuckers hit us."

Chief Engineer Basco said, "Damage report: shield containment needs flushed. Minor rad damage in forward sections, including Control. Outer hull breaches, count three, contained. Minor damage to drive antenna two. We've lost about point two G of boost capability."

That was an amazing shot. On the other hand, the UN ships weren't playing hard to see so were easy targets. The damage, though, would slow *Laconia*. *Quito* would have to take lead.

"Status on the enemy?"

"Unknown, sir. We've lost them. They apparently maneuvered after either or both detonations."

That bastard.

"Someone else should have data," he demanded.

"Sir, *Quito* was in our thrust shadow, and *Mirabelle* also took fire, though only close enough to act as a screen."

"That devious bastard," Ashton said in respect.

He addressed his staff. "Make your best guess on cones of potential and I'll do the same. We'll compare. Start scanning immediately. They may be damaged, too."

"Yes, sir."

Metzger studied the available sensor information. Light-seconds mattered.

"Bogey One is down slightly but measurably in acceleration. I think we hurt them with something."

Engineering reported by audio and display to him and the captain.

"C-Deck, I cannot authorize any more boosts over one hundred thirty percent. I was serious on my limits, and we've strained containment. You'll have to expect that to drop on future high-energy burns, too. I'd say I'm not happy, except I want us to win. We have to be alive to do that, though."

"Understood, thank you, sir," he replied. Yes, it had been a risk. They'd needed everything they could get.

Gods, he was tired. His eyes were getting gritty, and his guts sour. "I need something mild to eat."

"Banana?"

"Yeah, thanks."

He took a moment to color code all his envelopes to make it easier to grasp them at a glance. If . . . once . . . they got to green zones in those fascinating shapes, they'd be safe from intercept. They had the velocity advantage. Earth had three ships and less need to save power. They could call for refuel. Though much farther and they couldn't. They were reaching their own recovery envelope.

Worst case, we might take three more ships with us, the hard way.

They were incrementing toward green on Bogey One. It was going to get passed by Two shortly. If the UNPF was smart, it would stay in the race as recon, and he'd still have to deal with it.

He had three warheads, and three pursuers. He could drop five more VDAMs, and it was possible that had been what damaged Bogey One, though it could have been the warhead or even internal overload from the pursuit.

Someone handed him a banana. He ate it in three bites, then sipped cold tea.

Captain Hirsch said, "I would like to suggest you consider if further damage to Bogey One will cause Two to stop to rescue, and take both of them out of the running. Do you have anything against that?"

The captain was politely saying he was about to give an order.

Think. Think.

"Sir, unless we are able to damage life support or structural integrity, they can batten down on minimum and wait for rescue. I don't think we can reliably plan to effect that."

"You are correct. If that becomes a viable option, do take it."

He said, "Sir, I intend to cause as much damage as possible as we depart."

Hirsch replied, "And if we don't, I will cause them even more."

"I understand, sir."

Really, capture would probably be worse than death. Out here, very few civilian craft would detect anything. The UN could claim destruction for both PR purposes and cover, then do whatever it took to get intel out of every member of the crew, probably starting at the bottom. After that, space was an unfillable graveyard.

He asked, "Munitions, what effect would a VDAM have if detonated fractionally before and next to a warhead?"

Lieutenant Hadfield asked, "Are you trying for more ionization fuzz?"

"I am."

"It's not efficient, but it will work. You will get some congealed particles afterward, as well, but they will only be fractionally efficient for impact kills."

"Please configure the remaining warheads for that. That leaves us two more VDAMs I can use to jack off." The tungsten pellets were tetrahedrons, not quite jack shaped, but the joke was obvious and common.

"Now I am hungry," he suddenly realized.

Lalonde asked, "What do you need, sir?"

"I know it's off schedule, but any chance of that pot roast soup from last week?"

"I think I can have something in a few segs."

"Please."

At least he'd eat well as a condemned man.

Bogey One was going to drop out and be only a recon source. There was no reason for them to play a game, and they were farther back in the engagement envelope. Bogey Two was continuing to advance, and would eventually move out of envelope, if they didn't detect *Malahayati*. So far, so good.

Bogey Three's course was going to bring them a lot closer before receding. It was unlikely they'd avoid detection, even with the oblique, almost skew trajectories.

He ran sims on when that detection might happen, and what Two could do in response. Would it be best to maneuver again the moment they were seen? Or use incoming fire as another distraction?

He realized Lalonde had a bag of stew at his shoulder, and mumbled "Thanks." He squeezed out a mouthful and resumed figuring.

Calculations showed that given their own fuel margin and established trajectories, any further maneuver would slow their escape. The obvious fast curves would be attacked preemptively. If he waited for incoming, his available volume and options would shrink a lot.

"As soon as they detect us, we have to maneuver again. Realistically, that will be our last maneuver."

Hirsch demanded, "Elaborate, please."

Metzger ran through his reasoning and figures. "An immediate maneuver gives us the broadest envelope and them the widest search volume. If we wait, we have fewer options, and they will be slightly but relevantly closer."

"Understood. Maneuver as you see fit. After that, what is your call?"

"If they detect us after that, we're on a very tight fuel margin. We need enough to get us into phase, and to somewhere we can precipitate and expect help." If they dropped into normal space light-years from anywhere, it would take years for any message to get out.

"Please keep me advised on that margin," Captain said.

"Yes, sir."

If they couldn't do it, the captain was going to try to take at least one pursuer with them.

Really, there weren't any other options.

Metzger was the only one aboard who could prevent that.

"Sir, I think I can drop a loiter mine onto Bogey Two. The problem is, the residue of the detonation, microseconds as it is, will be enough for them to track this trajectory. Even with onboard maneuvering."

"Save it until you believe we're exposed."

"Understood. That increases the probability of a miss, however."

Hirsch acknowledged, "Yes."

"Confirmed."

Engineer Hazey reported, "Astro, we're losing efficiency. Adjustments require shutdown, so you need to assume loss of delta V. I've got a chart for you."

Metzger looked at the chart and clenched his jaw. He added the figures and reassigned everything. The envelopes changed and narrowed.

Werner said, "Incoming fire."

Metzger scanned the tank. There it was . . . "From where?"

Werner said, "Unknown. Bogey Four assigned, not identified."

"Stealth boat," he said. "There's no reason they don't have them the way we do."

That meant another set of sensors they had to evade.

"So the good news is, I can not bother evading behind their detonation fuzz. We can boost freely, then go silent after our screen."

Captain said, "I'm going to work with you on this. We need as much boost as we can get without shorting ourselves on the phase entry, but we also need to appear to not be concerned about energy consumption. That keeps their search envelopes larger."

"I agree and thank you, sir."

Captain asked, "The next question is why they revealed that boat by firing."

Good question.

"I expect it's a loiter missile. They want us to think the stealth is there and waste resources. But it doesn't matter where it is. Just that it can ID us."

Werner said, "That may be, but I'm doing everything I can to find emanations or occultations that might show their maneuvering . . . and I think I have."

Bogey Four showed in the tank. It would have come from forward of the jump point, even forward of the UN base there.

"So they have a secondary base we didn't know about, and most of them don't either."

Werner continued, "They also have really good missiles. It seems to have IDed us and locked."

Hirsch said, "And that's why they revealed the asset."

Werner replied, "Has to be expensive."

Metzger asked, "Do I need to waste a warhead?"

Werner wrinkled his brow. "I think you can stop it just with jacks. Add in flash and reflection chaff."

"Agreed, and done."

The charges were dropped in soft, deep vacgel that would make their signature even less visible than everything already was. All combatants were looking as much for dark holes in space where none should be as they were for emissions.

Captain Hirsch said, "I have a boost solution for you."

Metzger looked at it.

"That only allows us two more evasion burns."

Hirsch said, "Yes. I'm trying to draw them into wasting power in pursuit, and minimize our exposure time. If they think we're in more of a hurry, I'm hoping they get careless."

His eyes were beyond gritty, stung with sweat. He could barely visualize the equations. Everyone here had stayed on with him. The entire combat crew had to be wired. Third Chef Lalonde kept bringing food and beverages, Morgan brought stims. In between, some of them got combat naps. No one was going below decks at this end.

"I have no reason to dispute it, sir. Just noting we're limited on future evasion."

He brought thrust online and the frame hummed.

Twelve seconds of light lag time later, Werner said, "They're boosting in pursuit."

"Good. Now we see if it works."

The burns had been carefully selected to this point to align them with Jump Point Two. This was to encourage the UNPF to concentrate forces on each side of the point. The four pursuers were hoping to chase them into a blockade.

It was likely, though, that someone had assumed the possibility of phase drive, since several Freehold warships had it, which freed them from the fixed points.

Now was when they'd find out. If the enemy all planned to converge near the point, it would increase the safety envelope when *Malahayati* deviated farther from that course.

Captain Ashton saw the emission blip. "We have them. Thank *Gemdi* for the assist. Cut to minimum shipboard expenditures and chase those bastards down."

Rao asked, "Why would they head for the jump point?"

He shrugged. "Maybe they were towed in-system. Or damaged."

"Would they still have jump drive after a refit to phase drive?"

He shrugged again. "We don't know. I think that's more likely than them not being converted."

Engineer Basco asked, "Could they have ripped the phase drive out to reuse it, and plan to either lose this ship or slam the jump?"

That was a good speculation.

"Also possible. *Mirabelle* is going to cover the route to the point and prevent transition."

Alxi said, "Well they're visible now, and we're getting a lot more data. They can't win."

"No," Ashton agreed. "But they can't surrender, either. They're probably convinced we'd torture them to death or something, and they have to know we can't trust their intentions and will shoot to kill. So they may try to take someone with them. Between our ships, we have enough missiles. Fire when you have a solution."

"Will do, sir."

"Sir? They're firing."

Metzger was brought into a discussion between the captain and the engineer.

"Commander Hazey, is there any way at all to recover some of our drive power?"

Hazey said, "The only way to improve efficiency is to send an engineer aft to the reactor, under power, to make adjustments. They will die. And I guess if you're going to give that order, I'll do it, because I can't morally order anyone else to."

Metzger said, "I understand. We will try hard to avoid that." No, he could not request the captain give that order, not if there was any other choice at all.

"Thank you."

He said, "Then I guess it's time to make our last screen and burn, drop a loiter mine through the fuzz, jack off with everything we have left, and hope we power enough to clear system."

Hirsch said, "I see your envelopes. I have nothing productive to add. It's your mission, Astrogator."

"Understood, sir. We will initiate this maneuver on my mark. Countdown on screen."

Klaxons alerted the crew. Reactor power. Acceleration and boost. Danger-close detonation. Stand by.

The weapons rolled out, improving the ship's mass ratio fractionally. The screening warhead detonated, and boost cut in.

Engineer Hazey was going to be furious. Metzger had entered a command code to bypass the locks Hazey had set in place. The program pushed the reactor to 141 percent of max, well over emergency max of 115 percent, and his warning of 125 percent. It was all or nothing.

That boost tapered down to 125 percent, then 120 percent, then stopped. They were still inside the debris sheath from their own detonation. Metzger itched. It was psychosomatic, but he was inside a fusion explosion, or at least the edges of it.

"They'll track us out of that, eventually," he said. "Hopefully, they first think we scuttled, then draw some wrong assumptions."

Engineer Hazey came into the net.

"I want command to understand I am very, very unhappy with my recommendations being ignored. It should be noted at this point, if another vector change is needed, I will have to sacrifice a member of this crew to effect reactor repairs. I hope it was worth it."

Hirsch intercepted the call.

"I authorized it as an emergency measure, and felt it best not to alarm anyone with the status, in case of failure."

Damn, he was a good commander. All he'd said was for Metzger to proceed and Metzger hadn't said how far he was pushing it.

Hazey said, "Understood, and I comprehend the circumstances. Now please log my objection for the record, because this poor beast is going to need an overhaul if we survive."

But Bogey One was now out of reach, and Bogey Two was losing vector. Unless they had boost they hadn't exploited, they were probably out of it. Bogey Three could still potentially intercept, though they'd strain any known limit and need recovery afterward.

Bogey Four was still unknown, but a stealth boat likely didn't have the fuel ratio for any kind of chase like this.

Werner said, "Our loiter missile just went live. Intel on Bogey Four and Bogey Three. Not a lot, but it improves the estimates. Bogey Two is now evading."

And with that, Bogey Two dropped completely out of the race. No matter what they boosted, nothing known would let them pull enough G to intercept.

"Well done, Metzger," Captain said.

"Thank you, sir, but we still have Number Three."

Ashton clenched his jaw against very negative feelings. Anger, frustration, fear, all boiling over.

They'd evaded the contact envelope of the enemy missile, and in doing so, lost any hope of catching that ship. *Quito* had maneuvered around it, being that much closer, but between fuel margin and the vector changes, she was unlikely to catch them, either.

He muttered, "Damn whoever is flying that bucket. He's in league with gods, or devils."

He saw the updated data in the display and said, "It's bad, but *Mirabelle* has them. Exact current trajectory plotted. She'll chase them down and slag them."

Helm Operator Rao asked, "Sir? How deep have you ever gone? Because we're going a lot deeper before this is over."

He looked at the plot.

No ship he knew of had been this far out. They were well beyond the heliopause.

"It's been an impressive chase."

Rao said, "Are we going to offer them terms?"

"Those terms would be war crimes tribunals. They might win on a technicality. I doubt they want to risk it. They're going to run until we kill them. If they run low on power, they'll probably scuttle. I expect that ship is stripped to nothing."

Rao gritted his teeth. "Makes sense. We can't let them get away or they'll do this again."

"Exactly that. We'll keep scanning. Every bit of intel we get helps stop them now."

Bogey Three was moving farther into the green.

Metzger said, "We have a single warhead, sir. And a minimal amount of energy margin. We're already likely to need a tow and refuel on arrival home."

Captain said, "I see the figures." The two of them were the only ones with the coordinates of their base.

Hirsch continued, "Strip out any gram of mass we can spare. Dump oxy, water, anything. We'll use that missile as we leave."

The operations officer, Commander Cortes, said, "Yes, sir, though we already stripped almost everything."

Across the deck, Metzger could see the captain's gaze. "Then strip more. Uniforms. Underwear. Crew can manage in a single coverall. If we have to, we'll dump that. Shlippers only. Unclamp any backup equipment and have that standing by. We might need that more, but if it'll save us, it goes. If it can serve as reactor mass, get it in there. If not, queue it to jettison."

"Sir."

The order was given, and below, crew feverishly abandoned personal clothing and items, ripped out spare equipment, dumped containers. Reaction mass crept up slightly from a handful of material that was usable as fuel without reconfiguring the process. The rest showed on a graph, which corresponded to increase in delta V and thrust.

I've spent the last two day cycles staring at a screen full of math and coded graphs, Metzger thought. Most people would have no idea what they were looking at. To him, it was their life or death.

A short time later, Werner said, "Incoming. Can't ID the type, but it's got hellacious delta V."

Captain asked, "Can you call impact time?"

"Estimate only. The thrust is shifting continuously and apparently randomly within a range, more as it closes. We can't run."

"Can we evade?"

"If we do so just before detonation, we might spoof it."

Hirsch said, "Then configure that last VDAM and whatever chaff and decoys we have. Metzger, you and Werner make the call. Blow, jettison and boost."

"Yes, sir. Werner, what's our call?"

Werner said, "We'll have milliseconds in the danger-close envelope, and we need to call that conservatively."

"Can we evade now?"

"I expect it has enough range to track and follow. It's very active. We're zeroed . . . and now there's two more launches."

This was it. Either they reached that safe plateau in space, risked entry this close to the primary, or tried to evade high-yield warheads at fractional *c*.

Forcing steely calm into his response, he asked, "Can you give me a range on its expected detonation?"

Werner said, "It's on your feed. Updating as we go."

The missile showed as a dot with a glowing marker over it, fading from yellow to purple.

"Well, I think we can take a full second on the window. How fast can we get out of the envelope, allowing for response time?"

Lieutenant Hadfield said, "I think point five is pushing it. You didn't want to max boost again, did you?"

"Do we need to?"

Hirsch said, "Given your figures, one two five percent will suffice. One three five is better."

"One three zero. Split it." *And hope we don't blow up our reactor, or just render it incapable of powering the drive.*

Werner said, "Well, we're about to find out. It's on you."

"Alert, jettison and boost."

Metzger clenched up. G kicked, the ship's frame creaked, something thrummed as a too-close detonation caught them from the aft port lower. The dot in the display flashed bright, and figures scrolled. It was forty percent more than assumed, far beyond what they'd anticipated, and inverse-square law was their friend as they fled.

Aboard *Laconia*, Alxi shouted, "Detonation. I think *Mirabelle* got them!"

He then added, "Damn. *Gemdi* reports boost."

Ashton asked, "They got out of that?" The enemy crew were demons.

"Sir, we believe they were damaged, possibly severely. That missile got close enough they were in the plasma sheath."

"But not a hit."

Alxi said, "No, sir. That class of missile has been having frequent problems. A factory defect."

"So the contractors screwed us over again. The enemy is still maneuvering."

Alxi said, "Yes."

"So they got away."

Through clenched teeth, the recon officer said, "I admire and hate them at the same time."

Ashton asked, "What's the word on the rest of the salvo?"

Alxi looked at his display and carefully said, "Captain . . . nothing can reach them on their new track. All five will burn out and abort detonate."

"At least we haven't made it less safe with debris."

Oh, he was furious. They'd fired eight missiles and possibly caused some damage. Four ships were scattered across the Kuiper

Belt and would need support craft to recover, taking weeks in which they were known to be unable to protect assets. His ship was damaged. *Roeder* had been lost with all hands, three ships in repair, nine boats in dock, over thirteen thousand casualties.

And the enemy was now at an insane .06 *c*, too far out for anyone to reach with anything. By the time any updated sensor info reached the in-system defenses, even those powerful beams would be too late. The request was sent anyway.

Then, as they watched, the ship contorted inside a phase field and disappeared.

"Command is demanding a report."

Ashton felt a ripple of cold adrenaline.

"I'll take that in my cabin."

Command would probably understand. The media and the public would not. Captain Virgil Ashton and his peers were going to be crucified in the press.

Captain Hirsch said, "You're keyed in on damage report."

The report tumbled in and Metzger caught the important parts.

"Eight dead . . ."

"Fifteen critical injuries . . ."

"Reactor feed damage, containment shaping defect, max power down to eighty-nine percent . . ."

"Frame damage, hull damage, contained . . ."

"Life support holding . . ."

Completely out of context, he asked, "Captain, what's the fastest you ever traveled?"

"I'm guessing you're about to tell me."

"We're at almost point oh six *c*."

Even with a modern, well-tuned forceline drive, that took enough energy to power one of Earth's continents for a year only a couple of centuries before.

Werner said, "Three more launches. Tracking five. On your display."

Metzger looked. The five all showed as colored marks, vectored toward their own tag.

None of them had carets in the green zone. None of them could reach *Malahayati*.

"We're clear," he said. "Barring something our intel didn't find, farther out than anything else they have, we're clear. Sir, I request permission to secure and sleep until phase entry."

"Granted. Well done, Astrogator. You are relieved. Don't worry about phase entry. Second Astrogator Yukat and I can handle it."

"Thank you, sir. And all of you."

He rolled painfully out of his G couch and staggered aft. The surgeon assisted him to his cabin and onto his bunk.

With battle damage, short power, and massive velocity to counter, they barely made it. *Malahayati* precipitated rather farther from the base than Metzger intended. They were four light-hours out. It would be ten days on minimal power and half rations before anyone would reach them.

Four hours was 1.5 divs. It was that long again before a response came to their report and request.

"Fuel and drinks on the way. Welcome home, *Hate*. Congratulations on your mission."

That nickname seemed to fit perfectly.

Captain said, "Mister Metzger, I saved one bottle of sake for such an eventuality. Will you do me the honor of serving the command crew and yourself?"

"Yes, sir!"

A lot can go wrong when you're conducting research on Titan—even if you're only piloting a "homunculus" remotely on the surface while you hurtle through space in a colony ship. Add a young child with a vivid imagination into the mix, and a fairy tale ending of "happily ever after" is far from guaranteed.

HOMUNCULUS
★
by Stephen Lawson

THE YELLOW-ORANGE THOLIN haze above Titan's surface whirled around the chassis of a lighter-than-air research drone. A tiny carbon-fiber humanoid robot sat perched on its support structure, dangling his feet next to the drone's camera as it took pictures of the rocky surface below. The dirigible, designed to carry sampling probes and communication equipment, barely registered the stowaway's mass. Folded aramid-fiber wings fluttered on aluminum ribs on the bot's back as the breeze swept over the drone's chassis.

"Man, this place really does have atmosphere," Gavin whispered.

He snorted at his own bad joke.

It keeps out the cosmic radiation though. They have to live underground on Mars, like moles.

Gavin watched the haze roil beneath his tiny carbon-fiber feet. It wasn't really *him* of course. Gavin and his wife Lori were hurtling through the space between Earth and Saturn in a Goshawk Heavy Transport. The winged avatars through which they interacted with Titan's small colony would've only come up to his knee if they stood side-by-side. Nonetheless, six hour virtual reality workdays in the bubble box made the homunculus's carbon-fiber shell feel very much like skin.

Steady development in smartphone battery capacity and size had paved the way for the tiny twelve to fourteen hour lithium-ion battery nested in his back. The same was true of the dual micro-cameras that gave the homunculus crisp depth perception and picture, even in Titan's shrouded twilight.

Quantum entanglement communication—built on John Bell's experiments and tested from a satellite to Earth by the Chinese in 2017—had brought the *ansible* into the real world. It made instantaneous control of the homunculus possible, though the true breakthrough in quantum manipulation hadn't come until 2021 at CERN. That had earned two post-PhD researchers the title "Spin Doctors" in every major publication when they'd changed the spin of a pair of entangled electrons.

Gavin didn't wait twelve minutes, as the MarsX contractors had, to get an image from his avatar, or to send it a command. He was present—*now*—through the virtual reality goggles, surround-sound speakers, and the nest of tiny inflatable bubbles that rapidly expanded and contracted to provide haptic feedback in zero gravity.

The green qMail icon blinked twice in his visor.

He held his right thumb and index finger together to activate voice commands.

"Open qMail," he said quietly, and a stream of text overlaid the bottom of his view of the Kraken Mare's liquid methane.

Gavin, the message said, *please come to Greenhouse 3 as soon as possible. We can't find Jonah. We think he might be in a ventilation duct. Please hurry.* —Hope

That didn't sound good.

Gavin's hand moved up through the plastic bubbles to his left, and he felt the homunculus's hand grasp one of the airship's support cables as he pulled his tiny avatar to its feet.

"Add overlay," Gavin whispered, "—colony hub. Add building numbers. Add thermal signatures for humans."

Translucent blue lines shimmered around the plastic igloos two thousand feet below him. White numbers identified the nuclear plant, electrolysis facility, greenhouses, and homes. To the north, on Mayda Insula, a pair of blue outlines showed him the tidal generators that supplemented the colony's fast-breeder nuclear reactors.

Gavin turned his gaze back to the greenhouses. If he planned his glide right, he'd only have to put power to his wings for a few seconds before he touched down.

The tiny aluminum and carbon-fiber man leapt from the chassis that supported the lighter-than-air drone's camera and over-the-horizon communication hardware. Gavin tapped his left thumb and forefinger together, and the homunculus's wings opened.

He soared like a flying squirrel through the nitrogen-methane haze, S-turning left and right to match the shimmering blue optimal glide path in his visor. If he overshot too much, he'd have to swim out of the Kraken.

The flesh-and-blood colonists had tried flying when they'd first arrived. It was one of the great appeals of Titan—with a running start and some good hard flapping, a human could fly like an Earth-bird through the soupy atmosphere and low gravity.

The novelty wore off when they realized how many calories they had to eat after such workouts, and how few calories the greenhouses produced to supplement the monthly supply rockets.

There was, also, a limited amount of scenery to awe flying humans. Once they'd seen methane waves swelling under Saturn's tidal pull and a few cryovolcanoes spewing blocks of ice, they uploaded some videos to the interplanetary net's social media sites to impress people they'd never see at another high school reunion, and settled down to the hard work of colony growth.

It *had* grown—rapidly in fact—during Gavin's first three years in transit. Hydrocarbons like ethane (C_2H_6) and methane (CH_4)—so plentiful in Titan's surface and atmosphere—were easily transformed into hollow-core, vacuum-insulated polyethylene (C_2H_4) plastic building blocks which could be joined with resin to form domes. These plastic In-Situ Resource Utilization (ISRU) igloos rapidly replaced Titan2070's inflatable, less-insulated habitats.

The colonists had added two more greenhouses and had begun experimenting with gene-edited vegetables that wouldn't have survived Earth's cumbersome gravity. They'd bored a network of underground ventilation shafts as a contingency to the aboveground inflatable conduits, just in case the remnants of a micrometeor shower made it through the atmosphere.

Now, rather than flying humans, the fleet of semi-autonomous airships they'd built to map and study Titan circled the moon like zeppelin-Roombas, sometimes obscured in yellow-orange clouds, sometimes visible dropping tiny geo-samplers to the surface when the colonists found something that piqued their curiosity.

Gavin tapped his thumbs against his middle fingers to send battery power to his wings, which flapped on command. He decelerated rapidly before stepping onto the rocky surface outside the greenhouse.

In the ship's bubble box, plastic balls flexed rapidly against his feet, providing the sensation that he'd landed.

Good thing aluminum doesn't get brittle like steel or titanium in extreme cold, he thought. *It's lighter too—better for flying.*

He tapped his fingers for voice-command again while simultaneously folding his wings.

"Voice channel," he said. "Open comms—Greenhouse 3."

A chirp in his ear told him he'd been connected to the building's intercom.

"Hope," he said, "I'm outside."

The igloo's outer airlock door—also made of plastic—whirred open on servo motors. A safety circuit between the two doors kept one door locked if the other was open. Only intentional tampering would violate the igloo's climate control.

Air jets hissed in Gavin's ear as the pressure, temperature, and gas mixture equalized around his carbon-fiber skin. He turned to see if the meth picture was still up, which it was. Someone had taken an anti-drug poster from 2016, and written "ane" in black Sharpie to add a bit of humor to the airlock. "Meth(ane): Not even once," it said, above an addict's before and after pictures.

The inner door whirred open, and Gavin stepped into the greenhouse.

"Thanks for coming," Hope said. "I know you're busy building your—"

"No worries," Gavin said, with a dismissive wave. "Lori and I have two more years to make our home inhabitable. Once you figure out the brick-oven, assembly's pretty easy."

The homunculus leapt into the air and Gavin activated his wings to alight on a plastic workbench. Height disparities always made conversations awkward.

"Well, thanks just the same," Hope said. "The Earth-bound homunculus crew is on the far side of Titan still, researching a site for Hub 2. You're the only wee man within a week's travel."

"I don't understand why they wouldn't just build closer to Hub

1," Gavin said. "Resource pooling and all. You know how I feel about it. It makes rescue operations a bit easier too . . ."

"Yeah," Hope said. "Jonah's taken to crawling in the ventilation ducts the last week or so. I've tried to get him to stop, but it's hard to build decent child-proof gates out of polyethylene. Usually he comes out for meals, but I haven't seen him since yesterday."

"He's, what, six now?" Gavin asked.

Jonah had been the first "replacement colonist" allowed to be conceived onsite, after the death of the medical officer. Hope and her husband Scott had been overjoyed to be selected, even in the somber wake of Titan's first funeral.

When the Hub had achieved sustainability with backup power and surplus food, Gavin and Lori had purchased tickets on the next Reusable Launch Vehicle (RLV) to orbit from corporate headquarters. They left Earth's orbit in a robotically-assembled-in-orbit Goshawk Heavy Transport, with its counter-rotating toroid habitat sections and non-rotating, zero-G section.

Smaller, more frequent launches meant a steady operations schedule and supply chain for corporate, less risk in a single launch, and less resource strain per landing on Titan's colony. A crew of two was, in fact, nearly perfect from Titan2070's perspective.

"That's right," Hope said. "He's taller than any six-year-old on Earth, but way more curious. He gets into everything, and I can barely stop him reading to go to sleep at night. He's got a notebook full of fairytale sketches too—he's actually pretty good at drawing."

"Do you think he's embarrassed by something?" Gavin asked. "Maybe he's hiding. Has Scott—"

"We've looked everywhere for him, Gavin," she said. "Everywhere we can fit without tearing the ventilation apart. There are pry-marks on the floor hatch that goes underground, but I can't tell how old they are. He's either in the shafts, or he's—"

She didn't finish the sentence. Titan was more forgiving than Mars—its 1.5 bar surface pressure meant they didn't need the Martians' bulky pressurized suits—but a child without electrically-heated coveralls and closed-circuit air would certainly be dead by now.

"Okay," Gavin said. "I'll stay on this channel. Let me know if you find him while I'm inside, and I'll do the same if I find him holed up down there."

Gavin dropped from the table, fanning his wings halfway to the floor. He stepped to the vent, which Hope had opened. He wondered how long she'd yelled into the vent, praying for a response—how many times she'd tried to squeeze herself through the ninety-degree joints before calling for help.

He fluttered his wings again as he dropped into the darkness of the shaft, and landed on its floor, six feet below the surface.

"LED," Gavin commanded, and four tiny lights above and below his camera-eyes illuminated the horizontal shaft.

"Add overlay: underground ventilation."

Error M512 blinked in his visor. *Overlay not found.*

Dammit. I'm going to have to take notes so I don't get lost down here. Why wouldn't they put a virtual grid on the server when they dug the tunnels?

"Can you see where I am, Hope?" he asked through the radio.

"Let me check," she said. "No, sorry. The only locators anyone has are GPS-based, and our satellite constellation here is Gen 3. The ones around Earth are actually newer. There's no underground repeater system either."

Guess I'm on my own.

Gavin walked straight ahead in the dimly-lit tunnel, with its roof scant inches above his head. He found it hard to believe a kid would escape by crawling down here.

"Jonah?" he called, but there was a limit to how loud the homunculus would make his voice. The bots hadn't been designed for speeches or rock concerts, after all.

"Jonah?"

"Gavin?"

It was a woman's voice though, and not Hope's.

It took Gavin a second to realize it was Lori, and that he was hearing her voice through his own ears and not his synthetic ones.

Given how little she'd spoken to him in the last month, he excused himself for not recognizing her voice immediately.

Most long-duration spaceflight test groups experienced it—the emotional shutdown after months of confinement and sameness—so Gavin had poured himself into exploring while he waited for her to snap out of it. He was sure he'd get into a funk too at some point.

The homunculus stopped moving in the ventilation shaft.

"Hey, Lori," he said. "I'm—"

"You're not building," she said. "I know you love burning up battery power flying around or methane-surfing before shift, but we really, literally, won't have anywhere to *live* if we don't get this shelter built. I can't even get a ping-back for your location on the map."

In the ventilation shaft, the homunculus reached up to pull a non-existent helmet from its head. The shaft disappeared from Gavin's vision, replaced by the cramped interior of the *Goshawk 7*'s command module. Communication and systems computer screens lined the four walls.

"Lori—"

"Gavin."

She stared at him, waiting for an answer.

"Jonah's missing," he said. "Hope thinks he might be in the ventilation."

"If he is," Lori said, "he'll come out when he gets hungry."

"What if he's stuck or something?"

"Not really our problem," Lori said. "Just like building our house isn't theirs. You know how this works—how it's *supposed* to work."

It had been Hope's idea, when Hub 1 was still in the draft stage. The problem of the sheer boredom and cabin fever of multi-year spaceflight had plagued scientists and science fiction writers for decades.

"So," Hope had said, "the current timeline goes: send robotic probes and workers, pilot them from Earth, then spend five years in boring transit, and start the rest of the work when we land. Right?"

Everyone else had nodded, not sure what she was getting at.

"What if we do the work *while* we're flying? Quantum communication makes instantaneous control a possibility. Take the burden of robotic work off of mission control, and give it to the colonists during the long transit. It'll save time and resources on arrival too, since we can tend a greenhouse before we even get there if we send bots with seeds. Once the main infrastructure is set up, every new crew will be responsible for building their own home before they arrive. We don't know how much iron we'll have—and we won't have trees until we terraform—but the plastic bricks Ben designed are pretty easy to work with."

A few eyebrows had risen. Ben, the chief engineer, had been sitting across from her. His eyes had retained their hard skepticism.

"What kind of robotic vehicles?" he'd asked. "If you're suggesting virtual reality, you're also basically suggesting sending the same payload twice. Launching that much mass is a high-dollar proposition."

Hope had smiled.

"For one," she'd said, "robots in stasis don't need to eat or breathe, so that's half your payload gone. Since they're inorganic, you don't have to worry about lift-off force crushing them. You can launch the bots with a rail gun or whatever. They'd get there fast, and with renewable energy."

Ben's head had wagged to the side, as he half-heartedly acknowledged her point.

"For two," she'd said, "we don't have to make them full-size. Send homunculi, one for each—"

"Homunculi?"

"Tiny, little men," Hope had said. "I'm borrowing the term from psychology, and the shrinks borrowed it from alchemy. The sensory homunculus rides around in your brain experiencing the world. Maybe it's just time to turn that inside out and let the homunculi do the walking."

"The thing that's going to fry your motherboards—" another voice had said. All eyes had turned to Milton, the resident theoretical physicist. Milton had retired and come back from retirement so many times that at this point no one was certain whether he was getting paid to come to meetings, or just researching space for his own amusement. "Well, not *your* motherboards, perhaps, but your grandchildren's—is when we build something a bit bigger than a Goshawk Heavy and push out for an interstellar transit at something approaching, say, fifty percent the speed of light.

"Perhaps we'll have sent Hope's homunculi ahead, as I hope we'll agree to in this case, and they reach Betelgeuse before we do. With instantaneous communication *and* time dilation—since you'll essentially be in two places at the same time—will you watch your tiny avatar move much faster than you, as you slog your way through the expanded time of a slower point of reference? Will it react to commands before you realize you've given them? What if we had an artificial neural processor in one plane, and humans in another? Could they *think* for a thousand years while their bodies only aged ten?"

Ben had laughed.

"Maybe we should worry about getting to Titan f—"

"Milton," Hope had said, "do you realize the next implication of what you're suggesting?"

The old man had fixed her with an expression of patient curiosity, knowing she was prone to leaps of reason that took others hours to catch up to.

"Not yet," he'd said, "but I'm all ears."

"We can get information from the inside of a black hole," she'd said.

Milton had blinked several times behind his glasses before pulling them from his eyes. He'd polished the lenses with a microfiber cloth, stared at the floor, and after some moments, laughed softly.

"It looks like I'll have my work cut out for me while you're launching your homunculi, my dear," he'd said finally. "This is—well—it's not a done deal, but the theory's sound. Our probe would still be crushed as it neared the center of the gravity well, but we'd certainly get more data than we could with existing methods."

"I'll admit that I don't get it," Gavin had said. "Why can't we study the inside of a black hole now?"

"Light can't escape the gravity well," Hope had said. "So neither can radio, or post cards, or anything else we use to communicate. Quantum entanglement is *instantaneous* though, so the—"

"Ooooooooooh," Gavin had said slowly. "Never mind. I get it. Spooky action at a distance, and across relative planes."

"Yep."

Lori had elbowed Gavin at that point.

"I know it's easy to get excited," Lori had said, "and I really like the idea of being able to work while in flight versus, say, going into suspended animation or something, but—"

No one had asked, "*but, what?*"

Lori had a reputation for pragmatism and harsh reality, and Gavin guessed the others were half-scared to hear what she had to say.

"If we're building our homes while we're in transit," she'd said, "that means we're literally on our own on a new world until we start selling services back to corporate or the other colonists or whatever. It's like a straight-up frontier town, right? Rugged individualism and all that?"

"Well," Hope had said, "I mean in an emergency people are going to help each other. But yes, your log cabin is yours to build. Or plastic Lego-cabin. Whatever. The vent shafts, power connections, all that. You can rent greenhouse space in the mains or build your own."

"Okay," Lori had said. "I'm fine with that. It just seems like Ben and I are the only ones who realize this stuff costs *our* money and *our* sweat—that it's not just cool televised rocket blast-offs on a taxpayer subsidy."

"I do know how it's supposed to work," Gavin said. "Give me thirty minutes and I'll be at our build site, okay? We're ahead of schedule as it is."

"We're ahead on the *habitat*, Gavin," she said. "What if we have hang-ups with the greenhouse? I don't want to rent space to grow food. That wasn't in our budget."

"Thirty minutes."

"Fine," Lori said. "I'm going to make tea before I start then."

She pushed off from the bulkhead, pulled herself through the hatch, and disappeared into the food prep area.

Gavin replaced the headset, and the dimly-lit ventilation shaft became his world once again.

"—still there?" Hope's voice came through the speakers. "Gavin, can you hear—"

"Yeah," he said. "Sorry. I had to detach to talk to Lori."

"Oh," Hope said, her voice thick with maternal anxiety. "Okay."

Gavin moved his legs through the plastic bubbles that floated in the box, their limp, unflexed forms offering almost no force feedback. Beneath his feet, bubbles flexed each time the homunculus's feet touched the floor.

The tiny bot speed-walked through the narrow ventilation shaft until he came to a crossroad. Gavin looked left, then right, but saw nothing.

He thought, for a moment, he heard shuffling, but it could've simply been a shift in the air pressure.

Or it could've been a child.

Gavin turned left, which he knew would take him toward the long shaft that led to the tidal power station.

"Jonah?"

Nothing.

He heard another shuffle, and this time he was certain that it was the sound of cloth on plastic. He sped up, and the shuffling abruptly stopped.

Gavin rounded the corner, and found himself looking into the wide blue eyes of a young boy. The boy seemed startled for only a moment before his face broke into a broad grin.

"I found you!" Jonah said. "Or you found me. I thought you'd left me alone."

"Hello Jonah," Gavin said. "My name is Gavin. Your mother is—"

"Mama told me not to come down here," Jonah said, "but I knew you lived in the labyrinth. I knew I'd find you if I searched all the tunnels."

"Jonah," Gavin asked, "who do you think I am?"

The boy cocked his head to the side.

"Fair folk never tell their *real* names," Jonah said. "Names have power—even I know that. I just thought I'd gotten too old to play with you, or—"

"*Fair folk*," Gavin said. "You think I'm a fairy?"

"Where are Mr. Pickles and Lady Twilight though? Are they further down?"

The techs on Earth have been entertaining this boy, without realizing the consequences of their departure to research Hub 2.

"Jonah, you mom is really worried about you," Gavin said. "We need to go back the way you came. You're probably not going to see Mr. Pickles and Lady Twilight for a while because they're working on a project. And truthfully—because I feel like their make-believe is getting dangerous for you—*I'm* just a guy in a box with a remote control. I'm not a fairy."

Jonah frowned and sat back.

"This is a trick," he said. "You don't want me to find your secret underground kingdom. Wait—are you one of the bad fairies?"

"I'm not a—"

"You stay away from me," Jonah said. "I'm not big, but I'm bigger than you. I can smash you if I want to."

It was true, too. Durable as the carbon-fiber was on its aluminum frame, a few kicks would break Gavin's circuitry, leaving him incapacitated in the tunnel.

"Okay, Jonah," he said. "I won't try to come near you."

The plastic bubbles pulsed around Gavin, then pulsed again.

What was that? A malfunction in the bubble box?

Jonah's eyes grew wide again, so Gavin assumed he'd felt something too.

Gavin tapped his fingers together.

"Hope," he said through the radio, "there's something going on down here. The shaft just shook."

"I felt it too," she said. "Let me look at some things. I'll call Scott."

Gavin's homunculus took a step toward Jonah, but the boy scurried farther away.

"You can't scare me that easily," Jonah said. "If you use earthquake magic, you'll die too."

"Gavin," Hope said in his ear, "Scott says there's a small cryovolcano just south of here discharging ice. We might be feeling some of the seismic effects of—"

"How sturdy is this plastic, Hope?" Gavin asked. "If the solids around this thing shift . . ."

"You've got to get Jonah out of there, Gavin," Hope said. "Those shafts definitely aren't load-bearing. We have safety shut-offs at each end too, so if there's a breach or a leak, they'll automatically seal."

"He doesn't want to come out," Gavin said. "Some of the techs from Earth have been pretending to be fairies from Jonah's books. He thinks they're down here somewhere and that I'm a 'bad fairy' who's trying to keep him out of their kingdom."

"Let me talk to him," Hope said.

Gavin tapped his fingers for voice command.

"Direct audio patch," he said, "Greenhouse 3 to external."

In the shaft, the homunculus's voice changed from a man's to a woman's.

"Jonah," Hope said. "Jonah, sweetie, I need you to come out of the tunnel. I'm in the greenhouse, okay? It's not safe down there and I need you to come out."

Jonah kicked out at the homunculus with a speed Gavin hadn't expected. The boy's foot hurled him into the corner where the shaft turned. Plastic bubbles flexed against Gavin's chest and back almost simultaneously, and with a force that hurt. He moved to right the tiny avatar, and saw Jonah scrambling away from him in the shaft.

"You are a bad fairy," the boy said. "Good fairies don't use the sorcerer's voice."

Damn you, Arthur C. Clarke. "Any sufficiently advanced technology . . ."

Just then, the shaft shook more violently, and Gavin dove forward as he watched the polyethylene rupture under his feet. He heard the hiss of gas-driven emergency shut-off valves closing, and knew in an instant that the homunculus—and the boy—were trapped.

"This just got really bad," Gavin said. "The plastic's a great insulator, but with a rupture, it's going to get cold down there—quick. I don't know if the gases are sealed inside either. Is there an emergency override to open the shutoff valve on your end?"

"We designed these before I had Jonah," Hope said. "We weren't figuring anyone would be *in* them for any reason. The ceiling clearance was actually designed for the homunculi if we needed to do maintenance, and there are thin wires woven in to detect breaks. The locks don't deactivate until the electrical connection is restored and/or the gas sensors don't pick up anything but nitrogen, CO_2, and oxygen. Well, *trace* amounts of methane, obviously—we didn't want a fart to shut down the ventilation."

"The problem is, the longer we're sealed off, the more carbon dioxide we have—and less oxygen," Gavin said. "The rock that's poking through and the gases won't be as thermally conductive as, say, water, but it's still going to get cold in here."

Gavin examined the rupture more closely. A liquid rivulet in the fissure outside the plastic seemed about to form a droplet, but as the rivulet approached the break in the plastic, it evaporated into a haze.

"I've got liquid methane or ethane evaporating down here," Gavin said. "It's not a lot, but it's definitely getting in. The evaporation's making the air colder too."

"I radioed Scott," Hope said. "He's closest to our heavy tools, but he's still got to get into his suit and drag them over. The truck's broken down right now."

I'm not sure we have that kind of time.

I could extract oxygen, maybe, if we had water or ice.

It'd drain my power pretty quickly, but I could use the battery to heat my carbon-fibers—which probably wouldn't be enough to keep the kid alive anyway.

Gavin made his way back to the door and found a rupture worse than the one nearest Jonah. A gap in the rock had opened several feet below the opening, and he could see a liquid swirling and wisping into gas beneath the shaft's plastic. He tapped his fingers together.

"Spectrometer," he said, and a pale blue circle with a *sample area* label appeared in the center of his view. Given the homunculi's original expeditionary purpose, they'd been outfitted with an array of test equipment. Below him, he found ethane rather than methane evaporating in the cavity near the door. Gavin knew that ethane was heavier than air, and would remain trapped in the cavity. Methane would've floated up to fill the shaft, killing Jonah.

"How long until Scott gets here?" he asked.

"Thirty minutes, maybe," Hope said. "The suit, the airlocks—"

"It'll take another ten to fifteen minutes to get through that hatch with hand-tools," Gavin said. "The temperature's dropping by about a degree a minute, and I've got hydrocarbon gases evaporating in from several breaks in the shaft. Jonah didn't bring his respirator on his adventure to find his friends, nor did he bring his electric coveralls."

"Gavin, you've got to—" Hope said, but a sob caught in her throat. It was easy to be a calm, collected astronaut when it was her own life at stake, or that of another rational adult—one who'd volunteered to accept the risks. Her child was a different story.

He looked down at his tiny hands and up at the 8-inch-thick plastic safety door.

"What can I *use*?" he whispered.

"Yourself."

It wasn't Hope's voice this time, but Lori's, that came through the radio.

"Remember the early days of lithium-ion batteries?" she asked. "Cell phones, laptops—"

"I wasn't born then, Lori," he said. "Neither were you."

"Well maybe it pays to be a history buff," she said. "They used lithium-ions with other metals in the anodes rather than straight lithium because they were more stable and could be recharged. They still had problems though, especially with cheap knock-off batteries with bad separators. Sometimes the batteries would catch fire or explode. They were prone to thermal runaway. Our batteries have a gel electrolyte now, but they're pretty much the same design, Gavin."

"Good thing we have top-notch separators, right?"

"Lithium's still unstable, and if you connect the cathode and anode directly—"

"It would catch fire, but I'd probably just burn up inside the—" Gavin said, then paused. He looked down at the hydrocarbon gas pool building under the break near the door. "Oh. I'm just the detonator."

"I can be there in one minute's flight," Lori said. "I'll have to go in and pull the kid out once the hatch is breached."

"Hope," Gavin said, "this is your call. We can wait for your husband, and risk gas filling up this shaft while the temperature drops. I don't think Jonah will get hypothermia, but he may run out of air. We might get another tremor, too."

Gavin waited.

"What's the worst thing that can happen if you blow the door?" she asked.

"The *worst* thing is that I don't actually blow it, and maybe the tunnel around the opening collapses. As long as Jonah stays around the corner, there's almost no risk of shrapnel."

"Shrapnel?"

"Well," Lori said, "if we wait too long, the methane and ethane concentrations mean you'll get a fireball inside the shaft also. You pretty much have to do this now or not at all."

"No," Hope said. "No no no. Wait for Scott. He'll get here, and we can get my baby in a respirator, and—"

She stopped talking, as though her attention had been taken by something on another channel. Gavin thought he might've lost his radio connection.

"Lori?"

"Yeah," Lori said, "I'm here, but you might only have me on the ship's internal."

"Scott says there's a fissure outside the toolshed," Hope said finally. "The frame on the airlock split and the inner door won't open. The safety circuit won't allow it."

"Can he pull the circuit and hotwire it?" Lori asked.

"I think so," Hope said, "but it's going to take time."

"Hope—" Lori said.

"Okay," Hope said. "Do it. I'll put on my respirator and get Jonah's. The air's going to get pretty foul."

"I'm flying to Greenhouse 3 now," Lori said. "I'll take the other respirator in with me."

Gavin walked back to where Jonah sat huddled in the shaft.

"Hey buddy," Gavin said. "Sorry about all the bad fairy tricks earlier. You passed the test. We're going to let you into the fairy kingdom, okay?"

"I don't feel good," Jonah said. "My head hurts."

"Yeah," Gavin said. "We can fix that in a minute. My friend Princess Lori is going to come show you where the gate to the fairy kingdom is."

"Really?"

"Really," Gavin said. "I just need one favor from you."

"What?" Jonah asked, eying him with renewed suspicion.

"I need you to pull my wings off. I don't have the strength to do it at that angle."

"Why?"

"Honestly," Gavin said, "it's so I can open a door for you. Don't worry—they'll grow back. It's fairy magic."

Gavin turned. Either the kid would do it, or he wouldn't.

After a moment, he felt a tug in the bubble box.

Error R999—came up in his display—*catastrophic damage to*—

"Yeah," Gavin whispered, "I know."

He turned, and picked up the folded wings from the floor of the shaft.

"Stay here kid," Gavin said. "Princess Lori won't come if you see the magical gate open, okay? You should really cover your ears and close your eyes too. The overpressure can make your ears bleed."

"What's overpressure?" Jonah asked.

"More fairy magic."

"Okay."

"How big's this fireball going to be?" Gavin asked when he rounded the corner.

"Most of the pictures I've seen were about a twelve-inch radius," Lori said. "The electrolyte burns will hit the far walls though. I'm inside the airlock now."

Gavin stepped up to the break near the safety door and pulled up the corner of the ruptured plastic, widening the gap enough to wedge himself inside. The safety door was only about an inch from the homunculus's face.

"Little man in a great big world," Gavin said. "Only way to make a difference is to tear your wings off and set yourself on fire."

"Don't get too dramatic down there, Babe," Lori said. "It's not your real body."

"It feels like it."

Gavin stripped the aramid-fiber cloth from one of his wings and separated a rib from the frame. He popped open the battery hatch on his back, and in one smooth motion, wedged the rib across the anode and cathode.

Error F451. Battery short—

Then nothing. Gavin's goggles went black and the bubbles stopped bubbling.

Lori heard a *WHUMP* at the same instant the plastic safety door flew out into the ventilation duct. She took Jonah's respirator from Hope and ignored the desperation in the mother's eyes.

"Jonah?"

Nothing.

She stepped over the charred remains of Gavin's homunculus, and traced the path to where he'd said Jonah was.

"Jonah?"

The boy looked at her, and she saw blood at the corner of his ear.

Ruptured eardrum. At least he'll survive to figure out when to take good advice.

Jonah seemed to be in a state of shock from the explosion and resultant pain, which Lori was half-thankful for as he numbly accepted her fitting the respirator to his face and leading him through the cloud of toxic fumes.

★ ★ ★

Two months later, when Jonah's eardrums had healed, he watched the two homunculi he'd known as Mr. Pickles and Lady Twilight wave and then dance while video of their controllers on Earth livestreamed behind them. He promised his mother he'd never venture into the shafts again.

Gavin and Lori put the finishing touches on their main habitat, and began work on their power and ventilation. Gavin had been given control of another homunculus, and corporate put a replacement unit on the next resupply rocket. They'd finished ahead of schedule, since Scott had taken time away from teaching online exobotany classes to help them build, and the other colonists had begun pitching in whenever they could.

"Thanks for saving my son when I couldn't," Scott said, as they admired their day's work.

"Thanks for helping us build," Gavin said. He hesitated before adding, "This may sound horrible, but I'm actually kind of glad it happened."

"Why's that?" Scott asked.

"Lori had been in a funk for about a month," Gavin said. "There wasn't a reason for it apart from the mental exhaustion of routine and confinement. She—well, after we rescued Jonah—she perked up. She actually told me that, 'seeing your charred little robot body turned me on.' Can you believe that? No offense meant. Of course I wouldn't want to see Jonah in danger again."

"No offense taken," Scott said. "If you were the sort of people who thrived in dull routine, you would've stayed on Earth, right?"

"I suppose. Lori wanted to be a pirate until she was fifteen."

"Hey, I got something from corporate you're going to want to see," Scott said. "Milton sent it to Hope first, since they'd collaborated on it."

"What's that?"

"The first data from the inside of a black hole," Scott said. "It's not *quite* what anyone thought it was. Maybe that's your next big adventure."

"If Lori lets me live long enough to reach Titan, you mean."

"Obviously."

Awoken from cryosleep and told to prepare for battle, Carax and his fellow soldiers didn't know what they would find in the hull of the enemy ship. Extrasolarian mutants or Jaddian janissaries, monsters or pirates. Instead, they found themselves face-to-face with an enemy pulled from their darkest nightmares.

NOT MADE FOR US

★

by Christopher Ruocchio

"I THINK THEY THAWED OUT the whole Chiliad," Larai said at mess. She hadn't touched her food. The printed beef had gone cold on her tray. That bothered me. Can't say why, only that Larai usually put away her rations faster than either Soren or me—faster than anyone on the decade—which were crazy, small as she is. Not today. She just sat there, hands on her bald head. Hadn't spoken the whole meal. Not even touched her coffee.

Soren don't usually talk much, so I said, "You sure?"

She nodded. "Heard one of the medtechs say H-Deck was emptied out. Ninth Century's out of the ice. Guessing the Tenth's not far behind."

"That mean a big campaign?" I said.

"That means a *fucking* big campaign," Soren put in, setting down his fork.

Took me half a second to realize he was eying me. "What?"

"You've not had a proper campaign, son." He had this weird look in his eyes, like he were my da back on Aramis. I was about to respond when a voice came from my right. Gave me such a start I dropped my knife.

"My money's on annexation, lads!" I didn't see the decurion sneak up on us, but there he was: Peter Thailles in his black fatigues. He looked a little older than he had when I'd gone into the ice, making me wonder if he'd run up his clock somehow while we slept. Soren says officers always time-out faster than us groundlings. He noticed I'd dropped my knife and—clapping me on the shoulder all friendly—added, "Sorry, Oh-Four! You frighten that easy? Scarier than me's coming, you mark my words."

I didn't say anything. I don't like the decurion much. Probably shouldn't write that, never know when an officer will root through my things. He's a decent enough officer. Just don't like the way he talks to Larai and the other ladies in the decade, but he's my commander . . . and I guess that's what I should expect from some black-barred patrician like him. All the ego of a nobile, none of the sting—gives him a real chip on his shoulder. "Reckon it's Normans," he said, leaning in over his dinner tray. "Reckon brass picked out another one of their freeholds. We'll see how long they hold free, eh?"

"Hopefully good and long," Soren said, jerking his head at me. "Last annexation I was on took seven *years*. Weren't even hard. Those Normans can't fight for shit."

Decurion Thailles narrowed his eyes, "Language, Oh-Six. This isn't that three-bit whorehouse they raised you in."

If Soren didn't like the decurion talking to him like that, I couldn't tell. Old bastard grinned lazily at the officer and said, "Were a four-bit whorehouse, sir. Might be they cut you a discount."

I had to wait until the others started laughing before I joined in. Even so, I kept my eyes down on my tray and didn't look the decurion in the face. His eyes freak me. Too blue they are, like a bird's egg. Ain't natural. Earth and evolution didn't mean for men to have eyes like them, but the pats and the nobiles do what they want. Chantry lets them. Ain't that kind of pride a sin?

"They told you something they've not told us?" Larai asked the officer.

The decurion, he turned to her—and I still don't like the look in those eyes of his—and he said, "They're always telling me things, Oh-Five, but they haven't said a thing." He were in the dark much as us, then. That makes sense, right? Captain Vohra's supposed to give us a talking-to over internal comms, but no one's heard from her or Commander Kolosov. Shuttles have been going back and forth from the *Sword of Malkuth* and the *Prince Raphael,* though. Business as usual. I know it's been only four days, but am I wrong to want some kind of clue from on high? I've heard everything from pirates to

Extras to Thailles's Norman theory. One kid in the Third Century said something about Mericanii war machines like in the old stories, but his centurion gave him extra PT for saying that shit, so I doubt we're flying into the sort of hell they write operas about.

Going to sleep. Hope there's more answers tomorrow.

There's this moment, right after I seal the helmet on but before the cams come on, where it's completely dark and mostly quiet. You can hear everyone else kitting out: seals hissing in place, laughter, the grind of straps tightening, someone swearing at their tunic for not draping right; but you can't really hear straight. You're alone. Then the suit comes online, puts up a set of readouts in the peripheral: heart rate, blood pressure, charge levels on plasma burner and phase disruptor, communications channels with my triad, my decade, and up and up to Captain Vohra on the command line. Then the vision flips on, filling the inside of the helmet with a flattened-out version of the world. How they do it I don't know. Chantry swears there ain't no demons in the suit thinking for us, and they'd know, but the helmet's visor sifts out a lot of the crap: shadows, tricks of the light, that sort.

That moment—when I stop looking at the world with the eyes my mother gave me and start looking at the screen the Empire tells me to use—that's when it changes. I ain't me no more, or not just me. I'm *them*. I'm *Empire*.

The ten of us piled into our shuttle, pressed tight together, pauldrons grating as we get jostled by the thrusters firing. "Shields at full charge!" the decurion called from the back of the shuttle, behind his three triads. "Oh-One, you and yours start shooting the minute you're over the lip! You heard the captain, there are no friendlies on the other side of that door. Second and Third, fan left and right, secure a position near the shuttle—we may need to make egress fast." I wasn't looking at him—barely heard him through the blood hammering in my damn ears—but he must have turned to the pilot officer in back because he said, "You keep the engines warm, boy, and keep an eye out for anything coming at you down the hull. No idea what sort of hull defense they're fielding, but if you get jumpy, you scream."

Thailles kept talking, but I don't remember much of it. I was staring at the door. Perfect round, it was, and wide enough to fit three legionnaires shoulder to shoulder. When it opened, I had no idea what would be on the other side. Laser cutters on the outside could make a door just anywhere, cut through anything short of highmatter or the long-chain diamond they use on some warships. Our shuttle would clamp onto the outer hull like a burr don't come off, cut its way in without causing a leak. This was the sort of thing you think about when they scoop you up in the levies—or when they got you in the signing center like me. You think about seizing Mandari trade ships operating in Imperial space without papers, about putting down rebellious lords with as little loss of life as possible, about reclaiming stations captured by the Extras or bringing some colonists into the light of the Empire.

Something hit the ship then, or nearly did. Maybe it bucked our shields. I lurched sidelong into Larai, who shoved me straight again. Funny how little you hear things, just by the sounds pushed into the hull. Shrike shuttles are small, fast, ugly things not meant for the sky. Outside, they look like cigars, or like one of the sword handles the Imperial knights carry around—only bristling with little engines. They're fast. Damn fast. Suppression fields cut most of the inertial bucking, but someone out there was firing on us, and that changed things faster than the field could track, rattling us in our armor. Don't remember much else of the approach. Don't even know how long it was. I was watching the clock in the corner of my suit's visual field, but the numbers wouldn't stick. Only thing I remember's my breathing. I was sealed in my suit, sealed in that shuttle. It was all I could hear outside the groaning of the ship. I was breathing like I'd been at wind sprints, or sparring for a good hour. I looked back, past the three soldiers behind me and Thailles to where the pilot officer sat in his chair. Unlike the rest of us, I could see his face through his visor. He was gritting his teeth.

Then it went real quiet, and Soren said, "We close to the hull? Inside their line of fire?"

"Stow it, Oh-Six!"

"Wish we could get a look at the thing," I said.

"You wouldn't see shit anyhow," Larai said.

"I said stow it!"

We hammered into the side of the ship, and I had to hold to a loop on the ceiling to keep from falling on my face and knocking Oh-One into the door. Something high-pitched whirred like a metal demon in front, and I thought of little teeth chewing on whatever it was we'd clamped onto. I know that ain't right, but I can't shake it. *I* was shaking then, even though I didn't *know*. I was so scared. Like I said, that door could open on anything. Anything. I imagined Extrasolarian mutants all metal and slime, or Jaddian janissaries in bright silk and those mirrored masks of theirs. Maybe I was picturing monsters like the ones the lords keep for sport, or pirates like I used to play at as a kid on Aramis. And that were just the shit I'd heard of. I tried to tell myself I were ready for it, trained for it. It didn't matter. Back at camp on Orden they said you forget everything you learn the minute the shit hits.

I did.

The whirring stopped, the door opened. Just inside, the walls of the ship glowed like old coals where the Shrike had cut in, and all was dark beyond. Not that it mattered. Helmet cameras compensated for the low light inside, boosted visuals with infrared and sonic mapping. Everything looked gray, and there wasn't much to look at.

"Blackened Earth!" said Oh-One, leading the way in.

"The hell sort of ship is this?" Larai said.

Soren were praying, muttering under his breath just soft enough I couldn't make out the words. Someone told him to stop, and he did, turning left to look down along the hall. Everything looked green and granular. I kept my plasma burner down, arms straight, waiting.

The gravity felt off. Lighter. I didn't like that. Heavier's easier to deal with than light; suit's exoskeleton kicks in. Low grav means less control.

Thailles jumped down out of the Shrike. I could make him out in the light of the shuttle door, taller than the rest of us and with the two red dashes on the blank white plane of his visor above the right cheek to mark his rank. The left side of his visor was painted in, black with a yellow bird on in profile—his house's seal. The way he hefted his burner rifle, he looked downright terrifying, red cloak drifting in the micrograv. He oversaw deployment of the mapping drones—which went spinning off into the dark—and said, "Oh-Six, take yours down and right, I want to know what we're dealing with."

Soren gestured understanding and we went off down the hall, if you could call it that. The walls were like cave walls, and the floor was uneven and rolling, like we'd come into an asteroid someone'd dug out. My foot splashed in something.

"What kind of ship is this?" Larai asked, repeating the question from earlier. She shined the light off her plasma burner up at the ceiling . . . highlighting where huge pipes were bracketed to the stone. "There're no lights."

"Mining rig, maybe?" Soren put in, turning back to look at us. "You seen any doors?"

"No, sir," I said.

"You don't have to *sir* me, boyo." I could hear the grin in his words. "Stay sha—!"

I remember seeing him standing there, lit by the backscatter off Larai's and my plasma burners and green in my suit's viewfinder. Then I blinked and he was gone, knocked flat on his ass by *something* that came flying unseen out of the dark. Whatever it was banged off his shield, making the energy curtain momentarily visible, casting faint lights up the stone walls. I flinched away. Larai surged forward, weapon raised. Fumbling with the controls on my vambrace, waving my weapon round like an idiot, I dialed my suit lights all the way up to give her something to see by, ready with cover fire. Soren was a good two meters back from where we stood, struggling to his feet. For a second, I couldn't find whatever it was that had hit him, but Larai swore all kinds of fierce and moved off to his left.

"What the hell is going on?" Thailles's voice rattled in my ears. "Oh-Four? Oh-Four!"

"Something hit Oh-Six, sir!" I kept looking, weapon up, careful to keep Larai out of my line of fire. Spotted movement in the dark, turned toward it. I panicked, squeezed off a shot, plasma burner coughing violet light. "Contact! Contact!" The thing were small, and I must have missed, cause it came tearing into the light and straight at me, forgetting about Soren. It were a snake, a flying snake about as long as my forearm and just as big around. I saw its teeth flash in my face—and then I were flying, knocked off my feet just like Soren. Plasma light flashed and my head rang when I smashed into the wall. Larai stood above me, offering a hand. I took it.

"What in nuclear hell was that?" Soren asked, sounding a little worse for wear.

I followed Larai over to the smoking remains of what she'd shot, keeping my weapon—God and Emperor, I'd been useless—trained on the damn thing.

"It's a machine!" Larai said, nudging it with her boot, "Look!" She made a warding gesture with her free hand. Protection against evil.

Crouching, I looked. It weren't teeth at the business end of the snake, but bits like on the end of a drill. I swore, and said, "Imagine what that'd do, if it got past your armor."

Thailles came in over the comms, and Soren explained. "Oh-Four and me got knocked the hell down, sir. Some kind of drone . . ."

"You ever seen something like this?" I asked Larai, looking up from where I was crouched over the thing.

She shook her head. "No."

"Think it's Extras? They use all sorts of crazy-ass machines, right? Evil shit? Shit Chantry burns you for?"

"Could be." She straightened, checking the safety on her burner. "Never been up against them." She took a second, keyed up her own suit lights to match mine. Up ahead, one of the pipes was venting steam into the hall. Somewhere behind, I heard a *thud* banging through the wall and knew another Shrike cutter had grappled the hull and that somewhere another decade was on their way in. I could see the map of the ship taking shape in my suit's display, threads linking up like spider webs as the other decades deployed their drones.

"Best get moving," Soren said, "want to find a door or something."

Something screamed.

Earth and Emperor preserve me. The sound of it . . . like metal tearing ice.

I didn't want to be a soldier. Didn't want to leave Aramis. I done it for Minah. For the boy. I didn't want to be there. I wanted to throw down my gun and run back for the ship, hide there with the pilot officer until it were over.

They came out of the fog, and I still don't quite believe it. The stars ain't had anything like them around when I gone under. The worlds changed while I been froze . . . got . . . monsters in them now. And we got sent in to fight them without a word of warning.

At first I thought they was men. They had arms and legs like men. Walked like them. But as they got closer and got into the light, I saw they wasn't like us at all. They were tall. Taller than Thailles. And the arms stretched to their knees. And their faces—if they were faces—were like our visors. Smooth. White. With eyes big as my fist, black as space. No nose, no ears, but a mess of horns like on some devil from up on the Chantry walls.

I staggered back, mind locked up like I was some kind of idiot. Didn't even see the knife in its damn fist until it was on me. I couldn't think. I just froze, figured I was dead already.

"Carax! Down!"

My name got through to me. Not sure if it were Soren or Larai what said it. I fell into the wall and a shot flew past me, going wide as the *thing* lurched toward me. It stopped, pulled something from its waist, and threw it. One of those drone things. I heard someone cry out, tried to make myself aim, tried to control my breathing. I raised my burner and fired, hit the thing in the shoulder, but that didn't hardly seem to slow it down.

There were more of the things then, three or four coming out of the fog down the hall. Loping, doglike, only on two legs. Another shot went past. In the shaking lights off our suits, I saw teeth like broken glass snarling. It didn't go down. *It didn't go down.*

A huge hand grabbed me by the neck and pushed me up the wall. It squeezed, but the suit underlayment hardened and wouldn't let it choke me. I could feel the fingers tighten. I panicked, dropped my gun and tried to pull its fingers off me. They were like steel. And the face . . . Earth and Emperor, the *face*. I seen statues of Death in Chantry, all skull with empty eyes. Up close it were like that, like someone forgot to finish it, but poured white wax over a skeleton and called it done. Horns snarled above those huge eyes, curved back in a crown. We was nearly eye to eye, only there weren't nothing in its face, no light like a man has, no fire like a woman. Just empty. Flat. Like my da's eyes had been when I seen him dead as a boy.

That made me think of my boy and Minah, and I remembered my knife. I pulled it from my belt and brought it up under the monster's arm. Must have found something, because it hissed and dropped me. I fell like a bunch of sticks, slipped down the wall. Damn ankle went out from under me, and I think I yelled. Don't know what happened to the creature. Soren came out of nowhere, holding his burner out, one-handed, the other pressed to his side. The old man fired, shouted, "On your feet!"

That were when another loomed up out of the darkness, a long, white blade in its hands. I tugged my phase disruptor free from its holster, raised my arm. The thing hummed silent in my fist, and the energy current struck it blue in the chest. It went down spasming, long arms twitching as the disruptor burned out nerve channels and fried the creature in its own meat. Soren looked down at me. "Thanks."

I nodded, trying to find my wits. My first real fight. I wasn't ready. Not for this. I should have been back on Aramis. Should have lived to death with Minah. I could still run. Thailles would have me whipped, but whipped ain't dead, and the Shrike weren't far.

Thailles's voice was filling my ears on comms, shouting orders that didn't mean nothing anymore. Sounded like they'd found *them* too. It weren't real. This were just some nightmare I wasn't supposed to have. The hull around us shuddered like we was inside a metal drum. More Shrikes clamping on. More soldiers. Maybe that were the seals popping on cryofreeze. Maybe I was waking up.

"Carax, stand the fuck up!" Soren screamed. In a lull, he fiddled with his burner—swapping from shot to torch mode—then turned and sprayed a great stream of plasma fire over the things.

"Carax!" Larai added.

I was so gone I thought it were Minah for a moment, and that got me standing. The disruptor had no kick to it like the burner, so I pointed one-handed at another of the monsters, leaning against the rough stone wall. The energy bolt found its mark on the side of its head, and it went down smoking. Think I shouted something, because Soren glanced back over his shoulder. "Nice shot!" I could hear the grin in his voice. He sounded normal. Maybe he needed to sound normal.

Then it all went wrong. More wrong.

The wall blew apart in a flash of light and Soren were . . . he were just gone. Him and the demons. One second he was standing there, looking back at me, then nothing. The wind blowing out howled louder than the explosion. My ears rang. I couldn't think. I was ripped off the ground and thrown out the new hole. The wind froze around me and I spiraled out into the Dark. Something grabbed my leg. One of the demons, it had to be. I kicked, figured I'd smash its skull-face in. Only then the words screaming over my suit's comm got through to me: "Carax! Carax it's me!"

Larai.

You're not going back to the ship now, farm boy.

"It's not real," I kept saying. "It's not real. It's not real."

But it were. I tried to stop us tumbling, but as we got farther and farther away . . . I could see it. The ship—if it was a ship—was huge, so huge it vanished into the Dark, lit only by the running lights of a hundred Shrike cutter craft clamped on the outer hull. "Is that ice?" I remember it was the first coherent thought I'd had since the shuttle door opened.

"What?"

"Ice!" I tried to point. "It's covered in it." In the light of the shuttles, we could see pieces—just pieces—of a ship growing out of the Dark. Parts was metal, parts stone, all covered and glittering in a thick layer of ice. We was still getting signal fed in from the mapping drones on board, and I could see the full scale of the craft taking shape in the corner of my eye. It were huge. Bigger than the *Valorous*, bigger than any ship I'd ever heard of, so big it distracted me from the fact that Larai and I were careening out into naked space.

"Oh-Four, Oh-Five! Report!"

"Thailles?" I practically choked. "Soren's dead. Got hit by something from outside." Just then another explosion tore into the icy mass, and we saw flames spill out behind a blinding flash and fade to darkness. "Larai and I are . . . sir. We're dead."

I weren't scared. Maybe I didn't have no scared left in me.

"What?" Thailles said. "I'll have none of that. You two get the hell back here and help us hold until the whole Chiliad's on board this damn ship. I'm not losing anyone else. I—"

"We got blown outside, sir."

The Decurion swore. "How?"

"Something hit the outside," I said, "hull defense, maybe? Or one of ours? Didn't get a good look." The words was just spilling out.

Larai cut in, "You can't send the shuttle for us?"

Sounds of fighting over the line. The only sound in our world, except the breathing. I already knew what Thailles would say. Was thinking about Minah, about what it would be like to see her when the Earth comes again. And the boy. We'd be a family, right and proper. And there wouldn't be no demons.

"No."

Larai's hand tightened on my leg where she still held on. She swore. I had to shut my eyes, the spinning were making me sick, watching that impossible big ship get farther and farther away. I tried to guess the distance. We might have only been a thousand feet out, but that were good as light-years, unless . . .

Unless . . .

Unless I did something very stupid.

"You still got your burner?"

"What?"

"I lost mine when that . . . that *thing* grabbed me," I said. "Do you have yours?" I looked down at her where she held my ankle, and it were like I could see through her visor and feel her eyes watching me.

"What are you . . . ?"

"Just give it over!" I snapped, head going clear. Minah would wait. The Earth had not come back to us today, and even if the priests was wrong and the universe weren't made for us . . . I didn't think Soren would want me giving up. I'd already betrayed the old bastard's memory with my coward's thoughts, but I wasn't going to just let us die. We'd have to find our own way back to the ship.

It were harder than I thought getting the gun from Larai—without losing it or her in the Dark. Took longer, the stars all around, cold like eyes watching. I had both my hands free, and fed a cartridge into the side of the weapon.

I remembered that in orientation right before the freeze a couple of the others—I forget what decade they was—got busted racing in one of the null-G parts of the *Valorous* with fire suppressant tanks, using them to fly around one of them big storage bays. Got dressed down direct by the captain herself for that shit, rest of us had a laugh. This were the same thing, only the burner had a little more kick to it.

No air to pull out there, nothing around us but our suits. I switched the burner to torch mode and squeezed off a couple short bursts. The violet plasma streams slowed our roll enough that I could point the thing straight away from the ship. Larai got the idea and held on with both hands. I were not going to die out here, choking on my own fumes. I weren't going to let Larai go the same way. No.

Just had to get back to the ship. I tried to keep that in mind. *We just have to get back to the ship.* I tried not to think about the demons, about their white hands and those black eyes.

I fired, squeezed the trigger down for a good five seconds. "You all right?" I asked Larai, shouting despite the comms tying us. She nodded, but didn't answer. Maybe she thought she were going to be sick. I get that. We wouldn't be the only ones thrown out into the Dark. I tried not to think about that, about our brothers and sisters dying out there. Or about what else were dying with us.

The frozen ship got closer, flickering in the running lights off our shuttles clamped to its surface. I fired again. A good, long burn. The ship must have gotten closer, but it didn't seem to. A note blinked in my suit helmet, and I expelled the burner's plasma reservoir with a click that went all the way up my arm.

"Damn torch mode burns through the packs fast," I said, and slotted one of the replacement reservoirs into the gun. Fired.

Fired.

Fired.

"This the one we got blown out of?" Larai asked, pointing down into the hole. The ice around it was cracked, whiter than elsewhere in the light off our suits. The metal beneath tore inward, stone shattered. Debris drifted there, like it was floating underwater.

Peering over the edge of the hole, I shook my head. "No, don't think so. Don't recognize it." Not a hall inside. Looked like some sort of cargo hold. Red lights hung from what I guessed were the ceiling, faint as old coals. I wondered if these demons saw in the dark, or if they was blind. My da used to tell me things what live in space go pale over the years, living in the dark of their ships. Hadn't happened to me so I figured he was full of it, but I can't stop thinking about that white hand on my throat.

"Decurion?" I tried my comms. Nothing. "Decurion Thailles, this is Oh-Four. I have Oh-Five and we've made the ship again. Repeat, we've made the ship." I looked at Larai, tried to imagine her face through the visor of her helmet; those big eyes wide or narrowed. Were she scared? Or did she set her jaw that way she had? Seemed like she was taking this whole situation better than me.

She tried Thailles on her comms, then toggled over to the main channel.

Nothing.

"They jamming us?" I asked, not wanting to think about the other option.

"Must be, reckon we can only hear each other because we're right here. Give me my burner back, eh?"

I passed the gun to her. "Could try raising the *Valorous*."

"Done that," she said, swinging herself down through the hole. "We've got to find a unit. Any unit."

I followed on after her, stomach lurching as the gravity field inside the ship snagged us out of null G and dropped us to the floor. Storage containers and bits of trash and broken hull filled the hold—and more than a few bodies. None of them was ours, though. Just . . . them. I stopped a second, mindful again of the breathing in my own ears. "The hell'd they not tell us for? What we was getting into? Scaring the shit out of us don't make sense."

"Bet they didn't want us panicking aforehand," Larai shot back, checking the charge on her plasma burner. I wished I hadn't lost mine. "You imagine? Ship full of two thousand Legs learn they're walking into this? Captain don't want that."

That didn't sit with me, still don't. "You reckon they were afeared of mutiny?" Then another idea hit me, and I said, "You reckon this is *first contact*?"

I could see her shake her head. "I bet that happened while we were icicles, Carax. The world changed while we were getting our beauty sleep."

Tried raising Thailles on the comms again as we crossed the floor of the hold toward what looked like doors. Faint blue lights pulsed next to them, and I wondered if they was sealed up against the vacuum. They was, and Larai used her burner to cut through the black metal. Wind started whistling out—you could see it cooling the red edges of the hole she'd made. We forced our way through. I never heard such noise: the wind screaming out, weird alarm howling like a stuck pig, and us only still on our feet because of the rail inside the hall we pulled along.

". . . rendezvous at . . ."

"They're coming out of the walls!"

"—all back! Fall back!"

Snatches of comms chatter broke through as we pulled ourselves down the hall. Up ahead, I could see a massive bulkhead beginning to close. The blue lights flashed ahead even as the ship rocked under what I guessed were more collisions from Shrike fliers clamping on. I had to turn down the audio relays in my helmet—the static kept snapping in my ears. "Come on!" I shouted, doubling back to haul Larai past me and up the rail. The door was closing slow—way slower than they did on our ships during drills. Maybe it were old, maybe it were broken, maybe all those prayers I said in Chantry as a boy was worth something. We made it to the other side.

The alarm were still going, all high and thin sounding. Reminded me of the whistle Crazy Hector used to control his dogs back on Aramis, like there were more sound we wasn't hearing.

"The hell are we?" Larai asked, and I saw the problem. The mapping drones had done a merry job sketching halls and chambers in all kinds of details—but we wasn't on it. Whatever were jamming the comms were jamming our suits' telemetry, too.

"No idea," I said, more comms chatter crackling in my ear. None of it made sense. I went a ways up the hall, disruptor held straight-armed and ready. Couldn't hear nothing, couldn't see a thing outside what my suit lit up. Bits of cloth hung from the walls, black and blue, painted with these round symbols in white and red and pale yellow. They fluttered in the air—still not settled from the venting. Passages opened behind some of them. That scared me. Whatever these things was, they didn't seem to need their eyes much as Larai and me.

"Looks like we have to find a way up—" I broke off, the next thought hitting me like a tram. "I wish Soren were here."

Don't know why that didn't settle in sooner. Maybe it were because we were only just then getting time to breathe. There hadn't been time to really think about it until then. The old bastard hadn't even seen it coming.

I didn't get time to keep thinking about it.

"You cage!" something screamed. Or something like that. "You cage! You cage!" Then a bunch of sounds that made no sense. Then Larai shouted. One of the . . . *things* had emerged from a side passage and grappled her. It happened so fast. She hit the ground and it stooped over her like a revenant in the stories they used to tell us as kids. I didn't see a weapon, but it had its hands on her face. Them long fingers found the hardware clasps there and worked them free.

I heard Larai gasp as the seals vented, could hear the air hiss out as the pressures balanced. The faceplate of her helmet fell away, and the creature lowered its face to hers. She screamed.

I fired.

The disruptor burst caught the creature full in the back, and it slumped where it crouched over Larai. Thin gray coils of smoke rose out of my suit lights and away into darkness. I lowered the disruptor, stepping forward to look down at the beast. Only then did we see it were different, not dressed in the black armor the ones up top had been, but in simple gray clothes. There were a hole in the back of the shirt where the disruptor had taken it, smoking and black where the nerves had burned away.

"Are you all right?" I asked, crouching to hand Larai back her faceplate.

"It stinks in here," she said, taking the mask back. It took her a moment to shake herself free. Dead, the creature was all a tangle of limbs. Larai kicked it, ran a hand over her face. Took me a second to see she was shaking. "Its teeth . . ."

"I seen them," I said, checking behind one of the hangings.

"They go all the way back . . ."

"I said I seen them." Talking about it only made it worse. I couldn't listen anymore. All I could think on was getting back. Getting up. I decided I wasn't going to go out like Soren. It didn't matter if Minah was dead back home. Her and the boy. I were still fighting for them. For Aramis. For Earth and Empire—even if the Empire didn't give a shit about me. Even if all they do is tax me and ask me to die fighting their wars. Shit, they're better than these monsters. Anything was. And I weren't fighting for no Empress anyhow. I were fighting for home, for whatever family I had left— even if they didn't remember stupid old Carax who flew off to be a soldier. Wherever they were, whatever had become of them, I am still me. Still alive. I had signed up for them. I was still fighting *for* them. *That* hadn't gone anywhere, that hadn't changed—whatever else had.

Larai tried to get her mask back on.

"Black Earth! Bastard broke one of the seals." Still swearing, she tripped the catch at the base of her jaw and pulled the rest of the helmet off by the neck flange.

"Tiny gods, it's rank in here." She sniffed. "Smells like ass."

"I'll keep my helmet on, then," I said, forcing a laugh that failed to reach her. I was trying not to think about what her losing her helmet meant. About how vulnerable it made her. We hurried on, checking behind the hangings and around corners that branched off and wandered down into darkness. Off the hall, the rooms were more like little caves than real rooms. Here and there the natural stone would give way to a dead or blinking console, the screen so faint I couldn't see anything on them, even in the full light of my suit lamps. Once or twice we thought we heard something in the dark, but it were nothing. Larai stuck close.

After Earth knows how long like this, at last we found a passage leading up. It weren't no stair, but a sort of ramp spiraling up and out of sight.

"Smells like plasma burn in here . . . all cooked," Larai said. Without her suit, her voice sounded thick and muddy in the air. "Where is everyone?"

I spoke through my suit speakers. "Maybe they're higher up? Fighting the others."

We'd gone into a side room then, a series of small rooms behind a black hanging. Food—some kind of raw meat, looked like—lay on a table high as my chin. Storage cabinets in the walls made of some sort of flow-mold plastic. "I don't think this is a military ship, Larai." I'd found a tiny figure—bits of carved bone and metal pegs—shaped like one of the monsters. There were a faint blue flush in its hollow cheeks, and it had this sort of black robe. Dress. Thing. It were a toy, or I felt sure it must be. I put it in my sabretache with my extra air cells. It had a long knife in its hand, like the one I'd almost been stabbed with.

"Carax, come here."

I moved to stand by her. She'd climbed up onto a step by the table to get a better view of the food there. I swore. Meat, a huge piece of it, bones pulled apart and yellow-brown from the oven. When she spoke, her voice went all kinds of distant. "I recognized the smell." She reached out, turning the food a little on its tray. It had been roasted in its skin, the flesh crackled and leaking juice. As she turned it, the lines of a tattoo—some Mandari symbols—came into the light. She said again, "I recognized the smell."

I swore, "Earth and Emperor." From the size of it, she had been a woman. Once. Pieces of her were set on smaller trays about the table, half-eaten. "We interrupted their meal." I thanked Earth I couldn't smell, not through the suit. I wanted to throw up. To cry. To kill something. I staggered back, vision blurring a little. "Where did they get the . . . the body?"

"I don't know," Larai said. "Captured a ship before? Maybe that's why we're here? Revenge?" She shook her head. "Justice."

"Reckon there are more prisoners?"

I didn't hear Larai answer. The comms channel chose that moment to spit out more noise.

"What?" I said.

"I said did you hear—" She whirled, fired. The plasma left a glowing pockmark in the wall. "Something ran past us!" Then she was gone, back toward the hall. I followed, cursing to myself, but glad to leave that place and its terrible meal. Suit systems relayed an amplified model of the tunnels around, ghost paths off suit sonar showing the way around corners. I heard Larai shoot, saw the flash of plasma fire backscatter off the walls. When I caught up with her, she was standing in the middle of the hall, in an arch opening onto a massive space. At least, it felt big, I couldn't see the roof in my suit lights, even with my vision enhanced.

"Where'd it go?" I asked.

"Where do you think?" she hissed, jabbing her burner at the room ahead.

"Shit." I didn't like the look of it. We'd climbed a fair way since reentering the ship—and seen almost nothing in all that time—but this spot were so exposed, and there was only us two.

There weren't nothing for it, but had I known what were out there, I'd have liked to stay in that arch another hour, or gone back down and out again. I don't expect to be quit of the memory until they put me back on ice. But I didn't know that, and I opened my damn mouth. "We got to make a break for it."

"What?"

"Well, we can't stay here."

"If there's anyone out there, they'll see us. We should turn out the lights."

"Then we won't see shit. These things live in the Dark, Larai," I said. She swore, but in that way she had where I knew she agreed with me. She was all pale looking in the scant light, like one of Them. "You ready? Your shield still good?"

"Took a bit of a hit on the way outside," she said. Then, "Yeah."

I checked my disruptor, keyed up the spotlight under its slit of a barrel, and hurried out into the Dark at a jog. Larai moved past me soon enough, but held pace just in front of me, which was good. I still had my helmet, so my vision were better. I could see ahead more clearly. Even so, I didn't see the others until we were on top of them.

Until they screamed.

There must have been half a hundred of them, all gathered around the foot of a huge, black stone, between the arms of some shrine or altar built in the grotto. The darkness stretched out forever around us, and even the door we'd come through were lost. Red lights burned remote as dying embers on the arms of the shrine, cast upon the carved surface of the black monolith. Were they praying to it? Or only sheltering themselves, hoping to ambush us as we went by?

These was no soldiers. These was others like the one I'd shot in the back, dressed in simple clothes and not armor at all. But they was still monsters, still with slitted noses and black eyes the size of my fist, like I'd walked into some goddamned tomb. Larai fired before I could think, taking down two, three, four. The beasts hissed and drew back. But they didn't draw up like I expected, using their height to scare the piss out of me. They shrank down, away. Some fell over the others to get *away*.

"Wait!" I shouted, and were surprised when I didn't sound scared. I sure felt scared. "Larai, wait."

"What is it?" She'd backed up so we stood almost shoulder to shoulder. I reached up and unsealed my helmet, letting the mask slot back properly. "What in Earth's Holy Name . . . ?"

"They ain't soldiers. Look."

Without the flattening of the helmet's vision, I saw what they was. Monsters, yes, with glass fangs and those horrible, melted-skull faces. But with my own eyes I could see the way their nostrils flared, eyes wider than seemed possible. They was scared. Same as me. Or maybe their scared is different. They ran, scattered toward exits I could only guess at. The noise they made—high and cold—I haven't stopped hearing it. I put my helmet down on the floor, lowered my weapon. That's when I heard it. Shots. Plasma fire. Yelling.

Soldiers. Legionnaires.

Humans.

We stood there stunned, watching them go—watching still more huddle against the black monolith or against the arms of the shrine. I must have turned my head for two seconds, but it were enough. I heard Larai scream even as something huge hit me full in the side, and I went down with one on top of me. It shrieked like metal tearing, like cold wind.

I thought about Soren, about the meal we had found . . . about my Minah and the boy. The creature's arms were like iron about me, fingers wedged between the plates of my armor and the underlayment, tearing. I felt a clasp pop somewhere about my ribs. For a moment, I'd forgotten the disruptor was in my hands, forgotten the creature was not armored. Its breath hissed in my ear, and I thought it were going to bite me. I fired, insulated from collateral nerve shock by my suit. The creature went limp as a sack of wet oats, and I peeled it off me, staggering to my feet again.

Another of the creatures had Larai pinned down. Her burner'd been knocked away, and it had each of her wrists in its huge, long-fingered hands. It stooped over her, its face near to hers. I remembered their snarling, jagged teeth, and didn't hesitate. I were done hesitating. I squared my shoulders and fired. There were a flash of blue light and it fell on top of her.

Better to fight. Always better to fight.

I kept my disruptor raised, circling away from the shrine and the crowd of demons. Slowly. Sounds of fighting and gunfire came from up the hall. "Over here!" I cried. "Over here!" Then more quietly to Larai, "You all right?"

"Help me up!"

The beasts nearest me turned, unsure where to go. I could see the fear in them eyes, and knew it were fear like mine. One saw me and froze. Larai said something, but I couldn't hear her. I was watching the creature. Its huge eyes. Its horns. Its white hair tangled on its shoulders. It looked at me a good long time, flinching away. Not knowing why, I held out my free hand, above my head. I smiled. It cocked its head, took a step forward. Then I saw the stains about its mouth, on its chin. Red stains on the blue-white face.

"Carax, what are you doing?" Larai hissed.

"Quiet," I said, and moved slowly for my sabretache. I fished the strange doll out and held it out, keeping my disruptor primed, aimed at the floor beside me. The child—I don't know why I think it was a child, for it was taller than I was by a head—inched forward, raising its own hands, reaching for the doll I held. I weren't going to shoot. Monster or not, man-eater or not, I wasn't going to gun a child down. Fighting for the Empire was better than letting these monsters eat us, but I knew where I draw the line. I glanced at the helmet I'd left on the floor, then back to the creature. It looked me in the face, eyes narrowed, teeth bared.

And then it had no face. Only smoking ruins.

I don't think it were Larai who shot it. I think it were one of the others. One of the bone-colored Legionnaires in their red tabards looking like the enlistment posters. Faceless as the creature were now.

But they was a human kind of faceless.

A missing scientist. A secret lab. Corporate power-players jockeying for position in the mob-like ranks of the Syndicate Corporation. Enter SynCorp chief enforcer Stacks Fischer, a man who's not afraid to walk the mean streets of the Moon's Darkside.

THE ERKENNEN JOB
★
by Chris Pourteau

★ THE CONTRACT ★

TONY TWO-POINT-OH sat back in his chair and stared across the expanse of his English oak desk. I could see how much he favored his father when he did that. Same iron jawline. Same bony temple. Like someone had pulled an exoskeleton off a Martian assembly line and stretched skin over it. When he's angry, Tony's forehead ripples like liquid metal.

"It's a power play, pure and simple." His voice rumbled in the back of his throat. "Ra'uf Erkennen is making a move."

"Why not keep the marshals on the case?" I asked. Seemed like a perfect job for the Marshals Service, that bastion of law and order bought and paid for by the Syndicate Corporation. Like everything else in the solar system.

Tony shook his head. "When we thought Blalock had simply stolen tech, the marshals were fine. Now that we know Ra'uf is up to something . . . no, this secret lab in Darkside needs to stay a secret as far as the public is concerned. We need to handle this privately."

I nodded. By *we*, he meant *me*: Stacks Fischer, chief enforcer for SynCorp and Tony's personal assassin.

The Erkennen Faction had first reported that a scientist named Mason Blalock had committed corporate espionage and stolen research and dashed to Darkside with it. That's why the marshals went in. Now, we knew the situation wasn't so simple thanks to a whistleblower inside the Erkennen organization. Blalock was conducting secret research meant to upset the delicate, nuanced relationship of SynCorp's Five Factions. And meant to put the Erkennens at the top of the totem pole.

"What's this super-secret tech again?"

Tony had to look to remind himself. "Molecularly Enhanced Synthetic Hemp." He said each word deliberately.

"Developing a new drug in Darkside," I grunted. "Now there's a shocker."

Tony shrugged. "My little bird inside Erkennen tells me it's a game-changer. Ra'uf plans to use the new strain of hemp to take over," he said, stroking the plush arms of his leather chair.

"Using drugs as a weapon?"

Tony shrugged again. "How he plans to do it, I have no idea. But the fact that Ra'uf is working offline is already a violation of the corporate compact."

That was true enough. But each of the Five Factions maneuvered against the others all the time. This particular power play seemed to have Tony especially on edge.

"We need to set an example, Eugene." Tony gave me the unblinking eye, that look he reserves for his inner circle when he's passing along privileged Company knowledge. Or trying to intimidate the other guy.

"I reckon so," I said. But I wanted to be crystal clear on expectations. "You want me to bring Blalock back?"

Tony's eyes went cold. Ice-blue cold. Like his power core had just shut down, if he'd had a power core. "Kill the geek. Take the tech."

I stood. "I'll head out post-haste, Boss." How hard could it be to find one rogue scientist making new-and-improved pipeweed in Darkside?

"One more thing. Ra'uf Erkennen needs to be taught a lesson." Tony's words were gravel in a grinder. "Make it loud and clear."

"I'll get it done, Boss."

"I have every confidence, Eugene," he said with a wolfish smile. Tony's bone structure made the expression seem painted on again, like an undertaker had pinned his skin back to force a peaceful repose for respectful mourners. "Good hunting."

I thought about stopping by The Slate—my favorite watering hole on the orbiting station that served as SynCorp's headquarters—and pump Mickey Stotes, the proprietor, for information. But I figured whatever the Erkennens were playing at with Blalock was still far enough off-grid that even Mickey, usually a fount of useful knowledge, wouldn't know anything. If not for Tony's secret source inside the Erkennen Faction, neither would we. So I headed dockside and my ride waiting there.

From Tony's penthouse office in SCHQ, the vator ride down to the deck where the parking's cheap always takes a while. I don't mind. Gives me time to think, make sure I know what I think I know.

He's smart, Tony. Street-smart, unlike his father Anthony Taulke, who was a brilliant engineer and world-builder but not so smart when it came to managing people. Tony must've gotten his people skills from momma. As SynCorp's CEO and head of the Taulke Faction, he's a master at keeping the other four factions off-balance and everyone toiling toward the Company's bottom line. Maintaining the status quo means everyone wins.

That's what made this move by the Erkennen Faction even more odd. The Erkennens developed tech for the Company. That was their main contribution. But apparently Ra'uf Erkennen had decided to conduct this particular project off-book. He was risking a lot taking on Tony.

As the decks flashed by, I pulled my left bicep against my side to find the comforting curve of my stunner in its holster. Comforting yes, but stunners are new tech, only out a few years, and I don't trust 'em. That's why I carry backups. Strapped to my right wrist, my knife in a spring launcher. Inside my left ankle, my .38, what they used to call a police special a couple hundred years ago. The knife and the pistol were my old reliables.

Given what Tony wanted done, the stunner might be too humane anyway. The stunner tech, which I still didn't really understand, somehow causes a living being's EM field to shock them to death. It's a quick and supposedly painless way to go. And it requires less mopping up afterward.

But sometimes in this business you want to make a mess. The .38 would leave a weeping hole for everyone to gape at on CorpNet. I'd just have to make sure the wound was visible to make Tony's point for him: taking on Tony Taulke is no Sunday afternoon stroll with the family. It always has real consequences—deadly consequences. With that in mind, I walked off the vator appreciating Ra'uf Erkennen's testicular fortitude.

One quick valet delivery later, and I was back in the Hearse's cockpit. There are few places I feel safer. She's a fast, sleek little ship with black and silver lines and an oversized trunk for . . . well, you know . . . cargo. The Hearse—I named her myself—exchanged bona fides with SynCorp Control, and we were on our way to the moon and its main colony, Darkside. It'd be a few hours before I got there, so I went over the briefing from Tony again in my head.

The Erkennen Faction had first said that Mason Blalock, one of their own scientists, had stolen groundbreaking tech, maybe to hand over to the Resistance—called Ghosts because their favored way to resist is to gum up the works of the corporate machinery. Ghosts say they're fighting for mankind's freedom from the indentured servitude of life under SynCorp, but most of Sol's citizens are perfectly happy to let the Company run their lives. It wasn't forty years ago we all thought we'd expire right along with what was left of Earth. Then the corporations came along and saved us: colonized Mars, developed Titan's resources. So who can blame the citizenry if they trade a little freedom for survival of the species? When the Ghosts sabotage the assembly lines or blow up Company assets? Well, it strikes me as damned ungrateful.

When it looked like just another corporate espionage job by Blalock, SynCorp had dispatched the Marshals Service to set things right. But you only engage the marshals when you want the law enforced and the citizenry to see you've enforced it. When you need a message sent that's a little more direct—like to big-balled Ra'uf Erkennen, keen on taking Tony's job—well, that's where I come in.

I let myself relax a little and looked up through the Hearse's canopy. I was finally away from the bright blue marble, and the dark silver of the stars shone in. Other than the getting paid part, this was my favorite part of the job—traveling alone in the Hearse, carefully planning my next steps.

I still had hours to Darkside. With the starlight streaming in and my racing thoughts finally starting to calm, I pulled up the Hearse's reading library. This was my thing to do while I waited on the flight time. Waiting is ninety percent of my job. Some assassins play games on their padds. Some eat ravenously, mechanically. Some drink, but not too much. None dare to sleep if they want to stay alive.

Me? I like to read books. That's where I get my nickname from, by the way—my love for reading stacks of books. What, you thought it referred to how many bodies I've piled up in my career?

I pulled up Mickey Spillane. He'd do.

★ THE INVESTIGATION ★

FOUNDED AS DARKSIDE'S END, the largest settlement on the moon had once been the hope of humanity. It was supposed to be the first giant footprint for mankind off a dying planet, a springboard to a second chance among the stars. Then everything went to shit on Earth even faster than the experts predicted. Instead of a shining city on a lunar hill, the moon became a way station where people stopped off on their way to more important places like Mars. I remember a line from some old vid: *a wretched hive of scum and villainy*. That describes Darkside perfectly. Yeah, that's what everyone calls it now . . . no End in sight.

Once I landed, I headed for the Fleshway—a long, dirty bazaar of overpriced drinkeries and brothels, and peopled by pickpockets. If Blalock really was in Darkside, that's where I'd most likely find him, indulging in the local diversions. The Fleshway is so-called not only for peddling access to everyone's favorite fifteen minutes of the day, but also because foot traffic is so thick on the bazaar, it's hard *not* to stick your fingers in other people's pockets.

The smell of sweat, vomit, and other bodily fluids wafted up from the gray mud of the double-wide, prefabricated thoroughfare. The sounds of drunkards, hucksters, and a slurred desire for death sooner rather than later mixed in the murmur of the crowd.

I pushed my way through, heading for Minerva Sett's Arms of Artemis. The Arms is considered the best little whorehouse in Darkside, which isn't saying much for the place. The owner—Minerva, aka, Minnie the Mouth—and I were old friends. Whenever I prowled Darkside on a job, I'd stop in for a Scotch and a beer and sometimes help her muscle out a drunk john demanding more than he'd paid for. Though she never paid me for the service, Minnie was always grateful for my assistance, if you know what I mean.

I pulled my hat down when I entered the Arms. Last thing I needed was someone spotting me and tipping off anyone watching Blalock's back. I spotted Minnie holding court and angled in her direction. When she saw me, I jerked my thumb toward her office behind the bar. She nodded and began to wind down her conversation with the client she'd been chatting up.

Entering her office felt like slipping into an old coat. "This place looks the same," I said after she closed the door behind her. The fake friendliness of the negotiations under way in the front parlor, as Minnie called it, faded to a dull roar. "It's what I like about it."

"You and everyone else," Minnie said, amused. "My customers like to know what they're getting, each and every time."

I turned with a grin and noticed her absently wiping her lower lip. They don't call her Minnie the Mouth for nothing. Actually, for two things. I was here for the second.

"I need information," I said.

"Yeah? And Mars has two moons." Minnie strolled over to her desk with lazy legs that knew a paying customer wasn't watching. She kicked off her heels and flopped into a chair. "You know, you never come to visit when you don't need something. Not even a 'How you doing, Minnie? Business been good, Minnie?' first."

"No time for pleasantries. I need what I need and I'll beat feet out of here."

She blew out her disgust. "Typical male. What is it this time? Someone steal something from Tony Two-point oh? Make the Big Boss Man mad, did they?"

Maybe it's because every job I do is basically the same, or maybe it's because, after celebrating her fifth 39th birthday, Minnie has a lifetime of hard-earned expertise in reading people. But sometimes she hits the nail too squarely on the head for her own good. Someday it might get her killed. I decided not to add to those odds today.

"I can't tell you the what. I just need help finding the who."

"You're no fun, Stacks."

"That's not what you said last time I was here."

"I owed you for running those twin thugs out before they hurt another one of my girls."

"I remember."

"I felt I owed you big time."

"I remember. You delivered, too."

She smiled. "Yeah, I did."

"Does that shared reminiscence count as a pleasantry?"

"That particular one?" Minnie gazed off and closed her eyes for a moment. "Yeah, that counts." She reached across her desk and pulled the top off a decanter. "How much of a hurry are you in?"

"One drink's worth of a hurry."

Minnie filled two glasses with amber ambrosia and pushed one in my direction. I picked it up and said, saluting, "Bottoms up."

She saluted back. "If that's the way you want it."

That woman doesn't miss a beat. She downed the bourbon in one gulp. I followed suit out of courtesy. "What I prefer is Scotch."

"I prefer girls, and see where that's gotten me?"

That plussed my non for half a second. Minnie was diverting me, as was her wont. I set my glass down and said, "I'm looking for a man named Blalock. Mason Blalock. Ring a bell?"

Ignoring my pressing schedule, Minnie poured us a second round. I let mine breathe. She didn't.

"The EF geek that stole the super-secret tech?"

Shit. Minnie, you live a dangerous life. And I'm not talking about the daily need for antibiotics. My silence answered her question.

"I heard the marshals were hot on his trail," she said, still fishing.

"Where'd you hear that?"

"Whispers in the Basement."

Ah, the Basement—that second tier below the sanitized top layer of CorpNet—where only those who pay to play can get access. Taboo porn and SynCorp stock tips are the most popular search returns. And something called *The Real Story*, a series of non-stop real-time videos streaming the most recent rubbernecking eye-bait—whatever puerile happening will get viewers to tune in for the flash-ads that pop up in-between. The Company considers what shows up in the Basement as a safety valve for public angst. Sometimes SynCorp even seeds content to push public commentary in a certain direction. When things get a little too close to the truth, plugs get pulled. And I'm talking more than power plugs.

"Don't believe everything you hear," I said.

"Honey, I don't believe half of what I hear, and less than half of what I see. It's the only way to keep your sanity in a place like this"—she finished off her second bourbon. Then, chuckling—"and your sense of humor."

I nodded. I could relate. My line of work demanded a similar indulgence of the darker side of human nature. "Anyway, Blalock? If all you know is what's in the Basement. . ."

Minnie poured herself a third drink. Either it was the end of her shift or the beginning. Hard to know which one she'd need the liquid meds for more.

"Don't insult me," she said. "Do I question your professionalism?"

She watched me slowly shake my head over the rim of her empty glass. Sometimes I'm smart and keep my trap shut despite my knee-jerk tendency to mouth off. There were only the distant sounds of loud-mouthed braggarts and half-hearted gigglers bubbling in from the bar.

"Aw, hell, Stacks," she said finally, the bourbon already making her s's lazy. Beginning of shift, I guessed. Minnie prefers to work on an empty stomach. "I'm sorry. It's just that—"

"Don't mention it. Now, about Blalock?"

Minnie's a good kid and I didn't want to be rude, but I really was in a hurry. I had no idea what Ra'uf Erkennen's time table might be. But with the marshals called off, he might advance his schedule to move against the Taulke Faction. However that shook out, Tony was convinced it'd be in the public space, and it was real hard to put a bad-news genie like that back in the bottle. Any evidence of open warfare among the factions would only encourage the Resistance. The sooner I completed my contract, the better.

"I hear he's gone way deep," she said, kicking into business mode.

"The slums?"

"Deeper."

"Lower London?"

"Uh-huh. You gonna drink that?" She motioned toward my still-waiting glass.

"Help yourself."

I thought how that made sense. Lower London, wholly underground beneath Darkside proper. Originally built as sustainable housing by some Englishman and his millions. Now, like the rest of Darkside, it was a bleaker reality of its promised potential. Most people just called it the Sewer because, well, shit runs downhill, even on the moon. If you wanted to lose yourself among the refuse who populated Darkside, Lower London would be the best place to do it. No one stepped into the Sewer who ever wanted to come out again.

Minnie sipped her fourth dose of medicine and said, "The marshals were prepping for a raid on the down-below when someone called off the dogs. Though I hear all the hounds haven't stopped baying yet."

That woke me out of my pre-loathing about having to tromp through the Sewer. "What do you mean?"

She set the glass down. Her eyes lost focus for a tick, then set hard again. "I mean that sometimes a badger remembers why they're supposed to be wearing the star. Not everyone clocks in and out when the Company tells them to."

"A true-bluer?"

Minnie nodded, her eyes blurring again.

Nine out of ten marshals were just deputized muscle for the Company. Petty crime and enforcement of SynCorp law fell to them. And, most of the time, they did their job like you'd expect. Seeing that five-pointed star on a uniformed chest comforted the citizens of Sol, made them feel like some part of their old life on Earth really had made it to the stars with them. In reality, most marshals were on the take—either looking the other way during business hours or moonlighting as hired help for one faction or another.

But every once in a while, someone wore the star who actually *did* care. About their job. About justice.

I hate those guys. They make my work more complicated. SynCorp and even the Marshals Service itself didn't suffer them lightly. Being a straight shooter in a crooked game is the fastest way to feel the final embrace of Mother Universe.

"You're telling me some true-bluer is still bird-dogging Blalock? Even after Tony passed the word. . ."

I shut my mouth and glanced down at my empty glass. Goddamn it, Minnie's good. Good at getting information out of shmucks like me, information that can get her killed.

Minnie was smiling with her perfect mouth. "Now, Stacks, you used to be smarter'n that." She gave a lazy wink that, had she been less drunk and twenty years younger. . .

"And you're too damned smart for your own good," I growled. "That's all you're getting out of me tonight, Minerva. Got a name on the marshal?"

Her smile faded at my use of her given name. "Just a last one," she said, rising slowly from the chair. She was irritated. The bourbon had made her playful, and I wouldn't play. "Darrow."

"Darrow, got it. Any idea where—?"

Minnie had walked around the desk and now she leaned into me. She placed one hand on my shoulder to hold herself up. The other found my inseam. "Why not stay a while?" she asked.

"I told you," I said, the blood rushing south, out of my resolve. "I've got business."

"I can feel that."

"*Minnie*—where can I . . ." I cleared my throat. "Where can I find this Marshal Darrow?"

Her fingers stopped measuring me for a new pair of trousers. "You're no fun, you know that?"

I stood up abruptly, so fast it set her back on her wobbly heels. I grabbed her with a soft hand to keep her on her feet.

"Not tonight I'm not. Can you clue me in or not?"

"Sure, Einstein. I'd start with the marshal's outpost in the Sewer," she said, petulant and pouting. Minnie always seemed less the hardboiled madam and more the mean little girl when she was drunk. "Like I said—they were ready to raid when Tony Taulke called 'em off."

"Thanks." Rising, I headed for the door.

"Hey, Stacks?" she said behind me.

Turning, I watched her pick up the decanter of bourbon again. "Yeah?"

"Stop back on your way out of Darkside?"

I paused. Doubtful. Tony would want a firsthand report tout de suite, and in person. No way for the communication to be tapped, if I reported in person. The decanter clinked and clanked against the rim of her glass. I watched bourbon slop onto the desk.

"I've been getting stiffed by customers lately, and I don't mean in a good way," she said, adding a leer like drinkers do when they think the person they're talking to is as dull as they are drunk. "Now, when *you* stiff me—"

"I'll try to stop by," I said to stop her talking. I like Minnie; I like her a lot. We're two peas in a pathetic pod. Only I kill people for a living. She just screws them. "Thanks for the info, Minnie."

I beat feet before my sympathy for an old, drunk whore made me decide to stay.

If the up-top of Darkside smells like humanity overripe and underfed, the Sewer smells worse. SynCorp doesn't much care whether the artificial gravity works reliably on the moon, and that plays havoc with the waste reclamation located in the down-below. The corridors of Lower London, more narrow than up top, slosh now and then with gray filth when you walk. Lower London is like its namesake in older times, I guess. Minus the frilly Shakespeare clothes.

More like a toll booth than an outpost, the marshal's station was easy to find. It has a sign over the door. It's the brightest thing in the Sewer as you come off the ramp, so you can't miss it. I hiked my collar and lowered my hat when I got close.

"I'm looking for the deputy in charge," I said to the grizzled twenty-something on duty. Dark figures passed within the alcoves along the main corridor leading deeper into Lower London. Their feet stirred up the smell of the sludge around me. If I weren't armed to the teeth, I'd be concerned about the element I was stepping into. And I don't just mean the shit slurry on the ground.

"That'd be me," the grizzled twenty-something said.

He didn't bother to look up from his padd. The way his thumb was moving, I figured he must be either about to win the game he was playing or about to lose it.

"No, I mean, *really* in charge. Someone in command down here."

The sad sound effects of defeat spun out from his padd. Losing, then. Cursing, the unshaven whelp of a lawman looked up. "Name's Mustafar. And like I said, if you need a marshal, I'm the guy. You think they'd put a veteran with reputation down this shithole?"

Fair point. "Deputy Mustafar, then." I looked around. "Is there someplace we can have a private conversation?"

Mustafar gestured at the barely man-sized booth around him. "I'd offer you my office, but it's a little cramped. Now, what do you want? I'm busy."

I glanced at his padd but held my tongue. "I was just wondering if Deputy Darrow was around?"

His expression flattened. He wasn't much interested in playing games anymore, that's for sure.

"What do you want with Darrow?" He gave me a curious eye. "Do I know you?"

"Don't think so. Darrow and I? Old friends. Mutual acquaintance told me he was assigned down here. Thought I'd—"

"Old friends, huh?"

"Yeah."

"Well *she*—Deputy Darrow—is unavailable."

Shit. And I'd had a fifty-fifty chance of getting that right, too. Ah, well. Sometimes the best thing to do when caught in a lie is to own it with a smile.

I crossed my arms—an old trick, just in case I needed to draw—and smiled. "Hey, friend, you got me. I was just—"

"What do you want with Darrow?" he asked again. I watched him shift his weight to the right. I imagined him pressing a button under the lip of the counter in front of him. Seemed like his suspicion had touched on a memory. "Do I know you?"

My options were suddenly very limited. But killing a marshal, even in the Sewer, might blow back on Tony in the court of public opinion. Could even help Ra'uf Erkennen with his plan to take over.

"You know what?" I said, backing away. "I think I'll look for ole Darrow myself. Sorry to have interrupted your game."

"Hey! I do know you! Stop right there!"

Double shit. Out of options.

"You're Fischer! Taulke's assassin!" Mustafar fumbled beneath the counter.

I pulled my stunner. My eyes were on him, but at the same moment, I felt a shadow moving with purpose behind me. I hesitated on the trigger—and everything went real dark real fast.

★ THE TWIST ★

WAKING UP after being clocked from behind is a tricky thing. If you've got your wits, you do it slowly to get the lay of the land before whoever put your lights out realizes you're awake.

"You can open your eyes." A woman's voice. "Go on, Fischer, I know you're awake."

Well, no need to play possum then. I raised my head off my chest and felt a spider's web of pain shoot across the back of my skull. She'd cold-cocked me good, all right.

"Deputy Marshal True-Blue Darrow, I assume." I blinked away the blackout and took her in through the orange spots. She was slight for a marshal, almost comically so, though her size emphasized a kind of fierce beauty. The badge over her left breast hung like an oversized star on the too-small canvas of her uniform.

"And you're Stacks Fischer. Tony Taulke's assassin to the stars."

The orange spots had finally cleared out. "Since you know who I am, you know this little tussle can permanently direct the course of your career. Cut me loose and let me walk out of here, and I'll forget it ever happened."

Darrow thrust her hips to one side and crossed her arms. "Do I look stupid to you?"

"I try never to judge on first appearances."

"Funny."

I sat up . . . slowly . . . and rested against the wall. The room we were in had a film of something slimy on the floor. The seat of my pants felt soaked. Darrow had bound my feet, but that was all. I must've woken up too fast for her to finish tying me up.

"Maybe we should just space him, Glau."

I turned my head and found Mustafar standing there. He looked every bit the ten years younger than Darrow he was. Seeing them together, I sized up the situation real quick. Deputy Marshal Mustafar was into older women.

"Quiet, Amin," Darrow said. Then, looking at me, "Never tell the criminal element your plans."

I laughed, but the mirth was short-lived. The lump on the back of my head reminded me I wasn't in a laughing mood. "You're not going to kill me," I said.

Darrow cocked an eyebrow. She was good at the body language thing. Being short had helped her develop other necessary survival skills. "Don't be so sure," she said.

"Oh, I'm one-hundred percent sure." I stared at her straight. "For one thing, I woke up. If you wanted me dead, I'd be that way by now.

Second, you're smart enough to know you can't kill me and get away with it. Tony would put you in a decompression chamber and reduce the PSI for a week until your eyeballs finally exploded. Third—you're not a killer," I said, with a knowing look at her boyfriend, Deputy Big Mouth.

Damn. Darrow's ears had been distracted by my little speech, but her eyes had noticed my right hand flexing.

"Looking for the knife?" She moved aside and there, lined up on a table behind her, were my three insurance policies: my stunner, my .38, and my spring-blade.

"Not anymore."

"Let's just space him! No one will—"

"Shut up, Amin!" Darrow's voice was short and spoke of a growing irritation with her puppy-dog lover. At the look Mustafar gave her, Darrow's face melted into quick regret. She was in new territory having me as a prisoner. Life was getting more stressful by the minute. "Look, just go back out to the booth and keep watch, okay? Before Central notices you're gone."

"Fine," he said. Then, "I've put everything on the line for you, Glau."

"I know."

"Don't fuck this up."

"I *know*."

Mustafar threw a last leer my way, to which I puckered up and blew him a kiss. His look of disgust made its exit with the rest of him.

"I guess I wasn't out that long, then," I said. Even in the Sewer, an empty marshal's station would get noticed.

"No."

"Why *didn't* you kill me? Roles reversed, I would have done for you."

The look she gave me was pure hatred. Like I was a cockroach that had just crawled into her dead mother's mouth as she lay in the coffin.

"I'm sure you would. Maybe I'll kill you anyway."

I laughed again. "A true-bluer like you? There's no justice in cold-blooded murder."

"You should know."

I let her have her moment of smug satisfaction. "But anyway—let me go and we'll forget this ever happened."

"So *you* can kill *me*? Fat chance."

"Kill you? I have no intention of killing you. I'm here to fix a problem. That's all."

"Uh-huh."

I took a moment to collect my thoughts. Darrow's perspective on the puzzle fell into place fast. The top assassin in SynCorp steps into the Sewer asking after Deputy Marshal Glau Darrow, who's bucked the Company's directive to back off Blalock. In her mind, I was here to fix a problem all right: her.

"You think I'm here for you."

"I don't *think* anything," she said.

"I'm not."

"Uh-huh."

"I'm here for Blalock." I could have played coy, but Darrow struck me as too sharp to buy whatever I'd come up with. "We're here for the same reason, really."

She paused to consider. "If you're here, it's because Tony Taulke wants Blalock dead. I'm here to take him in for corporate espionage. Those aren't the same reason."

"You were told to stand down."

That made her eyes drop for half a heartbeat. They came back up with flames in them.

"I'm so tired of that crap," she said. "We're sworn to uphold the law—"

"Corporate law." Watch it, Fischer. Stay out of the pulpit.

"*Yes*, corporate law!" Darrow started pacing. "And half the time, just like with Blalock, we're denied our duty because Tony Taulke or some other faction leader decides they're *above* the law!"

"Look, kid," I said, "you know how this plays out. You're already in seven kinds of trouble, but the situation's still salvageable. I might even be able to help you out of the jam you're in."

Her eyes narrowed. "Why would you help me?"

Good question. Darrow was nothing to me except a potential headache with Tony. But, cold-cocking notwithstanding, I liked her grit. She was bucking her orders to bring in a criminal just for the sake of serving the law. We might walk opposite sides of that legal street, but I could admire her dedication to duty. We were more alike than she'd cop to. No pun intended.

"Young love sets my heart aflutter," I said by way of explanation.

Her forehead wrinkled as she translated. "Amin? You think I'm in love with Amin?"

"I think he's in love with you. Your little crusade is gonna get him killed. You too."

"Crusade? I'm doing my job!"

I was tempted to shout. Tempted to rail at the stupidity of Darrow's idealism. But I really was starting to like her, maybe because she *was* such an idealist. Quietly, without venom, I said, "Your job is what the Company tells you it is."

"My job is to enforce the law."

"SynCorp *is* the law!"

Darrow's eyes flared again, but her mouth shut up.

"There's more going on here than you know," I continued. "Blalock will never be taken alive. Whether it's me or someone else that does him, he'll get done. That's why Tony sent the marshals home—to make sure Blalock is taken care of permanently."

"What is it?" She sounded almost desperate to know. "What *is* going on?" Like knowing might somehow justify—literally—why she couldn't do her job. Like knowing would give her permission to let Blalock get spaced, to turn a blind eye.

"Can't tell you that," I said. "It'd only make you more of a target than you already are."

Darrow advanced, ready to get the story out of me one way or the other. Then, angry voices filtered in from outside. One of them was Mustafar's. He was doing his *I'm-the-marshal-you're-looking-for* bit.

I could tell in an instant it wouldn't be enough.

"Cut my feet free," I growled. "*Now.*"

She looked from me to my weapons on the table behind her, then toward the doorway and the ruckus outside. Mustafar's defiance had begun to lose its authority. And from the sound of it, he was outnumbered.

"Darrow!"

But she was already moving for the door, drawing her stunner. With her off-hand, without looking back, she snagged my knife from the table and shot it in my direction. I ducked as it thunked into the wall behind me.

Before her shadow left the room I could hear the sharp, potent *punk! punk! punk!* of stunner fire outside. Those marshals were both as good as dead. I didn't know who the loudmouths were, but Mustafar must've drawn on them like he drew on me, and they'd responded in kind.

I yanked the knife from the wall and cut the rope binding my feet. As I levered myself up, my ankles screamed in protest. I'd been sitting too long. Fuck being over fifty.

I flicked the knife back under my wrist, spring loaded. Blood began to fill my feet again, and I loped to the table. I filled both hands, one with my stunner and the other with the .38. I had no intention of getting involved, not really, and maybe I could just sit here and wait it out and steal away after the marshals were dead.

Punk! punk! punk!

Punk! punk!

But if I waited and the new players weren't friends, they'd be after me next. With all that shooting outside, I figured there must be at least a handful of them. Not good odds when you're cornered in a bare room with no cover. If I joined Darrow and Mustafar, I'd at least have them on my side. The enemy of my enemy and all that. Better odds.

Killing the lights inside the little room, I knelt beside the doorway and darted my eyes around the corner to get my bearings. I was across the dark alleyway from Mustafar's outpost in the same alcove Darrow must have jumped me from earlier. I spotted her behind a long, thin dumpster farther up the narrow alley. She was pinned down by fire coming from the near side. There was no sign of Mustafar.

Two of the shooters advancing on Darrow were crouched and moving from trash can to doorway. A third semi-strode down the middle of the alleyway like an Old West gunslinger.

Idiot.

I could flank them. They'd never see me coming, like I hadn't seen Darrow. Or, I reminded myself, I could just melt into the wall and go my own way.

"Firing on members of the Marshals Service is a capital crime! Cease and desist and throw down your weapons!"

It was Darrow reading from the marshal's manual again. I wonder if she really thought they'd obey her order or if she was just quoting herself some bravery.

Punk! punk! punk!

Their answer kept Darrow's head down. To drive the point home, a fourth shooter engaged from the marshal's booth. So, these guys weren't dicking around. Mustafar must be dead. In a few seconds, one of the three gunslingers would draw a bead on Darrow. The closer they got to finishing that job, the clearer they made my escape route.

Sorry, Darrow. You were a good kid. At least she'd die true to the principles she'd lived by.

I edged out of the doorway, my knees joining my ankles' chorus of complaints. I crept along the wall, Darrow's defiance hurling the scripture of the law like bullets at the bad guys behind me. But as I passed the fourth shooter, the one in the booth, I finally registered something. Like the three moving in on Darrow, he was wearing corporate blue coveralls, the kind the factory workers on Mars wear. But we weren't on Mars.

Punk! punk!

Those coveralls also happened to be the de facto uniform of the Resistance, since most of the movement's Ghosts came from the worker class. Why were they in Darkside shooting at—make that, *killing*—marshals at the same time the shit with Erkennen was going down?

I needed to know the answer to that question. Coincidence is too coincidental for my tastes.

I turned first on the one in the booth. He still hadn't seen me and was being cavalier about his cover. My stunner showed him the virtue of awareness. The others were too distracted by their target to notice me killing their buddy.

Punk! punk!
Punk! punk! punk!

Only, their buddy in the booth wasn't dead. I'd shot him point-blank and all it did was make him mad. My stunner had fired but to no effect.

Fuck! Never trust new tech!

He turned on me, drawing a bead.

Good thing I had my .38 in my other hand. The slug took him high in the chest, knocking him off his feet. If I hadn't been in a hurry, I'd have kissed my old reliable.

The report from my pistol got the attention of the other three. Before the first mook turned, I shot him in the back. The second had spun and crouched, and I flattened on my stomach in the muck. Her stunner fired fine but missed its mark. My .38 didn't. I watched Darrow take aim at the third guy and shoot him point-blank. Like the one in the booth, he seemed to shrug it off and turned on her. I did for him like the others, splitting his spine with a little old-fashioned lead.

As the three dead bodies settled into the sludge, silence was a strange sound after all that killing. Darrow darted forward from her hiding place, running past me.

"You're welcome," I said to her wind.

★ THE ALLIANCE ★

"AMIN!"

I could hear the anguish in her voice. I left her to it. I was more interested in the corpses at my feet anyway and why my stunner had misfired.

Blood from the three assassins leaked bright red into the gray muck. I kicked each in a kidney to make sure they were all good and dead. Not a grunt among them.

I noticed some of the resident Sewer rats poking their heads out of their holes. A few of them were pointing feeders our way. *The Real Story* gives those high-definition cameras away to anyone who wants one. They keep the show's insatiable video feed streaming 24/7. It wouldn't do to have my face all over the Basement, so I turned my back on the locals and knelt to get a closer look at the deaders.

They wore blue coveralls, all right. Two men, one woman. Nothing particularly remarkable about them, except . . . I picked up a weapon caked in gray shit and turned it over. A stunner, a Mark II by the looks of it. The Mark IIs were still pre-market. No one was supposed to have them. I was still carrying the Mark I, and reluctantly at that. But this new model—no one was supposed to have these yet. Hell *I* didn't even have one.

That made me curiouser. I unzipped one of the fellow's coveralls. Underneath, he was wearing finer sweat catchers than a Martian factory worker could afford. I looked at his shoes. Same story. These guys weren't displaced Resistance types a long way from home. These guys—and one gal—were professionals.

"Mustafar's dead," Darrow said behind me. I could tell by her voice that her eyes were getting wet. "And for what? Why?"

That same desperate need-to-know from earlier. I glanced sideways over my shoulder. "These guys weren't Ghosts." I wrinkled a lip at the irony.

There was a pause. "Why do you say that?"

"Too well dressed. Too well armed. See those pieces?" I gestured at the stunners laying in the sludge. "Pre-market. Ghosts use the cast-off weapons they can scrounge from reclamation. No way they could get their hands on pre-market tech like this. I doubt these are even on the black market yet."

"Maybe a patron—"

"He buy them silk undies too? And these coveralls—they're thicker than you'd expect for factory grunts moonlighting as terrorists. A heavier weave. Dyed to look like Martian worker duds, but more than that." Something tickled the back of my brain. Multiple things, actually, like puzzle pieces trying to fit together.

Darrow peered over my shoulder. "I see what you mean." The no-nonsense marshal had displaced the grieving woman in her voice. "What's that?"

"What?"

She pointed at the neck of the woman lying next to the man I'd unzipped. I reached over and pulled the gal's collar down to get a better look. "Huh." Those puzzle pieces seemed magnetized. They wanted to come together, but they weren't quite ready to yet.

"Huh what. . ."

"That's the Greek letter Epsilon."

Darrow stared at me.

"You should read more, Marshal," I smirked. "Epsilon is the Erkennen brand. All their operatives wear it tattooed to a body part. It's like their secret handshake." These assassins were on Ra'uf Erkennen's payroll. That explained how they had access to the Mark IIs, since the Erkennens supplied the Company's tech.

Darrow's eyes dawned. "You mean the Erkennen Faction sent a hit squad—"

"—to kill you. Yeah." I stopped there. She could do the rest herself.

"To keep me from tracking down Blalock. Because I wouldn't give up."

"Dressed like Ghosts. So any video that made it to the Basement," I said, nodding to the evermore curious rats in their doorways, "would make it look like the Resistance had hit the marshal's station. Two birds, one stone. The Erkennens stop you from messing in their business and the Resistance gets blamed, which makes SynCorp the victim. It's a headliner of a news story, tailor-made for CorpNet."

I stood and cursed my cracking knees. The Erkennens had gone to a lot of trouble to shut down Darrow and her puppy-dog lover. It didn't quite square with the risk they'd taken to do it.

Sticking the Mark II in a coat pocket, I gave her a minute to think it all over while I made the rounds to pick up the others' weapons. They wouldn't be needing them anymore, and I could resell them for a decent price after all this was over. Hell, maybe *I'd* start the black market for the Mark IIs.

"Amin's dead."

"Yeah," I said, not unkindly. I hate conversation as a rule. Sometimes I hate the silence more.

"Because of me."

And sometimes, silence is exactly what's called for.

"They failed," Darrow said.

"Failed? Well, yeah. You're still alive." Which reminded me . . . I looked around and, other than the eyes peering around corners, the corridor was empty. "The Service will send officers soon from the up-top. The first videos have probably already hit the Basement. Wheels are in motion here, Darrow. We need to beat feet. The marshals that come now won't be your friends."

"They failed," she said as if she hadn't heard a word I'd said, "because I'm going after Blalock anyway." Darrow glanced back at the booth. I could see Mustafar's marshal-booted feet around the lip of the doorway, heels up. "Amin's death has to mean something."

"Actually, it doesn't," I said. When she turned her flamers on me again, I tried not to feel bad. "Hell, we don't even know where Blalock is."

"I do." Darrow tossed it out like it wasn't the million-dollar answer to my prayers that it was.

I pulled her off to the side of the corridor, hopefully out of earshot of any expensive sound-catching equipment being aimed our way by the Basement trolls. "You know where Blalock is?" I whispered. That would certainly explain why the Erkennens had sent the hit squad dressed like Ghosts. They'd do anything to keep their little secret till they were ready to spring their trap on Tony.

"Yeah," she said, regaining some of her marshal moxie. "I know exactly where he is. And I'm not telling you shit, Fischer. You go your way. I'll go mine." She started to pull away and I stopped her. I got her stunner stuck in my gut for my trouble. Somehow, despite what I'd just seen in the shootout, I knew hers would work on me. That's just my goddamned luck.

"Hold up there, Marshal. Hear me out."

"Make it fast. You said yourself, we're about to have more company. And I have business to attend to."

"You need my help. Not only do you have the Erkennens gunning for you, but your own Service is out to rein you in."

"And it smells like shit down here. Tell me something I don't know."

"Point is—gunning for Blalock on your own ends just one way: you join Mustafar, forever embracing in the cold arms of Mother Universe."

When she glanced back at the marshal's booth, I knew I had her. What she said next didn't make a damned bit of difference, even when she burned me with those flamers again when she said it.

"I'll never work with you. Let them come and take me. Let the Erkennens kill me. At least I'll die—"

"Yeah, yeah, true to your goddamned ideals," I said. Darrow tried to jerk her arm free and I yanked her back against the Sewer's wall.

"Do that again, Fischer, and to hell with due process. I'll kill you right here and now."

She would, too. I could see clear intent behind the flames. She'd already tossed out the marshal's manual to focus on what justice demanded: *wergild* in blood for Mustafar. At this point, I was in her way. I gambled and let her go. A little trust might go a long way. She didn't bolt.

"Listen to me, Darrow. You might get to Blalock. And then what?

He'll never stand trial because no one—*no one*—wants him to stand trial. Not the Taulkes. Not the Erkennens."

"Why wouldn't the Erkennens want him to be arrested? He stole their tech!"

"No one stole anything!" I hissed. Mindful of the watchers, I pointed my .38 at the ceiling down the alley and fired off a round. More like turtles than rats, the locals pulled back inside their holes.

"This was all some kind of set-up by Ra'uf Erkennen. Whatever Blalock did, they let him do it—for their own reasons." I shook my head. "This is the bigger picture you never get to see, Darrow. And someone like you? Be glad of it."

The look on her face told me that wasn't enough. She was just confused. Overwhelmed. Not thinking or not able to think. I grabbed her arm again and dragged her closer to the booth, away from the rats. They were getting brave again.

I said, "Maybe the Erkennens sold Blalock a bill of goods. Maybe they promised to set him up on Titan for life. Who the hell knows? Point is, they're behind the whole thing."

"You're lying. Why would they do that?"

"Leverage! Against the Taulkes. To strengthen their own position, take over the Company. Hell, even I don't understand it all. One thing I *do* understand—your little crusade for justice doesn't mean shit to anyone but you."

She took it in. I could practically see the wheels turning inside her head. Her ideals as a marshal—extolled by the five-pointed star on her chest pledged to protect and enforce—battled a lifetime of living in a system ruled by the bottom line.

"Why do you think Ra'uf Erkennen sent these killers after you?" I pressed. "You need my gun if you want a chance in hell of setting things right for Mustafar."

The radio inside the booth crackled, demanding someone answer. More marshals were definitely inbound, probably to arrest Darrow. Once they had her, they were just as likely to kill her as incarcerate her—outside the public spotlight of *The Real Story*, of course.

She pulled away, and this time I didn't fight her. Darrow headed for the booth. She was going to tend to Mustafar, I figured. Maybe put something over his face or conduct some lawman's ritual; do one of those things we humans feel compelled to do when death takes someone we care about. As if the ritual is about their dignity and not our own need to cover up the fact that death's coming for us, too.

But Darrow surprised me and stepped right over him. I heard her opening cabinets in the booth. She came out with extra chargers for her stunner and a flash grenade, which she hung on a back belt-loop.

"Come on," she said. "Blalock's not that far."

★ THE JOB ★

THE HEADS OF THE TURTLE-RATS pulled back in their holes only to edge out again after we'd passed. They pointed their feeders for *The Real Story* at our backs. Their pale skin, damned near translucent in the dim light, was the brightest thing about them. Shaggy haired and clothed in rags, they kept to the darkness. They reminded me of the Morlocks from that old H.G. Wells novel, or maybe vampires with bad skin. Leaving them behind us made me edgy.

"These people trouble?"

Darrow gave a muffled laugh. "The Moonies? They're harmless. The last thing they want is trouble."

"Moonies?" I chuckled. "That's what they call themselves?"

"It's what they're called. Does it matter?"

"Guess not."

One of the palefaces got daring and tried to get a close-up. I stopped, turned on my heel and snatched the feeder from his hand. Without so much as a "Hey, that's mine!" he scurried back into his hole. I dropped it in my pocket. That should keep the rest of them from being so friendly.

"That's the most expensive thing that man owns," Darrow said.

"Not anymore."

She slowed her pace as we neared the end of the Sewer's main street.

"Which way?" I asked.

"Blalock is left," Darrow whispered. I started to move, but she reached a hand out. Big grip for such a little marshal. "We go right." She nodded back behind us. I turned my face in profile, just enough so my peripheral saw another Moonie pointing a feeder our way—but definitely from a distance.

"Scenic route?"

Darrow nodded and headed right. The narrow hallway immediately curved, and I could see her strategy. If the Erkennens or marshals were monitoring our progress via *The Real Story*, they'd think we were headed in the wrong direction. At least for a little while.

Without warning, Darrow darted left up a half-flight of muddy stairs. They led to a mid-level floor between Lower London and Darkside proper. The stairs dumped us into a cramped, deserted hallway of corrugated metal that felt more like a military ship than a livable community.

"You really know your way around here."

"Unfortunately." She angled her head up the hallway. "He isn't far."

We stepped off, quiet as mice. Thumbing slugs into my .38 I asked, "How'd you find him?"

"He's a science genius, right? Those types don't have jobs, they have obsessions. I scanned for nodes in Darkside placing excessive demands on the local 'net. Only the brothels in the up-top pull that kind of bandwidth. Until now."

I thought of the porn closets in Minnie's place and nodded. Their floors are sticky, but the booths are private. And cheap, considering the quality of the 3D video feed. Or so I've been told.

"Smart. But how do you know it's him?"

Darrow shrugged. "In the last two days, there's been a terabyte of data exchanged with a server off-moon," she said. "Either someone's opened a new porn franchise down here for an under-class that can't afford electricity on a regular basis, or it's Blalock."

"Good detecting, Detective, but that's a pretty big footprint to leave behind. Awful easy to trace."

"They think no one's looking anymore, remember?" She put her ear to the door.

"Maybe. This the only way in?"

Instead of answering, Darrow placed her fingertips against the rusty latch and slowly pushed down.

"This can't be that easy," I said.

She drew her weapon as the door inched open.

"Hey, something's wrong," I warned. "This is too—"

The door creaked open on metal hinges. A lone, fritzing lightbulb hummed in the ceiling, casting shadows into the corners of the room.

Darrow eased her way in. I followed despite my better instincts, drawing one of the Mark II's I'd taken off the dead Ghost. Maybe the latest stunner model would work and maybe it wouldn't. I had my .38 in my other hand, just in case.

The room was empty. It smelled like fish wrapped in a sweaty sock and left in the sun for a week. But for being only half a floor up from the Sewer, it wasn't too bad. Bare walls, rusty like the door latch. A floor mosaicked with decades-old dark stains. The room might've once housed school children specializing in ground-level finger-painting. Or it could've been a room where murder was done on a regular basis. Hard to tell under that sputtering yellow light.

I gave Darrow an inquisitive look as we moved deeper in. She shone a light on the far wall. Another door. She put her ear to that one too and stepped back quickly.

"Bingo."

My ear did its own recon. The rust flaked when I pressed against the metal. Low voices: bored and tired of smelling fishy socks.

"You're sure this is him?"

In answer, Darrow pressed the door latch down. This one was unlocked too. Yeah, it was too easy. *Way too easy.* But here we were, and Tony expected results . . . and soon.

"All right, here's how we'll play it," I said. "I'll go up top through the vents and—"

Darrow pushed every pound of her slight weight against the heavy door. It swung open, the scarred metal screaming.

"Marshals Service! Everyone stay right where you are!"

Cursing, I brought up my own artillery to cover her as she moved in.

Six pairs of surprised eyes turned to look at us. Four more of the Ghosts with new shoes and newer weapons. One doughy, bespectacled type who looked like he really needed to take a dump. And one very well-dressed corporate elite type. He looked familiar, even in the half-light.

One of the fake Resistance types started to reach for her weapon.

"Uh-uh," I said, motioning with my .38. "Slowly, butt first. I want them all lined up on the table over there. All of you."

The elite type smiled wide. "Welcome, Mr. Fischer. We've been waiting for you."

It's when he spoke that I recognized him. The mid-European accent sold it.

"Ra'uf Erkennen." Those puzzle pieces in the back of my head? They were gyrating like one of Minnie's girls after ten minutes.

The head of the Erkennen Faction made a slight bow. "And you must be the maverick marshal," he said to Darrow. "My dear, you have no idea how much trouble you've caused me."

"Not as much as you're gonna get," I said. "Now, you stooges, I told you already—put your stunners on the table."

"Do nothing of the kind," Erkennen said. Not that he'd needed to. They hadn't moved. "Fischer, put down your weapons. You too, my dear."

Darrow scoffed and tightened her grip on her stunner. Points for moxie.

"You have two choices," Erkennen said. "Drop your weapons or drop with them."

I've never been good at math, but I didn't need to be. There were five stunners pointed at us, and I knew, with my luck, they'd work like a charm. Darrow had hers and I had my .38, but I had zero confidence in the stunner in my other hand, even if it was new tech. *Especially* because it was new tech. Even if it did work, that was five shots to three in the first round of fire. We might get a couple of them but we were definitely going down.

"Darrow, do it," I said.

"Like hell!"

Erkennen exhaled boredom. "Shoot her."

"Wait! Darrow . . ." I nodded at her and caught her attention. My eye darted to her beltline. "No sense dying sooner than we have to. Do it."

She thought about it a moment longer, but she'd caught the hint I'd tossed her way. "Fine." Squatting straight down, she placed her stunner on the ground.

Smart girl.

I did likewise.

"Very good." Turning to the dumpy guy, Erkennen said, "How close are you to finishing the composition matrix?"

Dumpy guy shrugged, nervous. Had to be Blalock. Who else? "It's almost finished. The algorithm subroutines are populating the pattern, and once they're finished, the final formula—"

"I don't need the geek details," Erkennen groused. "Get it done."

"What's this all about?" I asked, playing dumb. I was good at that. I took a couple of steps forward, like from curiosity. "What's this mega-extra smoky hemp for? You gonna get everyone in the solar system high so you can take over?"

Erkennen gave me the strangest look. "What?"

"It's called Molecularly Enhanced Synthetic Hemp," Professor Geek corrected.

I motioned to him. "Whatever—the new drug he's making. How does it help you take over the Company?"

Out of the corner of my eye, I noticed Darrow getting fascinated. *Here's the bigger picture you were unaware of, Marshal.*

"You think we're making a drug here?" Erkennen laughed out loud. "Is that what Tony thinks? We're gonna smoke him out, eh?" The guffaws from his men filled the room, trying to please the boss. Even Blalock snickered, the brainy little shit.

"Hemp isn't typically a drug," Darrow said. "Same plant as marijuana but different purpose. It's typically used to make clothing."

"Very good, my dear," Erkennen said, pleased. "She's smarter than you and Tony put together, Fischer."

And that's when those magnetic puzzle pieces snapped together with seamless edges. I knew I had to stop this conversation right now, at least for the moment.

I stared straight at the head of the Erkennen Faction and marched across the space separating us. His goons brought up their guns, but their boss waved them off. I think he wanted me in his face. And to be in mine. As far as he knew, I was unarmed.

"Whatever this new tech is, you've got zero chance going up against Tony Taulke," I said. I was close enough to spit on Erkennen. I needed him angry. "Tony will grind you and your whole faction into the ground! That new wife of yours? Just wait till you're spaced. A kind word from Tony and—"

Erkennen stepped back to get strength behind it and cracked me against the side of the head with the butt of his Mark II. I went down harder than I had to and stayed there, shaking my head to make it look good.

"Say something else about her, Fischer," Erkennen growled. "I wanted to keep you alive long enough so you'd understand exactly what's going to happen to Tony Taulke. But maybe I can forego that bit of personal satisfaction."

I motioned with my hand like I'd had enough. Standing up slowly, rubbing my temple, I leaned against the wall and fake-breathed hard. "So, if it's not a drug strain, what is it he's making?" I asked again.

Erkennen jutted his head. "Tell him, Mason. He can take the secret with him into space."

Professor Geek stood up. He was proud of his creation. He wanted to give it its due. "Molecularly Enhanced Synthetic Hemp—or MESH—is a new kind of scalable cloth capable of absorbing and dissipating any catalyst used to ignite and direct electromagnetic current."

Blalock confirmed what I'd already guessed. Everything was crystal clear—what the tech actually was, why Erkennen had hidden it from the other factions, and how MESH, all by itself, could make Ra'uf Erkennen head of the entire Syndicate Corporation.

MESH wasn't a drug.

MESH was a shield.

A molecular shield that could be woven right into a person's clothing. A shield that protected against stunners and their ability to kill by capturing and amplifying a person's EM field to shock them to death. Those that wore it were protected. Those that didn't were just as vulnerable as ever.

"The faux-Ghosts in the corridor outside the marshal's post," I said, connecting the dots. "They were wearing a prototype? That's why my stunner wouldn't work on them."

Erkennen smiled. "Oh, and about that. I have to compliment you and the marshal for the show you put on. I couldn't have planned it better myself. The footage of Tony Taulke's main man and a renegade marshal gunning down Ghosts? All the rage in the Basement. Perfect recruiting material for the Resistance. And while Tony's stamping down that little grassfire, I'll move on SynCorp HQ. By the time the Taulkes or any of the other factions can react, I'll control the station."

The image of Erkennen mooks dressed in MESH-laden uniforms gunning down Taulke operatives filled my head. They'd be invincible with the new tech. While the other factions would steal it soon enough and make their own shielded clothing, that wouldn't happen in time to save Tony. Or keep Ra'uf Erkennen from taking over SynCorp.

"Humanity's just getting back on its feet!" Darrow said. "We're not even two generations out from damned-near extinction! And you'd risk turning all that inside-out for power?"

"Stick to your duties, my dear," Erkennen said. "Let the big boys do the big thinking."

"Yeah, Darrow," I added. "He's a smart guy. He's thought of everything."

Erkennen gave me a look. My words sounded right, but their smartassery was wanting. "And for all the dirty jobs you pulled for Tony?" He brought up his stunner. "On behalf of the other four factions, I'm about to pay you off."

I stood my ground. "Before you do—one more question."

"Make it quick."

"Can the Mark IIs get past the MESH?"

"Of course," Erkennen allowed. "But since we're the only ones that have both, it doesn't really matter."

"Well, I wouldn't say that," I said, nodding to the spot where I'd taken the dive earlier. "See that?"

Erkennen peered closely. When he saw the feeder where I'd put it on the floor, its red transmission light shining, his face went pale. His little scheme had just gone out live to anyone tuned in to *The Real Story*. As had the secret of the MESH and the new Mark II stunner. Every member of all Five Factions would now be seeking both techs in earnest.

I flashed him a toothy grin. "Now guess who's got a fire to stamp out?"

"Why, you sonofa—"

"Darrow, now!"

I saw the blur of her body duck and roll as I launched myself backward. The mooks in blue were caught flatfooted. Erkennen's shot hit the wall behind my empty air. Darrow lobbed the flash grenade from behind her back straight at Blalock.

I almost didn't clamp my eyes shut in time. The air brightened like a sunburst. Grunts and cursing followed. I grabbed up my Mark II from the floor and started firing.

Punk! Punk!

Two fake Ghosts became real ones.

Darrow angled at a third, still dazed by the grenade. With a lithe efficiency I took half a second to admire, she rolled to one of the newly minted corpses, snagged his stunner, and shot the third man dead.

Erkennen was no lightweight. Blinking furiously, he was back on his feet and sweeping his own stunner around the room, firing randomly. I ducked and scooped up the .38 and turned on him. Two shots later, he was short a kneecap and screaming on the ground.

I took a moment to enjoy his pain, and that was a rookie mistake. I felt the threat long before I saw it: the last of the hired help, his Mark II aimed point-blank at me, ready to give me the shock of my life. Slow motion took over, and I could feel the cold stroke of death's fingers on the back of my neck.

Punk!

His body convulsed, his stunner shot went wide, and he fell lifeless to the floor with the others. I caught Darrow's eye and nodded my thanks. First time I've ever had use for a badger.

That just left Blalock. The flash grenade had caught him full-on. He was just stirring, moaning.

"Watch him," I said to Darrow, pointing at Ra'uf Erkennen. He was inventing all kinds of four-letter combinations with my name sprinkled on top. "Put a tourniquet above his knee, if you can find something to use. I don't want him dying just yet." And I wanted to keep her busy. I had business to attend to.

Walking over to the feeder, I crushed it under my boot. Its work was done. Erkennen's plot to overthrow Tony had gone out live to anyone watching *The Real Story*, which had lived up to its name today, boy-o.

I turned to Blalock. "Is this everything?" I asked, pointing at his work station. "The formula, how to make it—all that?"

He was still blinking, still getting his bearings.

"Blalock!"

Startled, he tried to crawl through the wall. "Yes! Everything is there. The molecular formula, the thresholds for performance, the—"

He saw me pointing the Mark II at his head.

"Wait! You don't need to kill me! I was only—"

"—following orders, yeah, I know."

"Fischer! You can't murder him in cold blood!"

"I have my orders, too," I said. But I hesitated, and that's not like me. I think something inside me didn't want to disappoint Darrow. I liked her. Admired her, even. And she *had* just saved my life.

"Please!" Blalock cried. "I can help Tony Taulke! I can—"

"Geeks are a dime a dozen these days," I said, remembering my contract. "Which makes your example all the more necessary."

"*Please!*"

I pulled the trigger and Blalock's body stiffened, electrocuted by his own EM field. I heard Darrow gasp behind me.

"Goddamnit, Fischer," Darrow shouted, getting to her feet. "I'm arresting you for the . . ."

She trailed off when she saw me pointing the Mark II her way. Her eyes darted to her own weapon laying on the floor. She'd put it down to tend to Erkennen. Too far out of reach.

"Do it then," she said. "Just do it."

"I'm not gonna kill you, Darrow," I said. "I told you earlier."

She stared straight down the barrel of my fancy new stunner. "Then what?"

I thumbed the setting down. Technically, a stunner could be true to its name—it didn't have to be lethal. In my business, it was hardly ever used that way. "Sweet dreams," I said.

"Fischer—"

I pulled the trigger but was a hair too slow to help ease Darrow to the ground. She collapsed, but not too hard. I took a moment to wonder what her future might be with the Service, since she'd disobeyed orders from the top. They wouldn't kill her now, they didn't need to, and her mug had been all over *The Real Story*. Too high profile to get rid of, at least right off the bat. If they spaced her, it'd be after the hubbub from the livecast died down.

Ra'uf Erkennen had begun to move, gasping with every stretch of his limbs. He was reaching for Darrow's weapon. I kicked it away.

"Congratulations on ruining your faction, Ra'uf," I said. "Tony's going to absorb the Erkennens like a bad stain."

"Fuck you," he said through clenched teeth. "Taulke is still finished. Wait till Gregor hears what you've done here. He'll—"

"Your brother Gregor? If he knows what's good for him, he'll play ball with Tony. Maybe the Taulkes will even let the Erkennens live." As I moved to stand over him, Erkennen had to crane his neck. "Well, all but one."

The fear in his eyes, then. It seemed foreign. He'd been the big cheese for so long, giving orders and being obeyed. Now, he was just another rat about to be shot like the vermin he was.

"Last words?" I asked, bringing the .38 up. I'm nothing if not a traditionalist.

"*Fuck you.*"

"Good as any, I guess."

I plugged him right between the eyes, the blast echoing around the metal walls.

As he slumped, I took stock of the room. Four dead mooks, one dead geek, one dead faction leader too big for his britches, and one sleeping marshal. After she woke up, I knew Darrow would feel compelled to make an official report. Images of Ra'uf Erkennen's third eye would be all over the Basement before lunar sunrise, I figured. And most everyone would see it as justice served after that little confession he'd broadcast. Maybe even Darrow would come to see it that way in time. If she lived long enough.

I grabbed Blalock's padd full of the greatest invention since the stunner itself and headed for the door. Tony would be happy. Before stepping through, I turned and regarded Darrow one last time. Even unconscious, her fierce beauty I'd noted earlier, bolstered now by seeing firsthand her strength of dedication to right for right's sake, impressed itself on me. Part of me hated leaving her to her fate.

"See you around, kid. Good luck with the law."

★ THE FAVOR ★

"HEY, STACKS, how's life in the killing business?" Tony asked as I walked into his office.

"Tolerable," I answered, like always. It was our old way of greeting one another after a job.

I sat down and smiled. He *must* be happy, since he's calling me by my preferred handle. I *hate* Eugene. Tony happy? Everybody happy.

"Nice work out there," he said in a rare show of genuine appreciation. "And good work keeping your face off-camera."

"Thanks. I see Gregor Erkennen got out in front of the bad news."

Tony chuckled. Gregor had wasted no time disavowing his older brother after hearing Ra'uf confess. According to Gregor, the elder Erkennen and his super-scientist had pursued the MESH tech all on their own, outside normal Company protocols. Gregor's story explained both why Ra'uf had hid MESH's development in Darkside from his own brother and why the Erkennen Faction had originally reported Blalock's actions as corporate espionage. There'd been a power play *within* the faction too, discovered by Gregor after Blalock had disappeared. And Ra'uf had lost.

"You sure the Brothers Erkennen weren't in on it together?"

"I'm sure."

He said it in a way that raised my eyebrows. "Wait a minute. *Wait a minute.*"

Tony waited.

"Was Gregor Erkennen your little bird on the inside?"

Tony's face was uncharacteristically unexpressive. "Doesn't really matter now, does it?" Like usual, he kept his hole cards to himself. Tony doesn't like sharing secrets he doesn't have to, not even with me.

"Well, that opportunistic little. . ." I marveled at the human capacity for betrayal. "What about the MESH? What happens to it?"

"Gregor will have a distribution plan to me by Monday."

"Distribution plan?"

"Protection against stunners is an advantage," Tony said. Then, after a beat: "Unless everyone has it."

My eyebrows went up again. "So you're *giving* it to all the factions?"

"Along with the Mark IIs," he said. "My people are looking into how to upgrade the MESH to protect against the new stunner."

So Gregor Erkennen had uncovered his brother's plans after what looked like simple espionage by a wayward employee, plotted with Tony to get Ra'uf out of the way, and was now in charge of the family business. And set to make a huge personal profit when the other four factions ponied up for the new tech.

"Keeping the balance by keeping everyone without an advantage over the others," I said, impressed. "Mutually assured protection."

"Something like that."

"And you get to be the Company hero by handing everyone access to the new tech."

Tony was nothing if not a showman. A real natural at the theater of running the Company. He winked like he knew I was thinking that, and that sliver of human cleverness made the machinelike façade of his face all the more terrifying.

"Nice insurance policy for the status quo, too," I said.

Tony grinned. "I thought so too."

I sighed my satisfaction at successfully closing another contract. My bank account was bigger. My boss was happy. Life was good.

"What about you, Stacks? I'm feeling generous today. You got paid, sure . . . a bonus, maybe, or. . ."

He left the air empty for me to fill it with a favor. I thought it over. Whether he had a real desire to reward me or recognized an opportunity to do me a kindness he'd ask to be repaid one day, I wasn't sure. I decided it didn't really matter.

"Well, there's one thing."

Tony waited.

I cleared my throat. This would be tricky. "The marshal. Darrow."

"What about her, Eugene?"

Gah. Not a good start.

"She was a big help. Without her, I'd never have found Blalock. And even if I had—we were outnumbered and out-teched. I hate to see her rotting in a cell, stripped of her badge, for only doing her job."

Tony frowned. "She disobeyed a direct order from me. She's lucky to be alive."

"You asked what I wanted, Tony." I shrugged like it didn't really matter to me, like she hadn't saved my life while I reveled in Ra'uf Erkennen's pain. I hoped he'd buy it. "Up to you."

Tony Taulke eyed me for a moment: a hint of the cold blue mixed with the businessman's calculated stare. "If she's so good, maybe I should hire *her*, then, and pack you off to Planitia Prime."

It was an empty threat. I was the best corporate enforcer in the business, and Tony knew that. It's why I worked for the Taulkes and not one of the other factions.

"Retirement on Mars? Me?" I made a joke of it. "That'll be the day."

He held me in his steely stare a moment longer, then burst out laughing. "All right, then. I'll see that she's reinstated—only as a special favor to you, Stacks. But there need to be consequences for her disobeying orders."

"I reckon so."

"I'll leave that up to the Service to decide. Nothing career-ending, though."

"Fair enough." I rose and gathered my coat and hat. I'd have to get a new MESH set made, and soon. "See you around, Tony."

I left the boss's office and headed for The Slate to shoot the shit with Mickey Stotes and have a Scotch and a beer. Or maybe six. Quality downtime was something I've begun to appreciate more and more since passing the half-century mark. It's the sunnier side of becoming less patient with bullshit as you get older.

Maybe, after I slept off today's revels, I'd hop the Hearse back to Darkside and visit Minnie. She'd seemed anxious to have me spend some quality downtime with her. Up *and* down time, actually.

Yeah, exchanging pleasantries with Minnie might be just the thing—a pleasurable distraction until Tony called me in to execute a new contract.

Pun intended.

CONTRIBUTORS

★

James Beamon spent 12 years in the Air Force, 21 years married (and still counting!), and a lifetime playing video games, all of which somehow finds its way into his fiction. He's been in Iraq, Afghanistan, and on the Nebula Award's Recommended Reading List, and he figures all three are pretty respectable stamps on the passport of his life experience. He recently published his first novel, *Pendulum Heroes,* and is actively working on releasing the followup when he's not busy updating his bio. James lives and works in Virginia with his wife, son, and attack cat. Check him out on Twitter (@WriterBeamon) or his blog (https://fictigristle.wordpress.com/).

★ ★ ★

Brendan DuBois is the award-winning author of twenty-two novels and more than 170 short stories. He's currently working on a series of novels with bestselling author James Patterson.

His short fiction has appeared in *Playboy, Analog, Asimov's, The Magazine of Fantasy & Science Fiction, Ellery Queen's Mystery Magazine, Alfred Hitchcock's Mystery Magazine,* and numerous anthologies including *Best American Mystery Stories of the Century,* published in 2000, as well as the *Best American Noir of the Century.*

He is the author of the Dark Victory series, published by Baen, and his novel *Resurrection Day* won the Sidewise Award for Best Alternative History Novel of the Year.

His stories have thrice won him the Shamus Award from the Private Eye Writers of America, and have also earned him three MWA Edgar Allan Poe Award nominations. He is also a "Jeopardy!" game show champion. Visit his website: www.BrendanDuBois.com.

Richard Fox is a Nebula Award nominee and winner of the 2017 Dragon Award for Best Military Science Fiction or Fantasy novel. He's best known for the The Ember War Saga, a military science fiction and space opera series, and other novels in the military history, thriller and space opera genres.

He lives in fabulous Las Vegas with his incredible wife and three boys, amazing children bent on anarchy.

He graduated from the United States Military Academy (West Point) much to his surprise and spent ten years on active duty in the United States Army. He deployed on two combat tours to Iraq and received the Combat Action Badge, Bronze Star and Presidential Unit Citation.

Stephen Lawson served on three deployments with the US Navy and is currently a helicopter pilot and commissioned officer in the Kentucky National Guard. He earned a Masters of Business Administration from Indiana University Southeast in 2018, and currently lives in Louisville, Kentucky with his wife.

Stephen's writing has appeared in Writers of the Future's 33rd anthology, *Orson Scott Card's Intergalactic Medicine Show*, *Galaxy's Edge*, *Daily Science Fiction*, and at Baen.com. He's written two episodes of "The Post-Apocalyptic Tourist's Guide" (available on Kindle), which he also edits. His blog can be found at stephenlawsonstories.wordpress.com.

★ ★ ★

William Ledbetter is a Nebula Award-winning author with more than seventy speculative fiction stories and non-fiction articles published in markets such as *Asimov's*, *Fantasy & Science Fiction*, *Analog*, *Escape Pod*, Baen.com, the SFWA blog, and *Ad Astra*. He's been a space and technology geek since childhood and spent most of his non-writing career in the aerospace and defense industry. He administers the Jim Baen Memorial Short Story Award contest for Baen Books and the National Space Society and is the Science Track coordinator for the Fencon convention. His new novel *Level Five* is now available from Audible Originals. Find out more about his work at www.williamledbetter.com.

Suzanne Palmer is a Hugo Award-winning author whose short fiction has appeared in *Asimov's, Analog,* and *Clarkesworld.* Her first novel, *Finder,* is available now from DAW.

Chris Pourteau is the bestselling author of the sci-fi thriller novels of *The SynCorp Saga* (co-authored with David Bruns). If you loved the character of Stacks Fischer in "The Erkennen Job," he shows up as a major character in the Saga's second series, which begins with the novel *Valhalla Station* (see https://davidbruns.com/syncorpsaga/). A full-length Stacks Fischer novel, *O.R.P. (Optional Retirement Plan),* is currently under contract with Aethon Books.

Chris's first novel, *Shadows Burned In,* earned the 2015 eLit Book Awards Gold Medal for Literary Fiction. *The Lazarus Protocol,* the first novel in *The SynCorp Saga's* first series, placed in the Top Ten in Read Freely's 2018 50 Best Indie Book of the Year contest; it was the highest-rated Sci-Fi novel in the contest.

Want to know more about Chris? Sign up for his newsletter to find out when new books are coming out (and get free stuff!) at https://chrispourteau.com/newsletter and join his Facebook fan page at https://www.facebook.com/groups/842647879401279/.

Chris lives in College Station, Texas, with his wife, son, and their carnivorous zombie alert system (two dogs).

Christopher Ruocchio is the author of *The Sun Eater,* a space opera fantasy series from DAW Books, as well as the Assistant Editor at Baen Books, where he co-edited the military SF anthology *Star Destroyers,* as well as *Space Pioneers,* a collection of Golden Age reprints showcasing tales of human exploration. He is a graduate of North Carolina State University, where a penchant for self-destructive decision making caused him to pursue a bachelor's in English Rhetoric with a minor in Classics. An avid student of history, philosophy, and religion, Christopher has been writing since he was eight-years-old and sold his first book—*Empire of Silence*—at twenty-two. *The Sun Eater* series in available from Gollancz in the UK, and has been translated into French and German.

Christopher lives in Raleigh, North Carolina, where he spends most of his time hunched over a keyboard writing. When not writing, he splits his time between his family, procrastinating with video games, and his friend's boxing gym. He may be found on both Facebook and Twitter at @TheRuocchio.

New York Times bestselling writer **Kristine Kathryn Rusch** writes in almost every genre, and under a variety of pen names, including Kris Nelscott for mystery, and Kristine Grayson for romance. In science fiction and fantasy, she's published dozens of books, been nominated for almost every major award, won both the World Fantasy Award and the Hugo (twice). Currently, she writes two major sf series, the Retrieval Artist series, and the Diving series. A big book in her Diving universe, *Renegat*, will appear in September. The first (and only) female editor of *The Magazine of Fantasy & Science Fiction*, she now edits various publications for WMG Publishing, including acting as series editor for their premiere anthology series, *Fiction River*. She also edited *The Women of Futures Past* for Baen in 2016. Find out more about her work and read a free weekly short story at her website kriswrites.com.

Felix R. Savage's "The Scrapyard Ship" was written with interjections, complaints, and improvements from Walter Blaire, author of *The Eternal Front* and other sci-fi novels. It is set in the year 3416 in the M4 Cluster, where humans and aliens coexist in an uneasy peace . . . which is about to fall apart.

Dive deeper into the thrilling, richly-imagined universe of the Cluster with the first Mike Starrunner novel, *Lethal Cargo*. Mike is no stranger to trouble, but things get hotter than he bargained for when he lands on a planet occupied by Travellers. These grisly space pirates have a reputation so dire, even aliens won't mess with them. And they're about to attack Mike's home planet . . . *Lethal Cargo* is followed by *Dirty Job* and *Beast Mode,* with more novels and stories to come.

Born in South Carolina, Felix lives in Tokyo with his wife, two beautiful daughters, and two bad-tempered ex-stray cats with whom, it must be confessed, he identifies. Find all his books at http://felixrsavage.com, or sign up for his mailing list at http://felixrsavage.com/subscribe to receive FOUR free subscriber exclusive stories, not available anywhere else!

Brian Trent's work regularly appears in *Analog, Fantasy & Science Fiction, Orson Scott Card's Intergalactic Medicine Show, Terraform, Daily Science Fiction, Apex, Escape Pod, Galaxy's Edge, Nature, Pseudopod,* and numerous year's best anthologies. The author of the sci-fi novel *Ten Thousand Thunders* and the dark fantasy series *Rahotep,* Trent's story "A Thousand Deaths Through Flesh and Stone" appeared in *The Year's Best Military and Adventure SF's Volume 4* and is the prequel to this volume's story "Crash-Site." Trent lives in New England. His website is www.briantrent.com.

Michael Z. Williamson is retired military, having served twenty-five years in the U.S. Army and the U.S. Air Force. He was deployed for Operation Iraqi Freedom and Operation Desert Fox. Williamson is a state-ranked competitive shooter in combat rifle and combat pistol. He has consulted on military matters, weapons and disaster preparedness for Discovery Channel and Outdoor Channel productions and is Editor-at-Large for Survivalblog, with 300,000 weekly readers. In addition, Williamson tests and reviews firearms and gear for manufacturers. Williamson's books set in his Freehold Universe include *Freehold, The Weapon, The Rogue, Better to Beg Forgiveness . . ., Do Unto Others . . .,* and *When Diplomacy Fails . . ..* He is also the author of time travel novel *A Long Time Until Now,* as well as *The Hero*—the latter written in collaboration with *New York Times* best-selling author John Ringo. Williamson was born in England, raised in Liverpool and Toronto, Canada, and now resides in Indianapolis.